HEADHUNTERS

A John Milton Novel

Mark Dawson

To Mrs D, FD and SD
and to JD, sorely missed.

Prologue

Twelve Years Ago

THE BOMB-MAKER had his workshop in Manshiet Nasser, a vast slum that was home to almost half a million people. The locals called it Garbage City because the men and women who made their home there collected trash from the rest of Cairo and brought it back to be sorted, in the hope that they might find pieces to resell. Small children picked through the garbage all day, as did their mothers. Tens of thousands of people were crammed into rooms that were too small for them, in housing blocks that were in dire need of repair. It was a dour, joyless existence.

Ezbet Bekhit was a typical neighbourhood of Garbage City. Families survived on less than fifty dollars a month. Cooking and hygiene facilities were lacking. There was no electricity and very little drinkable water. It was a desperate place, poverty pressing down on it with a heavy hand, but, somehow, its loud and hectic spirit remained undaunted.

It was an excellent place to hide if you wanted to build bombs.

Life in the slum was difficult enough, but it had been made even more trying over the course of the last twelve hours as a sandstorm had blown in from the desert. Visibility had been reduced to twenty or thirty yards and the air was difficult to breathe. A thick film of sand had been deposited across everything, and the sun's rays had been weakened to a sickly yellow glow.

The bomb-maker's name was Ahmed and he had made an excellent reputation for himself as one of Hamas's most skilled technicians. He supplied the ordnance for the Izz ad-Din al-Qassam Brigades, the military wing of the organisation that had as its aim the destruction of the Israeli state. His nickname was al-Muhandis, which translated as the Mechanic. Shin Bet, Israel's internal security unit, had estimated that the Mechanic's bombs were responsible for the deaths of over three hundred Israeli soldiers and civilians. He was a high-ranking target and, when a defector had betrayed his location, the Mossad had dispatched two of its most dangerous operatives to eliminate him.

The agents on the ground were Avi Bachman and Uri Naim. They were assassins. They were not tasked with negotiating with Ahmed. They were not interested in capturing him, not even for the information they would have been able to extract during an interrogation. They were in Cairo to kill him, to make an example of him that would demonstrate, once again, that Israel did not consider international boundaries an impediment to the protection of its citizens, nor a shield to guard against its wrath.

Bachman was a man of normal height and stature, the sort of man who would be able to blend into most environments without drawing attention to himself. He was wearing a traditional Egyptian *gallibaya*, a loose robe that reached down to his ankles. He wore a long kaftan over the robe, a keffiyeh on his head and a light chequered scarf that was drawn up to cover his mouth and nose to protect them from the blowing sand. Bachman had welcomed the storm. It was a tremendous stroke of good fortune for them, providing the perfect excuse for them to obscure their identities. It also meant that the locals would be too busy suffering this latest privation to be particularly vigilant.

And more important yet, as far as Bachman was concerned, it would make it more difficult for the Mossad to confirm exactly what was about to happen.

There would be an assassination, but it was not the murder that they had planned in Tel Aviv.

Bachman's partner, Naim, was dressed similarly to him. They were sitting in the front seats of a Nissan that they had purchased from a dealer in Bab al-Louq. It was ancient and showing its age without grace: there were scratches and dents across its bodywork; the glass in the offside window had been shattered and the resulting hole had been covered over with a plastic bag that had been taped to the frame; the rear fender was tied on with pieces of wire. The car looked normal here, no better or worse than the other vehicles that struggled up and down the sandy street. They were parked behind a red Chevrolet flatbed truck that was overloaded with trash. Children had been scurried up into the load bed to start filtering it, separating the items that they could sell from those that had no value, but now the storm had forced them inside. There were large sacks of refuse and bales of recycled paper stacked up in the gutters. A few other locals were around, but most people were sheltering from the wind and the sand.

"Ready?" Bachman said.

Naim nodded. "Good luck, Avi."

"Thanks."

Bachman got out. The wind immediately whistled around his body, the tiny motes of sand blasting against his exposed skin. He put on a pair of old aviator sunglasses, slipping them between the scarf and the keffiyeh so that they might protect his eyes. He opened the rear door—it was stuck, and he had to yank it hard— and reached into the back seat. There was a black rucksack resting against the threadbare upholstery. It was heavy, and he could feel the strain in his tendons as he brought it out of the car. Inside the bag was a YM-II mine, the sort typically found in Iran and Iraq. It was a copy of the Chinese Type 72 non-metallic anti-tank mine, with a diameter of 270mm and weighing seven kilograms. Inside the plastic casing was 5.7 kilograms of Composition B explosive. Bachman had sourced the mine from a Mossad *sayanim* who operated in Cairo.

Fifty feet ahead of the Chevrolet truck was another car, a drab olive-green Renault, as decrepit as their own vehicle.

Ahmed's car.

Bachman felt the strain in his arm as he carried the heavy bag. He had made some modifications to the mine while Naim had been asleep last night. It was now much more suited to the purpose to which he intended to put it.

He crossed the sand-blown road and walked on.

* * *

MEIR SHAVIT started the engine of the yellow Volkswagen Kombi. Until he had stolen it earlier that afternoon, the truck had been used to deliver gas canisters to restaurants in the more upscale parts of the city. It was suitably run down and did not look out of place in Manshiet Nasser. None of the people who were foolish enough to be outside during the storm paid him much heed.

Shavit edged out into the sparse traffic and pressed down on the gas. He had been observing the two cars that were parked ahead of him on either side of the road: the Nissan that had brought Bachman and Naim, and the Renault that belonged to the bomb-maker. He knew that the man, Ahmed, was reputed to have his factory here, but that was of little interest to Shavit.

Ahmed was not the target of this operation.

He passed the Nissan and saw Naim in the passenger seat. He slowed, killed the engine and allowed the truck to roll to a stop. The Volkswagen was positioned perfectly, blocking Naim's view.

Shavit looked ahead and saw Bachman. He had reached the Renault.

He started the engine and then deliberately stalled it. He repeated the charade two more times. Shavit glanced to the left as Naim opened the passenger door and stepped out, gesticulating angrily, his words ripped away by the wind. He shook his head, shrugged and gestured toward the engine.

Naim walked to the truck.

Shavit looked forward again.

Bachman was on the other side of the parked car, on the pavement between it and the buildings it had been parked next to.

He was in position.

* * *

BACHMAN WALKED around the Mechanic's Renault. The wind had picked up and the sand was blasting against the sides of the buildings, including the warehouse where Israeli intelligence had suggested the man constructed his bombs. There was an alleyway between the warehouse and the building next to it. It was very narrow, almost as if the builders had erred when they were constructing the buildings and forgotten to fill it in. It would have been possible to touch the walls on either side without straightening his arms, and it was partially blocked with trash that had been heaved into it. Bachman and Naim had scouted the area the night before, driving by it a single time before turning and driving back in the other direction. They had been on station for less than five minutes, but that was enough: Naim had believed that they were reconnoitring the area in preparation for the operation. Bachman let him believe that. In truth, he had been looking to check that the surroundings would provide him with a means of escape.

And he was satisfied that they would.

He turned his head and saw the truck that had blocked the view between him and Naim. He saw Shavit in the cab. He knew that he didn't have long, so he moved briskly. He lowered the heavy bag to the pavement and nudged it with his foot so that it slid directly under the fuel tank of the car. Then, without turning back again, he hurried across the pavement to the mouth of the alley.

The storm howled as he reached into his pocket for the radio transmitter.

He turned it in his palm until he could feel the cross-hatched trigger against the pad of his thumb. He reached the alley, turned into it and squeezed it.

* * *

THE MINE DETONATED. The first explosion lifted the rear of the Renault from the road. It was followed, just a millisecond later, by a secondary explosion as the fuel tank ruptured. The gasoline inside fed the conflagration, boosting the rear of the Renault fifteen feet into the air. The car flipped through ninety degrees and then fell back to earth, its nose crumpling as it slammed back down onto the pocked asphalt.

Meir Shavit knew that the blast was coming, and had started to lower himself in the cab just as Bachman triggered it. He was twenty feet away from the seat of the explosion and the shockwave radiated out and engulfed the truck, swiping the windshield out of its frame and sending a storm of razored fragments into the cab. Shavit was sheltered below the dash and spared what would otherwise have been a certain death. When he heaved himself up again, he brushed glass fragments from his clothes. The upholstery of his seat, already worn and tired, was torn to shreds.

He looked out of the suddenly open windshield.

The Renault had been flattened by the blast. Its rear section had been separated from the rest of the vehicle, and the carcass was blackened and charred, coated with soot. It was burning with a ferocious flame, the conflagration feeding on anything that was flammable: the upholstery, the plastic dash, the rubber tyres. A thick black column of smoke emerged and was immediately flattened by the storm and blown into the street.

Shavit shuffled across the fragments of glass on the seat to get a better view of Uri Naim and the Nissan. The agent was on his back. He had stepped around the truck, exposing himself to most of the blast, and he had been picked up by the pressure wave and thrown backwards.

Shavit opened the door and dropped down to the surface of the road.

"Are you all right?"

The wind and the sound of the blaze were deafening.

He crossed the distance between them.

"Sir? Are you all right?"

The man had a furrow from the right-hand side of his temple all the way back into his scalp, and the wound was bleeding heavily. A piece of shrapnel. Shavit reached down for a pulse and found one. He was lucky to be alive. Shavit considered shooting him, but there were witnesses on the street and he didn't want to leave evidence that might contradict the narrative that he and Avi had constructed: this was a job that had gone wrong, a defective bomb that had detonated prematurely.

He left his pistol in its holster and, instead, reached down, slid his hands beneath the man's shoulders and dragged him away from the blaze. Naim's eyes flickered open, then closed again.

"Sir?"

He groaned in pain.

"Sir, are you all right?"

The man planted the soles of his feet and pushed away. He reached a hand to the ground and levered himself onto his feet. He looked at Shavit, confusion washing across his bloodied face, but he didn't say a word as he stumbled to the Nissan, slid into the open compartment and reversed the car away.

Shavit knew what the agent was thinking. Naim was an Israeli assassin deep in the heart of Cairo, caught in the aftermath of a hit that had not proceeded as planned. Was Ahmed dead? Was his partner? There was no way of knowing, and he couldn't stay to investigate. To be caught now would be the beginning of an international incident. Discovery was one thing that the Mossad could not contemplate.

Shavit knew all of this. He was a general in the Israeli Defense Force and he had known Avi Bachman for twenty years. When Bachman had appealed for his help, he had been glad to give it. Bachman was the son he had never been blessed to receive. He would have done anything for him.

He heard the sirens, their up and down yowling audible as the pitch of the storm descended just a little. He needed to be gone. He left the truck where it was and, as the sound of the approaching sirens grew louder, he headed away.

* * *

AVI BACHMAN hurried through the alleyway. He was hidden from the wind and its howling, allowing him to hear the sirens. There was more garbage than he had anticipated, and there were moments, as the passageway twisted around the back of the warehouses, where he had to plough through piles of plastic sacks that had been torn open, the fetid waste within them exposed for rats to gorge upon. His legs were quickly coated in foul-smelling slime.

He was committed now. There was no turning back. He had to trust that Uri Naim's view had been obscured by Meir Shavit's truck and the storm, and that he would be unable to confirm what had happened. What would he be able to say for sure? That the mine had exploded prematurely.

Bachman had no intention of being found. He had planned the operation for months, waiting for the perfect opportunity. This had been it. There would be no way for the Mossad to investigate the blast. How could they send their investigators here? They would not be able to confirm what had happened to him. He hoped that they would draw the obvious, easy conclusion: he was dead, killed in a freak accident.

The alleyway finally ended. It opened onto another street very similar to the one that he had fled: derelict buildings on either side, a truck with a fifteen-foot-high load of bagged trash lashed to its flatbed, religious decorations strung between the buildings high overhead, a celebration of Ramadan. The wind seized him again as he emerged from the lee of the buildings, and he rearranged the scarf over his mouth so that he could breathe more easily.

He reached his right hand under his left armpit and felt the bulk of the Glock that he carried in a concealed holster. He didn't think he would need it, but it was reassuring to know that it was there.

He set off, heading south. There was a car waiting for him in Nasr City. He would drive west to El Salloum, cross the border into Libya, and then continue through Tunisia and Algeria until he reached Morocco.

The thought of his destination filled him with anticipation. Lila was waiting for him there. Their relationship was the reason for all of this. She was a Palestinian, and he knew, with complete certainty, that their being together was dangerous. If the director of the agency, Victor Blum, discovered their secret, he would have them both killed.

It left them with two choices: agree never to see each other again or flee.

The first option was impossible. Bachman would not consider it.

They would run.

He had developed the plan. They would stay in Tangier for a week and then, after Shavit had reported the situation to him, they would take the ferry to Algeciras. They would pick up a car and drive north, through Spain and France, until they reached Paris. New identities were waiting for them there, together with an appointment with a plastic surgeon who would alter Bachman's appearance. Once the work had been done, both the plastic surgeon and the forger who would supply them with their new papers would be shot. There would be nothing to tie Bachman and Lila back to the people they had been before.

As far as the Mossad were concerned, Avi Bachman was dead.

He had died in a botched assassination in the Cairo slums.

Claude Boon would be born in his stead.

Chapter One

THE LAWYER left his office in Baton Rouge at eight in the morning. It was fifty-six miles to the Louisiana State Penitentiary. It would take just over an hour if the interstate was clear, but, since this was rush hour, he allowed himself two. The man he was visiting wasn't going anywhere, but he didn't want to be late. His client was frightening enough as it was, and he didn't want to antagonise him with tardiness.

The lawyer's name was Reed Scott and he was a partner in Renwick Chase Scott. Scott had been in the United States for thirty years since he had emigrated from Israel with his parents. He had an American wife and two small children. He took his son to see the Saints. He was active in his local community organisation, and thoroughly respected within the Louisiana legal system. Scott's caseload did not typically include criminal matters, so it had come as something of a surprise to his peers when he had accepted instructions from the suspected multiple murderer currently awaiting trial in the pen.

The roads out of Baton Rouge were quieter than those headed into the city and he made good time. He followed the Martin Luther King Highway to Highway 61 North and took the exit for Natchez. It was another twenty-one miles to St. Francisville. He turned left after passing the West Feliciana High School onto Highway 66. The twenty-mile-long highway ended at the front gate of the Louisiana State Penitentiary, otherwise known as Angola.

Reed Scott's usual clients were the men and women who worked in downtown Baton Rouge. He specialised in corporate law: mergers and acquisitions, reorganisations, employment matters. He was used to skyscrapers and gleaming offices, expensive marble lobbies and sleek conference rooms that offered wide panoramas over the city from a hundred feet up.

Angola? That was something else.

He doubted whether there was a worse place on Earth.

They called it The Farm. It had been a slave plantation a hundred years earlier, and the penitentiary was nestled at the heart of a tract of 18,000 acres that was larger than the island of Manhattan. It was penned in on three sides by the Mississippi and on the fourth by twenty miles of scrubby, uninhabited woods. It was said to be virtually escape-proof and Scott thought that that was probably true. More than 5,400 men were imprisoned within its razor wire. Most would die there.

There was a small yellow gatehouse and a homely red brick sign at the entrance that could have marked the gates of a national park. Scott drove through, noting the museum and gift shop where he could, should he have so chosen, buy a pair of miniature handcuffs, jars of inmate-made jelly, and mugs that read "Angola: A Gated Community."

Funny, right? He remembered it and allowed himself a small chuckle. It distracted him from the nerves that had settled, like a cold fist, in his gut. He always felt that way before interviews with this particular client. The man had something about him.

He drove on until he reached the main prison building. It was surrounded by several tall fences, the razor wire gleaming in the sunshine. He parked his car in the lot and made his way to the gatehouse.

There was a small queue of people waiting to get into the prison. He stood in line for the scanner, passing his briefcase to the guard so that it could be put through the X-ray machine.

"Come," said the guard on the other side of the security arch, beckoning him on.

Scott stepped through the arch. It remained silent. He smiled at the guard. The man looked at him, blank and bored and slightly unfriendly. Scott took his case and joined the queue for the kiosk.

He stepped up to the window.

"Name, sir?"

"Reed Scott."

"What's your business?"

"I'm here to see an inmate."

"Prisoner's name?"

"Claude Boon."

The woman tapped the name into her computer and scratched her head as she waited for the information to be retrieved.

"Relationship to Mr. Boon?"

"Attorney."

"ID, please."

Scott took his driver's licence and passed it through the slot beneath the window.

The woman looked at the licence and then up at her screen. She nodded her satisfaction. "That's it, I got you. Ten o'clock, right?"

"That's right."

"You know the drill?"

"Yes, ma'am. I do."

She reached down to press a button and, with the buzz of an electric motor, the door to the right of the kiosk opened. Reed swallowed, nodded his thanks, and went into the prison.

* * *

HE SAT DOWN, rested his briefcase on the table, took out his papers and arranged them before him. It was five to ten. He knew that his client was going to be on time. Claude Boon was professional and motivated. And where else was he going to go?

Scott looked up at the CCTV camera in the corner of the room. He had the sensation of being watched and appraised and, as usual, he felt vulnerable. He knew that his disguise was excellent. Indeed, it was *more* than a disguise. After all, he *was* a lawyer, and he had been for all of his adult life.

But there was more to him than that.

Scott worked for the Israeli national intelligence agency. The Mossad. He was a *sayanim*. The agency had *sayanim* across the world, local assets that remained in deep cover until there was a need for them and they were activated. Mossad field agents, or *katsas*, needed support as they prepared for operations in foreign countries. The *sayanim* provided it. Regardless of their allegiance to their country, each *sayan* recognised a more fundamental loyalty to Israel, and would do anything to protect it from its enemies.

Sayanim fulfilled many roles. A car *sayan*, running a rental agency, could provide a *katsa* with transportation. A *sayan* with an interest in property could provide accommodation on short notice and at no cost. A *sayan* inside a police department might provide useful information on investigations, and a *sayan* physician could treat injuries while keeping the identity of his or her patient secret. *Sayanim* received only expenses for their work, but they carried out their tasks because they loved their spiritual home, not because they wanted remuneration. In their turn, *katsas* could not operate without them. The agency itself depended upon them.

Scott heard the clank of the shackles from the corridor and unconsciously stiffened in his chair. His client was the sort of man who could make you nervous just at the thought of him. He had been indicted for seven murders and, in the three months that he had been in Angola, he had managed to kill one inmate and seriously injure another two. He was being held in solitary confinement. The measure had not been taken because he was being punished or even for his own protection.

Claude Boon had been put in the hole for the protection of the other inmates.

The door opened. The man who stepped inside the room was not imposing. He was forty-five and obviously in excellent shape. He had been fit before, but, now that he had little else to do save working out, he had added muscle to his frame. He had salt-and-pepper hair and was conventionally handsome. He was dressed in the standard-issue Louisiana Department of Corrections orange jumpsuit. His real name was Avi Bachman, but, for the purposes of the American judicial system, his name was Boon.

The door closed, and Scott was left alone with him.

"Claude," the lawyer said.

"Don't give me 'Claude' like we're best friends. What's happening? What the *fuck* is happening?"

"I know, I'm—"

"It's been two weeks since I last saw you."

"I know. And I'm sorry about that, but what you've asked is not a simple thing. You do know that?"

"I'm not interested in excuses. I've been in here for three months. I told you what would happen if you didn't get me out. Do they think I'm bluffing?"

He raised his hands in supplication. "No, Claude, they don't. They believe you."

Boon slammed his palms against the table. "So why am I *still* in here?"

Reed instinctively turned to the door, but there was no sign that Boon's raised voice had been overheard. "Calm down, please."

He leaned over the table, the chains rattling. "Don't tell me to calm down."

"Let me remind you of a couple of things. You're in a maximum-security facility. Not even including the inmate you killed, you're going to be put on trial for multiple homicides. The D.A. is up for re-election. He's on the record that convicting you is his number one priority. I mean, he's got a real hard-on for you. He wants the death penalty in the *worst* way. They know how dangerous you are, Claude. All those things taken into account, maybe you can see that this isn't a walk in the park, not even for us."

"Who's *us*? I asked and you never said. Who's on this?"

"The director."

"Blum?"

"He's supervising this personally. Believe me, he wants you out of here as much as you do."

He laughed bitterly. "I doubt that."

"It's true, Claude. I'm reporting directly to him."

"Stop calling me Claude," he said irritably. "We're not friends."

"I'm sorry… Mr. Boon."

Reed Scott leaned back again. He made the mistake of looking into Boon's eyes and wished that he hadn't. They were the eyes of a killer. There was no empathy there, nothing that suggested that he felt anything. They were a blank mirror. They sent a shiver of discomfort up and down his spine. They made him wonder how many men and women had looked into his eyes, appealing for clemency, right before he dispatched them.

Angola maintained a punishment unit known as Camp J. Scott knew a little about it. The block combined extreme isolation and deprivation. Normal visits were forbidden; prisoners were not allowed any personal items and their meals consisted of a lump of ground-up scraps known as "the loaf." The unit was plagued by suicide attempts. That was where they had put Boon.

"How are they treating you?"

"Tolerably. This is nothing to what I've been used to before. I've been in the Bangkok Hilton." He gestured around the room. "All this? Five-star luxury compared to that."

"Of course." He shuffled his papers and then looked

around with an exaggerated, knowing motion. The confidentiality between prisoner and attorney was sacrosanct, but he was not naïve enough to think that there was no chance that they were being eavesdropped on.

"Mr. Boon, listen carefully. You have an important hearing tomorrow."

Boon raised an eyebrow. "What hearing?"

"It's a preliminary thing. We're presenting evidence to the judge."

"When?"

"In the morning." He steeled himself to look straight into Boon's eyes, making sure that he understood what he was being told. "You'll be taken to Baton Rouge by the deputy sheriffs. They'll move you at eight or nine." He stared at him and gave a nod. "I'll see you at the courthouse."

Boon picked up the signal. "Is there anything I need to do?"

"You just need to be there. I'll take care of everything else." As he spoke, the lawyer collected his fountain pen from the table and removed the lid. A small device dropped out onto the table. It was about the size of a salad crouton. Boon saw it and covered it with his hand.

"Any questions, Mr. Boon?"

"No. I don't think so."

Reed stood, collected the papers from the table and slipped them into his briefcase.

Boon stood, too, his shackles rattling. "I've been patient. Three months is patient. But I'm still in here and *he's* still out there." He spat the word. "The thought of that, after what he did…" His anger scorched the rest of the words away.

"We understand, Mr. Boon, we do. Be patient. It's in hand." He raised his voice. "Guard!"

He walked to the door, putting his body between it and Boon. He watched, through the corner of his eye, as Boon put his hand to his mouth.

The door opened and the guard came inside.

"You done?"

"I am, thank you." He turned back into the room. "Goodbye, Mr. Boon. Get a good night's sleep. Big day tomorrow."

Chapter Two

THEY HAD two safe houses. The first was in Merrydale, north of Baton Rouge. Both properties had been rented two months earlier by a Mossad advance agent working with a local *sayan*. This house was designated Moaz, or "stronghold." It was a nondescript property in a middle-class street. It had been chosen because it was average, and because the neighbourhood in which it was situated was known for housing transient workers. It was the sort of place where newcomers would attract little in the way of attention. Perfect for what they had in mind.

The two agents had been in the country for three days. Their papers recorded them as Mr. and Mrs. Rabin, a young couple from Tel Aviv who had come to Louisiana for a holiday. They had landed at New Orleans, checked into a hotel, stayed there for long enough to be noticed by the staff, and then made their way west.

Malakhi and Keren Rabin were two of the Mossad's most effective *kidon*. The word meant "bayonet" in Yiddish, and the *kidon* comprised the Mossad's assassins. The unit included forty-eight men and women. They were all in their twenties and all of them were fastidious in ensuring that they remained in the best physical condition possible. They lived and worked outside Mossad's headquarters in Tel Aviv and in a restricted military base in the heart of the Negev desert.

The Rabins often worked together. Their status as a married couple had proven to be an excellent cover. Their last assignment had been in Paris. They had once again posed as tourists and had assassinated a prominent Iranian arms dealer who was alleged to have supplied Hezbollah with the Katyusha rockets it had been firing into northern Israel. They had carried out their orders and blended back into the background, just another couple of tourists enjoying the hospitality of the City of Light.

The house in Baton Rouge had been readied for their arrival. The equipment for the operation had been sourced and was waiting for them beneath the floorboards in the second bedroom. There were six Beretta 70s firing .22-calibre rounds. They had half-powder loads and suppressors to make them as quiet as possible. There were four Tavor assault rifles with plenty of ammunition. They would often have loaded out with Uzis, but, even though the Uzi was a great weapon, it was chambered in 9mm and a handgun round was less effective when shooting at vehicles. Glass and metal could cause round deflection, a problem that would not be encountered with the Tavor's high-velocity 5.56mm ammunition. There was a rolled spike strip fitted with a series of two-and-a-half-inch-long metal alloy spikes. The spikes were rugged, with three sharp-cornered edges, a half-inch wide at the base. Finally, there was a small netbook that had been installed with the software to monitor the GPS beacon that had been given to the man whom they had been sent to collect.

The advance agent had also rented two cars and a van for the purposes of the operation. The van and one of the cars had been put in long-term parking at the airport. The transport for the Rabins was a 2013 Honda Accord. It had been delivered to the house overnight, the keys posted through the letterbox.

They transferred their equipment to the trunk of the car before dawn when the street was quiet. They had a large breakfast, not knowing when they would be able to eat again, and then phoned to check whether the operation was still proceeding.

It was.

They locked the house, got into the car and set off.

* * *

THE RABINS arrived at the waiting area near the Tunica Hills State Wildlife Park at half past seven. It was a wide space that offered parking for a dozen automobiles. The lot was empty this morning save for their Accord. There were picnic tables, an information board that had been bleached by the elements, and a trail that led away into the trees.

Malakhi Rabin opened the driver's side door and stepped out. It was already hot, despite the early hour. He could see the buildings of a refinery in the distance, the smokestacks wavering in the hazy, polluted air. They called this part of Louisiana "Cancer Alley." The landscape was baked dry, the vegetation as brittle as tinder. Cicadas buzzed and birds, already addled by the heat, murmured their songs.

Malakhi was six feet tall and obviously muscular beneath the linen shirt that was already damp with his sweat. He reached into the car, took his sunglasses from the dash and put them on. He gazed at the horizon and the thick bank of black clouds that was gathering there.

His wife got out of the car. Keren Rabin was five eight and slender, her toned bare arms suggesting that she spent a lot of time in the gym. That was true, but she also owed her physique to hours of gruelling training on the wrestling mat. She was a skilful Krav Maga fighter. Many of the men that she had eliminated had taken one look at her striking appearance and assumed that she was just another pretty face. She came onto them, flirted with them, and they let their guards down. They took her somewhere quiet, somewhere they wouldn't be disturbed. And that was the last mistake that they made.

"Storm coming," Malakhi said.

Keren looked down at her cell phone. "They're saying it'll be here in half an hour."

"Going to get wet, then."

"Better wet than this. It's hotter than Hell."

Malakhi nodded his agreement. "Storm might be a

good distraction, too."

Keren glanced at the road. A van was approaching. It was an off-white Chevrolet Express. The Rabins watched as the van slowed and pulled off the road. Dust billowed from the wheels as it bounced across the uneven ground and drew to a halt alongside the Accord. There were four people inside the van: three men and one woman.

This was the second team. They were codenamed Mural. The four agents had been in the country for a week. They had arrived under the cover of students visiting Louisiana State University as part of an exchange programme. Their pseudonyms were Levy, Peretz, Biton and Dahan.

Malakhi went over to the van and opened the driver's side door. "Morning," he said.

Dahan stepped down. "We have a green light?"

"We do."

"How long?"

"Thirty minutes."

"Just in time for the storm."

"We were just saying that."

"It'll reduce the vis. That's no bad thing."

"We were saying that, too."

The female agent, Peretz, came around the van to the car. She nodded a greeting. "Do you have the gear?"

"In the trunk."

She reached into the Accord to pop the lid and then went around the back to open it. She took out the Tavors and the Berettas and distributed them to the other members of the team.

Dahan checked the mechanism on the submachine gun. "Same deal?" he asked.

Malakhi nodded. "I don't see any reason to change it."

"We know what we're looking at?"

"Not for sure. They think a van and an escort vehicle. Probably a sedan."

"And guards?"

"They'll take him seriously. At least two, possibly four."

Peretz racked the slide of her Beretta. "Rules of engagement?"

"As we discussed. The priority is getting him out. Anything you have to do to accomplish that is fine. We have carte blanche."

"Including lethal force?"

"If necessary."

"And that's from the top?"

"That's right."

She whistled her surprise. All of them shared the sentiment. This was an unusual assignment. Not the scope of it—that was routine—but the country in which it was taking place.

"It's not for us to ask why," Keren reminded them.

Dahan looked up at the sky. The clouds were closer now, a rolling shroud that was throwing shadow over the landscape.

Keren went back to the car. The netbook was open on the dash and an alert bleeped.

"Target is moving," she called out. "Ten minutes out."

It was eight o'clock.

"Move," Malakhi said.

Chapter Three

CLAUDE BOON was taken from his cell at seven that morning. He was transferred to a room by two guards. They were big men, both well over six feet tall and fifty pounds heavier than he was, yet they were visibly bothered by the prospect of being in a confined space with him. His reputation was well known. They all knew what he was capable of doing.

The guards told him to strip, and he did.

"Bend over," one of the men ordered.

"Seriously?"

"Just do it, Boon."

It was an imposition, and one for which he would not normally have stood, but he was happy to play along. There wouldn't be much more of this to put up with. He smiled at them both, a cold expression that left them in no doubt as to the length of his memory, but he did as he was told. They conducted a cursory body search and, quickly satisfied, tossed him a clean set of orange prison scrubs.

"Put them on," the man said.

He did. When he was finished, they cuffed his hands in front of him and then fastened a chain around his waist. The cuffs were looped through the chain to prevent him from moving his hands too far. The black box, with a padlock, was applied last. It prevented access to the keyholes of the handcuffs.

"When are we leaving?"

"Shut up, Boon."

He was taken to a loading facility. It was a large garage space, with several vehicles slotted side by side. One side was open, and Boon gazed out as rain slammed down against the asphalt. He could see a sliver of the horizon between the concrete ceiling and the wall that delineated the enclosed courtyard outside, and the sky was as black as pitch. Thunder boomed as the guards impelled him down a flight of steps to the floor of the garage.

He was to be transported to the courthouse in a van. There was a sedan waiting ahead of the van, the engine running and exhaust fumes drifting upwards. Boon counted four sheriff's deputies. They were all armed with handguns. He expected that they would also have at least one long gun per vehicle, either a shotgun or a rifle.

The two big corrections officers manoeuvred Boon around to the back of the van and helped him climb up inside it. He had wondered whether he might be transported with other prisoners, but it appeared that his status had won him the luxury of travelling alone. There were two doors to the rear: the main door and, inside that, a further metal door. The interior was simple, with a metal bench running along each side of the vehicle. The deputies up front were protected by a metal shield that divided the van into two portions. There was a grille in the shield that allowed light to enter.

Both rear doors were closed and locked.

Boon sat on the metal bench.

He heard one of the corrections officers speaking. "What do you know about him?"

"That he's a badass."

"Wouldn't guess from looking at him."

"I know, but he is. Killed an inmate the week he got here."

"We'll be careful."

Boon heard a third voice. "There's four of us and one of him."

"Believe me, you don't wanna take him lightly, buddy."

"Sure, but dude ain't Hannibal Lecter, is he?"

Nervous laughter followed that.

"You wanna know how he killed the man? Shanked him in the throat. Straight up. Did it like he was shelling peas. No emotion. No nothing. So when I say you need to take him seriously, that's what I mean. Don't give him a chance. He'll kill you just as soon as look at you."

The deputy laughed. "Relax, man. It's gonna be fine. A nice little drive, that's all. We'll have him back here again before you know it."

Chapter Four

BOON SAT with his back against the wall of the truck. He closed his eyes and concentrated on what he could hear: the sound of the engine, the rain battering against the metal roof, the muffled conversation of the driver and the officer who was riding up front with him, a radio playing country and western music. The truck was new and provided a smooth and comfortable ride, even with the cold, hard metal bench that he was sitting on. He opened his eyes again and looked down at the shackles. He raised his arms until the tether that connected the cuffs to the chain around his waist went taut. The bonds were solid. Boon was strong, but he knew that he would be unable to escape from them.

Boon had paid attention during his previous trips between Angola and the courthouse in Baton Rouge. He knew the route that the guards would probably take to get him there: southeast on LA-66, south on US-61 and the I-110. There was another way, but this was the most direct. He figured, this early in the morning, that it would take them between an hour and an hour and a half.

He knew the convoy would be hit close to the jail or close to the courthouse, but not too close to either. There was a good reason for that assumption. Being close to either the point of departure or the destination meant that the choices for varying the route diminished greatly.

The van crossed a railroad track, bumping and swaying side to side, and Boon planted his feet against the floor to steady himself. If he was planning the operation, he would do it sooner rather than later. He would do it round about now.

* * *

MALAKHI RABIN was soaked to the skin. The skies had opened, the deluge slamming onto the asphalt and quickly turning the baked mud on the margin into a quagmire. It was unpleasant, but, he reminded himself, fortuitous. The storm was so heavy that visibility was going to be drastically reduced. He could see only a short distance ahead of his position. The driver of the prison transport would be similarly disadvantaged.

Malakhi ducked down in the scrub that bordered the margin. The road bent around on a long and gentle curve as it switched from its previous easterly direction and emerged onto the southward stretch of road that was known as Tunica Trace. The terrain hereabouts was characterised by rugged hills, bluffs and ravines. The road dropped down a steep slope to the north and was heavily forested with dense stands of holly and beech to the south. The undergrowth included oak leaf, hydrangea and silverbell.

He was hiding inside a thicket of switchcane that stretched right down to the gravel at the edge of the road. It offered no protection from the downpour, but he put that out of his mind as he saw the glow of headlights as a car negotiated the turn onto the Trace. A large, dark-painted van followed behind it.

Two vehicles, just as they had anticipated.

He took a breath.

Malakhi turned back to the south. The Honda Accord was parked out of sight on an access road that ran into the forest. Keren was in the driver's seat, the engine running and the lights off. The Chevy Express was hidden on the apex of a switchback turn that led north to Pinckneyville.

Rabin couldn't see the van.

The drivers of the approaching car and van wouldn't be able to see it, either.

The car was a sedan, painted white, with a red and blue stripe on the door. The kind of car that a sheriff's deputy would drive. Malakhi saw the shapes of two men in the front seats. He couldn't see into the back. He estimated its speed as it approached, and guessed at a steady fifty miles an hour.

The sedan passed him, throwing up parabolas of spray against the switchcane.

Malakhi only had a narrow margin to act and he had to move quickly.

He reached down for the handle of the stinger strip.

The van was five car lengths behind the sedan.

He hopped out of the cane and deployed the strip across the road with a smooth bowling motion. It was articulated, and each segment sprang out with a click and a clack, the strip reaching all the way across the road. The van rolled right over it. The spikes pierced the rubber and detached from the strip. They were hollow, allowing for a controlled deflation that minimised the possibility of a sudden loss of control. He heard the pop of the tyres and then the screech of the wheels running on their rims. The van immediately slowed.

If the driver of the sedan noticed what had happened behind him, it didn't matter. The car was thirty feet farther down the road from Malakhi when Levy and Peretz stepped forward out of the clumped dogwood and sweetleaf that had been hiding them. They raised their Tavors and, as the car passed them, they opened fire. The rifles could fire nine hundred rounds a minute, and the agents were firing fully automatic. The windows were blown inwards as a storm of bullets sliced through the cabin. The officers were hit multiple times. They were wearing soft body armour and, although it might have protected them against handgun ammunition, it was no use against 5.56mm rounds. The driver suddenly and involuntarily yanked the wheel to the side and the car veered sharply to the left. It crashed through a thicket of blackberry, accelerated down the steep bank and slammed into the trunk of a big ironwood.

Biton stepped out of cover and fired into the

windshield of the van.

Malakhi yanked the spike strip back, clearing it from the road, and drew his Beretta as he sprinted in the direction of the crippled van.

* * *

BOON FELT the van run over the spike strip. The front tyres deflated first, the van tilting forward as it ran along on its rims. The rear tyres followed, and then the van decelerated with a suddenness that slid him forwards hard enough that he thumped up against the metal partition.

He heard the sound of panicked cursing from the driver's compartment.

And then he heard automatic gunfire and the sound of the windshield as it detonated. Five holes were punched through the metal partition, right at the top at the junction where it met with the roof.

He brought his knees up and pressed his chin against his sternum, wishing that he could cover his head with his arms.

* * *

MALAKHI RABIN SPRINTED HARD.

The van had rolled directly to the spot where Biton had been hiding and he had emptied almost all of his magazine into the cabin. He had aimed carefully, choosing his angle of fire so that the rounds sliced up through the cabin and passed through the roof, cautious to avoid the possibility of stray shots injuring anyone in the back of the truck. It would not do to injure the man that they had been sent to liberate.

Biton came out of the brush, his Tavor aimed cautiously at the van.

Malakhi slowed as he reached the driver's compartment. He raised the Beretta, holding it in a loose two-handed grip. He blanked out the rain that was pelting against his face, the water that was in his eyes and nose, held the gun out straight and approached carefully. He looked inside. The airbags had deployed, and the cabin was full of the fine blue dust that was packed with the bags to keep them pliable. There was a big splash of blood on the metal partition and the perforations of escaped 9mm rounds in the roof.

He edged around.

The driver was slumped against the deflated bag, resting against it as if he was just relaxing for a moment. His hand was pressed up against the window and, as Rabin watched, his fingers twitched against it like the legs of a crab. The glass in the window was still intact. Malakhi shattered it as he put two shots into the man's head.

Biton went to the passenger side. "Clear," he called.

Peretz had followed the sedan down into the ditch. The depression hid her from his view, but he heard the sound of two quick bursts of gunfire. She was making sure that the guards were out of commission. Kill shots.

Malakhi assessed. The guards were neutralised. He waved Biton to the rear of the van.

They were all wearing disposable latex gloves so as not to leave any prints. Rabin reached up to the handle, pulled it down and opened the door. The guard's weight had been up against it and, now that the door was gone, he lolled out, only prevented from tumbling to the ground by the locked seat belt. His arm dangled free, swinging a little until the momentum was arrested. Malakhi kept the gun level, just in case, and reached up with his left hand to the ring of keys on the man's belt. He unclipped the loop and went back to the rear.

Dahan was behind the wheel of the Chevrolet. He put the van into drive and jerked it out of its hiding place. He emerged from behind the trees that grouped around the apex of the switchback and sped forward, stopping alongside the van.

Biton had drawn his Beretta and was aiming it down the road to cover them in the event that any other traffic headed this way. The rain hissed, droplets bouncing back from the pitted asphalt.

Malakhi thumped his fist against the van's rear door. "Bachman," he called.

"I'm here."

He swiped the moisture from his eyes, took the keys and selected the one that looked like the best fit. He inserted it into the lock, twisted it, and heard the mechanism click. He opened the door to reveal the second, inner door. This one was on a latch. He flicked it up and opened it.

He had never met Avi Bachman before, but he had heard plenty. The man was something of a legend within the Mossad. The agency was not short of legendary operators, but Bachman stood alone when it came to his reputation for ruthlessness. They had all heard the stories about him.

It was difficult to impress Malakhi Rabin, and he was even more difficult to daunt, but he did not mind admitting that he was nervous as Bachman carefully stepped onto the lip of the van and then hopped down to the ground.

The man held up his shackled hands. "Get these off me."

Rabin swallowed and found that his throat was uncomfortably dry. He took the keys, found the one for the padlock on the black box, and opened it. He selected the key for the cuffs and opened those, too. Bachman rubbed his wrists as Rabin went around behind him and unlocked the belly chain. It fell free and clattered to the ground.

"We need to move," Rabin said.

"How?"

"In the car."

Keren Rabin had brought the Accord out of its hiding

place to collect them. Bachman nodded and the two of them jogged across the road. The other agents were preparing to leave. Biton opened the back of the van so that Peretz and Levy could get inside. Biton paused on the road and looked across at Malakhi. They were done here, so he gave a nod as he pointed to the south. Biton put up his thumb, clambered into the back and pulled the door closed behind him. Dahan put the van into drive and pulled away. The plan was for Mural to go right back to their cover stories. They would go to LSU, complete the exchange, and then return to Israel.

Malakhi got into the front, next to his wife.

There were no thanks. Bachman did not even acknowledge that he had spoken. "What are your names?"

"Malakhi Rabin."

"Keren Rabin."

"You're a couple?"

"Yes."

"Cute."

Malakhi could feel his wife tense. Bachman had the same effect on her as he had on him.

"What's your plan?"

Malakhi glanced at the empty road behind them. "We need to get you out of the country."

"Where are we headed?"

"You're flying out of Monterrey."

"What's that? Ten hours?"

"Thirteen."

"Fine."

"We'll drive straight through. Non-stop."

"I said it was fine."

Malakhi turned to his wife. "Go."

Keren put the sedan into drive and they pulled away.

Bachman looked out of the window at the devastation that they left behind them: the shot-up van with the shredded tyres, the sedan that had planted itself into the bank of the ditch at the side of the road. Four dead officers who wouldn't have had a clue what had happened to them. The driver of the sedan must have had his foot jammed against the brake pedal, for the car's taillights were still glowing through the murk.

"This is only part of the deal," Bachman said in an even tone. "The easy part. What about him?"

"Who?"

"Milton!" he snapped.

"We're looking."

"And?"

"It's in hand."

The car drove on. Malakhi wondered about what the Englishman could have done to deserve Bachman's hatred. He sat quietly in the car, staring into the rain, the abhorrence pulsing from him in waves. Malakhi found that his mouth was dry. He was still a young man, but he and his wife had already travelled all over the world, delivering Israel's justice to those who thought that they could escape it. He was familiar with death. He had seen plenty of it. But he did not think he had ever seen a man who was as single-minded as Avi Bachman. He was not concerned with his liberty. The only thing that mattered was that it had bought him the opportunity to go after the Englishman.

Malakhi did not envy John Milton.

Whatever he had done to Bachman, the Mossad would find him and then he was going to pay.

A reckoning was coming.

Chapter Five

IT WAS DAWN.

John Milton jumped out of the Jeep and took out his cigarettes. He had only one left. He had been surviving on nicotine and caffeine all night, but the effect was starting to wear off. He was tired. They had been driving for four hours. He took his lighter from his pocket, put the cigarette to his lips and lit it. The three other men he had been riding with jumped down, too. They looked exhausted. The dust had gathered on their boots; their work clothes were torn and dirty; their discoloured and stained parkas and duffle coats were draped around their shoulders to ward against the cool night air. They were covered in dirt, dried blood—some of it their own—and sweat. Milton glanced down at himself and realised that he looked just as bad as the rest of them. He held the cigarette between filthy fingers, the skin of his hand blackened with the detritus of a long week of work. His face was rough with stubble. He hadn't had a chance to shave for days.

Despite all of it, the deprivations and the back-breaking work, Milton felt good.

He took a long drag on the cigarette. The sun crested the bleak horizon of One Tree Plain. The outback spread out as far as he could see, most of it red and desolate, like the surface of Mars. The Lachlan River ran through the station, encouraging a little greenery near its fast-flowing waters.

Milton reflected that you only really got a sense of the scale of Australia when you were deep in the middle of it. He knew it was big, of course. He knew that if the country was overlaid atop North America, it would stretch from Manitoba in the north to Florida in the south, and from

San Francisco to New York. But being here, deep in the wilderness—that was when you got a true sense of its vastness.

Milton had visited the country before. The last time had been a babysitting assignment with an analyst from the Firm who was conducting business in Canberra. The capital was as bland and dull as Washington, D.C., a grid of clean streets, a place that emptied as soon as the legislative business was done. There had been no opportunity for him to visit the interior. Today, as he watched the sun rise, he was a thousand kilometres from the capital. He was deep in the outback.

Harry Douglas walked over to him. Douglas was the foreman. He was gruff and coarse, and Milton had known him for years. They had served in the SAS together. Milton was not in the business of having friends, and, since relationships were impractical for Group Fifteen agents, he had denuded himself of most of his attachments when he had been recruited.

Douglas had been medically discharged from the Regiment after he had broken both legs when his parachute had failed to deploy properly during a training jump. The two of them had been close, and they had commiserated about Douglas's discharge over a long night of drinking in Hereford. He had explained to Milton that he was going to go back home to Australia and work on his father's sheep station. They had emailed a couple of times while Milton was working in Florida, and when Douglas had suggested he come over for a visit, he had agreed. Miami had been pleasant enough, but it was a town that was full of distractions and temptations. He had been contemplating another cross-country trek to put those dangerous impulses behind him, but the promise of something completely different had been difficult to resist.

"All right, John?" Harry said.

"Yeah."

"You look done in."

"Don't look so good yourself."

Harry grinned. They were both competitive, and each had made no secret of the fact that he was a better man than the other. The score was most easily kept with the number of sheep that they were able to shear in the course of a day. Douglas was impeded by the limp he still suffered after his accident. Milton was more agile. But Douglas was big and strong, able to wrestle the sheep, and he had the benefit of years of experience. His best day saw him add 124 sheep to his tally. Milton lagged somewhere behind him with a best of 89. He kept trying, though. He was too committed to give up.

"Long day ahead. We'll grab a couple of hours of kip, get some breakfast and then go at it. You okay with that?"

"Of course."

They were at Booligal Sheep Station, a shearing shed on the outskirts of the town of Booligal. It was in deepest New South Wales, the last town on the road between Hay and Wilcannia. Milton had come to assess the size of a station by the number of shearing stands in the shearing shed. The station they had worked at for the last week had six stands. That wasn't unusual. Booligal had ten stands. It was a big station, and it promised an awful lot of sheep that were going to need to be sheared.

Milton reached back into the Jeep for his pack and followed Douglas and the others as they walked into the rickety building. Their accommodation was in a room adjacent to the mess. They each had a camp bed and a locker to store their things. Milton walked along the room to the single bathroom. There was a shower, a toilet and a sink. It had been given a cursory clean, but it was still dirty.

He didn't care.

Milton went back to the dormitory, dropped his bag on the bed and took out his dungarees and flannels. They had been new when he had been given them, but they had taken an almighty battering during the season so that they were almost rigid with the dust and dried sweat and blood. He sat down on the edge of the bed and prised off his boots. They had been new, too, redolent with the tang of fresh leather. They were cracked and beaten now, baked in the sun for six weeks. They looked ancient.

He undressed, took a quick shower, and then took out his copy of the Big Book and opened it at random. Milton read two pages, stopping to reread the sentence that he had already underlined on two previous occasions.

"The idea that somehow, someday he will control and enjoy his drinking is the great obsession of every abnormal drinker."

He thought about that for a moment and then put the book back into his pack. He had no intention that any of the others should see that he had it. They would just have questions and he had no interest in discussing his illness.

He lay down to rest. He was asleep within minutes of his head touching the pillow.

Chapter Six

TWO HOURS' sleep wasn't enough, but it was all he was going to get. He got up, washed his face and pulled on his dirty clothes once again.

Harry and the others were waiting for him outside. The other men in the crew were Eric, a brash Queenslander, and Mervyn, a Tasmanian who had lived up here for the last decade.

"It's Sleeping Beauty!" Harry announced as Milton emerged.

Milton raised a middle finger in acknowledgement.

They had cheese rolls and coffee for breakfast and then, when they were done, Harry drew lots for the shearing pens. He drew the first pen, the favoured one for this particular shed. Eric drew the second pen, Milton the third and Mervyn the fourth. They walked across to the shed.

The sun was already brutally hot. Milton put his hat on his head and tipped the brim to keep the sun out of his eyes. His gear was heavy and trapped the heat, and he was dripping with sweat within moments.

The shed left something to be desired. It was an old building, falling down in places. It was also built on stilts. There was no storage for the sheep at the back of the shed, as was the case in the best arranged facilities, so the animals were housed directly under the catching pens. That was bad planning. Milton knew from experience that sheep tended to excrete while they were being sheared. That meant that the sheep in the top pens would soil the sheep beneath them, and then Milton and the others would be covered in it when the time came for those sheep to be sheared.

"Ready?" Harry called out.

Milton laced his fingers and cracked his knuckles. "You're in trouble today. I can tell just by looking at you. You're exhausted."

"What? You're not?"

"Feeling all right."

"Fighting talk, John."

"Ten bucks says I do more than you today."

"Not a chance."

"You taking the bet?"

"Of course I am. You're on."

They started. The sheep were fully grown merino wethers, heavy and antsy animals who had no interest whatsoever in making the process easy. Milton got his first sheep and dragged it onto the board. He wrestled with it until he had leaned it back enough to shear a circle around its hindquarters; that way, if it defecated, the excrement didn't stay on the wool and attract flies. Most of the animals were infested with maggots and other insects. Milton was on the third animal when he noticed that he had sickly green pus that looked like a baby's vomit all over his hands and arms. He had sheared through a boil. He ignored it. No point in getting wound up about it. He knew that was just the start. There would be more to come.

And he had been right about the shitting and pissing. When he dragged a new animal onto the board, it dropped its guts onto the animal below. Within five minutes he had their waste over his clothes and his hands. Within ten minutes, he was covered in a sheen of sweat and sheep urine and pungent shit, the smell of it enough to make him gag even when he forced himself to breathe through his mouth.

He ignored it, working steadily, occasionally looking over at Harry in the next pen across. The big Aussie didn't have his agility, but he muscled the sheep with power and determination. He kept up a stream of colourful invective as he worked, as if their reluctance to do what he wanted was a personal affront to him. "Come on, you little bitch. Get over here. Don't... don't you fuckin' dare... don't you fuckin' shit on me, you little bitch..."

"What you got?" Milton called out as the sun was at its apogee.

"Ten," Harry shouted out. "What you got?"

"One behind."

His tone was surprised. "Really?"

"Nervous?"

He laughed. "You'll fade away. You always do. You don't have the stamina."

"Got plenty."

Harry shook his head. "No way, mate."

Milton had improved his technique day by day, and now he was able to shear a sheep in ten minutes from start to finish. You had to be careful not to cut the animal, for the manager would complain if his animals were sent back to him with too many nicks and scrapes on their freshly shorn flanks. It wasn't always easy to avoid, though. Some of the animals were old and wrinkled and the folds of skin were easy to catch with the blades.

They worked on, took half an hour to rest, and then worked through until dusk. The crickets were chirping as Milton finally pushed the last sheep down the chute, wiped the sweat from his eyes with the back of his arm, and leaned back against the wall of the pen. He was done in. Maggots writhed in the cuffs of his trousers and he had a mixture of blood and pus and lanolin on his bare arms and clothes.

He had wrapped tape around two of his fingers where he had sliced into the flesh with the blades. His wrist and elbow were taped for extra support. His legs were weak and he was light-headed from the heat. He needed a drink of water, a cigarette and a shower, in that order.

Harry was in no better shape. His arm was wrapped where he had an unpleasant purple boil. It had worsened during the day. He said, with no effort to conceal his distaste, that it was an infection that he had picked up from the sheep they had sheared at Red River Station last week.

"Well?" Harry asked as he walked over to Milton, Eric and Mervyn.

"Hundred and five," Milton said.

He grinned at him. "No way."

"Straight up." He had been marking each sheep with a stroke of his knife against the wood. The board was covered in notches.

"Good work, pommie," Eric said.

Milton looked at Harry with sudden trepidation. He realised, with an awareness of how foolish it was, that this actually *mattered*. "You?"

Harry grinned wider. "Hundred and ten."

Milton shook his head. "You're kidding."

"I told you you'll never beat me."

"He's not bad, though, gaffer," Mervyn opined.

Eric chipped in. "First time I saw you, I said to myself, ten minutes, I said, ten minutes is as long as you'd last. I said you'd be as useless as tits on a bull, ain't that right, Merv?"

"S'right."

"New at this, and a pommie to boot."

Milton's nationality was the main standing joke between them. Mervyn and Eric, tough and gnarled Aussies, returned to it again and again. They were fiercely nationalistic, proud of their country, and it was a source of great amusement to them that he was a foreigner in a foreign land. They didn't spare Harry, either. Their foreman might have been born in Australia, but he had been in the United Kingdom for long enough to have ceded at least a little of his heritage. He was, they suggested, infected with Englishness. He was a half-pommie.

"I'm glad I have your approval," Milton said.

"Don't get too comfortable. You've still got a face like

a kicked-in shitcan."

Milton shook his head and laughed. He took off his hat as they walked together to the outbuilding with the mess and their dorm. Harry was alongside him, unable to wipe the grin from his face. Milton had always been competitive. He hated to lose. He and Harry had spent hours in the range together when they were in the Regiment, each of them determined to demonstrate that he was more accurate than the other. Milton had won most of those head-to-head duels and, indeed, he had beaten him two nights ago when they had set cans and bottles as targets and shot them with the antique .310 rifle they kept in the Jeep. But the sheep were something else. He knew that he had picked a difficult challenge, and that, in all good faith, he was never going to be able to best him. But it didn't mean that he wouldn't give it a damned good go.

"Don't know about you fellas," Harry said, "but I could eat the arse out of a low-flying duck. What you say we get cleaned up and drive into town? We can get something to eat."

"You paying, skipper?"

"I'm paying."

"Hallelujah!"

Eric was kidding. Harry always paid for their food and drink after a hard day in the pens.

Mervyn looked over at him with a coy smile. "Matilda still coming?"

Harry answered with staged wariness. "As far as I know."

The grizzled shearer chuckled. "Best news I've heard all day."

Harry was protective of his kid sister. Mervyn knew that one of the best ways to wind him up was to make suggestive comments about her. Milton knew—and Mervyn knew it, too—that Matilda was more than capable of rebuffing those comments herself, but it never failed to get a rise out of her brother.

They reached the door. Harry barred the way ahead with his arm. "If you think Matilda is going to look at you twice, you're crazy. You'll have more luck pushing shit uphill with a rubber fork on a hot day. And if you annoy her, you'll have me to deal with."

"That'll be the least of his problems," Eric said. "She'd eat him for lunch."

Chapter Seven

THEY TOOK the Jeep into Booligal. The village was tiny, with a general store and post office, a cricket oval for the occasional social game, shaded eating areas and a playground. The Booligal Hotel offered food and drink. It was a tired, dusty business that survived on the back of the tourist trade. Townsfolk made the trek out to Booligal for an "authentic" cattle drive, moving stock through the outback. A drover's life would normally have been hard and uncomfortable, but the tourists were treated to floored tents with mattresses, hot showers and luxury food. A party was waiting to start their trek as they walked into the bar that evening. Eric and Mervyn made no attempt to hide their disdain, looking over at their table and making loud remarks about how they found the whole thing distasteful. Milton said nothing. He bought a packet of cigarettes from the bar and smoked them quietly by himself, happy to sit there and take it all in.

There were three other men in the bar. They were in their late middle age, broken-down old shearers bearing the scars of their profession like badges of honour. The fridge was on the blink, so the bottled beers were lined up on the bar and served warm. Harry went up and corralled three and a plastic bottle of water. Milton had explained to him that he had stopped drinking and, after a period spent trying to work out why he would do such a fool thing, he had eventually accepted it. The others had not been so forthcoming, and, as he took his glass of warm water, they made the usual suggestions as to his masculinity and then his sexuality. Milton was not bothered by any of it. He knew they were joking and, in any event, their ribbing was nothing compared to the continued serenity he found in abstinence. He would usually have felt uncomfortable in a bar—the AA line was that if you went into a barbershop, eventually you would get a haircut—but he didn't feel vulnerable here. He was in good company, with friends, and he felt satisfied after a hard day of work. And he knew for certain that the alternative was not appealing. He had woken up in enough gutters with no memory of how he arrived there to last a lifetime. He was not tempted.

They ordered plates of food and drank several more bottles of beer. Eric, whom Milton had quickly diagnosed as a man who could not hold his beer, quickly became drunk. His sense of humour, coarse at the best of times, became even more so. He kept glancing over at the table where the tourists were sitting. There were eight of them, five men and three women. It looked as if three of the men and the three women were couples. The remaining men, both slightly effeminate, looked like a couple, too. Milton could easily diagnose how well *that* was going to go down. They were all middle aged and, he guessed, they had paid a handsome price for the experience that they were about to have.

Milton's attention was drawn to the two guides who were sitting with them. They were authentic-looking blokes, dressed in khaki pants and shirts with the logo of the tour company stitched into the lapels. So far, so corporate, but it was the small details that Milton noticed that betrayed them: their hands were calloused, their arms and faces discoloured with small red blotches from the sun, their faces tanned a deep nutty brown apart from their foreheads where their hats would sit. They had the same complexions as Eric, Merv, Harry and Milton did. They worked outdoors. They looked tough.

Milton could see that Eric was getting worked up to start something. Harry could see it, too, and tried to redirect the conversation when Eric started making comments about how rich townsfolk would never be able to understand what it was really like to live and work in the outback.

It wasn't a question of being able to overhear what he was saying. He was making no effort to speak quietly. The sensible thing would have been for the tourists to ignore him. Eventually, he would have become bored of his sport and allowed the subject to be changed. But one of the men took offence to Eric's remarks, swivelled in his chair and told him to be quiet.

The mood changed.

"You what, sport?" Eric said.

"I said you ought to keep your opinions to yourself. You don't know the first thing about us."

"That's where you're wrong, see?" he said. "I know plenty."

One of the guides stood. "Leave it out, fella. Just enjoy your beer and mind your business."

Eric ignored the suggestion. Milton realised that he was drunker than he had suspected. He spoke quickly, his face was flushed red and there was a nervous tic in his cheek that danced up and down. "You ought to be ashamed of yourself, you fuck muppet."

"What did you say?"

"Leave it out, Eric," Harry said.

"Fuck that, skip. I ain't sitting here and taking bollocks from a dipshit like that."

"That's not necessary," said one of the effeminate men.

"Fuck off, you chocolate driller."

Milton groaned and rested his forehead in his hand. Eric laughed, turning to Mervyn and looking for a reaction. They shared a laugh. Harry scowled at him and told him to shut up, but it was too late.

The two guides had stood up.

Milton assessed them afresh. They were both a touch over six foot and, he guessed, fifteen or sixteen stone. Big, rugged men who looked like they knew how to handle themselves. The nearest one was wearing a big belt buckle with a steer design to hold up his moleskins. There was a half-finished bottle of beer at his place at the table, but he had been sipping at it and he looked clear-eyed. He wasn't drunk. Neither of them was drunk.

Eric most certainly was. He staggered out of his seat and bumped against the table as he approached the man. Harry tried to grab his wrist, but he brushed his hand away.

The two of them squared up.

"Sit down."

"Don't think so."

Eric threw the first punch. The guide deflected it with his left hand, cocked back his right and drilled Eric in the face. There was a splash of blood and a crunch as the bones in his nose snapped. Eric's legs went out from beneath him and he fell against an empty table, overturning it as he slid onto the floor.

"Any of you pig-ugly shearers want to make an issue of that?"

Milton was nearest to the guide. He sighed a little. This was the other reason he tried to avoid bars. He had been involved in brawls two times in the last twelve months, and both occasions had landed him in trouble.

The man was glaring down at him. "What are you looking at?"

"I'm not looking at anything," Milton said.

"You're looking at me, dickhead. You want some, too?"

Milton sighed again. He stood, very deliberately, and took a step to his right so that he was standing between the fallen Eric and the man. He didn't say anything, but he didn't have to. He was shorter and a couple of stones lighter, but there was an aura about him that made it very obvious that he wasn't a man to be crossed. He usually hid it, but, when required, it was as effective as it had always been. There was an almost physical quality to his confidence, a manifestation that made it very clear that he wouldn't hesitate to use violence and, if he was pushed, it would go badly for those in his way. And then there were his eyes. Pale blue, flinty, as lifeless as ice. There was no prospect of mercy or empathy or understanding. They promised pain.

The guide squared up to him for a moment, but then, as Milton cocked his head and stood his ground, the man took a step back.

"Fine," he said, bristling. "You keep your pal in line or there's going to be a problem."

Still Milton said nothing. He stayed where he was, staring at the guide until he backed away, returned to his table and sat down.

Harry was helping Eric to his feet. "You got what you had coming to you, you idiot. I don't know why I let you drink. That mouth of yours is always getting you into trouble."

Eric didn't respond; he was still woozy. Mervyn, who looked like he would have felt obliged to come to his friend's aid, now appeared to be relieved that the situation had been defused.

"Jesus," Harry sighed. "Well done, John."

Milton waved it off. It was nothing.

* * *

THE TOURING PARTY left the room soon after that. The atmosphere had been spoiled for them and it was obvious that they had no interest in seeing whether the brawl would reignite when Eric finally came around. Harry looked at Milton and shook his head: part apology, part wry admission of the foolishness of the whole situation. Milton had seen similar attitudes during the three months that he had been working with Harry across New South Wales. As an industry, shearing was, as Harry put it, "on its arse." It was assailed on the one side by the trend towards mechanisation and, on the other, by big corporate station owners who were determined to drive down their costs. Harry's family owned their station and that lent them some measure of security, but, as he had admitted at the melancholic end to a previous evening, that didn't mean that they would be around forever. Progress couldn't be ignored. Change was coming.

All of the shearers Milton had met had felt an affinity for each other through their shared vocation and the life they eked out of the wilderness. It was a harsh, difficult place to survive, and the sight of these soft, pampered tourists, backed up by a convoy of four-by-fours in the event that they should get tired, was a thumb in the eye.

Harry suggested that they should leave soon afterwards. Eric had been cowed by his embarrassment at the hands of the guide, Melvyn was half asleep, and Milton was happy to go along with the majority view. They finished the round, bought some travellers to drink on the way home, and headed back to the Jeep.

Chapter Eight

AVI BACHMAN had never been to the Adriatic coast before. He looked down from the plane as they circled for landing, deciding that the landscape was one of the most spectacular that he had ever seen. They traversed glassy bays, craggy bluffs, hidden coves and beaches, vineyards, olive groves, and forests of cypress and pine. It was wild and dramatic, the gathering darkness gradually prickling as the lights of Dubrovnik and the surrounding towns and villages were lit.

Bachman was tired. He had been travelling for the last three days and it was beginning to catch up with him. They had driven him west from Baton Rouge, following I-10 for eleven hours. They had passed through Beaumont, changed vehicles outside Houston and then swung to the southwest. They crossed the Mexican border at Laredo. That was the moment when he had been the most anxious. The breakout had made the national news and it was obvious that they would have circulated his details to the nearby airports. The border, though? The constant stream of traffic meant that it should have been easier to sneak across. He had hidden in the trunk of the car for the hour it took to approach the crossing and then get over it and, as it happened, the scrutiny they received was minimal. He had stepped out of the trunk as soon as they were five miles inside the border. The fresh air was a boon after the stuffy interior, rendered all the sweeter by the fact that he was breathing it in as a free man.

They drove on to Monterrey. The Rabins said that they were going to investigate a possible sighting of Milton and that it would be better if they travelled separately. Bachman was fine with that. He wouldn't have wanted them to travel with him in any event. He bought a ticket on an Aeromexico flight, changed planes at Mexico City and then, finally, managed a little sleep as he crossed the Atlantic to London. From there, he changed again to a third plane for the flight to Croatia. Bachman had travelled alone. He had no interest in a chaperone, and, although he knew that the Mossad would pick him up again as soon as he landed, it was pleasant to think, as he reclined in his first-class bed, that he had a little privacy for the first time in months.

* * *

THE PLANE landed and the passengers—a mixture of tourists and business people—disembarked. Bachman passed through immigration and, since he had no luggage, continued quickly through the terminal and took a taxi from the rank outside.

"Yes, sir?" the driver said.

"Villa Sheherezade, please."

He settled back in the car and gazed out the windows as the driver began the twenty-kilometre transit from the airport. Bachman knew the history. This had been a rough area for years, torn apart by wars and political strife, but, since the end of Milosevic and the outbreak of peace, it had been allowed to develop and take advantage of the bountiful natural advantages with which it had been bestowed.

Dubrovnik still bore the badges of its recent travails. As they passed through the centre, he saw the pockmarks of mortar fire against ancient walls and remembered that the Old Town, garlanded but not protected by its years of history, had been shelled during a long and damaging siege.

The driver spoke good English and he kept up a running commentary as they drove, despite Bachman's silence. The man was a proud Croat, he said, and the Dalmatian coast was destined to become one of the most popular and exclusive destinations in the Mediterranean region. He said that the Croatians had learned the lessons of those places, and would defend their town's heritage even as they marketed it as a new destination. Bachman looked out the window and did not share the man's optimism. The Old Town was gradually succumbing to capitalism. The menus outside the taverns were translated into English, German and Italian, and high-end boutiques had taken over the medieval lanes.

The driver tried once more to engage him in conversation, but he wasn't interested and kept quiet. In the end, the man took the hint and they drove the rest of the way with just the radio as a soundtrack.

* * *

VILLA SHEHEREZADE was ten miles to the south of the city. Bachman observed the road behind the taxi very carefully and, as they passed into the countryside, the traffic grew less busy until there were no other cars within visible distance. It was impossible to be sure, but Bachman was reasonably confident that they were not being followed. He had made it plain to the Rabins that he would treat surveillance as a breach of his agreement with Victor Blum. He was sure that the Mossad would have had someone on the flight with him, and perhaps a *sayan* waiting to pick him up at the airport, but, as the traffic thinned out it became more difficult for a tail to remain undetected. They could have called his bluff, of course, but it didn't look like they had. They knew he had unfinished business with Milton, and that he would need their help. Perhaps they were ready to trust that his desire to revenge himself was enough to prevent him from disappearing for a second time. That would have been a reasonable assumption. Bachman had no intention of going dark, at least not yet.

The villa was reached by way of a private road that

turned off the main route and sliced a path through a copse of trees. The road twisted for the final third of a mile until it ran along the edge of a steep cliff with a precipitous drop to the wave-pounded rocks below.

Bachman surveyed the property and concluded that Meir Shavit had done well for himself since he had left the army. The villa was nestled in a small depression amid a stack of steep cliffs that were themselves topped with lush greenery. It was three storeys tall, sleekly modern, and constructed from glass and the same stone that formed the cliffs. It overlooked a wide gravel parking area. A Jaguar was parked next to the house and there was a top-of-the-range Land Rover Discovery alongside that. A path snaked through beautifully tended gardens and led around the side of the house to, Bachman presumed, the cliff edge and the sea. He saw a large picture window on each of the second and third floors. A grand residence like this, in such an expensive part of the world, must have cost several million pounds.

His old commanding officer had done very well indeed.

Bachman paid the driver, waited until he had driven back to the road, and crunched across the gravel to knock on the door. He waited for a minute, self-consciously turning to look back down the access road, half expecting to see that he was observed.

He heard footsteps approaching across a wooden floor. The door opened. Shavit stood in the doorway and gazed out into the gloom. His expression changed from one of irritated enquiry to one of open-mouthed shock.

"Avi?"

"Yes, Meir. It's me."

The old man reached up and placed a leathery hand on Bachman's cheek. "Avi," he said, "you are out."

"I am."

"I thought I would never see you again."

"Don't be so foolish," Bachman said, allowing himself

a warm smile. "I always planned to come and visit."

"But it has been…"

"Too long."

"Ten years?"

"A little more."

They had spoken several times, most recently when Bachman had called Shavit from Angola. That had been only a brief conversation, necessarily so because he knew that they were being eavesdropped on by the prison authorities, and just long enough for him to provide the code word that Shavit needed in order to activate Bachman's failsafe. Upon receipt of the code, the old man had agreed to send copies of the files Bachman had given him to Victor Blum in Tel Aviv so that his threat could be demonstrated.

"I did what you said," Shavit said.

"I know you did. And I'm here. It worked."

"I have so many questions…" He paused, unable to hide the perplexed expression, before he shook his head and dismissed it. "But, no, they can wait. You have had a long day of travel, I think."

"Quite long."

"You are tired and hungry and I leave you on my doorstep." He tutted with theatrical gusto. "Please, *habib*. You must come inside."

Bachman followed him down a hallway and through the house to the kitchen. The rooms were airy, with vast windows that admitted the fading light and allowed views of the spectacular vista outside. The decor was modern and sleek, with expensively minimal pieces of furniture. Shavit led the way up a flight of stairs to the dual kitchen and dining room on the top floor. The sea was visible through the wide windows and Bachman went over to look out. There was a balcony outside and, below that, a series of terraces descending in tiers until they ended down at the water's edge.

"My housekeeper has left for the day," Shavit said

apologetically. "But I still cook. You remember? I was not so bad, no?"

"You don't have to cook for me."

"Don't be ridiculous, Avi. Of course I will cook for you."

He went to the fridge, opened the door and took out a plate with a large steak covered with cling film. Meir put the plate on the counter and unhooked a frying pan from a rack on the wall.

"Meir, you don't have to—"

He hushed him with a wave of his hand. "Medium rare?"

He stopped protesting. "Yes, thank you."

The old man poured a little oil into the pan and rested it over a lit burner. Bachman watched him as he worked. Shavit had aged since Bachman had seen him last. He had been vigorous before, still visiting Tel Aviv's Gordon-Frishman beach every morning to run along the sand and then swim in the ocean. Time had not been kind. He was more shrivelled than Bachman remembered him. His skull seemed to have shrunk, leaving his skin to drape over it in loose flaps and folds. His ears had sprouted clumps of hair and he peered through spectacles that he had not needed before. He was wizened in stature, too, all that vitality replaced with a hesitant shambling as he traversed the space between the hob, the central island and the refrigerator.

Meir Shavit had been Bachman's commanding officer when he had been a commando in the Israeli Defense Force. That was before he had been reassigned to the Mossad, when he was learning his trade. He had overseen his training and then they had worked together in some of the most dangerous places in the world. Powerful bonds could be forged in those crucibles and Shavit was his oldest friend. No, he corrected himself: he was his *only* friend. There were no others.

The room was soon filled with the smell of cooked

meat. Shavit took a plate of Dauphinoise potatoes from the refrigerator, peeled away the cling film, reheated them in a microwave and then put them, together with the cooked steak, onto a plate. There was a large modern dining table in the kitchen and the old man collected cutlery and made a place for Bachman to sit.

"You eat," he said. "We talk afterwards."

Bachman finished the meal quickly. He was hungry and the meat and potatoes were delicious. Meir Shavit sat opposite him and watched with a look that Bachman knew was paternal as he worked his way through the plate. He said nothing, letting him eat in peace, and, when he was done, he collected the plate, deposited it in the dishwasher and suggested that they retire to his study for a drink and a smoke. Bachman was tired—he would have been very happy to go to bed and deal with all of this in the morning—but he couldn't string his old friend along like that. He knew that Shavit would have questions. A lot of questions. He owed him answers to at least some of them.

Shavit led the way to a large study. The windows were huge and fitted on runners so that they could be slid to the side. They were open now, and a gentle evening breeze brought the suggestion of dampness and the smell of brine into the room. The murmur of the waves faded in and out, in and out, and Bachman became even more aware of his fatigue.

The muted light from a lantern outside filtered through the window. The old man flicked on a desk lamp and a standard lamp and then went across to a shelf that held bottles and glasses. He took down two shot glasses, collected a bottle of whiskey, opened it and poured out two generous measures. He handed one to Bachman, collected two cigars from a humidor on the desk and then led the way to two leather armchairs that had been arranged before a fireplace. The embers were red and glowing, and a book had been left open across the arm of one of the chairs. Shavit had been relaxing here when

Bachman had arrived.

"Sit, Avi," he said.

"I'm sorry if I surprised you."

Shavit waved it off. "Not at all. But you must tell me what happened. Where have you been? I hear nothing for years and then I hear you are in prison."

He leaned back in the chair, trying to relax the bunched muscles that were tight across his shoulders. It was a long story, and he was exhausted, but he was going to have to tell it sometime. It might as well be now, with a glass of whiskey in his hand.

* * *

HE STARTED with the aftermath of the explosion that they had engineered to fake his own death. Shavit knew of the events that had necessitated that course of action: Bachman's illicit relationship with Lila Arson, a Palestinian girl he had met in the West Bank town of Hebron. Shavit had been open minded when Bachman had explained that he was in love with the girl, as he had known that he would be. Shavit was a fierce warrior, but he was also a pragmatist and he had long advocated a dialogue with the Arabs rather than round after round of pointless wars. It was Shavit who had suggested that they would have to leave the country and make a life for themselves elsewhere. He had told Bachman that the relationship would have seen them both assassinated had it ever come to the attention of Victor Blum.

And Bachman knew that he was right.

Shavit had helped him to formulate the plan.

He had helped obscure the truth when he had triggered the bomb in Cairo. Bachman knew that the agency would question his death, but he only needed to create enough doubt that a full investigation would be rendered unnecessary. Bachman had given Lila instructions to leave her apartment, providing her with false papers and enough money to buy a flight and get clear. He had intended to tell Shavit where they were going, but the old man had insisted that he must not know. The Mossad knew that the two men were close. If Shavit really did not know where Bachman was headed, there was no way he could betray him under questioning.

After they had collected their new identities in Paris, they had gone to the United States. When Shavit asked him how they had supported themselves, he had answered with frank honesty. The admission that he had worked as a hit man did not faze him in the slightest. He nodded sagely and suggested that it made sense. Bachman had a very particular, and very lucrative, set of talents. What else was he going to do?

Bachman told him about New Orleans. He paused for a moment, taking a sip of the whiskey in the hope that it might disguise the thickening in his voice.

"There is a man," he said. "His name is Milton. I was asked to take him out. I didn't know it was Milton, not until I got to New Orleans. If I had known, maybe I wouldn't have taken the job. Maybe..." He swallowed another mouthful of whiskey and looked away for a moment, settling himself.

"Do I know him?"

"No. He used to work for the British government. He was a cleaner. Like me. He was good, too. You remember the hit on the Iranians? The reactor? He was on that team. It was us, the CIA, and him. He impressed me then. Very cold. Very clinical." He paused again. "It turns out that he was out of the game, just like I was. I don't know what happened to him, some kind of breakdown, but he was out. Just wandering. He ended up in New Orleans helping a woman who was interfering with my client's plans. They paid me to kill him. It didn't go down so well, though. Milton saw me coming. So I took this woman's brother, took him out into the bayou so the woman would back off, pull Milton back, but he found me. Took me by surprise. He attacked us. He killed Lila."

The old man's mouth fell open. "I'm sorry, Avi."

Bachman did not feel sorrow. He had never felt sorrow. That would come, in time, but there had been no space for any other emotion than the burning rage that had consumed him since that day.

Shavit reached across and laid his withered hand over Bachman's.

Bachman grimaced, angry with himself for showing weakness, and pulled his hand away. "I swore that I would kill him. We fought, I had him beat, but the woman he was working for distracted me and he hit me in the head with a crank. Put me down. When I woke up, Milton had handed me over to the police. They were preparing for a trial. They wanted to kill me. But that's not going to happen, Meir. Not while Milton is still out there, still breathing. It's not going to happen. He has to pay."

Chapter Nine

BACHMAN SLEPT well that night. The windows were open, letting in the cool zephyr that rose up from the sea and the sound of the waves as they broke against the rocks below. It was the most comfortable bed he had lain on for months, since he and Lila had left their New York apartment for the trip south to Louisiana. He thought of their apartment as he lay with his fingers laced beneath his head and his eyes closed, and the memories of his dead wife flowed back again. He indulged himself for a moment, remembering her face, concerned, as he always was, that he would eventually forget what she looked like and be unable to recall her beauty. He felt his mood start to darken and he caught himself. He didn't need to feel his anger to be energised.

Shavit was waiting for him in the kitchen.

"It is a pleasant morning. Shall we have breakfast on the terrace?"

Shavit opened a set of French doors to the balcony and led the way outside. To the rear of the house was the series of tiers that led down to the water. They followed steps from the balcony down to the first terrace, and then another set that had been cut into the rock, descending all the way to the foot of the cliff, where they passed a collection of jasmine and lemon trees from which emanated the cheerful chirruping of cicadas. There was an extensive covered terrace that, combined with an adjoining decked area, provided al fresco dining and relaxation space. The tide was tamed by a rocky outcrop that effectively provided a natural lagoon. The water within its ambit was still and, although it was a crystal blue, it was deep, too. There was a jetty at the end of the deck that reached out ten metres into the water. A rowing boat was moored to a post at the end of it, its fibreglass hull rattling against the pilings as it was gently buffeted by the current. There was a table and two chairs on the deck.

They sat down and, as if she had been watching, a middle-aged woman came down the steps with a tray of food and a jug of orange juice. Shavit introduced her as Mrs. Grgec, his housekeeper. The woman brushed a covering of fallen blossoms from the table so that she could set down plates of scrambled egg and toast. She poured them two glasses of orange juice, noting that it was freshly squeezed, before she set off back up to the house again.

"The food here is exceptional," he said. "The fish is superb. Shrimp, octopus, oysters. Wonderful wines." The old man started to wax lyrical, explaining how Italian cooking influenced the local cuisine, how risotto became *rizot* and prosciutto became *prsut*. Bachman remembered that his old mentor had always been motivated by his stomach, and that some things never changed. He let him talk, though, drinking his juice and enjoying the cooling breeze that hushed in off the sea.

"What do you think of it all?" Shavit said, encompassing his estate with a sweep of his arm.

"It's very impressive," he replied. "And I never thought I'd see you with a housekeeper."

"The private security business was lucrative," Shavit explained.

"Is that what happened after the army?"

"I quit a year after you left. I set up on my own. Western companies pay well to be safe in the Middle East. I hired ex-soldiers, people like you. We could charge a small fortune for personal security services. The company outgrew me in the end. I sold it to Manage Risk. Have you heard of them?"

"Of course," Bachman said. Manage Risk was an American multinational that was more like a private army than a security company.

"They paid me several million dollars. I've been living off that ever since. I have no children. No wife. No dependants. This life suits me very well."

"Why here?"

"Why not? I visited when I was a boy. I've always liked it. I get to swim in the sea every morning; I eat and drink very well. It is peaceful. I am not disturbed."

There was a pause. Bachman looked out at the water. "The files?" he asked.

"They are safe," he said. "Away from here."

"Where?"

"In a safe deposit box. It is safe."

"Meir," Bachman said, looking his old friend in the eye, "you can't go to get it now, not unless we mean to use it. I can't say for sure that I wasn't followed here. There will be *sayanim*. Agents. I was careful, but I'm just one man."

Shavit shook his head. "You would have been followed. But that's fine. They will not move against me."

"They'll know you're my fallback, now. That makes you a target."

"Perhaps. But they'll know that the consequences of going against you will be the same if they go against me. They don't know where the files are. For all they know, they could be ready to be sent to a newspaper. And I'm just an old man. What are they really going to do?"

"I just want you to be careful."

"Always."

"We will have a procedure," Bachman said. "I will call you every day between eleven in the morning and one in the afternoon. If I do not call, release half of the files. Save the rest. They will protect you."

Shavit nodded. He took a sip of orange juice and wiped his thin, bloodless lips with his napkin. "What's next?"

"Milton is next," he said.

"Yes. Has anything been done?"

"He's been found."

"Where?"

"Australia. He has a friend there. Someone from the military."

"And the plan? They will eliminate him for you?"

"No, Meir, they will not. They will collect him. But it has to be me. He will die at my hand."

He stood.

"I'm going to Australia."

"When?"

"I bought a ticket at the airport yesterday. My flight is at three."

Shavit nodded. "Then I will drive you."

* * *

THEY LEFT just after breakfast. Shavit led the way to the Jaguar. He turned the car around and drove up the drive and onto the road beyond. Shavit was quiet for the first twenty minutes. He turned on the radio and they listened together in silence.

They passed the sign for the airport when he finally spoke. "This Milton. How will it be done?"

"Hand to hand. One on one."

"He is good, though?"

"Better than average. Not as good as me."

"But you would give him a chance?"

He waved a hand dismissively. "Hardly. We've fought twice. I beat him twice. He's lucky he's still alive."

"But he is still alive, Avi. Why take the risk? Put him on his knees and put a bullet in his brain."

Bachman shook his head, and when he spoke, his words were loaded with anger. "I want to humiliate him. I want to beat him to within an inch of his life, put my hands around his throat and then squeeze the breath out of him. I want my face to be the last thing he ever sees."

Meir nodded. Perhaps he remembered Bachman's

temper and how frightening it could be. His vehemence stilled the conversation and they drove on in silence for another mile.

Bachman exhaled. "I know you mean well. But he's nothing compared to me. I'll crush him. I'll make him sorry he was born."

The terminal came into view to the right. "I know how good you are," Meir said, "but be careful. That's all."

Shavit pulled up against the curb in the drop-off zone and killed the engine.

"Thank you," Bachman said. "For everything."

Shavit waved it off. "Don't be foolish, *habib.*"

"Be careful. I mean it. You're in play now, too."

"I know."

"If you don't hear from me, assume the worst."

"I know what to do, my boy. You don't need to worry about me."

Shavit reached out his hand and the two of them shook.

"Good luck."

"I won't need it," Bachman said, "but thanks."

"Call me tomorrow."

"I will. Goodbye, Meir."

"Goodbye, Avi."

He got out and watched as his mentor disappeared into the light traffic. He wondered whether he would ever see him again. Probably not. Once Milton was disposed of, he would disappear again. He had money. He didn't need to work, at least not for economic reasons. He would still take jobs, though, because the urge to kill was something that had become entrenched deep within him, and, if he was going to do it, he might as well be paid for it. But he would do it from the shadows, out of the Mossad's sight.

He walked into the terminal and checked the departures board. Dubrovnik to Athens to Melbourne. He would be in Australia in twenty-two hours.

Chapter Ten

ZIGGY PENN looked through the windshield at the slow-moving traffic and the pedestrians that thronged the sidewalks. It was a stifling night, and Tokyo was busy. The heat was uncomfortable and the air-conditioning unit in his car was sporadic at best. His sweat had soaked through the fabric of his shirt and now it was stuck to his back. Ziggy was nervous. He had allowed himself plenty of time for the journey across the city, so punctuality was not the cause of his concern. It was what he was planning to do once he got where he was going.

A distant light turned green, the queue was released, and Ziggy got moving again. He took a quieter road through Minato until he reached Azabu, Tokyo's most upscale residential district. It was home to embassies and high-end businesses, and counted plenty of notable residents within its population. There were well-heeled ex-pats, diplomats and business people, the whole district awash with their money.

Ziggy found the address he wanted and turned off the road. He was at the top of a ramp facing the entrance to an underground garage. He took out his wallet and removed his faked credentials. The gate to the garage was operated by way of a security card. Ziggy had hacked the system, obtained the code and pasted it onto a magstripe that he had pasted onto a blank card. He lowered his window, reached out and slid the card through the machine. It worked, as he had known it would. The door retracted and Ziggy drove into the garage.

He drove slowly into the dimly lit space, found an empty bay and reversed his car into it. The garage was full of expensive cars: in the row opposite him he saw a Lexus, a Bentley and a Jaguar, each ensconced within a generously proportioned bay. He waited a moment, satisfying himself that the garage was empty. He was three cars along from the Ferrari. He had been given its registration and told where it would be parked. It sat there, in the corner of the garage, its red bodywork gleaming like a jewel in the dim light cast by a sconced light above it. It was a 458 GTB. Ziggy didn't care much for cars, but he knew that this one was expensive. There would have been very little change from $250,000.

He checked left and right again and, satisfied, reached across to the passenger seat and collected his MacBook. He opened it, waking the computer, and activated his homebrew software application. Ziggy was wearing forensic gloves, but the latex was thin and it didn't impede his fingers as they danced across the keyboard. It was custom software created for this specific purpose, and although he was confident in his coding chops, he was still a little anxious to put it to the test. He reached into the bag on the seat and took out the software-defined radio that he had built from off-the-shelf components for less than a hundred thousand yen. It was, effectively, a radio that could digitally emit or pick up a wide band of frequencies, including FM, Bluetooth and Wi-Fi.

He typed commands into the laptop, firing up the software. With the transmitter attached to the MacBook, along with an antenna and amplifier he had picked up in RadioShack, he was able to transmit on the same frequency as the key fob that the owner of the Ferrari used to unlock the doors and start the engine. He used that frequency to perform a brute-force attack. The software cycled through thousands of code variations at a rate of ten every second.

Five minutes.

Ten minutes.

The car's lights flashed and he heard the bleep that signified the doors unlocking.

He paused again and checked that the garage was still

empty. He put the laptop and radio gear into his bag, opened the door and stepped outside. He would leave the Nissan here. He had stolen it earlier that evening from a lot in Roppongi. It would be discovered, eventually, but it would be too late by then. He would be long gone.

He reached the Ferrari, opened the door and slid inside. He took a moment to familiarise himself with the layout of the instruments and controls and, satisfied, he took out his laptop and activated the software again. The keyless ignition activated and the engine turned over. Ziggy put the car into reverse and pushed down on the gas. He lurched backward, almost rear-ending the car in the bay behind him. He stamped on the brakes and then, applying pressure more carefully, pulled away. He negotiated the garage, ascended the ramp and pulled up at the gate. He pressed his fake credentials against the reader, waited for the barrier to be raised, and then pulled away. He turned onto the road that ran alongside the apartment block and pressed down on the gas a little more firmly. The car, agile as a cat and powered by a monstrously large engine, leapt forward.

Ziggy allowed himself a smile. He was not prone to doubting his abilities, but he wouldn't deny the quick flash of relief that he had successfully made away with his target.

Now to deliver it.

The identity of the recipient was more thrilling to him than the heist itself.

* * *

HE HEADED to another underground garage, this one beneath an apartment block in Ojima. He backed it into the space that had been specified, collected his things and stepped outside. That was that. The job was done. He walked back up the ramp, limping a little from the old injury to his leg, and exited onto street level. There was a taxi idling at a rank two hundred metres away from him and he put his fingers to his lips and whistled, loud and shrill. The driver flashed his lights to signal that he had seen him and started forward.

"Where to?" the man said in broken English. He had clocked Ziggy's ethnicity and assumed that he couldn't speak Japanese.

That annoyed him.

"The Park Hyatt," he said, reeling off the address in adequate Japanese.

"Very good," the man said, sticking to English, not even trying to hide the sarcastic little upturn at the side of his mouth.

Whatever. Life was too short to worry about the opinion of a patronising taxi driver, and Ziggy didn't push it. In any event, he was buoyed by the sense of anticipation that he felt. He rested his bag on the seat next to him and thought about the situation that he had found himself in. The arrangement was far from satisfactory, but it still gave him shivers of excitement whenever he thought about it.

He thought of Shoko.

Ziggy had been single for years, long since before he had made his way to Tokyo. It was one of those things that he had come to accept. Some people were in relationships; others were not. He was one of the people who were not. He had tried to persuade himself that it didn't matter and had immersed himself in his online world as a counterweight to the things he lacked in real life. And, for a time, it had worked. He spent hours lost in online games, using a hack he had written to level up a mage in World of Warcraft until he was so powerful that he was almost a God. When he bored of that, he made a name for himself on the forums where hackers met to buy and sell data. There were skilful coders there, but he knew he was better than all of them. He adopted a boastful online persona and defended his reputation against anyone who claimed that they had his measure. He developed a data packet that could be transmitted through forum posts, with the eventual consequence of wrecking the recipient's machine. A man of his talents could make himself rich beyond measure in a place like that, but he performed hacks mostly to inflate his status.

He thought that the distractions would be enough to take his mind off the fact that he was alone, but they had not. He still found himself drawn to porn sites, and he still found himself looking at couples who walked hand in hand in Roppongi with a hot stab of jealousy. In the end, he had to admit it to himself.

He was lonely.

He was determined to fix it just as he would fix any other problem. He would use data and logic to optimise his opportunities. He conducted a survey of the local online dating scene. It was big in Tokyo, and getting bigger. None of the sites he remembered from his time at home had been able to crack the market, but home-grown businesses, built on the same principles but with a Japanese slant, were gaining market share.

For someone with Ziggy's particular set of skills, that was an opportunity.

He chose the one with the best reputation. It was called JapanCupid and had the best-looking women in Tokyo, who, fortunately, were reputed to have a preference for rich Western men. Ziggy had the ethnicity and he could add money whenever he needed it by ripping off credit card information and selling it in the forums. The problem he had experienced during his first forays, however, was that women evidently didn't find him attractive. They ignored his profile and, when he did manage to meet a girl in real life, she inevitably turned up her nose, made her excuses and left him embarrassingly early.

Ziggy was not what would be considered good looking. He was short, with a thatch of untidy ginger hair that he had no interest in taming. His eyes bulged a little and, since he worked at night and rarely saw the sun, his complexion was as pallid as a ghost's, pitted with the old acne scars that had blighted his adolescence. At least he was self-aware enough not to pretend that he was attractive. He wasn't vain and didn't labour under the misapprehension that he was better looking than he was: he knew his appearance was a problem, especially in a culture where the women put so much store in a handsome mate.

He had considered using a fake photograph on his profile, but what was the point of that? He could string them along for as long as he liked, and that might be enjoyable to a point, but, in the end, he was going to have to meet them in the real world and his ruse would be busted in seconds.

No. He would be clever.

He improvised two workarounds that improved his efficiency. First, he registered with another dating site and posted a profile that targeted women in Nagoya. Far enough away that he wouldn't be found out, close enough that the women would share the same characteristics. He wrote an automated script that approached women who met a number of selection criteria. The script changed his profile picture and copy, switching through a series of eight, and then compiled the results of the split test so that he knew which combination of picture and copy was most likely to elicit a favourable response.

That was the first part. With that information in hand, he created an optimal profile and wrote a second script that contacted every eligible woman on the site in Tokyo. The script texted him every time he received an interesting response and, at a prompt, would begin pre-scripted conversations for him.

It had been effective. The script had contacted over five hundred women thus far. Fifty of them had replied. Five of them had graduated through the automated sequence and he had taken over the correspondence himself.

Two of them, in particular, were promising.

He met the first woman for dinner at Mikawa Zezankyo, and, over flawless tempura served straight from the wok to the plate, he had suffered through the most excruciating two hours that he could remember. The girl was self-absorbed and purely materialistic, and he had found her quite awful. He escaped as soon as he could, his wallet lightened and his confidence shaken.

And then he met the second woman.

Her name was Shoko Miyazaki.

And she was special.

Chapter Eleven

SHOKO HAD arranged to meet him at Kozue, a restaurant elevated above the bustle of the city on the fortieth floor of the Park Hyatt. The girl had expensive taste, and Ziggy had sold several lists of credit card details in order to afford their various rendezvous. This place, in particular, had proven to be one of her favourites.

She was waiting for him at the same table that they had been given before. It was at the window, with a vast view of the western hills. It had been daytime the last time they had visited and they had been rewarded then with a clear view of majestic Mount Fuji, its cone silhouetted in the distance. Tonight, it was dark, and there was just the suggestion of a dark mass beyond the glow of the neon that leached into the night.

Ziggy went across to her. "Hello, Shoko."

She was wearing a crop top and a pair of fitted jeans. Her hair had been coloured a vivid red and she bore that striking hue as if it were a badge to denote that she wouldn't be like other Japanese women her age. She never bowed, and her voice was natural and confident and without the high pitch that was a common affectation of local girls in the company of strangers. Ziggy looked at her. She was extraordinarily attractive.

"Have you been here long?"

She ignored his question. "Well?"

Straight to business today, he thought. Very romantic. "Yes. I got it. It's done."

"Where is it?"

"In the usual place."

Finally, she smiled for him. Her face, which had a tendency towards the stern, temporarily lit up. For that moment, basking in the glow of her beauty, he forgot just how foolish this whole scheme was. She reached across the table and laid a hand across his, and, as easily as that, his reservations became irrelevant.

"Very good, Ziggy. It was okay?"

He dismissed the suggestion that it might have been anything other than easy for him. "Simple."

"You are talented man," she said.

He felt his cheeks redden; she rarely praised him.

The waiter arrived. Ziggy took up the menu and searched through it as Shoko ordered sweetfish and matsutake mushrooms. He had shabu-shabu of marbled beef from premium wagyu cattle. He knew that the bill would be high, especially with the sake that he wanted to drink, but he didn't care about that. He had inflated his credit card limit to an obscene amount and he would just go into the bank's systems and reset the balance to zero when they were done.

He looked across the table at his date. She was young and headstrong, beautiful, with a disdainful curl of her lip that somehow made her even more attractive to him. Their first meeting had been difficult. He had known that she was out of his league and that, unless he did something to change the way she looked at him, she wouldn't be interested in seeing him again. She had mentioned in their online correspondence that she was interested in technology and, seizing that as a dying man seizes a lifebelt, Ziggy had begun to show off. He had been working on hacks to exploit the loopholes in car security for several months. Not because he was interested in stealing cars, but because he liked to challenge himself. He had demonstrated his software to her, thinking that his ingenuity would be a good way to woo her. He had been right. She had watched agog as he started the engine of her BMW from the window of the restaurant, and her reticence had—temporarily, at least—melted away.

He knew why now, of course. His talents and the opportunities she was interested in exploiting were a fortuitous combination. But it had bought him time, and her favour. She had pretended to show interest. Unfortunately, although Ziggy wasn't stupid and had known that she was stringing him along, he had allowed his lust to blind him. He should have disengaged there and then, before anything had the chance to develop. But he hadn't. He had stuck around, trying to develop a relationship with her even when he had known that it was a bad, bad idea. By the time he finally listened to his doubts, it was too late. She had settled on the notion that they were going to work together, and that was that.

The hacking software wasn't something that he would have followed up in a professional capacity, but she had been impressed enough that, when they met for their third date, she had a proposition. She had grown distant from him in the days preceding her visit, ignoring his emails and texts, but she promised that this offer would be a chance for them to become more intimate. They would develop a business relationship that could, she promised, be extremely lucrative for them both. Ziggy's instincts screamed at him to politely decline, to leave and then never speak to her again. His lust, though, would not be dissuaded. She said that a business relationship could lead to something else… and he was sold.

Shoko explained that her brother was involved in buying and selling cars. He would supply the details of vehicles that he knew he could sell; Ziggy would "acquire" them, and he would be paid generously for his efforts.

And, like the worst fool, he had agreed.

The Ferrari was the third car that he had stolen for her. There had been a Lexus and a Range Rover before that. He had brought them to the underground lot and left them there. Each time, she had made fresh promises to him, and he would be dragged just a little bit deeper under the surface.

Their food arrived and he watched her as she ate. She was stunning, and the haughtiness made her even more appealing. The fact that she was prepared to spend time with him was something that he couldn't quite understand. He knew it was the cars and the money he was making for her brother. The opportunities he was providing were the only reasons she tolerated his presence. But, on other occasions, when he allowed himself the luxury of dreaming, he wondered whether, just perhaps, there could be something else. He allowed himself that luxury now. That small bud of hope, so unlikely when set against all the rational evidence—the possibility that she might be attracted to him—drew him back, time and time again, like a moth to a flame.

He tried to engage her in small talk, but her replies were crisp and clipped and discouraging. He told her about a new hack he was perfecting, one that would allow him to infect a computer using ultrahigh-frequency sound waves, but she didn't seem particularly interested and he quickly gave it up. He resumed watching her as discreetly as he could, but she still noticed. She gave him a flat little smile and then looked past him into the restaurant. It was as if she were dining alone.

Ziggy was finishing his steak as he noticed a man enter the restaurant, pause next to the maître d', and then head toward them. He passed all the other tables that he might have stopped at until there was no doubt that he could only be headed for them.

Ziggy felt his stomach flip. "Shoko?"

"Relax."

"Who is this?"

"It is my brother." The man took an empty seat from the adjacent table and placed it next to theirs, between Ziggy and Shoko. "Ziggy," Shoko said, "this is Kazuki."

"I said I would only work with you," he protested.

The man sat. "I know what you said. But you knew my sister was working with me."

"That's not the point."

"I like to know with whom I am working. We are

sending a lot of work your way. It is reasonable that I assure myself that you are trustworthy."

"But it isn't what we agreed."

Ziggy started to rise. He would walk to the door and take the elevator down to the street. He would ignore Shoko, pretend that he had never met her. He would—

"Stay there, please."

Ziggy stopped. Kazuki was holding up a single finger.

"No. I'm going. I'm done."

As Ziggy paused, Kazuki wagged his finger from side to side. "You are not done. You stay. I want to talk to you."

"I've had enough," Ziggy said. "Your car is in the usual place. A quarter of a million dollars. Give me my money and we'll call it quits. No hard feelings, we all move on."

"No. We will not do that. I would like to talk to you. Somewhere else."

* * *

HE KNEW he couldn't say no. They took him to Roppongi in a BMW that was waiting in the street below. They parked the car and walked the rest of the way. The district was thronged with high-rises and drenched in neon, with vast electronic billboards projecting gigantic figures onto the flanks of the buildings. It was a sleek and futuristic cityscape that, nevertheless, did not obscure the area's sleazy underbelly. In just the last few weeks, a famous singer had been busted for supplying drugs to a groupie that led to her death, and two sumo wrestlers were disgraced after they tried to buy weed from undercover cops. The area was one of the main draws for foreigners, and their presence and the promise of their money drew in local prostitutes and illicit traders all looking to make a quick buck at their expense. Ziggy watched as a Lexus pulled up to the side of the road and a salon-tanned beauty in vertiginous high heels stepped out onto the pavement, her hands smoothing down her short skirt and just barely maintaining her modesty. A Westerner in a sharp suit slid out of the driver's seat and she anchored herself to him, clinging to his arm in a fashion that struck Ziggy as almost comically proprietorial. They passed a balding Westerner who was clearly drunk, his fly undone, leching after a local girl who, Ziggy assessed, could have only been legal by a few months if she was legal at all. He passed a karaoke bar, a Western salaryman slurring out the words to "Sex on Fire" while grinding his crotch against a waitress too jaded by the relentlessness of it all to give it even a moment of disgust.

Ziggy looked left and right, taking it all in, and moved on. It was a warm night, and the frantic buzz of activity that made Tokyo so special seemed as if it had been amped up a little by the heat and the humidity. The streets were busy with revellers passing between the area's bars and clubs. Ziggy was cautious. He scanned the faces of the men and women around him and saw no one that he recognised. He knew that he had to tread carefully. Recent events had reminded him that it was foolish to think that you could ever be too careful. He still felt the ache of the injury that he had suffered during his first trip to New Orleans, and he still remembered the beating he had been given during his second. Both served to remind him that bad things happened when he lowered his guard.

They reached the broad avenue of Gaien Higashi Dori. He saw groups of predatory local girls looking for prey, a raucous stag party, a drunken man who had been separated from his friends and now could only maintain his balance by clinging to a lamp post. An elderly woman leaned against the doorway of a building, trying to tempt tourists with Photoshopped pictures of girls in a laminated brochure. Drug dealers loitered on corners, their business transacted in darkened alleyways. He saw gorgeous Western women who, having failed at whatever it was that they had come to Tokyo to do, now made ends meet by offering conversation and sometimes more to the local salarymen who were enchanted by their long legs and foreign beauty.

Kazuki and Shoko stopped as they reached their destination. Womb was a well-known dance club and there was already a queue of youngsters waiting to get inside. Shoko made her way to the front of the line and told the bouncer that she had a reservation, and the man stepped aside so that they could get into the building.

The club offered non-stop performances by a cohort of up-and-coming DJs seeking their first breaks and jaded veterans who played for the free bar and wide-eyed groupies they could enjoy in return. It was a dark space on the second floor of an office block, accessed by an unreliable shoebox lift. As he stepped out of the lift into the steamy atmosphere of the darkened room, he saw that the place was jammed, the atmosphere soupy with humidity and the low ceiling dripping with moisture. Electronic dance music throbbed out of the big speakers, enough to rattle the unattended glasses on the table.

There was a hostess waiting at a lectern just inside the entrance. She had a louche, haughty beauty to her, her face perfectly made up and with a pair of discreet plugs nestled in her ears. She looked at Shoko and then Kazuki, and then him. As she regarded him, her expression changed to one of mild disgust. Shoko spoke to her. She nodded her satisfaction and, without a word, beckoned to another woman who was waiting inside the club. The hostess turned away without another look, as if the effort of looking at Ziggy was as much as she could stand. Ziggy had a momentary feeling of inadequacy and, self-consciously, looked down at the clothes he was wearing. He didn't normally care what he looked like, but now he realised that his moderately expensive jeans and shirt looked cheap compared to the outfits sported by the revellers inside the club. The hostess must have pegged him as someone without the means to be worth her time.

Well, Ziggy thought, she was wrong about *that*.

Never mind.

They followed the second girl, with Ziggy limping along at the back. Their table was on a raised area at the back of the room, access restricted by a rope. The woman unhooked the rope and wordlessly gestured to the table before leaving him to make his way to it.

He sat and looked out over the club. Strobes flashed, lasers swung across the room, the dance floor swayed and pulsed in time with the bass that throbbed out over everything.

Shoko and Kazuki sat down opposite him. The girl looked at him with a combination of disgust and amusement. Her brother's expression was more guarded, more difficult to read.

"I get you a drink, Ziggy?" he asked.

"No. I'm fine."

"You must relax."

"Just say what you have to say. I'll listen, and then I'm going to go home. It's late and I'm tired."

"You must not be so suspicious of me, my friend. We have been working well together, have we not?"

"I told Shoko I would only deal with her."

"Yes, I know. And I am sorry to have to change that arrangement. But, Ziggy, we have made excellent money, haven't we?"

"Yes, we have. But I'm through with it now. I don't want to do it any more."

"And I do not want to work with someone who does not want to work with me. That would be bad business. We can agree on that, at least. Yes?"

"Yes," he answered nervously.

"So we will part ways, as you suggest."

He knew that there was something else to come. "But it's not going to be as easy as that."

Kazuki smiled. "It will be easy. We do one more job together, and then we can stop. It is simple, just as tonight.

Nothing beyond you and your clever software."

"What is it?"

"Another car. I will provide you with the details. What it is, where it can be found, everything that you will need. And, because this will be the last time that we work together, I will make it even more profitable for you. We will split the proceeds sixty-forty in your favour."

"Why would you do something like that?"

"Because I am a fair businessman. And perhaps, when you see that, you will reconsider your decision."

"I won't," he replied quickly.

Kazuki leaned back against the chair and spread his hands. "But you will work with me this one more time."

His tone was rhetorical. It wasn't a question.

"Once more."

Kazuki beamed at him. He extended his hand across the table and, as Ziggy hesitated, nodded that he should take it. He did, and the man gripped it firmly. "Very good. I am pleased. Shoko will contact you with the details, just as before."

Ziggy stood.

To his surprise Shoko stood, too.

"I will come with you," she said.

She looked down at her brother and exchanged a glance. Ziggy caught it late, and couldn't discern its meaning, but he didn't know how to say no to her, even though he knew that he should. She reached down and slipped his hand into hers. It was the first time that she had done that. Her clasp was cold, her skin as smooth as polished ice, and, as she tugged him away from the table, he did not demur.

* * *

"WE GO TO YOUR PLACE?"

Ziggy flustered. He didn't know what to say. He couldn't go back to his apartment. It was in a shocking mess and, more important even than that, his memories of John Milton made him cautious enough to keep his address to himself. His brain locked and, even as he knew he was acting like a foolish schoolboy, he couldn't speak. He was about to ignore his reservations and give her the address when she put the car into drive and said, with a cold little smile, "It's okay. We go to mine."

She drove them back into Ginza. She didn't speak, her focus on the road and whatever it was that she was thinking about. Ziggy found himself fraught with nerves. He tried to start several conversations, useless small talk, but he didn't know what to say and whatever he tried sounded gauche. He let his hands slip down so that they were beside his legs and clenched the edges of the leather seat.

She drove them into a district of concrete apartment buildings, each garlanded by a fringe of Japanese maple trees that had been planted around and between them. The locals jokingly referred to them as mansion apartments, or "man-shi-yons," a euphemism that had been appropriated to describe this type of faceless concrete behemoth that provided accommodation to millions of people within the bounds of the metropolis. She slotted the car into an empty space in another underground lot before leading Ziggy to an elevator.

Shoko's place was on the fifth floor. It was a typical space with cramped dimensions. Many of the mansion blocks dated back to the sixties but, in a land that experienced frequent earthquakes, the concept of renovating an old building was alien. The preference was to tear down and start again. Shoko, it seemed, had rebelled. The apartment was divided into two rooms with tatami flooring separated by *fusuma* sliding paper screens and a Western kitchen. Without a word, Shoko went over to a closet, opened it and took out a futon and blankets. She unfolded the futon and arranged the blankets. Ziggy tried not to think what that might portend.

He looked out of the window instead. He could see the dark shape of Mount Fuji to the west and the glaring neon lights of a "love hotel" to the east.

Shoko took a bottle of Yamazaki Single Malt and poured out two measures. Ziggy was not a connoisseur, but even he knew that the distillery had recently been named as the best in the world, and that its products were correspondingly expensive.

She led him to the futon, which she had placed in front of the wide window. The view was stupendous, but Ziggy narrowed his focus so that he could watch the reflection in the glass: him and, close enough to his right that their legs brushed together, Shoko.

She sipped the malt and, without words, stood up, unbuttoned her top and pulled it over her head. Her stick-thin arms were covered, from the wrists all the way up to her shoulder, with a tattoo that wound its way to her chest and across her back. The design was of a female courtesan, a dagger clenched between her teeth. He had seen it before. It marked her out as connected to the Yakuza. Her brother was Yakuza, too. Ziggy didn't think he was senior—he was too young for that—but that was scant relief.

"If you want to see me, you must work with my brother. Do you understand?"

See me? He did want to see her, like this, more than anything else.

He said that he did, but that wasn't what he was thinking. One more time. One more car. That really was his limit, no matter what she said. He had known, of course, that he wasn't dealing with Boy Scouts. He had been stealing quarter-million-dollar cars to order. He had known that he was being drawn deeper into the underworld, and he had allowed it. It was Shoko. He couldn't resist her.

"You can trust me," she said. "You can trust my brother."

He didn't answer.

Deeper and deeper and deeper. He knew that he had to get out.

After this last theft, he would stop. He promised himself.

But then Shoko sat down beside him, her skin silken smooth and glowing in the muted light, and he forgot all about promises and intentions. He closed his eyes and allowed himself to be swallowed by the moment.

Chapter Twelve

THEY WORKED hard the following day. It was just the same: hot, uncomfortable and filthy. Milton and Harry contested each other once again, and the result was the same. Milton narrowed the difference to five sheep, but Harry said that he was holding back plenty in reserve and Milton knew that he was right.

They finished in the early evening. Milton wiped the sweat from his eyes and followed Harry towards the buildings. The sky was on the cusp between daytime and dusk, and they stopped at a broken fence to gaze up into the sunset. The sky was enormous here, a vastness that was cast about with little fragments of cloud. The dying light refracted through them, painting the clouds in burnt ochre.

"Beautiful, right?" Harry said.

Milton nodded.

"I'll never get tired of it." He leaned his elbows against the rail. "You remember the sunsets in the desert? In Iraq?"

Milton nodded. The two of them had served together in the SAS during the Second Gulf War. They had been dropped behind Iraqi lines and tasked with directing air strikes against Saddam's materiel. Harry had been with Milton when the botched strike against a Scud launcher had flattened a madrassa. Just thinking about that day was dangerous for Milton. It brought back memories that he had tried to obliterate with booze and, he knew, if he mused on them for too long, he would start to think about drinking again. It was a rabbit hole he had no interest in going down.

Harry looked over at Milton and realised that he didn't want to talk about it. "Sorry."

"Forget it."

Harry changed the subject. "We've got another day here before we've finished the last of them."

"After that?"

"We'll go north. There's about the same number of animals to shear up there."

Milton was happy to go along with him, and said so. They stayed there for a moment, resting against the broken rail as the sun dipped beneath the line of the horizon, its orange corona fading and then winking out.

The dirt track to the station was as straight as a die, and Milton saw a plume of dust just at the far reaches of his vision. It bloomed above the road, masking the dot within the cloud that must have been the approaching vehicle.

"Hello," Harry said.

"Matilda?"

"Probably."

"Want to go and tell Mervyn?"

Harry chuckled. "You know she'd kick the shit out of him, don't you?"

Milton nodded. "With one arm tied behind her back."

They waited. The vehicle was still ten miles away, and it took another five minutes before it was close enough for Milton to see that it was a Jeep, and another two for him to confirm that it was the dirty white Wrangler Renegade that Harry's sister drove. It was bouncing over the potholed road at a fair speed, dust and dirt streaking out from beneath the wheels. The Jeep barely slowed as it swung off the road and onto the track that led toward the station's outbuildings. It raced ahead for the final half mile, then braked with a suddenness that locked the wheels and sent a spray of grit in their direction.

Matilda Douglas was wearing the same old battered Aviators that Milton remembered from the last time that she had visited them. She had blonde hair, a little unkempt, all the way down to her shoulders. She opened the door of the Jeep and stepped out. She was wearing a pair of dirty dungarees; they were double lined around the knees because that was where the cloth took the most punishment from the burr on the sheep. She had a white T-shirt beneath the denim and a pair of heavy leather boots. She was twenty-five, full of sass and the kind of no-nonsense attitude that you could only get from being brought up on a sheep station, surrounded by ranchers and shearers in the arse end of nowhere. She did not stand on ceremony. She swore like a navvy. Everything that her brother did, she did, too, and said that she did it better.

"Hello, boys. Finished for the day?"

"Yep," Harry said.

"How many you do?"

"Hundred and three," he said.

"John?"

"Ninety-eight."

She sucked her teeth. "Getting better. He's gonna catch you up, Harry."

Douglas snorted. "Not a chance."

"You know a hundred wouldn't be enough to keep pace with me, though—right?"

"Want to put that to the test?"

She grinned at her brother. "You working tomorrow?"

"Thought I might. Where you going?"

"Up to Boolanga."

"When?"

"Driving up there tonight. We'll start work first thing in the morning."

"You got a pen for me?"

"You're full of it, Matty."

"We'll see if you're saying the same thing tomorrow."

Harry smiled at her. Despite all his gruffness and the sibling rivalry, Milton knew that he was devoted to the girl. He was fifteen years older than she was, and often more like a father than a brother. Their father, Harry senior, had drunk himself to death when Matilda was five years old.

Their mother had remarried another man with indecent haste and left them to fend for themselves. Harry had brought her up more than the woman had.

Matilda knew how to press all of Harry's buttons, but it was obvious that the ribbing and the mild abuse were all part of their relationship. For her part, while she pretended that Harry's paternalism was something that irritated her, she was just as devoted to him. They had an extraordinarily close relationship. They were bound together by their shared experience, the bonds forged in the fire of bereavement and then tested through early hardship. What was left was unbreakable. Milton envied it. He had nothing, and no one, like that.

She cocked her head in Milton's direction. "Want to join in tomorrow?"

"I'll be there," he said.

"I know. I meant maybe you want to put a little wager on the result?"

"Why not." He pushed away from the fence. "I'm going inside."

Matty winked at him and, just like the last time and all the times before that, Milton felt the little knot tighten in his stomach. He turned away, feeling the blood rise in his cheeks, and made his way to the dormitory. He took off his dirty clothes, wrapped himself in a towel and went through into the dingy shower. He cranked the faucet all the way around, waited for the hot water to run, and then stepped into the cubicle. The water sluiced across his body, rinsing the dirt and blood away, and soon the stream that was running into the drain was as black as tar.

Matilda was a very attractive woman, and he knew that she found him attractive, too. There had been an evening a month ago when she had been out to a station to shear with them. She had gotten drunk with the others, trying to tempt Milton to join them until Harry had chided her to leave him alone. She had been drunk, he knew that, but, in his experience, drink only made you do the things that you wanted to do. It loosened inhibitions, lubricated things, made them easier. They had been in a town whose name Milton had forgotten, in a tumbledown bar that reminded him of a Wild West saloon. He had gone outside onto the veranda to smoke and she had come with him on the pretence of cadging one for herself. She had flirted with him and then, before he could think about the consequences, she had kissed him.

He had let her do it, and kissed her back, before he realised that that was something that he could not do. Matilda was Harry's sister. Might as well have been his daughter. Milton had no idea how he would react, but it wasn't something he was willing to test. Harry was Milton's friend, and he didn't have so many of those that he was willing to risk the chance that he would see it as a betrayal.

But she had not given up. If anything, his reticence had made her try even harder. There had been several occasions after that kiss when she had found him on his own. After he had demurred for the third time, she had asked him what the problem was. He had explained: Harry was the problem, and what he might say. She had smouldered with anger, telling him that she was old enough to make her own decisions. He had explained that he didn't want to risk losing her brother's friendship, and her smoulder had caught light: she told him he was being pathetic, that she knew he felt the same way about her, and that he should be a man about it.

Still he said no.

She swore at him and left the station the next morning.

He hadn't seen her since.

But he had thought about what she had said.

And she was right. He *did* feel the same way. He found her attractive—very attractive—and he would have liked to spend time with her. But Milton was not one for prolonged relationships. He didn't value himself enough to think that he was worth the time of anyone that he admired and, more than that, he was a dangerous man to know. The idea of a real relationship with anyone while he had been working with Group Fifteen was so foolish as to be laughable. Being with him had not become a safer proposition since he had left the government's employment, either. He thought of what had happened to him from London to Juarez to San Francisco and then New Orleans. He'd left a trail of destruction behind him. People had died because of the mistakes he had made. He was trying to be better, but that didn't change the facts. He wouldn't risk the same consequences for her.

There had been a lot of reflection since he had put the bottle aside, and his conclusion had been reinforced. He was damaged goods. He remembered one of his favourite quotes from the Big Book of Alcoholics Anonymous. "It will take time to clear away the wreck. Though old buildings will eventually be replaced by finer ones, the new structures will take years to complete." It would have been selfish to think otherwise. He had heard a hundred drunks in meetings say the same thing. He had a lot of work to do.

And, if all that was true, all that he would be able to offer Matilda was something transient. If she wanted more, she would be the one who was hurt.

Harry wouldn't forgive him for that.

Chapter Thirteen

THEY HAD a two-hundred-mile drive to Boolanga to manage that evening. Milton changed into a clean set of clothes, packed up his bag and went back outside again. It was a hot, sticky night, and even the cicadas seemed dazed by the temperature. Matty and Harry were sitting on the ground next to the Wrangler, leaning up against the chassis. A coolbox had appeared from somewhere—Milton guessed that she had brought it with her—and they were both drinking from long-necked bottles of beer.

"Alright, sport?" Harry asked him.

"Better. Although," he said, picking his sodden T-shirt off his skin, "this was dry when I put it on."

"Hotter than a billy goat with a blowtorch," he said.

Milton looked down and saw that Matilda was staring at him with an amused upturn to the side of her mouth. He took a breath. She was going to make things difficult for him again.

"You riding with us?" she asked.

He couldn't very easily say that he would ride with the others. There was no reason for him to turn down her offer and, if he did, Harry would be suspicious. He was just going to have to manage.

"Sounds good."

"Got your gear?"

Milton nodded down to the bag at his feet.

"That it?" Matilda said.

"That's it."

"John doesn't like to be tied down," Harry elaborated with a chuckle, seemingly oblivious to the irony in his comment. He was a simple enough kind of bloke, not the sharpest tool in the shed, but was it possible that he hadn't noticed the way the atmosphere had changed?

"When are we off?"

"No reason to wait."

"The others?"

Matilda pushed herself upright, turned and pointed down the track. Milton saw the clouds of dust from the wheels of the other Jeep. It was already several miles away and he hadn't noticed it before.

"They left twenty minutes ago," she said. "Mervyn was getting on my nerves, so I told him to do one."

Harry got up, too. "And he did what he was told," he said. "Who would've thought a big bloke like that would be scared of my little sister?"

Milton collected his bag and tossed it into the back.

Matilda came across to him and rested her hand on his arm. "Ready?"

He took a step to the side, hoping that Harry couldn't see his awkwardness. "Whenever you are."

* * *

THE JEEP had two seats up front and another two behind on the flip-up tailgate. Milton knew that Matty would drive, so he started for the back.

"Up front with me, John," she said before he could get very far. "If I know Harry, he'll be asleep in ten minutes. I wouldn't mind someone to talk to. Keep me awake."

He gritted his teeth. He couldn't very well turn her down.

She had been right about her brother. He made some derogatory comments about her driving and then, before they were off the track and onto the road, he was quiet. Matty looked in the rear-view mirror and smiled. Milton craned his neck and looked back. Harry was asleep, his head lolling against the seat and his mouth open.

"Told you so," she said.

"I saw him sleep in places that were a lot less comfortable than this," Milton said.

"That right?"

"One time, he got forty winks in the back of an army Lynx while we were being shot at over Basra. I was sure we were going to get hit. He woke up like nothing had happened."

Matty took her phone and connected it to the Jeep's USB jack. She steered with one hand on the wheel, glancing up every so often as she used her spare hand to scroll through her music. She settled on Fleetwood Mac, and, after a moment, the opening of "The Chain" played through the speakers.

"This about your era?" she said, grinning as she rested the phone on the dash.

"Leave it out. You're about twenty years too early."

"What would you rather listen to?"

He leaned back in the seat and rested his boots on the dash. "The Smiths. The Stone Roses. The Happy Mondays."

"Who?"

He allowed himself the luxury of a smile and tried to relax a little. It was an easy and companionable silence. Good music, the warm breeze on his face. Matilda was a good driver, maintaining a fast pace as she picked the smoothest route over the pitted asphalt.

Fleetwood Mac finished and Guns N' Roses replaced it, the gentle introduction to "November Rain."

Milton almost thought he was going to get away with it.

"Last time," she said.

"Matty—"

She glanced in the mirror. "He's asleep. You know what he's like. A bomb could go off and he wouldn't wake. Relax."

He tried, but couldn't.

"Last time," she started again, and he let her finish, "I'm sorry about the things I said to you."

"What things?"

She looked over at him, her eyes reflecting the glow of the instruments. "I may have… questioned your manhood."

"No need to apologise."

"We didn't finish the conversation."

"We did. There's not much more to say. Nothing is going to happen."

"Why not?"

"It just… isn't."

"You don't want it to?"

"I didn't say that."

"So?"

"It can't. Your brother. Come on, Matilda. You know how jealous he is. If anything went wrong…"

"Why would it?"

"Because it always does, Matty, and, when it does, he'll kill me. He's my friend. I don't want to put that at risk."

They drove on for a minute in silence again.

"That's your final word?"

He sighed. "It has to be."

"All right," she said. "Fine."

"Fine?"

"I'm not going to shout and scream about it, Milton, if that's what you mean. I'm not going to flog a dead horse." She turned and smiled at him—an incandescent smile that sent a quiver up his spine—and added, the smile fading a little, "Your loss."

Milton looked up into the expanse of the night sky. There was no natural light outside the Renegade and the vast sweep of the stars looked like diamonds scattered liberally across velvet. The moon was full, casting its reflected light down onto the landscape and lending it a silvery sheen. There were hills in the near distance, and Milton heard the howl of a dingo. Another joined, and then another, a mournful wail that drifted down across the dusty plain.

It *was* his loss. He knew it.

"There was one thing I always wanted to ask you," Matty said.

"Go on."

"Why did you come here? I know you know Harry, but why did you come out here to work on the station with us?"

Milton was quiet as he considered what to tell her. "I wanted to get away from things," he said.

"Things?"

"Oh, I don't know—life, maybe. All the noise and the stress. I'm not best suited to it."

"This is the drinking thing?"

He hadn't told her about AA and his daily struggle to stay dry, but she knew that he didn't drink and he could tell that it was something that had piqued her curiosity. Perhaps Harry had said something to her. "It's to do with that," he said.

"You have a problem with it?"

"Me and drink don't make for the best combination."

"How long have you been sober?"

"More than three years now."

"But you know that a sheep station isn't the smartest place to go if you want to get away from booze, right?"

"I do now." He smiled. "But I can handle it."

"So it's just about that, then? The booze?"

He paused again. No, he conceded to himself. That wasn't it. He thought about Avi Bachman and the chaos that he had brought down upon Isadora and Alexander Bartholomew in New Orleans. He thought about Ziggy Penn, abducted and nearly killed. And then he thought about the beating that he had taken at Bachman's hands. But not just any beating: a thorough, comprehensive beating that had left him on his knees and just a few extra blows from death. Milton was not used to being bested like that, and it had shaken him. He had left Louisiana aboard a Greyhound bus to Florida, but the memory of what had happened was not so easy to leave behind. To have been beaten so easily had made him question the point of the daily struggle to stay off the drink. Why not just get drunk? What was the point in the struggle? It had made him question a fundamental part of himself. If that had been taken away so easily, was his struggle really worth the effort?

"John?"

"What?"

"There's no other reason?"

He realised she was probing for evidence of another woman, a failed relationship, some other reason why he would do something so extraordinary as swapping what she must have imagined was a comfortable life for a summer spent up to his knees in shit and sweat and blood.

"That's it," he said. "I just wanted a change."

Chapter Fourteen

THEY ARRIVED at Boolanga at two in the morning. Milton hit the sack and managed four hours of sleep, waking as the morning sunlight lanced through the uncovered windows. He lay still for a while, watching motes of dust as they drifted through the bright golden shafts, taking the opportunity to assess his body. He had the usual aches and pains that would be associated with a physical job, the stiffness in his muscles and the creaking of joints that had been pushed beyond their capacity. Beyond those were the injuries that had accumulated over the years of his previous life. The stabbings, shootings, the beatings that he had taken. His body had been put through it, the toll severe enough that he occasionally had to resort to medication to soothe the aches. He tried not to—he didn't want to exchange one addiction for another—but there had been days when he had no choice.

He closed his eyes and probed deeper. Avi Bachman had inflicted serious punishment: the dislocated shoulder, fractured ribs, a concussion so severe that he was still getting headaches two weeks later. Those wounds had all healed. Thinking about them recalled the fight again. He had only been able to save himself because Bachman had been distracted. Milton had taken a metal crank and swung it into Bachman's head when his back had been turned. It wasn't gallant, but he didn't care about that. Most of Milton's victims had been murdered without even knowing that he was there and, in this case, it was the only reason he was still breathing. Gallantry was a luxury that he couldn't afford.

Matilda, Harry, Mervyn and Eric were outside the dormitory. They were dressed for work. The air was baking hot already. The sheep in the pens were making an enormous racket, as if aware of the indignities that were about to be visited upon them. Someone had prepared bacon rolls. They were eating them and drinking from big litre bottles of water.

Harry tossed one of the rolls over to Milton. "Wakey, wakey."

Milton was starving. He bit into the roll and savoured the salty bacon.

"We were just saying," Matilda said. "We should make it interesting today. You still up for it?"

"Sure."

"We each put fifty bucks into the pot and whoever shears the most sheep takes it all."

"Fine," Milton said, ignoring the fact that gambling was another compulsive behaviour that he was probably not best suited to indulge in.

"You want," she said, smiling, "I could give the rest of you five sheep as a head start."

"We'll manage, Matty," Harry said.

She grinned. "This is going to be fun."

* * *

MILTON WORKED HARD. He settled into a groove, muscling the uncooperative sheep into his pen and wielding his clippers with a dexterity that he would have said was impossible just a few weeks earlier. The set-up at Boolanga was more amenable than at Booligal. The sheep were kept in a large corral, with an Aboriginal station hand responsible for shepherding the next one forward when there was a vacancy in the pens. Milton kept a tally, scoring a line on one of the wooden fence panels with the blade of his shears as he waited for the next sheep to arrive.

The first hour passed. "How many?" Matty yelled out.

"Ten," said Harry.

Mervyn had nine and Eric seven.

"John?"

"Eleven," he said.

"Fuck off."

"Straight up."

"Twelve," Matty called back, dampening his excitement. "Keep up, boys."

Milton glanced out across the pens. Harry was in the one next to him and Matilda was in the one adjacent to that. She had already bent back down to the next sheep and was stripping off the wool with easy, practiced strokes. She was wearing a muscle top beneath her dungarees and her skin was already awash with sweat, animal waste and wispy balls of wool that had stuck to her. She finished the sheep, ushered it on its way with a kick to its flanks and looked up. She noticed that Milton was gazing at her, and grinned.

"You all right?" Harry called across to him.

Matty winked.

Milton couldn't suppress the smile. "Yeah," he said. "Miles away."

"Looks like it. This ugly bastard is number twelve. You're falling behind."

* * *

IT GREW ridiculously hot as noon approached and Harry called out that they would stop for an hour to refresh themselves and shelter from the worst of the sun. Matilda protested, but not too much; Milton could see that she was suffering as much as the rest of them. They revealed their tallies and Harry had forged ahead by four animals. Milton was in third, behind Matty but ahead of Mervyn and Eric. That did not go down well.

They got back to it again. The afternoon dragged on. The heat was oppressive, a crushing weight that lay across them all. Milton's wide-brimmed leather bush hat offered a little shade, but did nothing to take the edge off the volcanic temperature. His sweat soaked into the leather and, after a while, he stopped trying to deter the swarms of flies that gathered around the squealing animals from alighting on his face. Harry seemed to be struggling with his legs, cursing as he wrestled a difficult ewe into position. Milton marked each shorn animal on the wood, and, when Harry called out that he had just finished his eightieth, he saw that he was five ahead of him. Matilda was still working with steady efficiency, but she was quiet, not announcing her tally, and Milton couldn't see across Harry's pen well enough to see her count.

The last animal was ushered into Mervyn's pen a little before six. The sun was low in the sky, but it was still blazing hot. Milton finished his sheep, shooing it out of the pen and carving the final notch into the wood. He counted and then recounted his tally: he had managed one hundred and eleven animals. His shirt was sodden with sweat and he was bleeding from several small cuts. One particularly obstreperous ewe had bitten him on the wrist and the indentations from its teeth were starting to turn a dark red. He was exhausted and he needed to sit down.

"Done!" Harry called out.

"How many?"

"One hundred and three. You?"

"One eleven."

"Piss off, Milton."

"I'm serious. One eleven."

"Well, fuck me sideways," he said, shaking his head. "You beat me."

"By eight. It's your legs."

"Fuck off, John. No excuses. You beat me."

Eric and Mervyn finished and reported numbers of ninety-seven and ninety-nine.

They waited for Matilda. She was finishing her last sheep, stripping the wool away in two neat sections and tossing it aside. She booted the sheep up the arse and watched it trot to the others, bleating its dissatisfaction.

She leaned back against the pen and wiped the sweat from her eyes. When she brought her arm away, she was grinning and Milton knew that he had lost.

"How many?" Harry asked.

"One fifteen."

"Serious?"

"One fifteen. Money's mine, boys. Drinks on me."

Chapter Fifteen

MILTON WASN'T quite sure what happened next. The plan had been for them all to drive into the nearest town for food and drink. Then Harry decided he was done in, saying that he was going to pass and get an early night. Mervyn, who had been struggling with a hangover all day, took that as permission to decline the festivities himself, admitting that the idea of another night of booze was not something that he had been relishing. Without his wingman, Eric very quickly backed out, too. Milton knew that he would also have had an eye on the prospect of being an interloper on a night where it was only Matty and Milton to keep him company. The two shearers might not have been the brightest, but it seemed obvious enough to Milton that they had noticed the atmosphere between the quiet pommie and their foreman's kid sister. Milton let the thought play out: if *they* had noticed it, then surely Harry had noticed it, too. And Harry didn't have a problem with Milton and Matty going out together. Did that mean he didn't mind the idea of them having a relationship? Milton shook his head at the way his thinking was leading him. Milton had never been the most empathetic of men, and this was confusing him.

He decided to back out himself. It was a bad idea. He went to find Matty to tell her. She was in the Jeep, the engine running. Before he could even open his mouth, she raised a hand to stifle his protest.

"Relax," she said. "Just a drink. Well, a drink for me, and whatever you want—water or whatever—for you."

"That's it?"

"Yep. That's it. I'm going out anyway. I've got money in my pocket and I need a beer and a change of scenery. You can either come with me and make sure I don't do something stupid, or I'll go alone and God alone knows what'll go down."

"Fine. I'll come."

* * *

THE TOWN OF BROKEN HILL was thirty miles away. The road was decent once they got off the station, and they made good progress, heading west on the A32. Matilda was in a good mood, her spirits buoyed by the day's events. She jabbed at Milton with a little good-natured gloating. He didn't mind. It was good to see her smiling and, the tension between them at least temporarily defused, he was able to relax. He had no intention of taking a drink, and knowing that he would be sober all night, he was confident that he would be able to deflect her should her new-found resolution when it came to their relationship start to waver.

"I'll take you to a restaurant I know," she said. "It's called the Silly Goat. They do these amazing burgers. My mouth's been watering all afternoon just thinking about it."

Milton stretched out his legs as far as he could and allowed himself a smile. His life wasn't really so bad. He was fortunate enough that he wasn't driven by material things. He wasn't ambitious, either. He just wanted a quiet existence, the opportunity to try different things and experience the parts of the world that he hadn't visited before. He had known that coming here would prove to be a good idea, and he had been right. He had no obligations, no responsibilities, and he could find tranquillity through the medium of hard work. The harder he worked, the more tired he became, and the easier it was to silence the demons in his head. And then, as a pleasant bonus, he had evenings like this to enjoy.

"Look," Matilda said. "Up ahead."

Milton looked. It was dark, and the headlights of the

car at the side of the road were bright in his eyes. He squinted and saw a silhouetted figure standing in front of them, waving an arm up and down. They drew a little closer and he could see that the hood of the vehicle had been raised. He could see a figure hunched over the engine.

"We better stop," she said. "This isn't the kind of place I'd particularly want to get stranded in."

Matilda flicked the indicator and touched the brakes. They rolled off the asphalt and onto the gravel margin, the tyres crunching. The man at the front of the car straightened up. There was enough vestigial light for Milton to see that he was wearing a suit and a white shirt that looked as if it was damp with sweat. The second man walked to them. He was wearing a suit, too, and he had black hair and glasses.

Milton got out, meeting the man halfway.

"What's the problem?"

"I don't know. Think it could be the fuel injector."

The man gestured back at the car. It was a big Nissan Navara. The figure who had been looking under the hood was a woman. She stepped away from the engine, wiping her hands on a rag. She was of average height and slender. She was wearing a white blouse, the sleeves rolled up to her elbows, and a skirt.

"Where are you headed?"

"Broken Hill."

"Not a good place to break down."

"Tell me about it."

"What you doing out here?"

"We work for BHP."

Matilda was out of the car, too, now. "Mining?" she said.

"That's right. Visiting the facility."

"Where from?"

"We left Dubbo last night."

"Dubbo?" she said with surprise.

"Yeah," the man said ruefully. "We thought it'd make a change from flying."

"That's miles away."

"I know it is. And never again."

Matty went over to the car. "You want me to have a look at it?"

The man nodded. "Sure," he said, a little uncertainly.

She looked at him with amused disdain. "What? You think I can't fix it because I'm a woman?"

"I didn't—"

"Don't worry. I'm a mechanic. I fix all our trucks."

The woman stepped aside. Matilda walked across to the open hood and bent over the engine. She poked around inside, muttering to herself.

"Doesn't look like the carb," she said. "What was it doing before it packed in?"

Milton realised, too late, that something was wrong.

No, he corrected himself. *Four* things.

First: the tyre tracks on the dusty margin on the other side of the road.

Second: the Nissan was clean. Compared to the dusty Wrangler, it was spotless.

Third: the man said they were executives.

Fourth: the clothes they were wearing were clean.

He connected the deductions just a moment too late.

The tracks suggested that the Navara had originally been travelling east along the A32 before looping across the road and changing direction so that they were pointing to the west, towards the town. They were lying about their direction of travel. They had been coming *out* of Broken Hill, rather than heading *into* it.

Dubbo to Broken Hill was a straight run of 750 kilometres. A marathon drive like that would take eight hours. The truck should have been filthy. It wasn't. It was clean, as if it had just been driven off the lot of a rental company.

And how likely was it that a couple of executives

would drive through the outback, rather than flying? Not very likely, despite what the man had said.

Finally, their clothes were clean. The creases were still in the man's trousers and his boots looked like they had only been out of their box for a few hours.

Milton looked at the woman standing by the front of the truck next to Matilda. He must have betrayed his suspicion, for there was a flicker of recognition in the woman's face as her hand slipped into her jacket, right about the spot where a holstered pistol would be kept.

The man had paused while Milton had walked on, and now he was just behind him. Milton felt a jolt of adrenaline, but before he could make use of it, something solid with sharp edges clashed against the back of his head. The impact was sudden and unexpected, and it dropped him to his knees. He blinked his eyes to try to clear his vision, and when he looked up, he was staring into the barrel of a pistol. It was a Beretta. It looked like an M9. The man had struck him with the butt of the gun.

Matilda turned, but the woman next to her had drawn a pistol. She pointed it at her. "Don't do anything stupid," she said from behind her gun.

Milton was on his hands and knees. He looked down, waiting for his fuzzy vision to clear, and saw spots of blood as they fell down into the dust. They were red against the dirt, visible even in the gloom. He reached up to his scalp and pressed it with his fingertips. When he looked at them, they were stained with his blood.

The man spoke again. "Do anything I don't like and the first thing I'll do is put a bullet in your right knee. And then I'll put one in your left knee."

"All right," Milton said. "I get it."

"What happens next is up to you."

"I'm not going to do anything," he said, making sure that his voice was calm and reassuring. He didn't know what was happening, but he wasn't about to precipitate something by spooking whoever these two were.

"Very good." The man took a step back, ensuring that there was more than enough distance between them for him to shoot before Milton could get to him, but not so much that there was any chance that he would miss.

"What do you want me to do?"

"Not just you. Both of you."

The woman by the car looked over at her companion. Milton saw the unsaid exchange. It was a look of question, as if a decision had just been taken on the fly. The man who had hit him had made the decision. That meant that he was more senior than the woman by the car. Milton filed that little piece of information away. It might be helpful.

The man raised his aim just a fraction so that Milton was looking right into the inky little hole. "Let's get some ground rules set up right now. You do what we say. No questions. Bad things will happen if you don't. We clear?"

"We are."

"Excellent. Now, then—you got a cell phone?"

"No," Milton said truthfully.

"And you?"

Matilda didn't answer.

"Give it to her," the man said, nodding to the woman.

Milton looked to her and nodded that she should hand it over. Her eyes burned with fury as she reached into her pocket, took out her phone and gave it to the woman.

"Thank you. Now—into the car."

Milton watched the man's finger on the trigger of the Beretta. It hadn't moved. Milton kept an eye on it as he edged slowly around to the side of the Nissan. He opened the rear door and held it for Matilda. She got in, sliding across to the right-hand side of the car. Milton looked at the man and woman again. The man gave the pistol a gentle flick, suggesting that he needed to be getting inside, too. Fine. He ducked his head, slid onto the seat and shuffled along. The woman shut the door and went around to the driver's side. The man got into the passenger seat, arranged himself so that he could look back into the cabin, and raised the pistol again. The driver started the engine, put the Nissan into drive and gently fed in the revs. The car rolled off the margin and onto the bumpy road, turning through one hundred and eighty degrees and gently speeding up as it started to the east.

Chapter Sixteen

THE DRIVER, the woman, concentrated on the road ahead and said nothing at all. Her companion covered them both with the pistol. He made them sit all the way back in their seats to make sure that there was plenty of distance between his gun arm and his two captives. Milton would have to lean forward and then stretch in order to get to the gun; the man would be able to shoot him three times before he could get to him. Milton didn't like those odds. He would play the long game.

"What are you doing?" he asked.

"No talking. Keep it shut unless we ask you a question."

So Milton observed them both instead. This wasn't a robbery. If it was, they would have taken whatever they wanted—the Wrangler, perhaps—and left them on the side of the road. It wasn't a hit, either. They would already have been dead if it was.

So, it was something else.

He watched how they presented themselves. The two of them were professional. Very professional. They were cool and calm, they didn't get agitated, and they were firm with what they wanted Milton and Matilda to do. It all spoke of them being well-trained and experienced operators.

They had held their weapons easily. The guns themselves were nine-millimetre automatics. The one aimed at Milton now was a brand-new Beretta M9, as he had suspected. Milton was familiar with the weapon; it had been the weapon he had considered along with the Sig Sauer P226 when he was choosing his own sidearm. It was a full-size service pistol, with a 4.7-inch barrel, an aluminium alloy receiver and a steel slide. It had a mechanism that allowed for loading and unloading with the safety activated, along with a long twelve-pound double-action trigger pull for the first shot. That pull might buy Milton a fraction of a second of extra time, but that wouldn't be long enough to close the distance before it was fired. The gun was oiled and looked like it was carefully maintained.

Milton narrowed his focus. It was a large gun, with the length of trigger reach and the diameter of the butt making it suitable only for medium- to large-sized hands. This man was of average build, and the gun looked comfortable in his grip. The safety was flicked off and the man's finger was inserted loosely through the trigger guard, the trigger resting lightly on the pad of his index finger. The man's right arm was braced across his left. The muzzle of the gun would tremble if he was nervous, but it did not; it was steady and unmoving.

That was useful information: both of their captors were comfortable with their weapons. That, too, suggested that this wasn't their first dance. It suggested that this wasn't something impetuous, that it had been planned.

And so what did that make them?

Milton thought. It made them either criminals or government operatives.

It wasn't difficult to think of criminals who might have a motive for wishing him harm. There had been dozens through the years who had fallen within his ambit; plenty of his victims had been dispatched because they were too powerful to be vulnerable to traditional law enforcement, or immune to the prospect of a guilty verdict at trial. He had crossed the Mafia several times, both in the United States and in Italy. There had been assignments that had seen him decapitate the leadership of triad factions that had extended their malign influence into British Chinatowns. And, of course, it wasn't that long ago that he had killed El Patrón, the paterfamilias of La Frontera, the Mexican cartel that dominated the border town of

Ciudad Juárez. These two didn't look like the type who would work for the cartel, but Milton knew that there were plenty of professionals who would be available for hire, and the really good ones looked like regular guys, just as these two did. They were "grey men," like Milton, the sort who could just drift away into a crowd and become anonymous.

Government operatives? The list of state actors with a reason to bear a grudge against Milton was even longer. He could have wasted an hour trying to consider all the people who might want to see him dead, but there would have been no way of knowing. There was no profit in idle speculation, so he put it to one side and continued his study of the man and the woman.

The man with the gun was facing him, so he started there. He had been the one who had done most of the talking, so Milton made the assumption that he was in charge. He was broad and thick, with a round head that looked heavy atop his shoulders. Forty or forty-five years old. His hair was cut short and he wore stubble on his chin. He had evenly spaced eyes, heavy brows and a squashed nose that looked as if it had been broken a few times. He was calm, breathing easily. If he was nervous, his breathing would have been shallower and faster, but it was even. There was no sign of sweat, and his eyes stayed on the two of them in the back and did not flicker or deviate in the way that Milton would have expected if he was anxious. His fingernails were not chewed. He was tanned, although the skin around his eyes was a little whiter, as if he had been wearing sunglasses.

The driver was tanned, too, but Milton could see the patch of peeling skin on her forearms. Milton guessed that she and her partner had only been in the country for a short time. A local would have had a deeper, more even tan and would not have been peeling. She was slender, and Milton noticed that she held the wheel with long fingers. Her blouse looked new, and the collar still had that starched stiffness that made Milton think that it had probably still been in its cellophane wrap this morning.

Milton switched his attention back to the man. He looked relaxed, as if they were just going for a pleasant Sunday drive. Milton looked up from the gun to the man's face.

"Where are we going?"

"I told you—"

"I know what you said, and I'm being cooperative. But it would make me relax even more if you told me where we were going." He indicated outside the window. "I know we're going east."

The man gave a little nod of his head down to the Beretta. "Where we're going is for me to know and you to keep your fucking mouth shut about." His eyes showed no emotion and his mouth was fixed in a tight line, his lips thin and cruel. He spoke evenly, without raising his voice, but there was authority and purpose there that Milton did not mistake. He had been concentrating on the sound of the man's voice rather than the message, which had been easy enough to predict, after all. He didn't speak with an Australian accent. Nothing about the man suggested that he was native. He spoke with a hard intonation, glottal, harsh-sounding. Milton tried to guess where he might have originated, but he couldn't place the accent.

Milton pressed him, trying to get a reaction. "Back to Dubbo?"

"I'm not telling you where we're going, so stop asking me. If you keep talking when I've asked you not to, there will be consequences for both of you. Are we clear?"

Matilda reached across and laid her hand over his. "Do what he says. Stop talking."

Milton didn't take his eyes off the man. "We're clear," he said.

He opened his hand and let Matilda's slip inside. He squeezed it tight.

Chapter Seventeen

THEY DROVE EAST on the Barrier Highway for two hours until they reached the town of Wilcannia. The town was located where the Barrier Highway crossed the Darling River. The A32 bent to the south here. The terrain was arid, bordering on desert, although the landscape—studded with river red gum, yellow box and lignum—suggested that it was prone to flooding when the river was in full spate.

Milton looked out the window as they passed into the town. It was dark, and there were only a few streetlights, but the moon was bright and it cast enough illumination for him to see that it was a small place. There was a clutch of buildings centred around the junction of the highway, with a pub, café, post office and general store. The buildings were all painted in washed-out yellows, the colour bleached out of them by the fierceness of the sun. They passed a neat and tidy residence that announced itself as the council chambers of the Central Darling Shire, and then took a side street to the south.

They ran on, the ground undulating down as they reached the river. There was an abandoned building on the water's edge. It was a large brick structure with a tin roof and looked as if it had, at some point several years earlier, been a warehouse. The name of the business had been painted across the top of the second storey, but the black paint had faded away into illegibility. A second painted message, more recent, warned that fire should be kept away.

The driver angled the car off the road and into the dusty space between the building and the river. There was a wide set of double doors and, at a quick toot of the horn, two men came around the corner of the building and opened them.

Four of them now? Their odds were getting worse.

The driver nudged the Nissan ahead of the doorway, put the shifter into reverse and backed up until the car was inside. The doors were closed almost all the way. The only illumination now was the silvery moonlight that filtered inside through the gaps and the glow of the instrumentation on the dashboard.

The two men who had opened the door had flashlights. They switched them on and Milton used the fresh illumination to glance around. It was an empty space, with exposed rafters above and a bare brick wall that showed evidence at regular intervals of brackets that would have supported some sort of industrial equipment. There was nothing else inside save for a white panel van that had been parked against the north wall.

Milton searched for any other means of egress. There was a mezzanine level at the rear of the structure, with an opened door just dimly visible beneath the half landing. The windows were all bricked up. The two men outside stayed next to the doors, and Milton could see that they each held handguns with their flashlights.

The man in the car with them opened his door, stepped out, and came around to the rear of the car on Milton's side. With his Beretta held in his right hand and aimed through the glass at Milton's head, he reached out with his left and opened the door.

"Out."

Milton had hoped that the man might make a mistake, get in too close so that he could take his wrist and force the gun away, but he was too careful for that. He stayed back, out of range, covering him with the same steady aim as he got out of the Nissan. Matilda followed.

"This is a mistake," Matilda said. "Whatever this is, you've got the wrong people."

The man had his eye on Milton and didn't respond.

Matilda's temper overwhelmed her anxiety. "Talk to

me!"

"Sit down, please, Miss Douglas."

Milton registered that: they knew her name, too. He already knew that this wasn't a random thing, but there was the confirmation. They had done their research. He filed that away with everything else.

Matilda did as she was told and Milton sat down next to her.

"Don't worry," he said quietly to her.

"No talking."

"Stay calm. It'll all be all right."

The man came all the way up to Milton and pressed the gun right up close, in the centre of his forehead. Milton was thinking about that extra few pounds of pressure that he would need to exert to fire the first shot, the fractions of a second that that would buy him. The man was close enough now for Milton to gamble, jerk his head out of the way, sweep his arm up to try to knock the gun away. The man left the gun there for five seconds, long enough for the muzzle to leave a faint indentation on his skin, and Milton thought about taking action for every one of those seconds. He decided against it. He was confident that he would be able to disable the man with the gun, but there were three others now.

"I said be quiet," the man repeated. "I meant it."

Milton raised his hands in surrender and the man stepped back again. One of the men from the door walked over to him and the two conversed. They spoke quietly, and Milton was unable to eavesdrop. Instead, he looked over at the van. It was parked in a particularly dim part of the warehouse, but there was enough light from the flashlights for him to see that it bore the livery of UPS. He could guess why they had brought them here. They were going to be transferred from the Nissan to the van. It would be easier to transport them covertly in the van. It would have been more difficult to be discreet with them visible in the rear seats of the four-by-four. They had chosen to leave the van, collect them in the Nissan and then make the exchange here. If their abduction had been less smooth, and if a chase had been necessary, the powerful Nissan would have been a much better bet to catch Matty's Jeep.

More planning. Milton was impressed.

It looked like the man with the gun was in charge of the two new arrivals, too. He said something, his tone assertive, and the other man went to the van, opened the hood and checked the engine.

The leader turned back to Milton and Matilda. "You want to use the bathroom, now's the time," he said. "We won't be stopping again for several hours."

"Where are we going?" Milton said.

The man smiled humourlessly and ignored the question. "Her first."

Matilda got up and followed the man to the back of the room.

Milton was about to stand, but the man waved the gun as an indication that that would not be a good idea. He stayed where he was and watched them.

Matilda was five minutes. When she came back, the man asked whether Milton wanted to relieve himself.

"Yes," he said.

The two newcomers followed Milton to the bathroom. He took a closer look at both of them as he made his way past them. One was around six feet tall, around the same height as Milton, with a head of curly black hair. He was handsome. The other was not; his hair was a messy thatch and his eyes black nuggets, mean and cold, sitting just a little too close together. They followed behind him, their weapons drawn. They had new Berettas, too, he saw. They all did.

The bathroom was a room with a bucket. There was a thin aperture in the wall, just below the line of the ceiling, and a little streetlight was admitted through it. The floorboards had been taken up and he had to step over the exposed joists. He could see from the discoloured earth in the corner that the bucket was just tipped out when it was full. There was enough waste there for him to guess that the men had been here for a few days. This appeared to have been a base for them.

Milton relieved himself into the bucket, zipped up his fly and turned back to them. There was no play for him. They had him covered, and Matilda was alone in the main room. Even if he had been able to disable these two, he wouldn't have been able to leave without her. Any kind of move would put her in great danger. It was impossible. He dutifully led the way back to the van. The rear doors had been opened. He paused and felt one of the Berettas pushed into the small of his back.

He couldn't see Matilda.

"Get inside."

He was pushed, hard, between the shoulders and stumbled against the tailgate. Matilda was already in the back of the van. She had the bracelet of a set of cuffs around her left wrist. He pulled himself into the van and sat down on the floor next to her.

"Put the cuff on," the man ordered.

Milton put the cold metal around his wrist and pressed it together until it locked with a click. "Done."

"Show me."

Milton shook his hand to demonstrate that the cuff was secure.

The man swung the door shut. The interior was swamped with darkness.

The chassis rumbled as the van's engine started.

He heard Matilda give a little sob.

Milton reached out until his hand was atop her knee. He squeezed it. "Don't worry," he said. "It's going to be fine."

"I'm scared."

"I know. It's fine to be scared. But if they were going to kill us, they would've done it here."

"So what's going on?"

There was nothing else for it but to be honest. "I don't know."

Chapter Eighteen

THEY SET off immediately. There was no light now, and he couldn't see a thing. He could feel Matty sitting next to him. She had pressed herself up close. He spent the first five minutes probing the cuffs, but the mechanism was solid and he knew that he would be unable to unlock them without a tool. There was no point in struggling, so he moved on to making them both as comfortable as possible. They had pressed themselves up against the wall, with the arch of the back right wheel up against Milton's right side. Milton brought his legs up a little to brace himself against the swinging motion of the van. His right wrist was connected to Matty's left, and they laid their arms down with only a little play between them.

He stretched out his free hand and pressed as much of the wall as he could reach. It felt solid.

"It'll be okay," Milton said. "Try not to worry. I'll get us out of this."

She didn't respond, and Milton didn't press. He used the quiet to think. He couldn't narrow down the list of people who might want to do this to him. It was a long list, and no one stood out any more than anyone else. He let his mind wander over the problem and realised that he had been too restrictive in his thinking. What if it wasn't anything to do with him? What if this was something to do with Matilda, instead?

"Matty," he said.

"What?"

"Can you think of anyone who might have a reason to kidnap you?"

"Me?"

"Think. Is there anyone who holds a grudge against you?"

"No. A couple of ex-boyfriends I didn't split with on the best of terms, but they're not the kind of guys who'd want to do something crazy like this, not even for a joke."

"What about Harry? Has he upset anyone recently?"

"You know Harry. He's too nice to have enemies."

"What about rivals to the business? Any disputes, anything like that?"

"No. I mean, there have been some issues with the unions, but that's usual."

"What kind of issues?"

"There was a strike six months ago. The shearers said they wanted double the pay and stopped work until they got it. But they're already making a lot of money, and the way Harry saw it, they weren't growing the wool or looking after the sheep or the land—they just came in at the arse end of it and made all the money. Anyway, Harry and the other graziers near Booligal flew in Kiwis to take over. You can imagine how that went down. There were a lot of problems. Lots of fights between the locals and the Kiwis, and those lads are tough bastards."

"And?"

"And the strikers backed down."

"You think they resent Harry?"

"He was the one who was on the TV. He was the spokesman. If they were going to go after anyone, I guess they'd go after him." She paused. "But that was six months ago. It's been good since then. Things have been patched up. I'll give you two examples: Eric and Mervyn. They're union boys, and you know how much they grumble. They were some of the first to stop working. Six months ago, you ask them what they think of my brother and they'd tell you he was a capitalist bastard screwing down the honest hard-working shearer. But you look at them now. Happy to have a beer with him, laugh at his jokes, best mates again." She stopped. "No, John. I can't see it. It just doesn't sound like the kind of thing that they would do."

Milton thought. It seemed unlikely, but it was worth keeping it in the back of his mind. Both of them had begged off coming out tonight. It wasn't like either of them to turn down a night on the beer, especially one where Matilda was along for the ride. Maybe they wanted to get themselves out of the way. Was it possible? Maybe.

If he could understand the motive, it would help him work out the best way to proceed.

The van rumbled along and they were quiet for a moment.

"What about you?" she asked.

"What about me?"

"Anyone who'd want to do this to you?"

He paused. She knew nothing about what he had been doing for the last decade. Harry didn't know, either, at least not the specifics. He had explained to him that he had been recruited into the intelligence services, but he had purposefully left it vague after that. It was better for all concerned, and there were some questions that Milton did not want to be asked. He realised, as he sat there next to Matilda, that he especially didn't want her to ask him those questions.

"I've upset a few people through the years, just like anyone else."

"And?"

"And I can't say any more than that. Maybe this is about me. Maybe it isn't. Maybe it's about Harry. Maybe it's about you. We just have to stay calm, do what they say, and keep our eyes open."

Chapter Nineteen

TIME PASSED. Milton estimated that they had travelled for another hour and, as far as he could tell, they were still heading east. There was no pausing, no stopping for junctions or stop signs. There *were* no junctions out here, not for hundreds of miles. It was difficult to be certain, but he knew that the road was straight and he knew that he would have been able to tell if they turned around. An hour, travelling at between fifty and sixty miles an hour. He tried to picture a map of the area in his head, and tried to work out where that kind of distance would put them. In broad strokes, it was somewhere in the outback between Wilcannia and Dubbo. He tried to remember the map he had studied with Harry in the shed at Boolanga. There was nothing out here on the A32. It was just thousands and thousands of acres of outback and the long, straight arrow of the road cutting through the heart of it. It was a wilderness, one of the harshest places on Earth.

They had to be going to Dubbo.

He was grateful for one thing: it was night. It didn't bear thinking about what the inside of an unventilated van would be like once the sun came up. They could only hope that they reached wherever they were going before dawn.

Milton wasn't prone to worrying about things that he couldn't control. It was a waste of energy. He had considered all the angles and concluded that there was nothing to be done. He would fall back on his training. Conserve his strength. Observe and assess. Be ready to strike when the opportunity presented itself. And there would be an opportunity. It might only be a slight lowering of the guard, but there would be a moment when his captors became more vulnerable. If Milton decided in that moment that the risk of inaction was greater than the risk of resistance, he would take his chance.

* * *

MATILDA HAD been quiet next to him. He had no idea what she must have been thinking. She had rested her head on his shoulder and, for a moment, he wondered if she had fallen asleep. But then, he felt her shift, pushing away from him until she was upright again.

"Can I ask you a question?"

"Of course."

"What is it with you and drink? You never really said."

"What do you mean?"

"Why do you have a problem with it?"

He would have preferred to say nothing, but he felt that he owed her something.

"There are some things I'd like to forget."

"What?"

"Some things that I've done."

"I don't understand. The army?"

He fidgeted uncomfortably. "No. After that."

"You never told me what you did after."

He was anxious to get her off this subject as quickly as he could. "I know I didn't. There are some things I can't talk about."

"Why can't you talk about them?"

"Legally. It would be against the law to talk about it. What I did was secret. It still is."

That was partially true. It wasn't the main reason, though. He couldn't talk about what he had done because she would hate him if she ever found out.

She laughed drily. "What are you saying? You were a spy or something."

"Or something," he said.

The van started to slow. That was odd.

"What's happening?"

"I don't know," he said.

"Are we stopping?"

He doubted it. They couldn't be near where they were going. Not yet. Dubbo was still hours away. Why would they stop out here?

He was concerned. "Is there anything else out here between Wilcannia and Dubbo?"

She thought about that. "Poopelloe Lake? That's about it. The rest is just the outback."

"And what's there?"

"At the lake? Nothing really. I think you can fish. Not sure if there's anything beyond that."

The van's suspension rattled as they ran off the asphalt and onto the pitted surface of a track. They started to slide forward, toward the cab.

"We're going downhill," Matilda said. "A lake would probably be in the bottom of a depression. Maybe the road runs above it."

Milton hated to guess, but guesses were all he had. "The lake," he urged. "Think. What's there?"

"I don't know. I've never been. I saw something on the TV once. Something to do with fishing. That's all I know."

He tried to listen for anything that might give him an idea what was happening, but the only sound coming from the driver's compartment was the muffled noise of music. The throb of the engine obscured everything else. The van bumped over uneven ground and they were thrown together. The van took a sharp corner and Milton reached out to grab the wheel arch to prevent them both from sliding across the floor.

The van slowed to a crawl and turned sharply to the right.

Matilda reached for Milton's hand and, when she found it, he grasped it and squeezed tight.

"Try to take it easy," Milton said.

"Are you nuts?"

"They don't want to kill us. There's something else that they want."

"So what do I do?"

"Whatever they say. Don't give them any attitude. If they think we're going to be compliant, they might let their guard down."

"And then?"

"I won't need asking twice."

"To do what?"

"To get us out of here."

The brakes applied again and the van rolled to a full stop. The engine was still running. Milton heard the passenger door open and then, shortly afterwards, the sound of rusty hinges squeaking.

"It's a gate," he said.

The passenger door slammed again and the van set off. The surface beneath the tyres was gravelled, crunching as they proceeded onward, the driver keeping to a slow speed. Milton estimated that they travelled for another ten minutes, although there was no way of telling whether it was to the north, south, east or west. Finally, the engine changed back down through the gears and the brakes were applied again. This time, the engine was switched off. The two doors ahead opened and slammed shut and they listened to the sound of footsteps on the gravel. After that, too far away to decipher, came the sound of voices. Milton held his breath and tried to listen, but it was just a low murmur.

The conversation stopped and footsteps approached the rear doors.

Milton squeezed Matilda's hand.

The mechanism cranked and the door was pulled back.

Blinding light.

A powerful flashlight. It lit up the interior. Milton couldn't see anything behind it. He looked down quickly, knowing that he would compromise his vision for moments that could prove to be crucial if he looked into it for too long. He raised his hand to shield his eyes and, as the flashlight jerked down a little, he looked up again. He thought he caught sight of trees and, perhaps, a body of dark water.

"We're here," the man holding the flashlight said. Milton recognised the voice: it was the man who Milton guessed was in control.

"Where's that?"

"Doesn't matter. All you need to know is that we're finished for now."

"Can we get out?"

"You're staying in there tonight." A jerk of the flashlight indicated the van.

"Come *on*," Matilda protested.

"No arguments."

"What are we waiting for?" Matilda snapped.

"You don't have too much longer to wait. This will all be settled tomorrow."

"What does that mean?"

Milton squeezed her hand again. He knew that there was no point in trying to negotiate. Better to focus on the concessions that he could win. "We need water," he said. "And if we're staying in here, we're going to need somewhere to relieve ourselves."

"Piss in the corner."

"At least let her have a moment outside," he said. "I'll stay here."

There was a momentary pause as the man considered the request.

"All right," he said. He jabbed the flashlight at Matilda. "Come forward."

"Go on," Milton said, wishing that he could tell her what he needed her to do, and trusting that she was smart enough to do it without needing to be asked.

Matilda shuffled to the door. Milton had to move with her.

"Far enough," the man said.

Milton stopped and stretched out his arm so that Matilda could continue far enough to allow her to dangle her legs over the tailgate. His eyes had adjusted to the glare. There was another man next to the man with the flashlight. He was carrying a shotgun and it was aimed into the back of the van. It was level with the floor. If the man pulled the trigger, the buckshot would pepper his legs and stomach. If it didn't kill him outright, the injuries it would cause would end him soon enough. He would bleed out in the back of the van. There would be a chance, but this wasn't it.

The man with the flashlight took a key from his pocket. He had to lower the flashlight to get to it and, while the glare was out of his eyes, Milton took the opportunity to look around properly. It was dark, but the moon was high overhead and that, plus the glow from the flashlight, cast out enough illumination for him to see that the van had come to a stop in a wide clearing. There was a fringe of straggled underbrush and then the occasional black stripe of a tree trunk. The ground looked like the orange-red gritty sand of the outback, gradually becoming less arid as the ground dipped down to the body of water that spread out to the left of the van.

The flashlight was brought back to bear and Milton had to look down again.

The cuff was released from Matilda's wrist and she dropped down to the ground.

The shadow of a woman appeared behind the beam of the flashlight. Milton recognised her: the woman from Broken Hill. She stepped forward, into the light, and tossed a big two-litre bottle of water into the van. It bounced once and then rolled to a halt against Milton's legs.

"Take her around the back," the first man ordered.

"Come on." The woman grabbed Matilda by the forearm and led her around the side of the van.

"There'll be someone outside all night," the man with the flashlight said. "If you or the girl try to get out, you'll be shot. Understand?"

"Who are you working for?"

The man ignored the question.

"Come on. Throw me a bone."

"You know better than that, Milton."

"Look at me. What am I going to do?"

"The less you know, the better for everyone. All you need to know is that if you do anything stupid—and I mean *anything*—I have authorisation to finish you right here."

"Authorisation from who?"

"Forget it."

"Who are you waiting for?"

"Enough talking, Milton."

Milton shuffled back a little. "You killed anyone before?"

The man laughed. "Come on. Seriously? What is that? You trying to get into my head?"

"Would that be a waste of time?"

The man with the shotgun joined in the laughter.

"Here's a bone for you, Milton, since you asked. Yes, I've killed before. Not as often as you, maybe, but enough that it doesn't bother me. Pulling the trigger on you would mean nothing. I wouldn't lose a wink of sleep."

The man with the shotgun emphasised the point by shouldering the weapon, raising the muzzle to aim squarely at Milton's chest.

The woman returned with Matilda. Her hand clasped around Matilda's bicep and she hauled her forward, sending her stumbling against the tailgate. Milton saw that Matilda's lip was cut, with a gobbet of blood rolling down her chin.

"Get in," the woman said.

"All right?"

"Little bitch thought she'd make a run for it. She won't

do it again."

Matilda pressed up so that she could get into the back of the van. Milton caught her beneath the shoulders and helped her the rest of the way.

"I was going to let you have the cuffs off," the first man said to Matilda. "You've blown that. Put them on again."

Milton took the open bracelet, fixed it carefully around Matilda's wrist and pressed it closed. He held up his hand, demonstrating once again that the cuffs were properly fastened.

The first man closed the door and Milton heard the lock slide home with a metallic *thunk*.

"Are you all right?"

"Fine," she muttered.

"She hit you?"

"Not before I got one in myself."

"I told you," he said, as calmly as he could, "no struggling. We do as they say."

"Until when?" she fired back. "What are we waiting for?"

"I don't know."

"I saw a chance. I thought if I could get into the scrub—"

"No, Matilda. What would you have done? There are at least four of them. They would have locked me in here and all of them would've gone after you. We don't even know where we are."

She didn't answer immediately, hawking up a mouthful of blood and then spitting it away to the side. "I do," she said. "I know where we are."

"Where?"

"It is Poopelloe. I saw a sign. We're next to a fishing cabin."

"What else? Everything, Matty. Everything you saw."

"The water is twenty feet to the left of us. There's a clearing and a track heading south—that's what we came in on."

"What's the cabin like?"

"Small. Looks basic. One room, from the look of it."

"Any other vehicles?"

"The Navara."

"How many of them?"

"The two who stayed with you, the woman who took me, and one other in the Nissan. He was speaking to someone on a phone. I don't know how—there's no signal out here."

"How big was it?"

"What?"

"The phone? How big?"

She parted her hands. "This big."

"A satellite phone, then."

The more Milton heard about their captors, the more he was convinced that this was a government-sanctioned operation. The organisation, the equipment. It all suggested it.

"What do we do now?" Matilda asked.

"We sleep."

"You think I'm going to be able to sleep?"

"You need to try. We both need to be rested."

She sighed, but fell silent. Milton shuffled back to the side of the van and, as the cuffs went taut, she followed. They both arranged themselves against the metal walls. Her breathing deepened and then grew shallow and, as she slipped into slumber, her head fell against his shoulder. Milton closed his eyes and listened. He heard the murmur of conversation from outside, but it was too distant for him to be able to make anything out. After a while, even that noise stopped. He heard the hungry calls of dingoes and the chatter of a nocturnal cuckoo. Milton directed his thoughts to the Twelve Steps, and, as he recited them back to himself, he only made it to the Seventh Step before the words became a jumble in his mind and, finally, he slept.

Chapter Twenty

MILTON HAD no idea of the time when he finally awoke. The temperature had climbed inside the back of the van and it was beginning to get stuffy. He opened his eyes and saw lines of sunlight edged around the sides of the doors and little shafts piercing through holes and gaps in the bodywork. The sunlight lent just enough illumination for Milton to be able to see around the inside of the van. It had been cleared out thoroughly, and he couldn't identify anything that would help him remove the cuffs and get out. Matilda's head was against his shoulder. He craned his neck around so that he could look down at her. Her hair had fallen across her face in a curtain that reached down to his elbow. Her breathing was relaxed and even, with a gentle sighing each time she exhaled.

He didn't want to disturb her.

He conducted a quick assessment of his own body, starting with his head and scanning down to his feet. All the usual aches and pains were present, almost reassuring in their constancy. It was something to focus on, and as he sat there in the back of the van, waiting for something to happen, it was a helpful distraction. He decided to let Matilda sleep, stretched out his aching legs, and settled in to wait.

* * *

HE GUESSED that it was another fifteen minutes before he heard the voices again.

"Get ready."

He heard the lock turn and the doors were thrown open. Light flooded inside, and Milton had to look away until his eyes adjusted to it.

Avi Bachman was standing in the sunlight.

Milton blinked the glare away.

"John," Bachman said.

Milton quickly mastered his surprise. He had entertained the possibility that this might have something to do with Bachman. But Bachman was locked up in Angola, awaiting trial for multiple homicides, and it looked very much like a life behind bars was the very best sentence he could hope to receive. However, Milton hadn't dismissed the prospect, not completely. A small part of him, buried deep, had always entertained the notion that Bachman had a hand in this. And, now that that suspicion was vindicated, other details became apparent.

This *was* a government operation.

Somehow, Avi Bachman had been released from custody and had enlisted the assistance of his old employer to seize Milton.

The Mossad.

And that meant Matilda wasn't part of the deal. She was collateral damage. Wrong place, wrong time, but that was scant consolation for her now. Bachman wouldn't spare her. And if he thought that hurting her would hurt Milton, things would get even worse for her.

It took a lot to make Milton frightened, and he was frightened now.

"Surprised to see me?"

"Of course. I thought you were in Louisiana."

"Things change. We've got unfinished business."

Bachman was not a big man, perhaps a shade taller than Milton, but he was powerfully built. Milton thought that, if anything, he was a little bulkier than he had been the last time he had seen him. Bachman had had a lot of time on his hands. He had clearly spent some of it in the penitentiary's gymnasium.

"John," Matilda said, "who is this?" She stirred and tried to sit up.

Bachman's attention had been fixed on Milton, but, now that she had spoken, he turned his cold eyes on her. "I heard we had another passenger. Who are you?"

"Matilda Douglas. And who the fuck are you?"

Bachman laughed. "Feisty. Like the girl in New Orleans. Right, Milton? Just like her."

The mention of Isadora reminded Milton that if Bachman was out, then she and her family were in danger, too. Anyone who knew him—anyone who could say that they were friendly with him—was in a great deal of danger. "She's the friend of a friend," he said, trying to deflect attention away from her and knowing that it was a futile gesture. "I know her brother. I was working for him."

Bachman gave Matilda a little tip of the head. "My name is Avi. Has John mentioned me?"

"No."

"Can't say I'm surprised. We're not really friends."

"That has nothing to do with—"

"He killed my wife. No reason why he'd tell you that. Doesn't paint him in the best light, though, does it, John?"

"I didn't—"

Bachman's seeming affability vanished in the blink of an eye. He raised the pistol and aimed it at Milton's head.

"Deny it one more time."

Milton looked at him, at the mask of fury that had fallen across his face, and knew that he should pull back, but he couldn't. "I didn't kill her, Avi. I told you what happened. She was killed by a ricochet. From one of your rounds."

"Say that one more time." He came forward and jammed the gun against Milton's head.

"Take it easy."

Bachman pushed hard until Milton's head was pressed up against the side of the van. The muzzle of the pistol pushed against his skull, just above his ear, and he thought of the bullet nestled in the chamber, two inches away, so close.

"How well do you know John, Matilda?"

Bachman held the pistol in place. Milton's arm was outstretched from the position he had been forced into.

"Not very well."

"No, I doubt you do. I can't imagine that you'd want to have anything to do with him if you knew what he was really like. I'll tell you a few things, shall I? See what you think then."

"Avi—"

"He used to be an assassin. He's a murderer. A professional killer. He tell you that?"

"No," she said, her voice wavering.

"I know he didn't tell you that he killed Lila, but he did. Lila—that's my wife. He shot her. And she's just the last that I know about. You killed anyone since, John? Anyone else Matilda should know about?"

"No."

"That's the thing, Matilda. Psychopaths, the worst ones—they're good at hiding it. Someone like Milton"— he pressed harder with the gun—"someone who seems like he's just another guy, just another ordinary guy... You got to ask, what kind of person is it that can hide like that?"

Milton pushed back, straining his neck until he had moved his head away from the wall. Bachman let him do it, but he left the gun still pressed there.

Milton stared into his face. "Shoot me or don't shoot me," he said. "I don't care. But, please, for God's sake, just shut the fuck up. If you believe a word of that, you're even more insane that I thought you were."

Bachman held the gun in place for another long second and then brought it away.

There was glee in his face. Milton looked into his eyes and saw madness.

"I'm not going to shoot you. You know me, John. That's not my style. Too easy. We're going to finish what we started in the fairground. You and me. Man on man. No weapons. No one else." He stepped back, handed the gun to one of the other men and then took off his jacket. "Get him out of there, Malakhi. Take the cuffs off and take them both down to the lake. I was going to wait, but we might as well get this over with now."

Chapter Twenty-One

MILTON WAS dragged out of the van and held at gunpoint while the cuffs were removed. The bracelet had been fastened to his wrist for hours and it had chafed and scraped the skin. He kneaded the flesh, trying to encourage the blood to flow back into fingers that were a little numb. The bracelet was removed from Matilda's wrist, too, and the female agent grabbed her arm and pulled her aside.

Milton was left with Bachman and the other man he had addressed as Malakhi. He took a moment to get a better look at his surroundings. He saw the slope down to the lake, the vegetation that grew more abundant the closer to the lake it was. There were three vehicles: the UPS van, the Navara and an Isuzu D-Max. Milton guessed that the last vehicle was the one that Bachman had arrived in.

Bachman pushed him ahead of him and told him to walk down to the water's edge. Milton did as he was told. He knew he was in a dangerous situation. Bachman was an immensely gifted hand-to-hand fighter, trained to a high level in Krav Maga, the combat system devised by the Mossad. They had fought once before, in New Orleans, and Bachman had bested him without much bother. He had beaten him to the edge of unconsciousness, and it had only been the intervention of Isadora Bartholomew that had provided Milton with a momentary distraction. He had taken advantage of it, using a metal crank upside the head to put out Bachman's lights.

The ground descended to the edge of the lake. The shoreline was wide and open, with a surface of damp sand. There was a slight breeze, just enough to send ripples across the otherwise glassy water, tiny waves that lapped over the sand and then quietly retreated. Milton felt two strong hands on his shoulders as he was propelled ahead, stumbling a little as he stepped ankle-deep into the water.

The water gave him an idea.

He turned.

Bachman had removed his jacket. He was wearing a white T-shirt, cut high to his shoulders, the garment revealing the sleeves of tattoos he wore down both arms. If Milton had suspected that he had added weight during his incarceration, now he was sure. His shoulders were stacked with slabs of muscle, the join between them and his neck now difficult to discern. His biceps bulged as he flexed his arms, and the hunks of his pectorals pushed out against the white of his shirt. Maybe ten or fifteen extra pounds of muscle since their last encounter. He had outweighed him then; this made it even more of a physical mismatch, and that ignored the fact that Bachman had already outmatched him once in combat.

Milton shook out his arms and rolled his shoulders, trying to give the impression that he was loosening up. He was not. He was looking for a way out. He hadn't lasted as long as he had by taking on impossible odds. He would fight Bachman, but it would be on his own terms.

But there was nothing.

Bad enough that they were in the middle of the wilderness, with no easy means of transportation. Even if he could win a moment's advantage over Bachman, there were the other agents to consider. They were a little way up the slope. Worst of all, they had Matilda. He wouldn't be able to leave her here.

Somehow, he had to beat Bachman.

His opponent stepped forward, closing the gap between them.

"Come on then, John. We'll finish this now."

* * *

THEY LOCKED UP, Milton fixing Bachman in a bear hug and trying to force him to the ground where he wouldn't have to contend with his arsenal of kicks and punches. Milton could barely contain him, but he managed to lock his fingers and started to force him down to his knees. He started to drag Bachman backwards, one step at a time, the water reaching up to his knees and then his thighs. Bachman realised what Milton was trying to do and Milton could feel his body go taut with tension. He heaved again, as hard as he could, and managed to drag him into water deep enough so that it reached above his waist. Bachman found a new reservoir of strength, drew back his head and butted Milton in the face, loosening the hold with the first strike and then forcing it apart with a second.

Milton bit down on his lip, blood squirting onto his tongue. He stumbled away, wiping the blood from his mouth, just barely able to raise his defences to block away the right and left punches that Bachman swung at him. Bachman came around to the side and attacked again, forcing Milton away and back to shallower water. He stepped toward the water's edge, his feet sucked into the damp sand, trying to stay out of range as he decided upon another tactic. Bachman followed, aiming a kick at the right side of his trunk that Milton was able to block with a downward slap of his hand. Bachman hopped onto the other foot and kicked into the other side of Milton's body. He blocked with his arm and the blow caught his elbow joint, sparking a jolt of pain that made him gasp aloud.

It was hot and close and Milton was already covered with a sheen of sweat. Bachman was, too. But where Milton's breath was already reduced to quick and hungry gasps, Bachman's was still easy.

He jabbed with his right, probing Milton's defences, and then unleashed a kick that he couldn't block in time. Milton crumpled over the blow, sagging to one knee and getting his arms up just in time to block a roundhouse that Bachman launched next. It was tremendously powerful, the natural strength augmented by the momentum of the spin, and Milton fell back onto the sand.

"Come on, John," Bachman said. "This is too easy."

* * *

MATILDA WATCHED with mounting horror the beating that Milton was taking. She knew that he was fit and strong—she had seen more than enough evidence of that in the shearing pens—but this new man, Bachman, was of another order of magnitude entirely. He threw his punches and launched his kicks with an economy of movement that was almost beguiling to watch. He didn't draw back his fist before throwing a punch; the blows just fired out as if his arm were a jackhammer. Milton had managed, so far, to prevent a punch or kick from finding its way through to his head, but she doubted he would be able to keep absorbing the impacts against his forearms and shoulders for long. It was obvious that each assault was full of power and force, since Milton gasped every time one of them landed.

She was standing with the man named Malakhi and the female agent, a little way up the slope from the scene of the one-sided brawl. The woman was nearest to her, her fingers resting against Matilda's triceps as a reminder that she was not to do anything foolish. Malakhi had referred to her as Keren and Matilda had noticed an easiness about the way they spoke to each other that made her wonder whether they were a couple. Malakhi had a pistol in his hand and Keren held a shotgun, the barrel pointing down at the ground, her left hand grasping it just below the stock.

Matilda was desperate to do something. Milton had not said anything directly to her, but she had seen the way that he had reacted when the reality of their situation had been underlined by Bachman's arrival. He had been frightened, and it was obvious to her that he was not the kind of man to frighten easily. She didn't need to guess what would happen to her once Bachman had disposed of Milton. She would be next. Milton would be beaten to death and she would be shot and they would both be tossed into the lake.

She thought of Harry. He would never find out what had happened to her. The thought of his anguish was unbearable.

She had to do something.

But what? She knew that she was no match for Malakhi or Keren: anything she did would just make things worse. What little chance Milton stood against Bachman would be squandered if she distracted him.

She had no options.

Milton was her only chance, and he was getting beaten black and blue.

* * *

BACHMAN KEPT coming on, relentlessly aggressive. Milton's arms and shoulders had been turned into one painful, livid bruise, and every time he blocked one of Bachman's blows he was rewarded with a searing burst of pain. Two blows had beaten his defences; he had jerked his head away from the first, just enough for Bachman's knuckles to sink into the fleshy part of his cheek rather than against his nose, but the second had connected flush on the point of his chin. A black curtain of dizziness had descended over him and, for a moment, he had thought his knees would buckle. He had fought to stay upright, knowing that to fall now would be the end of the fight. Bachman would lock him up on the sand and choke the life out of him.

Milton kept backing away.

"Come on, Milton. Fight me!"

No, he thought. *You're too much for me. Something else.*

Milton took three steps up the slope, away from the

water, covering ten feet. It brought him closer to the two agents and Matty. He played up his injuries, feigning that he was more dazed than he was and dropping to one knee.

He heard Bachman chuckle softly, almost hungrily.

Milton's attention was split: most of it was on Bachman stalking toward him, but he was also keenly aware of the group behind him. They had shuffled back to compensate as he limped up the slope, but Milton had narrowed the gap between him and them to six feet.

He hoped that it would be enough.

He rested his hand on his bent knee and pushed himself upright.

Bachman's arms were hanging loose at his sides. He was relaxed. Confident.

Milton looked up. "That all you got?"

"You have balls, Milton. I'll give you that."

"You want to know something?"

"What, John?"

"You want..." He paused, shaking his head as if clearing it of cobwebs. "You want to know how your wife begged me not to kill her?"

He was changing tactics now: he wanted Bachman to become so angry that his bloodlust would consume his reason.

Replace his tactics with mad rage.

"She begged, Bachman. On her knees. Just before I shot her."

It was a gamble.

And it worked.

Bachman lowered his head and charged up the slope at him. Milton allowed him to close, but, just before he could crash into him, he took two hops and then launched himself backwards. The agents behind him were backing away, but Bachman's rush had distracted them and they were too slow. Milton slammed into them, his shoulder catching Keren on the chin. She fell to the ground.

She had been holding the shotgun, and now she

dropped it.

Milton saw it fall and scrambled for it, but he never really had a chance.

Bachman was too close. He fell on him before he could get to it.

Milton tried to get his arms between their bodies, but Bachman was much too good to let him do that. He locked his legs around Milton's hips and worked around so that he was on his back and Milton was atop him. He locked his arms around his neck in a hold that Milton recognised as a *Hadaka-Jime*, or guillotine choke. Milton's head was forced beneath Bachman's left arm, the crook of Bachman's elbow pressed tight to the side of Milton's neck. Bachman's right palm was pressed against his own chest; he gripped his wrist with his left hand and pulled upward with both arms. He pulled again and pushed down with his legs, exerting huge pressure on Milton's throat.

Milton felt Bachman ratchet up the pressure again. Milton heard his voice in his ear, a harsh and compressed whisper that was full of fury. "Fuck you, Milton." He pulled again and Milton was swallowed in a tide of darkness that swelled and swept over everything. "Fuck you."

Milton couldn't draw breath.

Everything started to fade.

"Back off!"

The pressure relaxed, just a little, and the darkness receded.

Had he heard that? A voice? He couldn't be sure. He couldn't be sure at all—about that, or the clamour of angry voices that he thought he could hear now.

Bachman squeezed again, and the darkness closed in once more.

* * *

"BACK OFF!"

Matilda raised the shotgun and aimed it dead ahead of

her.

Bachman tightened his grip. She looked down. Milton's lips had started to turn blue.

"Let him go or I'll shoot."

The woman, Keren, was dazed. The impact with Milton had cut her lip, and now blood was running freely down her chin.

"If you shoot," Bachman said, "you'll hit both of us."

Malakhi had pulled a pistol from its holster and was aiming it at her. She was aware of it in her peripheral vision: the glint of the metal, the infinite black circle of the muzzle.

"If I don't shoot, you'll kill him anyway."

"True," Bachman grunted, cinching the hold in more securely as Milton struggled, weakly now.

"I'll shoot," Malakhi called out. "You and Milton will both be dead. All for nothing."

She tried to ignore him. Bachman kept the hold fastened tight across Milton's neck, the lines of his tendons standing out across his forearm.

"I'm serious," she yelled. "You've got three seconds to let go."

She had to bluff it out.

"Three."

How much did Bachman value his own life?

"Two."

"Put it down!" Malakhi shouted. She tried to ignore the gun.

"*One.*"

Bachman loosened his grip, just a little. Milton gasped for breath before Bachman tightened it again, getting his feet beneath him and then rising, dragging Milton back with him.

"Let him go."

Bachman was edging away, using Milton as a shield. She had no idea what he would do. She thought that she would be unable to pull the trigger, but, as she felt it nestle between the joints of her finger, she wondered if she had underestimated herself.

She didn't have to find out.

"All right," Bachman said. "Malakhi, relax. Don't do anything stupid."

Bachman released his grip and, raising a foot into the middle of Milton's back, propelled him back toward her again.

Milton fell forward, stumbling to his hands and knees in front of Matilda. He braced himself with both arms and struggled upright, coughing as he gasped for breath.

Matilda kept the shotgun trained on Bachman.

"Look at her, John," Bachman said. "I think she might have shot us both, you know. She might have done it. There's something to this one. Some backbone. That's impressive."

Milton got to his feet. "Keep the gun on him," he told her, his voice rasping.

Matilda had no intention of doing anything else.

Bachman turned his attention to her. "Seems like we've got ourselves a little stand-off, Matilda. If you shoot me, my colleague will shoot both of you. That doesn't suit any of us, does it? And it doesn't need to happen like that. My friend isn't going to fire first, are you, Malakhi?"

The man didn't answer.

"*Are you, Malakhi?*"

The man spoke through gritted teeth. "No."

Even as he answered, Keren drew her own pistol and took aim. Matilda tried not to think about it. It was overkill, anyway. Two pistols made no difference. One would have been more than enough.

"Easy," Bachman said.

"Give me one good reason why I shouldn't do her right now," the woman said, lisping a little through a thickening lip.

"Because you know what happens if I'm not around to keep making phone calls. You think Victor will be happy?

You need me to remind you?"

Matilda kept her attention, and her aim, on Bachman, but she could hear a whispered instruction from Malakhi to Keren.

"Do what you have to do," the woman muttered.

Bachman kept his own attention on Matilda, but he nodded his satisfaction. "Good. Now, then, Matilda. Let's keep things civil, shall we? They're not going to shoot you and you're not going to shoot me, although I can see that you would like to do that very much. You know why I know you're not going to do anything?"

"No," she said, edging around a little so that Milton could get behind her.

"Because you're not a fool and you don't have a death wish. Right?"

"That depends on you," she said.

He laughed at that. "You have some balls on you," he said. "You hear that, John? She has some balls on her." He paused, edging around, Matilda covering him every step of the way. He spoke again. "This is what we're going to do. You just bought John a little more time. There's a car over there, up by the van. Where are the keys, Keren?"

"In the ignition."

"Take John with you. You'll be fine. The spread on that shotgun is more dangerous to us than the pistols are to you. Malakhi and Keren won't fire."

She started to back up the slope.

"Keep the gun on him," Milton repeated.

"I am."

"You get in the car and drive away. But it's just a postponement. John knows I'm going to find him again and kill him, one way or another. You've been lucky twice, haven't you, John? Hiding behind someone's skirt for the second time."

"I'll drive," Milton said to Matilda, his voice low and imperative. "I'll go around, get in, wind down the passenger window and open the door for you. You're going to get in, rest the shotgun through the window and keep it trained back at them. All right?"

"Yes," she said.

"You get a head start, but where are you going to go? Look where you are, John. There's one road out of here. You could go east or you could go west. How hard is it going to be to find you again?"

Malakhi and Keren still had their guns on them. Bachman stayed where he was, allowing a distance to open up between him and them.

"You know who he is?" he called out. He was talking to Matilda. "You know who he really is?"

"I know who he is," she said.

"Don't let him get in your head," Milton said.

Bachman pressed on. "John Milton. The British government's most bloodthirsty assassin. You know how many people he's killed? I bet he hasn't told you that. Men and women, maybe children too. I don't know."

"Don't listen to him."

Bachman's voice was full of sarcasm. "What is it, John? How many have you killed? A hundred? Two hundred?"

Matilda and Milton kept backtracking; Bachman started to follow them.

"How many, John?"

He didn't answer. She dared not look behind her, but she heard the sound of a car door opening, then the sound of an engine turning over and an electric window winding down. She heard the click of the door as it was unlatched and the squeak of a hinge as it was opened.

"Get in."

Matilda backed up until she felt the chassis of the car against her back. She heard Milton put it into gear.

It was the Navara. She ducked down and lowered herself onto the passenger seat.

Milton had the car in gear and floored the pedal.

She heard shots.

Two shots.

The windshield shattered and Matilda shrieked.

They swung around, the rear wheels sending up twin scads of gravel and scree.

More shots. The rear windshield was blown onto them.

Matilda poked the barrel of the shotgun out of the window. The agents were spread out on the slope between the clearing and the water's edge. They dropped to the ground as she fired. The buckshot spread tossed up scads of dry earth and vegetation and she thought she heard a cry of pain.

She pumped the shotgun, ejecting the spent round and chambering a fresh one.

Milton wrestled the car into a straight line and they barrelled ahead.

They passed the van. Matilda aimed and fired into the engine block. She pumped again, leaning out of the window so that she could jack around and aim at the Isuzu. The Navara bounced through a pothole just as she fired, and the jerk ruined her aim. The spread went low, the edge blowing out the front offside tyre and scoring tracks across the hood.

"You all right?" he called out.

She didn't answer.

He swung around and looked at her. "Matty? Are you hit?"

She realised that she hadn't taken the opportunity to check herself over.

She checked now.

"I'm all right."

Milton swung the wheel, the rear of the vehicle sliding across the gravel until the wheels found purchase and they bolted forward.

"What did you hit?"

"The van isn't going anywhere."

"The four-by-four?"

"I think I blew a tyre out."

"Well done, Matty."

They roared up the track that led back to the Barrier Highway. There was a single bar gate at the end. Milton told her to hold on and punched the gas. The Navara lurched ahead and then slammed through the gate, ripping it open. Milton spun the wheel again and the car slid out onto the asphalt, heading west.

"We need to move," Milton said. "They'll change that wheel and come after us."

"Where?"

"Broken Hill," he said.

"And then?"

"I'm going to have to work on that," he said.

Chapter Twenty-Two

MILTON DROVE the Navara as quickly as he dared. It was a fine balance. He knew that Bachman would be in pursuit, and he couldn't allow him to catch up. On the other hand, if he drove the car too fast through a pothole and buckled a wheel, he was going to have to stop, and Bachman would reel them in. How long would it take them to change the wheel on the Isuzu? Not long. He pushed the car up to sixty, blooms of grit and dust spraying out and, he knew, visible for miles behind them. Nothing to be done about that. He couldn't slow down. And Bachman was right. There was no way they would be able to lose them out here.

Matilda was grim-faced next to him, bracing herself against the dash as the car bounced and leapt.

Milton stared ahead, his face locked in concentration. The sun lanced down, blinding shafts that he had to squint into, trusting that the glare wouldn't blind him when he needed to see.

The engine roared.

Milton squeezed down with his foot.

Eighty-five.

A little more.

Ninety.

"John—" Matilda said.

Milton didn't reply.

"What are we going to do?"

"We run. If we stay ahead of them, we'll be fine."

"They'll come?"

He nodded. "He won't give up."

* * *

MILTON REALISED how they were going to escape as the buildings of Broken Hill appeared from out of the heat haze. The road had been joined by the tracks of a railway for the last twenty miles and, as they raced ahead at seventy, they caught up with a train. It was enormous, almost a kilometre from start to finish, and the Nissan was travelling more quickly. They passed carriages with people gazing out of the window at them, a dining car, and, eventually, the squat-shouldered engine. The driver pulled his horn as they raced ahead, the mournful up and down blare echoing away across the vast plains.

"Do you know where the station is?" he asked.

"This side of town. Why?"

"It's our way out."

Milton kept up the speed. The track ran five metres from the road at one point and Milton had seen a large plaque on the side of the engine that announced it as the Indian Pacific.

"What do you know about that train?"

"It runs east to west, from Sydney to Perth. It only runs once or twice a week."

Milton guessed that the train would need to stop for a while to replenish its supplies, but he couldn't guarantee it, and he didn't want to spoil their chance of escaping on it by arriving too late.

Matilda had opened the glovebox and was rifling through it. "How are we going to pay for tickets? I don't have anything on me. No money or cards. You?"

"No," Milton said. "Nothing."

They would have to stow away. How practical was that? It was a big train. It would surely be easy enough to get onto the platform and, once they were on the platform, they would be able to find their way aboard. How long would they be able to stay there?

"What stop comes after Broken Hill?"

"Adelaide."

If they had to get off, they would get off there. Then

what?

"Check that," Matilda said.

"What?"

She was holding up a wallet. She opened it and took out a wad of banknotes.

"Lucky us."

That was fortunate. But it made him nervous. Luck tended to even itself out, over time. Where were they on the scale now? Ahead or behind?

* * *

MILTON FOLLOWED Matilda's directions to find the station. It was an old Victorian building, with two large wings joined by a single-storey run with a veranda. There was a large parking lot that was mostly empty save for a handful of vehicles parked next to the entrance. He slowed and looked for people. There was a single man leaning with his back to the wall, a cell phone pressed to his ear. No one else.

Milton parked and asked Matilda to wait. He took the wallet and walked across the lot toward the building. The man with the cell phone was lost in his conversation. Milton paused at the door and glanced quickly to the side; the man didn't react, glowering into space and raising his voice as, presumably, his conversation took an unwelcome turn. If he was with the Mossad, he was good. Very good. Milton didn't think it was very likely.

He opened the door and stepped into the building. It was air-conditioned, and the cool washed over him. He was hot, sticky and dusty, and the change in temperature was welcome.

He went into the bathroom and looked at his reflection in the mirror above the sink. Bachman had landed a series of blows on his face and the damage was evident: dried blood clotted his nostrils, there was a cut above his right eyebrow and a contusion was forming on his left cheek, darker marks within the purple evidencing Bachman's knuckles. Milton had boxed in the army, and had been good, and he had received thorough combat training in the SAS and then the Group. But Bachman was on another plane entirely.

Milton was not used to being beaten so comprehensively, and Bachman had done it to him twice now.

But Milton knew that Bachman had one weakness. The two of them had met before, years before their altercation in New Orleans, when Bachman was working for the Mossad and Milton was an operational Group Fifteen asset. The CIA, Mossad and MI6 put together a joint black operation, beyond top secret, to infiltrate the Iranian nuclear weapons industry. There was a factory in the Zagros Mountains responsible for the development of Iran's Shisha missiles. They assassinated five key scientists in an audacious coup that put the fundamentalist bomb back by five years.

The mission had involved a trek through the mountains and, during the journey, it had been necessary to ford a fast-flowing river. Each member of the team had been carrying a full combat load of weapons and other gear, and crossing the chest-high water had proven to be difficult and dangerous. Milton had gone first, working hard against the flow, concentrating on maintaining a solid footing, and had made it without incident. Bachman had waited and had gone last of all. He made it across, but it was obvious that he was uncomfortable. As they continued the trek on the other side of the river, both of them damp and cold, Bachman had sheepishly admitted that he was a poor swimmer and that he had always been uncomfortable in water.

Milton had tried to exploit that weakness at the lake, but Bachman had been wise to his ruse.

There would be a third confrontation. Bachman wouldn't give up, and it wouldn't be safe for Matilda until he was out of commission. Milton would have to take him out, one way or another.

He filled the sink with cold water and stooped to dunk his face. The sudden chill was invigorating, sending tingles across his skin, and he stayed there for a moment and waited for it to bring him all the way back around. He stood again, took a tissue from the dispenser and began cleaning the blood from his face. The water in the sink darkened as his blood dissolved in it. When he was finished, he was left with a swollen eye socket and a litany of bruises, but he looked a little less frightening.

He drained the sink, splashed another handful of cold water on his face and then took the wallet from his pocket. He withdrew the notes and counted them. Three hundred dollars. He slipped it into his pocket. There were three credit cards in the name of Paul Watson. An American Express, a Visa and a MasterCard. He knew that they would all be fake and that, even though he would have been able to draw down significant funds by using them, doing so would be too dangerous: Bachman would be able to trace each transaction, probably in real time, and although it would have been useful to have more money, it wasn't worth the risk. He put the cards back into the wallet and dropped it into the trash.

Then he went back outside.

There was a woman being served at the ticket window. Milton joined the queue. The woman seemed to know the clerk and the two of them were having a very pleasant conversation about a shared acquaintance and how he was recovering from a recent stroke. Milton tapped his foot, and then cleared his throat. If either of them noticed his impatience, they did not show it.

Milton felt a twist of anxiety.

Bachman was following. Had to be. Milton didn't know how far behind them he was, but it couldn't have been more than half an hour. The road was straight, and he hadn't seen anywhere that he might realistically have hidden during their eastward flight. Given that, he guessed that Bachman would have continued. It wouldn't be long before he caught up. Ten minutes? Would he check the station, or would he assume that they would carry on and keep driving west? It was impossible to guess, but Milton would feel anxious until they were moving again.

The woman finally shuffled out of the way and Milton stepped up to the window.

"Afternoon, sir. Where to?"

He had been considering their destination. There was one given: they had to get out of Australia. But where would be the best place to do that?

"Next train to Sydney?"

"Direct train leaves in six hours."

That was too long to wait. Bachman would be in town much sooner than that. And it was the most obvious choice. He tried to put himself in Bachman's shoes. It was most likely that Sydney had been the staging post for the Mossad agents. If they had others with them, or if there were *sayanim* working with them, that was where they would be stationed. They would be routed to the airport to look for him.

Too dangerous.

"When does the Indian Pacific leave?"

"They're just resupplying it." She looked up at the clock on the wall behind Milton. "It'll be off in thirty minutes."

"Two tickets, please."

"Where to?"

"Perth."

Milton took the money. The tickets cost $295. He pushed the notes beneath the window and watched as the woman counted it out, returning a single five-dollar bill. That was all they had to last them until he could find another source of funds. He would worry about that later.

"Enjoy the trip, sir."

* * *

MILTON WENT back to the car.

"We're good," he said.

"Where are we going?"

"Perth."

She leaned forward and rested her head against the dash. "Perth," she mumbled.

"We need to get as far away as possible. And we won't make it if we drive."

"I don't believe this is happening to me."

"I'm sorry, Matty, but it is happening. The train leaves in twenty-five minutes. We're going to be on it."

He took the keys from the ignition and went around to the rear of the car. Twenty-five minutes was good in that it would allow them to prepare for the trip, but it was bad in that it might be enough time for Bachman to find them. He thought about that again. Would he guess that they would risk the train to increase the distance between them? There was no way to predict that.

They had twenty minutes. He got back into the car and drove the short distance into the centre of town. They found a clothes store and quickly found fresh jeans, shirts and shoes. They got changed in the dressing rooms and then walked out of a door at the back of the shop. The proprietor was taking a delivery and didn't notice them. They hurried back to the car and Milton drove them back to the station, parking in a side street a hundred yards from the building. He would have preferred to have left the car a little further away from the station—if Bachman found it, it would be a simple enough deduction to guess where they had gone—but he was happy enough. It was obscured from the main road and would be difficult to find.

They walked briskly across the parking lot. The station building was empty and the only people on the platform were a family who were transferring their luggage inside. A guard poked his head out of a window three carriages ahead of them and a cloud of diesel fumes from the engine drifted back to them. The heat was crippling, almost dizzying, and Milton was anxious to get inside. He checked again that they were not observed—the family were too chaotic to be anything other than authentic— and, satisfied, he opened the door and waited for Matilda to get inside.

A guard emerged onto the platform and put a whistle to his lips. He blew, long and shrill, and the engine grumbled as the driver increased the power. Slowly, and with rattles and jangles as the carriages were coaxed into motion, the huge train parted ways with the station and continued its long journey to the west.

* * *

THE TRAIN ran between Perth and Sydney, taking three days on a mammoth trip that also included stops in Adelaide, Port Augusta and Kalgoorlie. It was 2,698 miles from point to point, one of the longest railway lines in the world. The train was, in effect, a rolling hotel, with rooms, a restaurant and several lounges.

There were three levels of travel: economy, gold and platinum. Economy had open seating, and gold cabins were split into twins and singles. Milton had paid for a gold ticket. He found their carriage and opened the door. They had a twinette sleeper. The sleeping car had a corridor along one side, with compartments opening off it. Each compartment had an upper and lower bunk that folded away to reveal a sofa for daytime use. There was a tiny private bathroom with a hot shower, toilet and washbasin. It was neat and tidy and clean. It would serve them well enough, he thought.

Matilda went inside. Milton followed and closed the door.

She sat down on the sofa. "All right, John. You need to

tell me now."

"Tell you what?"

"Who was that?"

"I'll give you everything," he said. "But I'm tired. You're tired, too. Can we get some sleep first?"

"No. I need to know."

"Please, Matilda. I'm exhausted."

"John—"

"I'll tell you everything, I promise. I just need to close my eyes for a couple of hours."

She looked at him, and, eventually, she relented. "Fine," she sighed.

Milton reached up and lowered the top bunk. There was a metal ladder beneath the bottom bunk, and he fixed it into its brackets and clambered up. It was a narrow cot, with a miserly mattress, but, after the events of the last few days, it felt luxurious. He lay down, feeling the aches and pains in his body from where Bachman had beaten him, the throbbing from his cheekbones and nose and eye socket. He had taken a lot of punishment and he would, he knew, look even worse as the bruises came out properly. No time to worry about that. There was nothing he could do.

He closed his eyes and concentrated on the clatter of the train as it ran across the rails. It was regular, almost hypnotic, and he was aware of his breathing as it went from deep to shallow, ushering him ahead into sleep.

Chapter Twenty-Three

IT TOOK MILTON a moment to realise where he was. He looked up and saw a ceiling that was close enough to touch with his arm only halfway extended. He closed his eyes again and heard the wheeze and rumble of wheels passing across track and then heard the blare of a horn.

He remembered. *The train.*

He turned onto his stomach and reached down for the curtain that he had pulled across the window. He twitched it aside, just a little, and looked out to a burning hot afternoon. He looked at his watch. It was half past twelve. He had been asleep for five hours. They were passing through a red and orange landscape, rocks and boulders strewn by the side of the track and, beyond them, the gentle ascent of uplands that were dotted with the occasional clump of desert pea or blaze cassia. He saw one tree, a myall, atop a hill that looked down over the wilderness like a sentinel.

That's right. They were on the train, headed west.

And then he remembered.

Bachman.

He winced from the aches in his hips as he swung his legs off the side of the bed and descended the ladder. Matilda was asleep in the bottom bunk. She had taken off her shirt and the dark nutty brown of her shoulders was vivid against the thin white sheets.

Milton hopped down to the floor as quietly as he could and went into the tiny bathroom. It was designed with some ingenuity so that it could fit into the compact space. The toilet bowl folded down for use and there was also a fold-down sink. There was a vanity with power points, a small cupboard and, overhead, a showerhead. Milton took off his new clothes and stood under the shower for five minutes. He found a sachet of soap and used it to scrub the dirt and dried blood off his skin. The water that ran into the drain was a mucky brown, and it took a minute to run clear. He scrubbed at his scalp, feeling the grit of the sand. There was a disposable razor in the cupboard and he used it to shave away his bristles.

By the time he was done, he almost felt human again.

The towels were in the compartment. He opened the door a little and peered out. Matilda was awake and staring right at him.

"Towel, please?"

She smiled at him, the first that he had seen from her for what seemed like an awfully long time. "Come and get it," she said.

"Matty, come on."

She grinned, relented, and tossed one of the towels across the room.

He snagged it, wrapped it around his waist and came back into the compartment. He dressed while Matty used the shower, and then he called through the door that he was going to go and find coffee.

* * *

HE FOUND a café at the end of the third carriage along. There were four tables between seats upholstered in blue and yellow material. He gazed out the window while he was waiting and watched as a kangaroo kept pace with the train for fifty yards before losing interest and coming to a stop.

He spent the rest of his money on coffee and Danish pastries and asked the server how long it would be until they were in Adelaide. The woman said that they arrived at three. Not long. Milton thanked her and returned to their compartment. Matilda was sitting on the lower bunk.

Milton gave her the coffee and pastry.

"So?" she said.

Milton knew what she meant. He sat down next to her. "His name is Bachman. Sometimes he goes by Boon. I knew him a long time ago."

"Who is he?"

Milton sighed. There was no way he was going to be able to change the subject this time. She had just been abducted, hauled across the outback and threatened with death. She deserved to know everything.

"He used to work for the Mossad. You know what that is?"

"I don't know. Maybe."

"The Israeli Institute for Intelligence and Special Operations. Their Secret Service. Israel's not exactly in a friendly neighbourhood, and they've always fought dirty. Very dirty. The Mossad is one of the most dangerous organisations in the world. I've been around them, once or twice, and they scare the shit out of me. They have a lot of blood on their hands."

"So why are they involved with you?"

He shrugged. "Bachman hasn't worked for them for a long time. He was supposed to have died in Cairo, years ago. That's what they said, and it's what I thought, too, until I saw him again in Louisiana."

"That's where you were—before here?"

"I was helping a friend. She runs a charity replacing houses that were wrecked by Katrina. She got into trouble with a corporation who wanted to build on the charity's land. She wouldn't do what they wanted, so they hired a man to get rid of her. That was Bachman."

"I still don't understand. Get rid—"

"Bachman is a hit man. He kidnapped her brother. I found him and got him out. There was a firefight. Bachman's wife was killed. He thinks it was me, and now he wants me dead."

"But it wasn't you?"

"No," Milton said. "He shot her. There was a ricochet. I've tried to tell him, but it's the last thing he wants to hear. He's angry and someone has to pay. He thinks it has to be me."

"And he's dangerous?"

"Very." *The most dangerous man I ever met*, he thought. A psychopath, a killer who kills because he likes it. It would be difficult to pick a worse man with whom to have a feud.

She paused and bit her lip. "The Mossad. You said they had a lot of blood on their hands?"

Milton knew that they were coming to a crossroads. He knew where the conversation was going, and, knowing that it was about to become difficult for him, he answered quietly, "Yes."

"And him?"

"Yes."

"Like you?"

There was a saying in Alcoholics Anonymous: they said that you were only as sick as your secrets. Milton determined that he would have no secrets with her. She didn't deserve dishonesty. He would tell her the truth and whatever happened, happened.

He took a breath. "Yes," he said. "Like me."

"What he said was true?"

"Yes."

"I don't understand…"

"After the SAS, after I met your brother, I was recruited to join an organisation in London. We called it the Firm. The part of that I worked for was called Group Fifteen. Some people in the Firm called us headhunters. I suppose you could say Group Fifteen was similar to the Mossad in that regard."

"You killed people?"

"Yes," he said.

"How many people?"

Milton looked out of the window.

"How many, John?"

"I don't know," he said.

"How many?"

"A lot."

He could remember them all.

She stood, a look of disgust and terror on her face.

"Please, Matty. Sit down. Let me explain."

She backed away.

Outside their compartment, a conductor opened the door to the car. They heard him call out that he was going to need to inspect tickets, and then heard him knock on the door of the compartment next to theirs.

"Please, Matty," Milton said. "Sit down."

"No!"

She flung the door wide. The conductor was standing there. She hurried out.

"You all right, miss?"

"What's the next stop?"

"Adelaide in five minutes."

"Thank you." She took out her ticket and showed it to him.

The conductor took the ticket, stamped it and handed it back. "Is everything okay?" he asked, looking into the compartment at Milton.

"Thank you," Matty said again, hurrying away down the corridor.

The man stepped into the compartment, bracing himself against the doorway to anchor himself against the swing of the train.

"I don't want any nonsense on my train."

"It's fine," Milton said, handing the man his ticket.

The conductor looked at it dubiously, as if there had to be something wrong with it. Unable to find a fault, he stamped it and gave it back.

Milton stood and the conductor put out his arm and rested his hand on Milton's shoulder.

"Like I was saying, no trouble."

Milton clenched his fists, but took a breath to stay his temper. "There won't be any. Now, please—get out of my way."

The conductor held his hand there for a moment before he looked up into Milton's eyes. The authority of his position melted away; he stared into Milton's cold, implacable gaze, and decided that if there was going to be any trouble, he didn't want any part of it. He stepped back out into the corridor. Milton thanked him and walked quickly to the next carriage.

Matilda was ahead of him. He made his way as quickly as he could. He caught up to her just as she opened the door to the carriage with the café.

"I've got nothing to say to you."

"Then just listen."

"Does Harry know? About what you did?"

"Not as much as you do."

She turned, ready to walk away again. Milton reached out and took her shoulder.

"Let go of me!"

"I can understand why you're angry with me."

"It's not just anger, John. I'm scared."

"You don't need to worry about Bachman."

"I'm not just scared of Bachman. I'm scared of *you*."

He stopped. "You don't have anything to be frightened of from me, Matty."

"You're a *killer*, John."

"No," he said. "Not any more. Not for a long time. That's why I came here. I've been running from my past ever since I got out. I've been trying to do the right thing. Help people, rather than hurting them."

"*Helping* people?"

"Putting things right. That's why I was in New Orleans."

"You call this helping? Because of you, I've been abducted. Because of you, they threatened to kill me. And now, because of you, I'm on a train running away from my brother. If this is your idea of help, I can manage on my own."

The train started to slow. They were approaching Adelaide. Milton knew he had only a few minutes to persuade her.

"Hear me out," he said.

"I don't want to hear any more."

"Just give me until we get to Perth. If you still feel the same way, fine. Go your own way."

He knew that abandoning his protection would be a terrible option for her, but he couldn't say that now. That battle could wait until later. He had to win this one, first.

"I'm not going to Perth, John."

"Fine," he said. "We'll get off here."

"I'm getting off. I don't care what you do, but you're not coming with me."

Adelaide station came into view as the train rounded a corner and drew alongside the platform.

"*Please*, Matty."

The train slowed to a halt and the door opened, a blast of heat washing inside. A male passenger stepped down onto the platform. There was a woman waiting with a young girl, and, as Matilda made for the exit, the child ran down the platform and threw herself into the man's embrace.

"Goodbye, John."

"It's not safe."

"I'll take my chances."

She started for the open door. Milton thought about trying to stop her, but he didn't. It would cause a scene, and the last thing he needed was that. She climbed down the three steps to the platform. Milton couldn't just leave her here. She had no money. And she was far from safe. He climbed down and followed her.

Chapter Twenty-Four

ADELAIDE PARKLANDS TERMINAL was three kilometres from the city centre. Milton had read about it in a corporate magazine he had flicked through on the train. It was adjacent to the suburb of Keswick and had been developed as a dedicated long-haul station. It was the only station in the world where passengers could catch trains for three distinct transcontinental routes: the Ghan ran to Alice Springs and Darwin; the Overland went to Melbourne; and the Indian Pacific, their train, between Sydney and Perth.

Matilda was on the platform, making her way to the exit.

"Matty!"

She turned, her face livid with anger. "What are you doing?"

"Please, Matty. Don't."

"Leave me alone."

"I can't. It's not safe. I know you're angry with me— that's fine, but you have to trust me. They're looking for both of us."

"Not here, though," she said.

She broke into a trot and he matched it, keeping pace with her. "You don't know that. Matty, please."

"Leave me alone, John."

A flight of stairs ascended from the platform, offering access to a bridge. She climbed them quickly, Milton just behind her.

She reached the top and turned to face him again. "I'm serious. Leave me alone."

"I can't."

She turned and nodded towards the gate line. A guard was checking tickets.

"If you don't, I'm going to tell him that you're stalking me. How do you think that's going to look? If you follow me, I'm going to have you arrested."

She headed away from him.

Milton believed her. He held his ground, watched her go through the gate, but then followed fifty feet behind. He gave his ticket to the guard and then angled away so that he could skirt the edge of the building and stay out of sight. She walked straight through the terminal and out through the doors into the brightness outside. He kept the same pace, slowing in the lobby to allow his eyes to adjust to the glare from the open doors so that he could fix her position in his mind. As he came to a stop, he realised that he couldn't see her. He opened the tinted glass door and stepped outside into the broiling heat. The building was new. It was a single-storey construction opening out onto a parking lot and then, beyond that, Wikaparntu Wirra park.

Milton stayed in the shelter of the doorway and scanned left and right.

Matilda was a hundred feet away, waiting to cross the road that would take her to a taxi rank. There was a line of cars, a truck waiting to turn at a red light, and a handful of passengers milling about outside the station.

He didn't know what to do. He could try to persuade her again, but she was stubborn and it was difficult to deal with her once she had made up her mind. But if he didn't do that, what was he going to do? Leave her? Could he really do that? He mused on that, wondering whether there might be a measure of safety for her after all. He saw a bank of telephones and thought that perhaps he could call Harry, tell him what had happened. Matilda would go back to Boolanga. He would tell Harry that he needed to keep his sister safe.

Milton had almost persuaded himself when he heard a scream.

He had taken his eye off Matilda for a moment, and, in

that time, one of the group of passengers had disengaged from the others and approached her. It was a man; Milton was too far away to get a good look at him, and he was facing away, but he looked as if he was of average height and build. He was wearing a ball cap, a red T-shirt, a pair of cargo shorts and sneakers. There was nothing about him that looked unusual for a place like this. Milton hadn't registered him when he had seen him before. Now he had his hand around Matilda's wrist. She was trying to jerk her arm away, but it looked as if his grip was too strong.

Milton's urge was to run, but he stalled. Haste would be dangerous. The guy would be armed, and he knew that the Mossad often sent their *katsas* out in pairs. They were looking for him, and, while this might be an opportunistic snatch of one of the targets, he couldn't ignore the possibility that she was being used to bait a trap. He could blunder into the middle of it and make things worse. Instead, he took a step back into the lobby. There was another door farther along the building that offered access at a point adjacent to the taxi rank. Milton sprinted for the door.

He covered the distance in twenty seconds.

He arrived at the door as a car raced along the road that adjoined the station. A red Mazda CX-5. It came to a sudden stop and, before Milton could do anything, the man hauled Matilda to the rear door, bundled her inside and got in after her.

Now Milton moved.

The Mazda had set off to the east, along Greenhill Road in the direction of Veale Gardens. The road outside the station was busy, with two lines of traffic halted there by a red light. Milton ran. There was a Toyota Corolla at the back of the queue, and he made for it. He slowed to a fast walk, careful not to draw attention to himself if the agents in the Mazda were looking behind themselves, as was very likely. The Toyota was in the outside lane, next to a metro stop where a clutch of people were waiting for their tram while trying to shelter from the sun. He approached it from behind a parked Land Rover, using the bulk of the four-by-four to hide him from the Mazda.

The light changed to green. The Mazda pulled away.

Milton opened the driver's door of the Toyota. It was being driven by a middle-aged man in a business suit. Milton didn't waste time with negotiation. He reached over to unclip the safety belt and then hauled the man out. The people waiting for the tram were right alongside. None of them was brave enough to intervene, but Milton knew that they would all have got a very good look at his face. He didn't have time to worry about that now.

He got into the car, put it into drive, and hit the gas.

* * *

THE MAZDA stayed on Greenhill Road. Milton stayed a safe distance behind. He was aware that this could be a ruse: taking Matilda to draw him away from the people at the station, perhaps lure him to a location where they could muster reinforcements. The other possibility was that they hadn't seen him. He guessed that it was a two-man team: one carrying out surveillance on the station and the other standing by with transport. They had seen Matilda and taken their chance. The most likely explanation was that this was an opportunistic snatch. They would interrogate Matilda for his location and, if she didn't know where he was, they would use her to flush him out.

The Mazda merged onto Glen Osmond Road and picked up speed. It settled at sixty-five and followed the route to the southeast. They passed through Frewville and Glen Osmond. Milton stayed ten car lengths behind them, hiding in a moderate flow of traffic. He looked up at the signs as he flashed beneath them, looking for anything that might give him a clue as to their destination. If they broke out of Adelaide and continued to Mount Barker or Murray

Bridge, at some point the traffic would thin out and an agent with even the most rudimentary grasp of counter-surveillance would be able to make him. He decided that if it looked as if they were heading out into the open country, then he would go on the offensive before he lost the element of surprise, assuming, of course, that he had ever enjoyed it at all.

The Mazda continued through Glen Osmond and then, at Urrbrae, it followed the majority of the traffic onto the M1. It was scorching hot, and, even though Milton had the air conditioning pushed all the way up to maximum, he still found that he was damp with sweat. He closed in a little, leaving six cars between the Mazda and his Toyota. A sign reported that Mount Osmond was ahead. Milton knew about the town from a previous visit to the area when he was operational with Group Fifteen. It was a suburb of Adelaide, located in the foothills that marked its eastern boundary. There was a golf club there, he recalled, a high-end one that attracted a lot of money to the area and had ameliorated the reputation for roughness that had been generated by the town's previous reliance on mining.

The Mazda took the exit that was signed to the town. The road executed a sharp switchback and then, as it straightened out, it began a steep ascent.

There was only one car between them now, and Milton had no choice but to drop all the way back.

He hoped that he would still be close enough to see them if they turned.

They continued to follow the road, the golf club passing by on the right-hand side and then, as he passed onto a stretch of clear road, Milton looked to the left and saw Adelaide spread out in a spectacular view. The Mazda passed a sign that welcomed drivers to Mount Osmond and then took a sharp left, turning onto Sherwood Terrace. Milton stopped at the end of the road, leaving the engine to idle, and watched. The road was residential and, as he observed, he saw the Mazda's brake lights glow as the car decelerated, and then the indicator flashed as it turned off the road and onto a driveway.

Milton waited, wiping the sweat from his eyes. The driveway was steep and shielded by a hedge and a telegraph pole. Only half of the Mazda was visible. The rear door opened and the man who had taken Matilda stepped out. Milton was too far away to see whether he was armed, but, as he saw Matilda's arms half raised as she slid out of the car after him, he knew it was safe to assume that he was.

The man took Matilda's wrist and led her up the drive and out of sight.

Chapter Twenty-Five

MILTON WAITED for five minutes. He saw the driver get out. It was another man. He made some assumptions. He guessed that these two were *sayanim*, the sleeper agents that the Mossad had in every city of every country around the world. He guessed that they had been activated when he and Matilda had escaped from Bachman. There would have been assets waiting for them if they had gone to Sydney and, most likely, Canberra, too. He wondered whether they would have had people waiting as far away as Perth. Maybe. Probably.

But there was no point in worrying about that now.

Milton got out of the car, leaving the keys in the ignition. He looked up and down the street. It was residential, with a number of single-storey properties arranged in generous grounds. The nearest had a smart whitewashed wall with metal bars between each pillar, and a gate made of similar bars between two gateposts. The property beyond was set into the sloping hill, its neighbours perhaps fifteen feet higher and lower than it was. The sidewalk was swept clean and the recycling bins that were pushed to the kerb looked fresh and new. A female jogger with her phone strapped to her arm strode alongside, quickly overtaking him. Another woman walked a Labrador. The cars parked in the driveways were expensive, and the only vehicles on the road belonged to tradesmen. This was an affluent area where people could afford to hire in their help.

The road descended sharply. Milton approached the house with the red Mazda in the driveway. There were no hedges or walls that he could shelter behind. If he was going to surveil the front of the property, he was going to have to go and get the car and drive by.

He was about to do that when he heard the sound of a scream from inside the house. It was loud, but quickly muffled; if anyone else had heard it, the silence that followed would have persuaded them that they must have imagined it.

But Milton heard it.

It was Matilda.

Then there came a crash, and the sound of something heavy falling to the floor.

All thoughts of a careful surveillance were abandoned.

Milton would be cautious, but he didn't have the luxury of time.

* * *

MATILDA OPENED AND CLOSED her fist, stretching out the fingers and trying to ease the stinging in her knuckles. She had punched the man in the face, a straight right jab that had landed full on the mouth. It was a strong punch, given extra impetus by fear and anger and the indignity of being hauled off the street by these two strangers. The man had stumbled backwards, his hand reaching to try to staunch the blood that had bubbled up from the spot where his teeth had bitten down on his tongue. He had tripped over the edge of a rug and fallen into a table, overturning it so that the glass top was dislodged to smash into bits against the parquet floor. He was still on the floor, brushing fragments of glass from his clothes. Matilda would have taken the opportunity to try to get out of the house, but the other one, the man who had taken her from the street, had drawn his pistol and was pointing it steadily at her head.

"You silly bitch," the other man said, struggling back to his feet.

Matilda didn't answer. Her fist still stung, but she would have hit him again if it wasn't for the gun.

They had brought her out of the car and into the house

through a side door. It looked like a typical suburban property, perhaps a little more expensive than average thanks to its size, its proximity to Adelaide and the beautiful vista that it offered of the foothills and the city beyond. Matilda had been ready to run, but the man kept close to her, his left hand around her arm, and the gun, in his right, pushed discreetly into her ribs.

The door had opened into the kitchen. They had taken her through it and into a room at the rear of the house. The windows looked down onto the view and the city in the distance, but the driver had closed the blinds. Matilda had noticed the front door to the house when they had approached in the car, but she assumed that it was locked. She had looked for another way out, but she had been unable to find one. She would have to get back to the door through which they had entered.

The driver spat a mouthful of bloody saliva onto the floor. "You know the reason I don't take that gun, shove it in your dirty little mouth and pull the trigger?"

Matilda clenched her jaw, her teeth pressing down hard, and said nothing.

"The only reason I've put up with your fucking *attitude* is because you're going to help us find your friend. But if you do that again, so help me God, you're going to wish you hadn't."

Matilda had studied both of them during the drive from Adelaide. The driver was effeminate. He was plain looking, built solidly, and wearing sensible clothes that had seemingly been chosen with the heat in mind. The other man was similarly average and could have been an accountant or a lawyer. They were both blandly anonymous. They spoke with the easy, abbreviated style of a couple who have known each other for long enough to be able to dispense with unnecessary communication. They wore rings, and she guessed that they were married, or at least pretended to be.

The second man raised his left hand in a placating

gesture. He kept the gun in his right aimed squarely at her. He had been more even-tempered than the driver during the ride. They were both professional and comfortable with what they were doing, but he exuded a strange mixture of calmness and menace. It was a cool confidence that reminded her of Milton.

"Calm down," he said.

"You saw what she did."

"I did," he acknowledged. "She's frightened. This is not a pleasant thing to have happen to you. It's fine. Doesn't have to be unpleasant."

The two of them spoke with broad Australian accents. The others, the ones who had taken her and Milton, spoke without one. Matilda didn't know what that all meant. She thought of what Milton had said, about how it was the Mossad that was behind this. These two were working with the others, surely? Local agents?

"Come on, Matilda. Let's be reasonable. What do you say?" He indicated the gun. "Can I put this away?"

"What is this? You're the good cop and he's the bad cop? You can both go fuck yourselves."

The careful, thoughtful part of her mind told her to be pliant. Respectful, even. That, surely, was the best course of action, given the circumstances. But the angry, fuming part, the part that was furious with what had happened to her since she went into town with Milton, well, that part was loudest, and it drowned everything else out.

The man, if he was annoyed with her reaction, did not show it. "You're going to be staying here with us for a while," he said. "Might be a few hours, might be a few days. You can make the time shorter by helping us."

"Put her in the basement," the driver said. "Let her think about it for a bit. We can ask her later."

"Relax," the man chided gently. "I'm going to be as civil about this as I can. I don't see why we can't have a conversation about this now. Right, Matilda? We can have a conversation now, can't we?"

She kept her jaw clenched shut.

"My name is Paul," he said. He pointed to the driver. "And this is David."

"Those are your real names, are they?"

He smiled. "No, but they'll do for now. We know this has got nothing to do with you. You're just unlucky, getting caught up in something you don't deserve to get caught up in. That sound about right, Matilda?"

She clenched her fists again.

"The man you were with—John Milton. Where is he?"

She said nothing.

"Was he on the train with you?"

She said nothing.

"Is he in Adelaide?"

She said nothing.

Paul smiled at her, trying to get her to relax. "If you tell us where he is, we can stop all this right now. Once we have him again, there's no more need for you to be involved. You can just walk away. Go back to your brother and forget all about this. What do you say?"

She had to say something. They knew that she must know something about Milton, and it seemed more sensible to give them something rather than put them into a position where they had to force it out of her.

"We had an argument," she said.

"About?"

"What do you think? About him dragging me into this." She waved her arm around, encompassing both of them. It wasn't difficult for her to be credible. Her anger was authentic and she meant every word.

"And where is he now?"

"I don't know where he is."

"Your best guess."

"Broken Hill."

"He didn't get on the train?"

"I told him I didn't want him to. So he didn't."

Paul gave her answer some thought. "Are you sure

about that? If we're going to be friends, we need you to be truthful."

"We're not going to be friends," she said.

"Last chance."

"That's how it was."

"All right. Is there anything else you think we should know?

She shook her head. "That's it."

"Fine. It'll do for now."

He inclined his head to his partner and gave a nod.

There was a small leather pouch on the sideboard. David collected it, unzipped it and reached inside. He took out a moulded plastic case that looked as if it might house an expensive pen. He opened it and withdrew a syringe and an ampoule containing clear fluid. He gave it to Paul, who turned to Matilda.

"Your arm, please."

"What?"

"Give me your arm. I'm afraid we're going to have to sedate you."

"No," she said, her pep draining away. "I'll be quiet. I'll do whatever you want."

"It's better this way. Please, Matilda. Don't make it more difficult than it has to be."

She knew, even before she acted, that what she was going to do was reckless and would probably get her killed. It was a combination of things: the gun that had been pointed at her head, being hauled across the outback, Milton's lies. She knew she should play along, but the anger overwhelmed her good sense.

She feigned compliance, letting her shoulders slump so that her arms fell to her sides.

Paul stepped up to her.

She threw herself at him, her nails reaching for his eyes and gouging down his face. He staggered back as she drew back her fist and struck him in the nose, then wrapped her arms around him. The surprise bought her a moment's advantage, but it was quickly lost. He was strong, shrugging her off and then shoving her away with his forearm. Space opened up between them, enough for him to bring his right hand up to whip it across her forehead. The impact was sudden, the pain an intense flash that sent starbursts across her vision. She blacked out for a fraction of a second and, when she came around, she found that she was on her knees.

Paul was standing over her. She had scored three weals down his cheek, each of them brimming with blood. If it was painful, he didn't show it. "You're full of it," he said. "Normally, I'd say that was a good thing, but you might want to reconsider it today. Playing ball with us will be much better for you."

Matilda backed away until she felt her back against the wall. Paul and David approached. Paul left the gun on a table and raised his arms, his hands open, ready to grab her. She shuffled to the side, but space was limited and there was nowhere to go. He lunged at her, both hands fastening around her biceps, and twisted her around so that he could wrap her in a bear hug. Although she bucked and jerked and scraped the heel of her boot down his shin, Paul did not release his hold. David anchored her arm and rolled up her sleeve. Matilda gave a feral shriek as she tried to fight her way free, but it was no good. Instead, she hawked up a mouthful of phlegm and sprayed it into David's face.

He wiped it away. "She's nuts," he said, the expression on his face saying that he couldn't believe just how crazy she was.

They held her arm steady between them. Matilda strained, but, as the needle scraped across her skin, she realised that it was pointless and that she would do more damage to herself if she struggled. She relaxed. She felt a sharp sting as the needle slid into a vein. The barrel depressed and a sensation of icy cold passed up her arm. She felt an uncomfortable throb in her arm before a wooziness took hold. Her strength faded away and she felt her head dip, her chin resting against her sternum as Paul lowered her carefully to the floor.

Chapter Twenty-Six

MILTON SPRINTED up the drive and hid behind the red Mazda. The engine was ticking as it cooled. The wing, baking in the sun, was warm to the touch. He shuffled along the car until he reached the hood, and glanced around the chassis. There was a door in the side of the house. That must have been the door through which they had entered. He could use it, assuming that it wasn't locked, but he preferred a different way in. He glanced ahead. There was a window adjacent to the door, but the blinds were down and he couldn't see inside. There was a fence with a gate and then, he assumed, the back garden.

He waited a moment, checked that the side door was still closed, and, satisfied that it was, he stayed low and left cover. He hurried forward, pressing himself down beneath the line of the window and reaching out to try the handle of the gate. The latch opened. He pressed the gate aside with his fingertips, saw the large garden beyond, and slipped inside.

He heard another impact.

This one was nearer and clearer. Two impacts. The first was a fleshy thwack as something was struck. The second was the sound of someone falling to the floor.

Milton felt his heart beat faster, his breath accelerate. Adrenaline pulsed and he felt the familiar twitch of impending violence. He paused, reasserting a sense of calm, assessing his surroundings again.

The garden.

A pool, covered.

A hot tub next to it, also covered.

A brick barbeque with a bag of charcoal on the ground next to it.

A window in the wall overhead, the room beyond

hidden by a blind.

He pressed his back against the sun-warmed bricks and listened.

He could hear voices.

The words were muffled. Double glazing, perhaps. He couldn't make out the sentence, but the reaction—a cry of alarm—was obvious.

He looked again. He was taking too long; he had to move more quickly than this. Almost the entire width of the house was taken up by a decked area, twenty feet of space that ended with a wooden balustrade and a drop down to the garden below. A huge set of sliding glass doors at the other end of the deck gave access to the house. He climbed up, poked his head around the doorjamb and looked inside. It was the kitchen. Modern and expensive, granite work surfaces, a large double range, expensive equipment. The doors, when opened, would create one enormous inside-outside space.

He tried the door.

A lucky break.

It was open.

He pushed the handle all the way down and carefully slid the door wide enough to slip inside. It was new and the runners were lubricated, easing back without a sound. Milton stepped inside. It was woozily hot, like a greenhouse. The air conditioning had been left off; he wondered how long the occupants of the house had been away. He could feel the sweat rolling down his forehead, salty in his eyes. He wiped it away and stayed low, passing an easy chair and a small kitchen table until he reached the shelter of a large island.

He looked up. He saw a knife block with an array of knives on the counter on the opposite side of the room.

He was about to move to it when he heard voices.

A man: "What do we do now?"

A second man: "We wait."

"No—with *her*. What do we do with *her*?"

"She's not going anywhere. We'll put her in the basement."

The voices came closer. He heard the sound of two sets of feet.

"This place is like an oven," the first man said. "I can't believe you left the air-con off."

"There was a rush, remember?" This voice was a little effeminate.

"True."

"Nothing for six years and then drop everything and get to the station."

"You know how it is. Don't ask questions, just do as you're told."

"I know."

"At least they'll be pleased. We got one of them."

"But not the one they want. You believe what she said?"

"I don't know. Maybe. Look, there was just the two of us and we only just got there in time. I think, given the circumstances, they should be pleased."

"It's Bachman, though. You know what they say about him."

"Half of that is just gossip. Legend."

"That still leaves the other half. All I know is, he's a bad man. And he's got them running around like this, running his errands."

"Must be true, then, right?"

"What must?"

"What they said. That he's got operational data. That's what he's holding over Victor."

"Maybe. Maybe not. Either way, he's not someone I want to disappoint."

"Fuck him," the first man said. "We deliver the woman to them, and we're done. Back to normality like none of this happened. How long can we keep her here with the kids?"

"Won't be very long. I was thinking, until they pick her

up, you could take them camping for the weekend. I'll come when they've come to collect her."

"I guess."

"I'm thirsty. I need a beer. You want one?"

Milton looked up. There was a big American-style refrigerator adjacent to the end of the island. If the beers were in the fridge, whoever came to get them was going to see him. There was no way he would be able to leave the kitchen without being seen. There was only one possible outcome now: confrontation. He pressed himself tight up against the edge of the unit, feeling the familiar tingle of adrenaline as his body readied itself for action.

He heard the sound of someone approaching, the sound of shoes on the floor.

Milton bunched his fists. He thought of the man who had abducted Matilda. Average height and build, forty to forty-five years old, looked like he kept himself in shape. He had only glimpsed the other man, the driver, as he got out of the car.

Milton held his breath as the man came into view from around the side of the island. It was the man who had taken Matilda. He was still talking, his head angled back in the direction from which he had approached, and, as he reached out for the handle of the big unit, Milton knew that he wouldn't see him in time. He pressed up and out, closed the short distance between in a single stride, grabbed the man's left shoulder with his left hand and took a fistful of his hair with his right. He powered the man's forehead against the metal door. He felt the man's legs go weak, and, as he dropped him to the floor, he looked up to see his colleague.

He was on the other side of the island, ten feet away. Slim, of slighter build than Milton and thirty pounds lighter. He was next to the block of knives, and, before Milton could get to him, his hand whiplashed to the side and yanked out a cleaver.

He raised it and came forward.

Milton stepped back, over the first man's recumbent body, and saw a rack of saucepans suspended above the range. He reached up for one and took it down as the second man rushed him, swinging the cleaver in a wide right-handed swipe. Milton brought the saucepan up and blocked his swing, the impact ringing out. Milton noticed that the man's stance was excellent, his weight evenly distributed between his feet so that he would have optimal balance. He had certainly seen some training in his time; he wouldn't underestimate him.

The man switched the cleaver between his hands, trying to keep Milton guessing and off guard. He came forward, backing Milton away from the island, and swung the cleaver again. Milton blocked it a second time and, using the brief moment that the man needed to readdress himself, hopped forward, grabbed the man's wrist, thrust his elbow into his gut, and, reaching his right hand between the man's legs, lifted him up onto his shoulders and then crashed him down again, dropping him onto the table near the sliding door. The man slammed down onto it, the glass shattering and the sudden weight buckling the legs, the metal screeching and scraping against the tiles as the man bounced off it and landed on the floor.

Milton felt a blow to his back as he turned away. The first man was up again, and he had swung a standard lamp at him. The china base was heavy, and it drilled the breath from his lungs, stunning him. He dropped the saucepan and stumbled away, steadying himself with a hand against the back of one of the two easy chairs. The man's head was already showing the signs of a large contusion from the impact with the fridge door, the discolouration reaching from his closed right eye up into his scalp. Seemingly oblivious, he settled back into an easy ready position, his hands raised.

There was no conversation. No offer for him to surrender. They must have been told who Milton was, and what that meant. Milton shook his head to clear the dizziness away and then put up his guard, his fists clenched.

The man attacked first, a blisteringly fast series of rights and lefts that Milton blocked with his forearms. The flurry forced Milton onto the defensive, and he stepped away from his attacker, opening up enough of a gap so that the man could change to kicks. He went low, hard right and left strikes that bounced off his thighs and calves, aiming for the weaker junctions of cartilage and bone at his knees. Milton blocked.

The man aimed higher, his right foot slamming into the left side of Milton's torso, but he had been anticipating it and, ignoring the fierce blare of pain, he clamped his left armpit down over the man's ankle and, grabbing his shin with his right hand, he yanked and spun at the same time, lifting the man off his standing foot and corkscrewing him in the air until he landed on his face with a heavy thud.

The cleaver was on the ground. Milton stooped to collect it and turned, looking for the second man.

He had a gun.

He fired.

The bullet went wide, only just, drilling a neat hole in the centre of the wide pane of glass and striking the wall outside with a puff of chewed-up masonry.

Milton threw the cleaver. It streaked between them, end over end, the blade burying itself in his assailant's sternum.

"*No!*"

A rending, anguished cry. The first man was back on his feet. He sprang at Milton and buried his shoulder in his stomach as he wrapped his arms around his waist and propelled him backwards. Milton's head bounced against the edge of a cupboard, but he managed to hold onto the man, using his dead weight to pull him down to the floor as he wrapped his legs around his waist. He held him tight and squeezed, trying to restrict his movement, but the man reached a hand up between their bodies for Milton's eyes. Milton jerked his head back at the last moment and butted the man, hard, square in the face. With his legs still pinning the man's left arm to his side, and with his right hand fastened around the man's right wrist, Milton drew back his left and pummelled him with a series of crisp, stiff jabs.

One.

Two.

Three.

Four.

Five.

Milton fired in a sixth and then seventh blow. Blood splattered across the man's face from his hopelessly shattered nose and lacerated lips until with the eighth— and as Milton feared he was about to kill him—he gave a groan, his strength dissipated, and his eyes rolled back into his head.

Gasping, Milton looked over at the other man. He, too, was struggling to breathe. He had removed the cleaver from his chest, and each time he tried to draw a breath, the air was sucked into the pleural cavity between his chest wall and lungs, where it stayed trapped. With every breath, more air was drawn inside, and the pressure increased. There was nothing Milton could have done for him, even if he had been so inclined. The pleural cavity would fill until the pressure collapsed the lungs. The pressure would continue to build until it pushed on the arteries and heart. Milton watched. The man's blood stopped flowing and, as Milton rolled away and got to his feet, he gasped once, twice, and then lay still.

Chapter Twenty-Seven

THE MAN whom Milton had knocked out was still unconscious. Milton found a washing line in the garden outside, used a knife from the kitchen to sever two metre-long lengths, and, working quickly, lashed them around the man's wrists and ankles. He dropped him into one of the kitchen chairs and lashed him to it. Satisfied that the man was secure, he took the dead agent's pistol, a Glock 22, and quickly searched the rest of the house.

He found Matilda in the lounge. She was laid out on the sofa, breathing with regular, shallow breaths. He gently tapped his fingertips against her cheek and, when that elicited no response, squeezed the tender flesh in the crook of her arm. Still she did not stir. Milton looked around and, on the table, saw a syringe and an empty ampoule. He picked them up. The barrel of the syringe was empty. The ampoule was empty, too, the label describing its contents as midazolam hydrochloride. It was an anaesthetic, usually reserved for surgery. If they had hit her up with the full 10mg/2ml solution, she was going to be out cold for several hours. Milton laid her out into the recovery position, making sure that her airway was unobstructed, and then checked the rest of the house.

He was confident that they were alone, but, since there was a chance that someone might have hidden, he moved carefully and thoroughly. He started on the first floor and cleared each of the remaining rooms one by one, entering with his gun aimed and ready to fire, sweeping right to left and then checking behind doors and inside and underneath furniture. Moving to the second floor, he found four bedrooms and two bathrooms. Three of the bedrooms bore the signs of use. One, the largest, was obviously the master suite. There was a picture of the two men on the dresser, smiling happily into the camera. The second was a storage room, with unpacked crates stacked against a wall. The other two rooms were occupied and, judging by the posters on the walls, the books in the bookcases and the toys stuffed into colourful plastic boxes, they were occupied by children.

Milton hadn't thought of that, but there was no reason to think that the couple would have been childless. They were *sayanim*, and what better way to merge into the locality than by having kids? He went downstairs again and noticed a portrait on the wall that he hadn't seen before. There they were: the two men and two children, a boy and a girl, a nice little family unit.

But now? Not so much.

Milton felt a moment of regret, and, knowing that dwelling on it would only lead him closer to taking a drink, he closed his eyes and waited until the moment had passed.

They had brought it upon themselves.

He searched the downstairs more thoroughly. There was an occasional table in the hall and, on it, next to a hands-free telephone, he found a stack of bills. The family name on the bills was Hughes. David and Paul Hughes. Fake names? Maybe. A mundane existence, a mortgage and utility bills, nothing out of the ordinary. Yet they were *sayanim*, and they had put themselves in his way.

He opened the cupboard under the stairs, and, behind a stack of boxes, he found a gun safe. It was a metre tall and half a metre wide wide, the kind of safe that would be used to store a couple of broken-down shotguns. He tried the door, but it was locked and much too substantial for him to think about forcing. On a whim, he went back to the kitchen and took the bunch of keys that he had noticed on the counter. There was a key for the side door and another for the Mazda, but a third, smaller than the others, looked as if it might fit the safe. Milton tried it and, with a satisfying click, the lock opened. The door swung open on well-oiled hinges and Milton looked inside.

He was pleased with what he found.

There was a Tec-9 semi-automatic handgun chambered in 9x19mm Parabellum. A Swedish weapon, discontinued now, but favoured by the US market as an inexpensive open-bolt semi-auto. There were two more Glock 22s, with boxes of ammunition for the pistol and the semi-auto. It was a good haul. Milton felt a little more prepared knowing that he would be properly armed when he and Matilda left the house.

He went back into the kitchen.

* * *

THE MAN was beginning to stir. Milton glanced at him briefly and searched the kitchen. He opened the refrigerator and found another three bottles of the midazolam hydrochloride that they had used to sedate Matilda. Returning to the front room, he checked that she was still comfortable, collected the empty syringe and then went back to the kitchen.

He frisked the man. He had a wallet in his pocket with two hundred dollars and a collection of credit cards. Milton pocketed the wallet, then filled a glass with water from the tap and took it back to the man. He poured the water over the man's face and waited as he regained consciousness completely.

He groaned as he was assailed by pain from the battering he had taken.

"Mr. Hughes, wake up."

He opened his eyes as far as he could; the right was already half-closed by the incipient bruising.

His voice was thin and weak. "My…" He didn't finish the sentence.

"Dead."

Hughes looked away, his larynx bobbing up and down. His voice was choked and husky when he spoke again.

"You're a dead man, Mr. Milton."

"Let's not do that. It'll be easier if you just answer my questions and I can be on my way."

"You think it will be as easy as that? The Mossad wants you. Avi Bachman wants you. You know what that means?"

"Avi and I will have a chance to discuss all of this, believe me."

The man laughed bitterly, humourlessly. "You're deluded."

Milton went to the island to collect a chair. He placed it in front of Hughes and sat down.

"We are going to have a discussion. It's going to go like this: I'm going to ask you some questions, and you are going to answer them."

"Go to Hell, Milton. I don't know anything, and even if I did, I wouldn't tell you."

"I thought you might say that."

Milton stood and went to the cupboard next to the refrigerator. He took out the small culinary blowtorch that he had seen earlier. He went back to Hughes and sat down again.

"Do what you want to me," he said. "It won't make any difference. I can stand a little pain."

"You think you know about pain?" Milton said. "You don't. Not yet. I'll start with this, and then we'll move onto your fingernails and then your fingers."

"Go fuck yourself."

"And it's not just about the pain, though, is it? You can't be thinking clearly. What about your children?"

Hughes didn't answer this time, but Milton saw that he was gripping the arms of the chair.

"Jack and Ella, right? I had a look in their rooms while you were out. Where are they now? School?"

Hughes clenched his jaw tight.

"I'm going to assume that they are. And, since it's one thirty, I'm going to assume you've got an hour or two before they come home. Who are you? Paul or David?"

"Paul."

"You have a choice, Paul. You can cooperate with me, and I'll leave you in one piece. Or you can play games, and we'll do things the other way. But if we have to do that, there's a good chance I'll still be here when they come home. And I don't know about you, Paul, but that's not the sort of thing I'd want my kids to have to watch."

Milton opened the gas on the blowtorch and squeezed the trigger to ignite it.

Hughes blanched, and Milton watched as beads of sweat appeared on his brow. He brought the blowtorch closer so that its icy blue flame was just an inch from his scalp. He moved it closer still until the ends of his hair began to smoke. Hughes squeezed his eyes closed and, for a moment, Milton thought he was going to try to resist. Milton did not enjoy inflicting pain, but he wasn't bluffing. Hughes had brought this on himself. They had tried to kill him. They had mistreated Matilda. He didn't want to have to torture Hughes, but it wouldn't have been his first time, and he would have done it.

The flame had started to blacken the skin of the man's scalp when he gasped out in pain and said, between ragged pants, "Stop! Stop!"

"Want to talk now?"

He gasped, and Milton let him gather his breath.

"Ready?"

"Ask your questions."

Milton pulled the blowtorch away and extinguished the flame.

"I don't have many," he said. "Why is the Mossad doing this?"

Hughes paused for a moment, his eyes watering from the pain Milton had inflicted. "It's Bachman. I don't know what you did to him, but he wants you dead. They could've put a bullet in the back of your head in the outback except for the fact that, whatever you did to him, he wants to do it himself."

"How did he get out of prison?"

"They broke him out."

"What?"

"You don't pay attention to the news?"

"I've been trying to avoid it."

"They took out the convoy that was transporting him from Angola to Baton Rouge. Killed the guards, got him out. It's a big story. The FBI and the CIA know it was us, but no one is going to admit it. The truth doesn't suit anyone."

Milton felt the anxiety in his gut. It was getting worse. The Mossad had staged an attack on American soil just to free Bachman?

"Why?"

"Why what?"

Milton gripped the man's chin and turned his face so that he could look directly into his eyes. "Why is he getting help?"

He shook his head, and Milton let go. "You tell me, Milton. I haven't got the first idea."

"Don't waste my time. You were talking. I heard you. You said he's using something against them."

"It's a rumour. But they're not going to confirm anything to us. That's not how this works."

"What rumour?"

"They said, when he got out, he took a copy of the Black Book with him."

"What's that?"

"The active operational database. Details on agents in the field. Aliases, photographs, their assignments."

"But he's been out for years."

"Don't be naive, Milton. Even if it was ten years old, or twenty, it's still dynamite. Some of those agents will still be in the field. They were junior then. Think what they could be now. He could tear down years of work if he ever put that out here. The agency is not doing this willingly, I know that much. Whatever Bachman has, it's important enough for them to take massive risks to keep him happy."

"How far up does this go?"

"All the way."

"*All* the way? To the director?"

Hughes nodded. "All the way."

"Have you reported to them? That you found Matilda?"

"I called it in when we were driving here."

"What's the procedure now?"

"They come to pick her up."

"Here?"

"Yes."

"When?"

"Tomorrow."

"Will it be Bachman?"

"I don't know. I didn't speak to him."

Milton ran the thought through his head and started to assess the angles. Where would Bachman be? Would he have followed them to Broken Hill? Where would he have gone next?

"Logistics," Milton said. "How many people are in Australia? How many *katsas*?"

"Four agents."

"Malakhi and Keren?"

"I don't know their names, so don't ask."

"What about *sayanim*?"

"Everywhere. Dozens. The Mossad knows you're dangerous, Milton. Everyone is looking for you."

"And what about the girl? What do you know about her?"

"We had her picture. They said that you might be travelling together. They think you're a couple."

Milton grimaced. That was bad news. If they thought that, they would go after Matilda as a lever to use against him. She couldn't be left alone now. If she was still minded to run, he would have to persuade her otherwise. That might not be easy.

"Okay. We're getting to the end now, Mr. Hughes. Can you get in touch with Bachman?"

He looked down. "Yes."

"How?"

Hughes sighed. He had already given up plenty of information. His cover was gone; he was finished as a *sayan*. His partner was dead. And, as far as he was concerned, he was clinging onto his own life and to the lives of his children. Milton knew, now, that the man was broken. He would give him everything that he asked.

"I can call the agent who's with him."

"Do it."

"My phone," Hughes said. "It's in my jacket pocket."

Chapter Twenty-Eight

MILTON LET Hughes find the number, the phone laid out flat in his hand so that he could see exactly what he was doing. The number was stored in a blank contact form, with no indication that it was anything of any import.

He put the phone on the counter and went back to Hughes. He took the syringe, popped the cap from the end of the needle, and slid the point of the needle through the pliant plastic sheath. He drew 5ml of midazolam into the barrel and then depressed the plunger a little to expel the first few droplets.

"I'm going to put you under. By the time you wake up, we'll be gone."

"My husband? I don't want my kids to find him."

Milton looked over at the still body on the floor. "Do you have a room you can lock?"

"The garage," he said. "The key's on my key ring."

"I'll put him in there and lock the door."

"What about all this?" He nodded down at the washing line that secured him to the chair.

"I'll cut you free and leave you in bed. They'll think you're asleep."

Hughes didn't thank Milton—he had no gratitude for him, under the circumstances—but he gave a nod, a little acknowledgement that he had been kinder than he might have expected.

Milton took the syringe and slid the point into the vein on the back of Hughes' hand. He pushed the plunger all the way down, watching as the fluid disappeared, and waited the ten seconds it took for the man's head to loll woozily, for his eyes to shut, and for the muscles in his neck to relax so that his chin was pressed up against his chest.

He moved quickly. He had no wish to be there when the children returned from school.

He moved the body of the dead man into the garage. There was enough space inside for a car, the rest taken up by unopened storage crates and the detritus of daily life. There were two children's bicycles; Milton tried not to think too hard about what they represented as he laid David's body on the concrete floor and covered it with a span of tarpaulin. He made sure that the roller door was locked, then went back into the house and locked that door, too. He found a mop and bucket, filled it with soapy water, and washed the bloodstains from the kitchen floor. There was a lot of it, and it smeared and streaked, and the job took him longer than he would have liked. He checked that Paul Hughes was unconscious—he was—and untied him. He hoisted him over his shoulder and carried him upstairs to the bedroom, laying him out on the bed.

He went downstairs again. Matilda was still asleep. He left the house through the side door, ran back to the car he had stolen and drove back with it, reversing into the drive so that it was adjacent to the door. He went inside, scooped Matilda into his arms, and carried her to the car. He laid her across the back seat, looking down at her face for a moment. She gave out a peaceful exhalation, but didn't move. Milton clipped the seat belt to anchor her to the seat, shut the door and went back into the house.

He collected the Tec-9, two of the Glocks and filled a plastic carrier bag with boxes of ammunition for both.

Outside, he locked the side door, got into the driver's seat, put the car into drive, negotiated the downward slope of the driveway and set off.

* * *

MILTON STOPPED the car at a lay-by when he was beyond the Mount Osmond city limits. He stepped outside into the burning heat and took Hughes' mobile phone from his pocket. He quickly scrolled through the messages for anything that might have been useful, but there was nothing of note. Hughes had been too careful to leave anything in the memory that might be incriminating.

He navigated to the contacts and found the blank page with the single number that Hughes had identified.

He pressed CALL.

"Hello?"

A terse, tight voice. Milton thought he recognised it. Malakhi.

"I want to speak to Avi Bachman."

A pause. "Who is this?"

"John Milton. Put him on now."

Another pause. Milton could hear the sound of muffled conversation, none of the words distinguishable.

The line cleared and the sound on the other end became a little more distinct. A hand removed from the microphone, perhaps.

"Milton."

"Avi," Milton said.

There was a pause, just the crackle of static on the line. Milton waited.

"Where are you?" Bachman said. "Adelaide?"

"I was. But not any more."

"The girl?"

"Don't worry about her."

"She's your girlfriend?"

"No," he said. "I know you think I'm saying that because I want you to leave her out of this, but it's the truth. But I'll be honest: she is important to me. I won't let you hurt her."

"I'm sorry, John, you should have thought about that before you shot my wife."

Milton sighed, his grip tightening on the phone. "I'm going to say this one more time. I didn't shoot her. You did. You pumped fifty bullets into that container. One of them ricocheted."

Bachman shouted down the line at him: "You're fucking lying!"

Milton paused. "I know that's hard for you to hear, but it's the truth. And I know there's no point in us talking about it any more. You're not listening to me, so I'm not going to waste my breath. You can think whatever you like."

"Why don't you tell me where you are? We can meet and talk about it."

"I don't think so."

"So why are you calling me?"

"I'm giving you a warning. One of the *sayanim* who found the girl is dead, and the other one is only alive because I decided to spare him. I'm giving you notice, Avi. I know you're not listening to me. I know you need someone to blame for what happened to your wife and that you blame me. And that's fine. I know you're not going to stop coming for me, but this isn't going to be one way any more. I'm coming for you, Avi, and anyone else working with you. You're all fair game. I just wanted you to know that."

He expected Bachman to explode with rage, but, instead, he heard a bitter chuckle. "Nice try, Milton. But it's not just us. Me and you. It's the Mossad. *All* of the Mossad. How long do you think you can run from that?"

"I don't have to run," he said. "I just have to take you out. I know about the Black Book. If you're not a threat to them any more, why would they risk coming after me?"

"Not as simple as that."

"But that's why I'm calling. I'm giving you notice. I'll see you again, but it'll be on my terms."

"Didn't go very well for you the last two times we met."

"We're not going to fight. You know what I can do. I could end this from five hundred yards away."

He ended the call.

197

He didn't know whether Bachman would buy it. Probably not. He just wanted to give him something to think about. Something that might, maybe, slow him down.

It was a diversion. Milton had a plan. Something that Bachman wouldn't expect. He just needed the opportunity to put it into action.

Chapter Twenty-Nine

MILTON PULLED into the lot of the Playford Tavern. He had found it with a quick search on Hughes' phone and selected it because it was outside the city and a half hour's drive away from the house. It was a basic motel, with clean and functional rooms. There was a restaurant for guests and, as Milton surveilled his surroundings, he saw a couple emerge from the door to their room, cross the veranda and enter the large room. Matilda was sleeping in the passenger seat, still deep in the grip of the narcotic, but he didn't want to leave her for long. He walked briskly to the reception, where he booked a room for one night and paid in advance with the cash that he had taken from Hughes. The room was fifty bucks, which left him $250 once the transaction had been completed. That wasn't going to be anywhere near enough to get out of the country. He would have to think about the best way to find more.

He paused at the exit, checked left and right, and, confident that he was not being observed, he cautiously crossed the lot to the car. He had been allotted a room at the end of a long row, and he parked the car directly outside the door. The room was small and basic, as he had expected, with a double bed, two chairs and a television that sat on a cheap bureau. A door opposite the bed opened into the rudimentary bathroom.

It would serve their purposes.

He returned to the car and, after checking once again that he was unobserved, opened the door and stooped down to Matilda's recumbent body. He released the safety belt, slid one arm beneath her legs and the other behind her back and lifted her out. Her muscles were relaxed and her head rested against his chest. Milton crossed the veranda, entered the room and closed the door with a backwards push from his foot. He laid Matilda down on the bed, closed the curtains and locked the door, fastening the chain for added security.

He took out the Glock and rested it on the table. Then he took out Hughes' cell phone and opened a window in the browser.

He had business to attend to.

Chapter Thirty

MILTON'S SLEEP had been fitful. He had been unable to relax, still afraid that they had been followed and that, at any moment, the door would be kicked open and armed *katsas* would appear to take them both. It was an irrational fear, given life by his fatigue and the state of restless torpor that would not quite allow him to slide all the way into sleep. His mind raced with thoughts and images: murderous bloodlust on Avi Bachman's face, the sight of Matilda lying unconscious in the front room of the house in Adelaide, and, as he was just about to cross the margin into sleep, the memory of what had happened that day in Iraq, a replay of a personal movie that had driven him to the bottle in order to forget.

He awoke with the dawn. He was in the chair, his legs stretched out before him. He didn't feel particularly refreshed, and, as he came all the way around, he became aware of the throbbing from the injuries that Bachman had inflicted on him and he remembered the full scope of the predicament that he was in.

Matilda was still asleep.

He went to the vending machine outside the office and bought a packet of cigarettes. He went back to the room, checked that Matilda was still asleep, and then went back outside to watch the sunrise and smoke. He needed to think.

He had made his plans the night before. He knew that his best option was to run. He could slip back into obscurity again and stay out of sight. He was trained to do that and, if he determined that it was the best course of action, he was confident that he could make himself invisible to Bachman regardless of all the help that he had somehow managed to summon. He would go to Africa or

201

South America, just as he had when he had fled from Control and Group Fifteen, and simply erase himself so that he was impossible to find. He could live out a life in Durban or Rio or Buenos Aires and never have to think about Avi Bachman again.

He could do that.

But Matilda could not.

How could he ask her to exchange her life for one spent watching shadows? A life where she had no choice but to abandon her brother and her friends and accept that she could never see any of them again? She had done nothing wrong. This was nothing to do with her. Her involvement was because she had been unfortunate enough to have crossed his path, just as others had been unfortunate in the past. And some of those people were dead.

Milton swore to himself that that was not going to happen to her.

Thinking of Matilda had crystallised his thinking. He couldn't keep playing defence. At some point, he was going to have to bring the fight to Bachman. The only way he could guarantee her safety was if Bachman was gone.

But to do that, they would need to travel.

The sun's rays were already strong and he took off his shirt and hung it on the door handle. He looked out at the vast Australian landscape and the buildings in the far distance that marked the edge of the city. He thought of David and Paul Hughes and all the other *sayanim* that the Mossad could call upon to find him. He thought of Bachman and the agents with him.

Where were they?

He stretched, smoked the last of the cigarette and ground the butt beneath his shoe. He wished that he still had his copy of the Big Book, but it was still in his pack at Boolanga, most probably lost forever. He would have liked to read a few of his favourite passages, but he would have to do without it. He closed his eyes and meditated, reciting the Twelve Steps to himself and allowing himself a moment of reflection. He needed the peace and tranquillity that it brought; he knew that there would be no other opportunity for that today.

He went into the room, collected the pistol and slid it into the waistband of his jeans. Matilda had shifted position so that she was on her side, her face angled toward him. The anaesthetic had knocked her out all day and all night. She had stirred, once, at three in the morning and let out a sudden fearsome shriek that shocked Milton awake, but the moment had passed and she had quickly fallen back into the grip of her drugged slumber. Milton had rearranged the covers over her and returned to the chair.

He would have liked to let her sleep off the remnants of the drug, but they had to get moving.

"Matilda, wake up."

She shifted, her legs sliding down the bed, her eyes opening for a moment and then closing again.

He knelt beside her and rested a hand on her brow.

"Matilda, wake up. It's John."

She mumbled something that he couldn't understand, but he could see that she was starting to come around. He had left a glass of water by the bed for her, but she hadn't touched it. He took it into the bathroom and refreshed it. When he came back into the bedroom, she was awake, rubbing the sleep from her eyes.

"Where are we?"

"In a motel. Just outside Adelaide."

She didn't answer, lying there quietly for a moment, but then the memory of what had happened came back to her and her eyes went wide with fright. She pressed down with her legs, shoving her body all the way up the bed until her back clattered into the headboard.

Milton reached out and put a hand on her shoulder. "Relax. It's fine."

"They drugged me."

"I know."

"They were at the station. They took me. They… What happened?"

"I saw what happened. I followed them."

"Where are they? I—I…"

"It doesn't matter."

She looked at him and, for one heart-breaking moment, he saw that he was the cause of the fear in her eyes. "What happened to them?"

"One of them is dead."

She remained where she was, the colour leaching from her cheeks, but then, with a suddenness that took Milton by surprise, she surged out of bed and staggered into the bathroom. He saw her fall to her knees, her head over the open toilet, and heard as she retched.

He wanted to go and help her, but he stayed where he was. She vomited again and again, eventually standing and closing the door behind her. He heard the tap run and the splash of water and, when she re-emerged, her face was wet.

"Matilda," he said, "I had no choice. They would have killed you."

She didn't respond. Instead, she sat on the edge of the bed, saw the glass of water, and drank it down.

"We need to talk."

She replaced the empty glass on the table.

"Matilda, we need to leave the country."

That brought her around. "What?"

"It's not safe."

"I'm not—"

Milton cut her off. "Listen to me. Please, for once, just *listen* to me."

Fresh blood coloured her cheeks and her eyes flashed, but she stopped.

"You saw what happened. It'll keep happening until I'm dead. They'll come for both of us."

"This is a big country."

"Yes, it is. But there are a lot of them, and they have backup. Until they're satisfied, you won't be able to go back home. You won't be able to see Harry. You are leverage, Matty. They know that if they have you, they'll have my attention. They know I'll come for you."

Her voice was ragged. "Why did you do this to me?"

"I'm sorry. I should never have come."

She paused, biting her lip. The fight drained out of her and, for a moment, he thought that she was going to cry. "So what do we do?"

"We leave."

"To where?"

"Tokyo."

"What? Why?"

"I have a friend there. Someone who can help us."

"Tokyo," she mumbled.

"I know I don't deserve your trust. I'd understand if you never wanted to talk to me again. None of what has happened to you is fair. But you know I care for you, Matty. I won't let anything happen to you. I swear it to you on my life. I'm going to fix this."

"How are you going to do that?"

"We're going to stop running. We're going to fight back."

"But we are running. You want to go to Japan."

"We're not running. There's a man there who can help us. Someone I worked with before."

She bit her lip. She looked washed out and weak, the bloom of indignation that had suffused her cheeks quickly dissipating again. The vigour and pep that Milton liked about her so much was gone now, and she looked young and vulnerable. Milton hated himself. He was the cause of the change.

Eventually, she gave a small nod. "Okay," she said uncertainly.

"You'll come with me?"

Her throat bobbed as she swallowed, but she nodded.

He was relieved: he had anticipated that it would be more difficult to persuade her. But securing her assent was just the first obstacle to clear.

"How do we get there? I don't have a passport."

"I know a man. We need to get to Perth."

"How are we going to do that? Drive?"

"No. I don't think that would be safe."

"How, then? I can't fly. I've got no money."

"No," Milton said. "I have an idea."

Chapter Thirty-One

MILTON WENT outside, checked that they were unobserved, and started the car. Matilda was watching through the window and she hurried out at Milton's gesture and strapped herself into the passenger seat. He put the car into drive and they set off.

He had noticed the goods yard as he had driven to the motel. It was in Regency Park, toward the northern edge of the city, a confluence of railroads that accommodated several big diesel engines, each of them at the head of a long line of freight boxcars. It took half an hour to drive there; traffic had slowed to a crawl as rubberneckers gawped at a wreck on the side of the road. Milton drove carefully, watching his mirrors, but he noticed nothing out of the ordinary.

They arrived at the yard. The facility was protected by a wire fence, but stretches of it were in poor condition. There was a tyre iron in the trunk of the car and Milton was able to use it to prise the fence open wide enough for them to ease through. He knew that the yard would be protected, especially after 9/11, and he waited to ensure that there was no one in sight. Finally satisfied, he led the way and they hurried across the open ground, stepping across the lines, and reached the nearest boxcar without being seen.

The boxcars were identical. They were fifty feet long, with aluminium panels fitted to a yellow steel under-frame, and two big wheels on the front and rear axles. There was a door in the middle of the car in front of them. Milton unlatched the lock and hauled himself inside. The boxcar had been loaded with sacks of cereal. Milton examined the sacks until he found a bill of lading that identified the destination.

"We got lucky," he said as he reached down to help Matilda into the boxcar.

"Melbourne?"

"Yes."

"When?"

"The delivery date is for tomorrow. So I'm guessing it'll be soon."

* * *

THEY HAD TO WAIT. Milton kept the door open just a crack, not quite enough to be noticed from the outside but enough so that he would have warning if security drew too near. A white pickup went by on two separate occasions.

It was dusk when they finally heard the hoot of the horn and, with that, they felt the jolt as the boxcars were heaved into motion. Milton had wedged the door open with the tyre iron and opened it a little more now so that he could watch as the train picked up speed. They crawled through the suburbs, but, as they broke out into the outback once again, the engine opened up to full power and they accelerated.

It was more than seven hundred kilometres to Melbourne, and Milton estimated that it would take the train eight hours to cover the distance. They sat with their backs to the wall of the boxcar, the rumble of the wheels settling into an even and almost hypnotic rhythm. They had stopped at a garage shop on the way to the freight yard, and Milton took out the supplies he had purchased and arranged them: two bottles of water, packs of sandwiches and bars of chocolate. He tore the wrapper off a Cherry Roll bar and started to eat.

"How long did you do what you did?"

"Ten years."

"And why did you stop?"

"Because I hated it."

"But only after ten years. You didn't hate it before?"

He thought about that. "I thought I was doing the right thing. The people... the targets... they were bad people."

"So?"

"I didn't ask questions when I started. You didn't. You got your orders, you carried them out, you were debriefed and then that was it. You had a break and then it started again. I was a soldier for a long time before I was transferred. You don't question orders, not unless you want a court martial."

"You haven't answered my question. Why did you stop?"

"Because I *did* start to question my orders." He shook his head. "I can't believe I'm telling you this. I haven't spoken about it before, not to anyone."

He paused then, wondering whether he should go on. He hadn't spoken about it, not to the psychologists who were employed by the British government to make sure the agents remained sane, or to the drunks who were in the meetings with him after he quit. But Matilda was watching him, her face open, softer than it had been since they had been abducted. He remembered the mantra that ran through every meeting: *we are only as sick as our secrets.* Milton had had too many secrets for too long.

"There was a job," he said. "There were two scientists working on the Iranian nuclear program. They were set up. They thought they were meeting someone who would supply material for them. But it wasn't what they thought. They were meeting me." He paused again, his throat dry, and took a swig of the water. "I was waiting for them. I shot them both, and then I shot a policeman who shouldn't have been there." He stopped again, looking to her face for a reaction, but there was none. "I went to check the car that they arrived in, and there was a kid in the back. A little boy. He was just staring at me. Standard procedure was clear: you didn't leave witnesses. Didn't matter who it was: no one who could identify you could be left alive."

Now she reacted; her lips parted a little, and there was the glint of something—horror?—in her eyes. "You—"

"No," he interrupted. "I didn't. I couldn't. He reminded me of another kid I saw, just like him, years ago, with your brother. When we were in the desert."

"I know about that," she said quietly. "The madrassa."

"Harry told you?"

"He said you were nearly killed trying to save him."

"I don't know about that." Milton was silent for a moment, just listening to the rattle of the wheels on the track.

"What happened next?"

"I went back to London and told them I quit. They didn't like it. They tried to persuade me it was a bad idea, and when I told them I wasn't going back, they tried to kill me. More than once. It would have kept carrying on, with me hiding and them trying to find me, but my old commanding officer died and they replaced him with someone who trusts me. I thought I might get some peace, but then I ran into Avi again."

The train rumbled on. Neither of them spoke for several minutes. It was dark now, and Milton slid the door all the way back to let in some air and what little illumination was still in the day. When he turned back into the boxcar, he saw that Matilda's eyes were closed. When he went over to check, he saw that she was asleep. The dregs of the sedative, perhaps. He took off his jacket and draped it over her shoulders, and then went back to the open doorway and sat with his feet over the edge. He had bought cigarettes at the shop, too, and he lit one, blowing smoke out of the door. The smoke was torn to pieces in the slipstream.

Chapter Thirty-Two

MILTON CAUGHT four hours' sleep, but no more. He knew how long the journey should take, and, as dawn broke the next day, he was watching through the open door as Melbourne came into view. Matilda had slept through the night, another eight hours, and, when he gently shook her awake, she mumbled groggily and tried to go back to sleep. Milton persisted, his hand on her shoulder and, eventually, she gave up and allowed herself to be roused.

"Where are we?"

"Just coming into Melbourne."

The train started to slow when it was several miles from the yard. The wilderness became more and more urbanised, with scattered dwellings and farmsteads and then paved roads and denser concentrations of buildings. Milton had no intention of their being seen at the train's terminus, and so, as it slowed still further, he told Matilda that they were going to have to jump.

He looked ahead and saw a sharp bend in the track, and waited again as the driver braked and bled more speed away. The track passed through a deep cutting, with a short span of gravel and then a grass slope that was covered with heavy vegetation. Milton pointed to the short ladder that descended from the boxcar and waited as Matilda climbed down. She paused at the foot for a moment and then, eyes closed, jumped clear. She hit the gravel, tried to run, tripped, and fell onto her side. She bounced up quickly and waved that she was okay.

Milton lowered himself to the bottom rung, aware of the huge steel wheels that were turning behind him, and jumped, too. His feet dug into the sharp gravel and he, too, very quickly found that he couldn't match the train's speed. His foot caught and he fell, rolling over the sharp stones, his hands and knees scraping against the rough edges.

He came to a halt and checked himself over. Nothing damaged.

Matilda appeared beside him.

"You okay?"

"All good."

"Not hurt?"

"Just my pride."

They clambered out of the cutting. They were on the edge of the city, and, after ascertaining the direction they needed to travel, they walked for an hour. They came across an industrial park with a series of warehouses and depots. There was a parking lot that offered a place for the workers to leave their vehicles. Milton assessed it, found a space that was not covered by CCTV cameras, and walked along a line of parked cars until he found an old Nissan that he knew would be easy enough to start. He tried the door. It was locked. He could have been subtle about gaining access, but the lot was remote and unobserved and he was in a hurry. He found a rock that was the same size as his hand in the margin of rough ground at the edge of the lot and used it to punch through the glass. He reached in, unlocked the door and opened it.

Milton swept the fragments of glass from the seat and opened the glovebox. There was a small pouch of tools there, including a flat-head screwdriver. He lined the tip of the screwdriver up with the ignition slot and gave it a firm strike with the palm of his hand. The screwdriver slid home, ruining the ignition cylinder, but, as Milton turned it, the starter engine fired and the car spluttered into life.

"Subtle," Matilda said.

"You drive."

She looked at him with mild surprise, but didn't demur.

Milton went around to the passenger side and slid into the cabin.

"Where to?"

"You know the city?"

"Never been here."

"I have," he said, "but it was a while ago."

He tried to remember the geography.

"Head into town," he said. "South."

Chapter Thirty-Three

THEY HAD jumped from the train a few miles north of Gisborne. Matilda drove them south, along the C705 through Toolern Vale and into Melton. They reached the interchange with the M8 and merged into the gentle flow of traffic, following the road east toward Caroline Springs.

They were on the outskirts of Deer Park when Milton saw what he wanted.

"Pull in there."

Milton pointed out the strip mall as they approached. There was a business that groomed pets, a hairdresser's, a dry cleaner's, an insurance office, a small supermarket and a bank. Victoria Savings & Loans. It was a local operation with branches around the Melbourne area.

"Why?"

"I need a bottle of water."

"Get me one, too," she said.

Milton had found a baseball cap inside the glovebox and a pair of sunglasses in the holder behind the rear-view mirror. He put them on as he stepped outside.

Matilda leaned out of the broken window. "And a sandwich. Cheese and something."

"Okay."

Milton made his way across the lot to the entrance of the supermarket. There was a telephone in a booth next to the wall, and inside was a directory. He flipped through the pages until he got to H and then tore out two pages with listings for local hotels. He folded the pages and stuffed them into his pocket.

He paused, looked back to check that Matilda was distracted and, seeing that she was, he continued past the supermarket and made his way to the bank. He had been thinking about what they were going to do for money on the train. There was no other way around it. Something like this was going to be necessary.

He pretended to busy himself with a leaflet that advertised a new savings product. It offered five per cent on savings if the saver didn't touch the cash through the course of the year. Whoever wrote the leaflet seemed to think that was a pretty good deal judging by the enthusiastic copy and the eager young couple who were beaming out from a big photo on the front. Milton turned the leaflet over and made a good show of reading it.

But he wasn't reading it. His attention was on the room.

It was small. He had entered through an automatic glass door. Beyond that was a thin counter that ran down the centre of the room, separating the space so that customers at the glass-fronted counters had privacy from those waiting behind. The counter bore several collections of leaflets offering the bank's products. Behind it were two offices carved out of the space by a glass wall. Milton saw stylised pictures of the Australian landscape on the walls inside the offices. There were two cashier windows, and only one was staffed. The cashier was talking airily with the customer before him. The man had asked for a transfer to be made between two accounts, and the cashier was trying to upsell him a new product.

Milton checked again and saw the cameras mounted on the walls and behind the counter. There would be no way to escape being photographed, but he would worry about that later. It was impetuous, but he had to do something. They were out of money, and they needed funds to keep Bachman at arm's reach.

The man finally disentangled himself from the cashier's attention and walked away.

"Next, please."

Milton put the leaflet back and went forward. The clerk was a middle-aged man with ginger hair and a beard that needed a little attention. He had a half-eaten sandwich on the desk. Milton looked down at the badge attached to the man's lapel. It said his name was George.

"How can I help you, sir?"

"I'm very sorry about this, George."

"About what?"

Milton reached behind his back and removed the Glock. "You see this?" Milton said, giving the gun a little jerk. "It's a Glock. It fires 9mm rounds. The bank probably told you that that glass is bulletproof. Trust me, it's not. This close, the bullet is going to go through the glass and then it's going to go into your head." He nodded down at the man's right hand, which was slowly crawling across his side of the counter towards his lap. "No alarms, George, okay? We do this nice and quickly and I'll be on my way, no harm done. But if you give me any problems, any attitude, then I'm going to pull the trigger. Do you understand me?"

Milton spoke with calm, easy confidence. The clerk looked back at him, transfixed by the Glock, his eyes wide and a nervous tic suddenly twitching in his cheek.

"George?"

"Yes. I understand."

"Good. Now, nice and quickly, I want you to put all of your high-denomination bills into an envelope for me. Can you do that?"

"Y-y-y-yes," he forced out.

"Start with the bills from the top of the drawer. Hundreds first, then fifties, and twenties last if you have room. Come on, George, let's go. The sooner you finish, the sooner I'm gone and the sooner you can enjoy the rest of that sandwich." Milton nodded that he should get to it, and then trained the gun on him as he started. "That's it. Keep going. Fill it up all the way."

Milton looked over his shoulder. The branch was still empty and, in the lot outside, he could see the car with Matilda inside. He didn't know how long it would take the police to respond to the alarm that George was going to press as soon as he was out of the branch, but he didn't expect he would have much more than five minutes. He needed her to stay where she was. If he was left outside with no transportation in a town that he didn't know, he knew it would be difficult to make it away. And if he was caught, Bachman would find out. And if he was in custody, he would be a sitting duck.

"It's full," George said, shoving the bulging envelope through the opening at the bottom of the window.

Milton took it and pushed it into his pocket.

"Well done, George. No alarms, okay? If I hear police, I might have to come back in here again. You wouldn't want that."

"No alarms."

"That's great. Enjoy your lunch."

He turned and went outside. Matilda had the engine running.

She saw him coming out of the bank, the gun in his hand. He opened the door and slid inside, putting the gun and the envelope on the dash.

"You fucking didn't…"

"Shall we talk on the road?"

"Seriously, Milton. You're turning me into an accessory to a bank robbery now?"

The hum of rush-hour traffic was split by the up and down shriek of an alarm.

"Matty—drive, please."

She threw the car into drive and they lurched out of the parking lot and onto the empty road. In the distance, Milton heard sirens.

* * *

MATILDA GAVE him a hard time for the first mile and then, with a weary shake of her head, she let it go and concentrated on the road ahead. Milton didn't know what he thought of that. He had expected worse. But, he reminded himself, robbing a bank was merely the latest in a series of unfortunate incidents for her. Her abduction. Being drugged. The things that she had learned about him.

She drove with a determined set to her face. Milton knew better than to push his luck, so he said nothing until ten minutes had passed and they were away from the bank. He reached into his pocket and snagged the edges of the pages he had torn out of the directory. He unfolded them and skimmed the details. There was an old satnav in the glovebox. He plugged it into the cigarette lighter and tapped in the details of the hotel that looked most promising.

"What's that?" she asked.

"Hotel."

"We're staying?"

"We need a base. There are some things we need to sort out."

"Like?"

"Like passports."

Milton had six fakes, but they were all in his pack, and that was back at the sheep station. Matilda didn't have hers. Perhaps it was at Boolanga, too. There was no way they were going to be able to return—he knew Bachman would have left a team there in the event that they did something as stupid as that—so they were going to have to improvise.

Chapter Thirty-Four

THEY STOPPED at the Harbour Town Shopping Centre and Milton sent Matilda inside to pick up some photo paper and a phone with a camera that they could use. There was a Vodafone branch inside, and she came back with a brand new cell phone. They drove on and reached the hotel after another ten minutes. It was part of a chain and was as soulless and anonymous as he had expected it would be. They could have been anywhere. That was fine. Milton wasn't interested in a high-end establishment. Those places tended to be more careful about checking their guests, and the last thing he wanted was a clerk to identify him from the description of the bank robber that he expected would be broadcast on the local news. Far better to find someone who was badly paid and bored with their job to take care of the initial pleasantries. The clerk who took him through the procedure was just that kind of person, and she made no comment as Milton paid in advance with one of the stolen hundred-dollar bills.

He spent half an hour on the Internet in the hotel's business centre. He took out the phone and downloaded ID Photoprint, an app that promised to deliver passport photos, and used it to take a picture of Matilda. She reciprocated and took a picture of him. He exported the photos to the camera roll, connected the phone to a wireless printer and printed the pictures on two sheets of the photo paper. He waited for the paper to dry, cut the photos out and put them in his pocket.

He called a cab and they waited for it in the lobby. Milton was nervous, much happier to wait inside and look out than stand outside on the street. His description would have been circulated by now. The police would be looking for him. Their car would most likely have been flagged, too, but he had parked that in the hotel's underground lot away from the main flow of traffic. He was happy enough that it would be safe there and, in any event, they were not going to be here for very long.

The cab arrived. Milton opened the door for Matilda, got inside himself, and told the driver to head for St. Kilda. He had visited the area before and remembered that it was the kind of place where he would be able to get what he needed, but it was a long time ago and he had no idea how much things had changed. Melbourne was as prone to gentrification as any other big city, and he knew that there was a good chance that the streets had been cleansed and the red-light district relocated to another area. But he had to start somewhere, and, at least as far as his memories went, this was as good a place as any.

The driver slowed the car as they reached Greeves Street. "This is as far as I'm going to go," he said. "You know this is the red-light district, right?"

"Thank you," Milton replied, giving the man a twenty. The fare was ten and, instead of leaving the change as a tip, Milton waited for him to give it back before peeling off two dollars and passing them back to him again. The man shrugged, neither overly grateful at his generosity nor annoyed at his parsimoniousness; Milton was satisfied, since he didn't want to stand out either way.

Matilda and Milton stepped out of the cab and waited as it drove away. Milton looked around and assessed. Greeves Street was mixed use, with low-rent accommodation and business premises vying for space. They were opposite a meat wholesaler's, the only operating business in a line of vacant and boarded-up factories and warehouses. There was a clutch of women on the street corner, dressed in cheap and revealing outfits, all of them displaying the emaciation of dope fiends. A car rolled slowly down the street and then, as they set off to the north, it passed them again. Milton watched as it drew to a halt, coming to rest adjacent to the women. One of the group peeled off and, clacking on scuffed heels, she crossed the pavement and leaned down with her arms on the sill of the open window so that she could speak to the driver. A transaction was discussed and agreed on, the woman went around to the passenger side and got in, and the car drove away.

"Lovely places you bring me to," Matilda said.

Milton stayed close to her as they continued along the street. There was a pub five minutes up the road, with no sign above the door. Milton examined it from the other side of the street. More working girls congregated around the picnic tables that had been arranged in the concrete space that served as the garden, and pimps and pushers hovered menacingly, their faces lit by the red glow from their cigarettes and joints. There was no sign of the police. Milton had visited before and knew that law enforcement would treat the pub with kid gloves. Better, they would say, for the dregs of society to be drawn to one particular place where they could be monitored, rather than closing it down and dispersing them so that it would be more difficult to keep a tab on them. No effort had been made to tidy the place up, and that, they would hope, would be enough to steer the unknowing to another street and another place to get a drink.

Milton crossed the road and, with Matilda behind him, went inside.

There was a single low room with a bar at one end and the start of a corridor at the other. Milton checked for ways in and out, as was his habit, and saw only two: the way that they had entered and, provided it was unlocked, the door at the end of the corridor. There were open windows, too, wide enough to serve the purpose if it became necessary. It could have been worse.

He felt the baleful eyes of the regulars on them. They regarded them with unhidden hunger. Most likely they thought that they were easy marks, maybe tourists who had wandered in the area looking for Melbourne's boho quarter, ready to be ripped off or rolled. Milton had the Glock shoved into the waistband of his jeans, the butt hidden by the untucked tails of his shirt. He felt secure enough, even in a room like this, but that didn't mean that he was relaxed. He was confident that he would be able to protect them both, but the last thing he wanted was a confrontation that might attract the attention of the police.

"What a dive," Matilda muttered.

There was a table at the far side of the room. It was away from the door, which did not please him, but it was arranged so that he could see all of the room if he sat with his back to the wall. Milton guided Matilda to the other chair and then asked her if she wanted a drink.

"Do I have to?"

"No. But I'm thirsty."

"Bottle of water."

He nodded and went to the bar. The bartender was a big man, with a furze of rough black hair down his arms and disappearing beneath the folds of a sweaty and torn Hells Angels T-shirt. His biceps bore a sleeve of prison tattoos and his nose had the flattened aspect of one that has been broken a few times too many.

"What do you want?" he asked as he turned to address Milton.

"Two bottles of water."

"You serious?"

Milton held his eye. "Two bottles of water."

The man shook his head, reached down into a below-counter fridge, and took out two cold plastic bottles. Milton took the moment to look over his shoulder. There was an open door behind him that looked like it led into a stockroom. Milton saw a man in the doorway with a crate of beer in his arms. The man was skinny and tattooed and Milton recognised him at once. Their eyes met. The man looked confused and then, as realisation dawned, he looked frightened.

"Five bucks."

Milton paid the barman. "Could you get Walter for me, please?"

"Who?"

"Walter," Milton repeated. "The owner. Get him for me."

The man squinted at him. "Who are you?"

"My name is Smith."

"That right?"

"John Smith. Walter knows me."

"I'm sorry, Mr. Smith. No one called Walter here."

The man turned to serve another customer, but Milton reached out quickly across the bar and took his wrist. The man turned back to him again, a threat ready on his lips and anger wrinkling his brow, but Milton dug his thumb and index finger into the man's pressure point and the anger warped into a blast of pain.

"He's in the back," Milton said, nodding his head to the open door where he had seen the other man. "I just saw him. Tell him I don't want to have to go in there and bring him out."

Milton released his hand. The man's anger was exchanged for unease, badly masked with feigned annoyance. He took his wrist in his other hand and massaged it.

"Now," Milton said.

He took the bottles back to the table.

"I've been in some dives," Matilda said when he sat down, "but this…"

"Not the most pleasant," Milton agreed as he twisted off the lid of his bottle and took a long draught. He was taking a second drink when he noticed that Walter had come out of the storeroom. He was watching him. Milton set the bottle on the table and looked over Matilda's shoulder at the man, holding his gaze.

"What is it?"

"The man we've come to see is about to introduce

himself."

Walter started across to them. He didn't look like very much at all. He was tall and slim, wearing a dirty pair of jeans and a muscle top that exposed skinny arms that were decorated from wrist to shoulder with a sleeve of lurid tattoos. More prison ink. His hair was thinning, pink stretches of scalp catching the harsh fluorescent light overhead, and his attempt at a moustache was an embarrassing wisp of fluff. Genetically, he had been dealt a very disappointing hand.

"Hello, Walter."

"Mr. Smith."

Milton nodded.

"And Mrs. Smith?"

Matilda turned so that she could look at him, and Milton caught the sneer of disgust on her face. Now that he was closer, Milton could see the tracks on his arms and the unpleasant welt that had developed in the crook of his elbow. That was a new development. The vascular damage and the weeping wound were the unmistakeable badges of an addict who couldn't hide the evidence of his addiction any longer. Milton had expected that this might be unpromising, but it was worse than he had feared. If he had a choice, he would have stood up and led the way out of the bar. But he didn't have a choice. If they wanted to get out of the country, this was about as good as it was going to get. Walter was their main hope.

"Didn't think I'd ever see you again."

"Sit down."

Walter did as he was told. Milton knew that Walter was frightened of him, and that was with very good reason.

"What can I do for you?"

"I need your help, Walter."

"I ain't into that business any more."

"You can get back into it again. One-time deal."

"No," the man said. "This is my business now. The bar. Look around. Going well."

"Come on, Walter."

"No, Mr. Smith, I'm serious. I don't do none of that no more."

He started to stand.

"You really want to annoy me, Walter? How short is your memory?"

The man lowered himself back into the chair again, his resistance gone. Milton had known that he would only need a little prompting. He had been in the passenger seat of the car that afternoon, down by the docks, and had ended up with the blood of his charge sprayed all over his face and a close-up look at the business end of Milton's pistol.

"What do you need?"

"We need to get out of the country."

"So go to the airport. I'll call you a cab."

"I'm not in the mood for jokes, Walter."

"You want me to help you? After last time?"

"That wasn't your fault. He was careless."

That seemed to give the man a small jolt of confidence. "Yeah," he said. "It wasn't my fault. I told him to stay in the hotel and he didn't."

"No," Milton said. "He didn't."

"And you clocked him."

"We did."

He scrubbed his fingers through his thinning hair. "So why can't you use the airport?"

"No questions, Walter. You know better than that. Do you still have a hook-up at the port?"

"Sure I do."

"And the paperwork?"

"What do you need?"

Milton reached into his pocket and pulled out the passport photos that he had prepared earlier.

"Everything. Passports for both of us, anything else you think we might need."

They had moved on from their unfortunate beginning,

and now Walter was telling Milton what he needed to do. He found a little assertiveness in a topic he knew well, and Milton, hiding his irritation, knew it would be better to give him his head.

"You're an ugly bastard," the man said, glancing down at the strip with Milton's likenesses. He turned the page and angled his head to Matilda. "But you're as pretty as a picture."

"How soon can you do it?" Milton asked, intervening in an attempt to save him from the denunciation that he could see Matilda was about to deliver.

"Usually takes a week."

"We don't have a week."

"So it'll cost more, then. When do you need to go?"

"Tomorrow. How much?"

"Two grand for the passports. Twenty to get you out of the country."

"Twenty?"

"Each."

He felt Matilda prickle.

Milton let it ride. The money didn't matter. They had enough. "I'll tell you what," he said. "I'll give you fifty if you can get us out tomorrow. And that's for the premium service. Full discretion. You understand, Walter? What happened before—he was careless, but I'm very, very good at what I do. You remember that, don't you? You know I'm good at finding people, and what happens when I find them."

Milton was keenly aware that Matilda was beside him. He didn't want to threaten Walter in front of her, but it was important that the man understood the consequences of disappointing him. Milton needed him to be on his game. Walter did understand, and his new-found assertiveness drained away as quickly as it had come. Milton could see that the memory of their last encounter was still fresh.

"You don't need to tell me twice, man. I understand."

"That's good," Milton said. "Where do you want us to come?"

"Here. Tomorrow. Six in the morning."

* * *

THEY LEFT the bar and walked back to more civilised streets.

"You know him?" Matilda asked.

"Unfortunately."

"How?"

"He's a smuggler. Contraband, mostly. But he'll move anything if it pays well enough."

"People?"

"Yes."

"So?"

"Three years ago, when I was… working for the government." He paused for a moment before choosing the verb, unwilling to be more graphic, but knowing at the same time that she would know exactly what he meant. "There was a man in Australia who was involved in Islamic terrorism. A recruiter. He was responsible for several British Muslims going to fight for al-Qaeda. I was given orders to find him and… stop him."

"Stop him?"

Milton bit his lip to stop from wincing. "Neutralise him."

"And?"

"This man knew that he couldn't use the airports. He knew he would be found. So he used Walter. He was going to smuggle him out aboard a ship. It might have worked, too, but he got sloppy and we saw him outside his hotel. We followed him to the docks. That's where I met Walter."

"When you shot the other man?"

"Yes."

"But not Walter?"

"It had nothing to do with him. He was just a third party."

It wasn't quite as cut and dried as that, although Milton didn't elaborate. But he remembered that his first instinct had been to shoot Walter, too. He had seen Milton's face. Milton had aimed the pistol at his head, ready for the instinctive double tap into the head and body. If it had been at the beginning of his career with the Group, he would have followed through with it. The rules of engagement were clear: headhunters left no witnesses. But he wasn't at the beginning of his career, fortunately for Walter, and he had begun to develop the burden of guilt that would eventually become too heavy for him to bear.

They crossed onto Nicholson Street. The area was more smartly bohemian now, away from the grit and squalor of the red-light district. Milton saw a taxi waiting at a nearby junction and flagged it down. The cabbie flashed his lights to acknowledge him.

"Is that how we'll leave the country?" Matilda said as the cabbie pulled up next to them.

"Yes," Milton said.

"And you think he can do it?"

"What I said to him was true: what happened before wasn't his fault. It would have worked. The guy came out of his hotel and he was spotted. We'll be more careful."

He hoped that he was right. Milton knew he was gambling. Walter had allowed himself to slide into squalor in the time since their paths had crossed, and Milton would not have trusted him as far as he could throw him. Then, too, he suspected that the police would circulate his picture from the bank's security cameras. What if a reward was offered? What if it was more than the fifty thousand that Milton had offered Walter? What then?

Chapter Thirty-Five

THEY WERE back at the bar at six, just as Walter had instructed. The sun was just appearing over the tops of the low buildings and the streets were quiet. The bar was empty and had yet to be cleaned from the night before. There were empty glasses on the tables and spilt beer on the floor.

Walter was waiting for them.

"Well?" Milton said.

"It's been arranged. You need to leave now."

He took them outside and around to the back of the bar. There was a large dusty square of ground that had once, from the look of the charred debris that remained, accommodated another building. A tractor and semi-trailer had been parked in the space. A freight container had been loaded onto the trailer.

"Your ticket out of Australia," Walter said, indicating the container with a sweep of his hand.

Matilda stopped in her tracks. "You're kidding."

"What?" Walter said, confused.

"I'm not getting into *that*."

Milton understood her reaction. Her memory of the trip across country in the back of the van had probably not lost any of its edge.

"That's how you're getting out of Australia, darling."

"No. Find another way."

"How long do we need to be in it?" Milton interceded.

"The container gets loaded, you wait on board, the freighter sails."

"When?"

"Tonight."

There were no two ways about it, Milton thought: it was going to be unpleasant. The container would collect and amplify the heat, and Walter wanted them to stay inside it all day. They would cook.

"We don't have a choice," he said to Matilda. "We need to leave. This is the safest way."

She held his eye, sighed, and shook her head. "This is ridiculous. All day, in there?"

"I know. It's not going to be much fun, but there's no other way. We can't stay."

"We can't fly?" She spoke with resignation, already knowing the answer to the question.

"They'll be covering the airports. They might be covering the ports, too. This way, there's no way they'll see us. We'll be invisible."

"And cooked half to death."

"There are holes drilled in it," Walter offered, "for ventilation."

"Praise be," Matilda said, turning her back to him. She looked at Milton, shook her head and mouthed, "Fine."

Milton turned back to Walter. "What happens then?"

"The crew will get you out when you're at sea. You'll have a cabin."

"Where's the freighter headed?"

"Auckland. Six days."

"Documents?"

"Here."

Walter took a large envelope from his pocket. Milton opened it and took out the two passports inside. They looked legitimate, with the simple dark blue covers embossed with the Australian coat of arms. The photo page was microprinted with horizontal lines of text drawn from the lyrics to Waltzing Matilda. Milton's name was David Anderson. He opened the other passport and flipped through it. Matilda was Miriam Shepherd. They would serve, he thought.

"Need anything else?" Walter asked.

"No. That's good."

"There's food and water in the container. Enough for

two days. The captain is reliable. You won't have any problems."

"That's good to know, Walter."

The man put out his hand. "Money?"

Milton had counted out the fifty thousand earlier, stuffing it into the cloth bag that the hotel left for dirty laundry. After paying Walter, he would have just ten thousand left.

He held out the bag, but as Walter reached for it, he drew it away again. "You know who I work for, Walter."

"I know."

He reached and Milton drew it away again.

"You know what will happen if this doesn't go just like you've described it."

"Take it easy. I got the message, okay? I understand."

Milton flipped the bag at him. Walter caught it, his eyes lighting up with an avidity that was all Milton needed to know that it would be spent on whatever it was he was injecting into his arms. That knowledge did not make him any more confident. He was trusting their escape to a junkie.

Walter opened the bag and reached inside, pulling out the bundles of notes. Milton thought he was going to count it, but he didn't; instead, he went around the back of the truck and yanked down on the big handles that sealed the doors. He pulled them back, exposing the inky blackness inside. Milton laid his hands on the sill and vaulted up. He turned and extended a hand to Matilda. She took it and Milton hauled her up after him.

"There's a flashlight inside," Walter said.

Milton turned and saw it propped next to eight one-litre bottles of water that were sealed together in a plastic sheath. There were packets of sandwiches and bags of chips next to the bottles. Milton had only just picked up the flashlight when Walter slammed the doors together. The lock clicked into place with an ominous finality.

He heard a muffled shout from outside and then the

rumble of the truck's big engine. The air brakes hissed and the container rocked a little as the truck pulled out.

Milton felt vulnerable now.

Chapter Thirty-Six

MILTON USED the flashlight to examine the interior of the container, and then, satisfied that he had it fixed in his mind, he switched it off to preserve the battery. If Matilda was unhappy about that, she did not complain. She was quiet throughout the brief journey, allowing Milton the chance to listen carefully. Sounds were muffled inside the sealed container, but the drilled ventilation holes meant that the noise of the city was detectable. He heard the hum of traffic as they passed through busy streets, the wearied anger of car horns, the occasional snatch of shouted conversation. Then, twenty minutes later, the quality of the noise changed. The engines he could hear were deeper, more guttural, more like the one that belonged to their truck. He heard the boom of a ship's horn and, throughout, the regular caw and chatter of gulls.

"The docks?" she said.

"Yes."

Milton took his phone from his pocket. He had split it open as soon as he had finished taking their pictures and had taken out the battery. He knew he was being cautious, perhaps even paranoid. He couldn't think of a way that Bachman would be able to track a phone that they had only just purchased, but he didn't want to take any chances.

Now, though, he needed it again. He put the battery into the compartment, slid the lid across until it clicked shut, and powered it up. He dialled a number that he had memorised and put it to his ear.

It rang six times, then seven, and then Harry Douglas picked up. "What?"

"Harry."

"What? Who?"

"It's me. Milton."

"Shit…" Milton heard the sound of sudden motion. "Milton, shit."

"Everything's okay."

"Where are you? It sounds like you're underground."

"I can't say where we are."

"We? You've got Matty with you? Where are you?"

"Harry, listen. Something's happened."

Now there was panic: "Matty?"

"It's okay. She's fine. She's with me."

"You've been gone for days. You better tell me what the fuck's been going on. If you—"

Milton spoke firmly. "Shut up, Harry. Shut up and listen."

He paused, and the line crackled as Harry held his tongue. "Go on," he said. "I'm listening."

"We were attacked on the road outside Broken Hill. A man and a woman at the side of the road. We stopped to help. They pulled guns on us and put us in the back of a van."

"Jesus—"

"Matty's fine, Harry. *Listen.* This is all to do with me. There's a man I used to know, a long time ago. He thinks I killed his wife, before I came out here. I didn't, but he doesn't believe me. He tried to kill me before and I managed to get the better of him. Now he's trying again."

There was a pause, static crackling on the line.

"So we take him out."

"It's not as easy as that. He's ex-Mossad. And I don't know how he's managed it, but he's got them to help. There's a full team with him."

The tone of his voice changed from anger and fear to something approaching stupefaction. "Mossad?"

"Yes."

"What have you *done*, Milton?"

He ignored that. "We can't take them head-on. We wouldn't last five minutes."

There was a pause. Milton found that his stomach was tight and that he was gripping the phone hard.

"So?"

"We're going to be clever about it."

"Where are you?"

"I can't say," Milton replied. "I can't be sure this line is secure."

"Where is she?"

"She's here. She wants to speak to you."

Milton turned away from her so that she could have a little privacy. He gazed into the darkness and then took the opportunity to walk across to the doors and run his fingers against the seal. It was secure. This was potentially a crazy idea, but he was all out of alternatives. He had to hope that it would work. If not... or, if Walter betrayed them... well, they wouldn't last long.

He turned back after a minute. He didn't want to leave the line open for too long.

"Matty."

She held out the phone to him.

"He wants to talk to you again," she said.

He took it.

"What the *fuck* is going on? If anything happens to her..."

"Nothing's going to happen."

There was another long pause. More static.

"All right," he said, finally. "When will I hear from you again?"

"A few days. But be careful. They might be watching you."

"I can look after myself."

"I know you can, Harry. But they won't hit you straight up. Just watch out."

"You too."

"I'll call when I can."

"Look after her, John."

"I will."

"Promise me."

He turned the beam of the flashlight away so that Matilda couldn't see him and said quietly, "You have my word."

* * *

AVI BACHMAN was in the same bar as Harry Douglas. Indeed, he was just two tables over from him, arranged so that he could observe him without making it obvious that he was watching. Bachman was close enough to overhear Douglas's side of the conversation, and it was that that probably saved the man's life. It was obvious that he was speaking to Milton and it was similarly obvious that he had no idea where Milton and his sister had gone. Douglas spoke with animated fluency, his expression passing through several very distinct stages: relief, confusion, anger and then, finally, concern. Bachman sipped at his bottle of beer as Douglas continued the conversation, interrogating Milton as to the whereabouts of his sister and what had happened to them both, and, obviously, getting very little in return.

Lucky for him.

Douglas had been put under observation as soon as Milton and the girl had escaped them. Bachman had led the chase all the way to Broken Hill, but Milton had too much of a head start and he had been able to shake them off. He had stayed in the town, knowing that it was pointless to continue the pursuit until he had a better idea of where they had gone. There was the train, of course, but it was already thirty minutes to the west by the time they had arrived. There were other possibilities, too; he might have stolen another car or taken a bus. There were routes out of town to all points of the compass and no way of knowing what was most likely. Bachman didn't have enough manpower to chase down every possibility, so Malakhi Rabin had alerted the *sayanim* to watch the stations and termini in Perth, Melbourne, Adelaide and Sydney. That done, he took a hire car and drove back towards the sheep station.

There was the possibility, however slim, that Milton might try to surprise them by looping around so that he could return to Boolanga. There were weapons in the trunk of the car that he had taken to escape, but he had no travel documents and no easy way to get out of the country. Milton was resourceful—Bachman knew that from bitter personal experience—but there was the chance that he would assume they were looking elsewhere and return to collect his documents.

The news that the girl had been found in Adelaide, and the call that had followed from Milton to warn him off, had changed all of that.

Douglas finished the call and put his phone away. He sat at the table for a long minute, staring into space, his fingers absently picking at the label of the bottle. And then, a little resolution flickering into his expression, he stood, laid ten dollars on the table, and made for the exit of the bar.

Bachman left money on his own table and followed him outside.

He tailed him into the street, staying twenty feet behind him. Douglas was a decent-sized man, but he was lame, favouring his right leg. Bachman made the assessment automatically and knew that he would comfortably outmatch him in a struggle. But it wouldn't come to that. He could feel the reassuring bulk of the pistol in its shoulder holster. It would be a simple enough thing to follow him out of town, force him to stop and then put a bullet into his brain. He was wearing a knife in a scabbard that was strapped to his ankle and, he thought, if it came to that, he would favour the blade over the pistol. It would be more personal. More enjoyable. He had a wellspring of frustration building up inside him, and the expression of primal violence was, in his experience, the best way to release the pressure.

Douglas took a right turn, heading away from the busier part of town and toward the parking lot where he had parked his Jeep. Bachman had parked his own car on the other side of the space. Apart from their vehicles, the lot was almost empty. There were no other people around.

Bachman felt the twitch of adrenaline and picked up his pace. Douglas was a hundred feet away from his Jeep. Bachman was thirty feet behind him and quickly closed to twenty.

Bachman heard Malakhi Rabin's voice in his ear. "Bachman, what are we doing?"

He wore a tiny microphone attached to the collar of his T-shirt. "Hold position," he hissed.

"Not here."

"Hold."

"At least let him get out of town first. You'll be seen if you—"

Bachman clenched his fists with fury. "Hold position and shut the fuck up."

Douglas reached the Jeep and stood for a moment, fumbling in his pocket for something. He pulled out a packet of cigarettes and a lighter.

Bachman reached into his own pocket and took out the packet of Longbeach he had bought earlier that afternoon.

"Excuse me," he called out.

Douglas looked up at him, an expression of wariness on his face. "Yes?"

He held up his unlit cigarette. "You got a light?"

"Sure."

Bachman stepped closer to him, put the cigarette to his lips and dipped his head a little to touch the end to the flame. He inhaled once and then twice, waiting for the cigarette to catch light, and then straightened out.

"Thanks."

"No problem."

He gazed up into the sky. "Hot tonight."

Douglas lit his own cigarette and nodded at that. There was a pause between them, uncomfortably long, before Douglas frowned and asked, "You need anything else?"

Bachman dragged on the cigarette. He clenched his fingers, balling his hands into fists. He thought of the gun. He thought of the knife. Malakhi Rabin was watching from somewhere behind him, and, in the unlikely event that Bachman was observed, he would take care of any witnesses. They *could* wait until they were out of town, but what was the point of that? Why wait? Why not do it now? Bachman was frustrated beyond patience.

"You all right, sport?"

Bachman snapped back into awareness. He pinched the cigarette between thumb and forefinger, slipped it from his mouth, and smiled. "Yes," he said. "Fine. Just a million miles away. Thanks for the light."

Douglas shrugged it off and took a half turn toward his car.

Bachman wondered, for a final time, whether he could afford to indulge himself, but he decided against it. Killing him now would be a foolish thing to do. There would be some short-term gratification, but that would pass and, when it did, he would have eliminated the best opportunity they had for picking up Milton's trail again. Milton had called Douglas. Perhaps he would call again. Perhaps he would arrange to meet him somewhere. And Douglas had asked Milton where he was. Bachman had heard him ask the question. Perhaps Milton had told him something, given him some hint. Maybe, maybe not. But Milton and Douglas were friends. That meant that Douglas was leverage.

It was frustrating, but Bachman needed Douglas to be alive.

For now, anyway.

Douglas paused and looked back at him with a quizzical expression. Bachman nodded farewell and set off.

Later, he thought.

Later.

There would be time to release the frustration later.

Chapter Thirty-Seven

AZABU WAS Tokyo's most expensive residential district. Its appeal was partly geographical since it bordered the fashion district of Aoyama, the Akasaka business district and the similarly upscale Hiroo residential area. The area had a village feel and Ziggy had passed a number of small eateries that charged extortionate prices as he made his way to the address that Shoko had provided. The real estate here was some of the most expensive in the world. There were a number of embassies here, too, and that meant that there was a reasonable police presence. Ziggy had researched that and was confident that it wouldn't be an insurmountable problem.

Ziggy parked his rental next to Azabu Gardens. He had researched the development as he planned the best way to complete the assignment. There were sixty luxury apartments nestled on a quiet, tree-lined street.

He reached across to the passenger seat and took his MacBook from his bag. He rolled down the window; it was another hot, muggy Tokyo night, and the interior of the car was stuffy. The garage was protected by a roller door with a control unit on a metal stalk sunk into the concrete on its approach. He had waited outside the block all yesterday afternoon until a resident had arrived to open the door. He had captured the frequency used and now, as he held up his transmitter and aimed it at the unit, the code was fired back and the door unlocked and rolled up.

Ziggy checked the street, saw nothing that concerned him, and rolled his car down the ramp and into the darkened garage.

The cars inside were all expensive, but the car he had been tasked to collect was the most expensive of all. It was a Bugatti Veyron. It was wide and low-slung, pressed down to the asphalt with the promise of immense power. It was the fastest street-legal car in the world, with a top speed of nearly 270 miles per hour. It was also the most expensive. This model, Ziggy knew, would have cost its owner more than two million dollars.

He found an empty bay with a line of sight to the Veyron and parked. He took his laptop and activated the software. He targeted the car and set the software to find the correct frequency. The algorithm sped through the millions of variations, slowly identifying the components of the activation code. The software's timer displayed the interval it believed it would take to crack the code: nine minutes.

He had fretted about the wisdom of this misadventure for several hours after Shoko had sent him the details on behalf of her brother. He knew that he had been fortunate so far. He was careful, and he could minimise the risks of detection, but it was inevitable that the spate of high-end car thefts would eventually attract the attention of the police. Ultimately, cars like this one would be kept under surveillance. It wouldn't matter how careful he was: he would eventually be caught. He knew that the sensible move would have been to decline the offer and put the whole silly episode behind him. He should have gone back to his apartment, packed up the things that he could not afford to leave behind, dumped the rest, and left. South Korea sounded good: highly technological and with the fastest domestic broadband system in the world. It was the kind of place that would suit him very well.

And then he thought of the night he had spent with Shoko and his resolution crumbled.

He would compromise.

This one more time.

That was it.

One more job for one more night.

And then he would leave.

The price for that night was the Veyron that sat in the

lot ahead of him.

The timer counted down.

Three minutes.

He reached down and, without realising that he was doing it, rubbed his hand against the ache in his leg. He knew it was psychosomatic, but it always felt worse when he was stressed.

The software bleeped. It had isolated the code with two minutes to spare.

Ziggy took the transmitter, looked around the lot to ensure that he was still alone, and then fired the data at the Veyron.

The lights flashed, the wing mirrors folded out and he heard the *clunk* as the locks disengaged.

He slid the laptop and transmitter into his rucksack, opened the door and stepped out. He crossed the quiet space to the car, opened the doors and slid inside.

* * *

ZIGGY PULLED off the road, rolled down the ramp to the underground garage and pressed his pass against the reader. The barrier was raised and he drove ahead, turning to the right and then parking in the usual spot. Shoko's BMW was opposite. The grumble of the engine echoed off the concrete floor, bouncing back at him, and, for a moment, it sounded uncomfortably loud. He pressed the button to kill the engine and closed his eyes, assailed by a sudden bout of lethargy. He felt brittle and bone tired.

The doors to the BMW opened and Shoko and her brother stepped out.

He did the same.

"There you go," he said, indicating the Veyron with a sweep of his hand. "Not a scratch on her."

Kazuki went over to the car and stroked his fingertips over the hood. "It is a nice car. Very nice."

"For that much, it better be nice."

Shoko glanced over at him. Her expression was dismissive, as usual.

"Who are you going to sell it to?"

"That is a matter for me. You need not concern yourself."

"My money?"

"We need to talk about that."

"There's nothing to talk about. We agreed—"

Kazuki shrugged. "I will be honest with you. There is no money for you. Not this time."

"We said—"

"What we said is irrelevant. You disrespect me, Ziggy. You disrespect my sister. I pay no money to a man who treats me with disrespect. And, for a man who disrespects my sister, there must be a reckoning. Do you understand my English? Do you know what I mean by that, you arrogant piece of shit?"

Kazuki undid the buttons on his jacket and let it fall open. Ziggy saw a shoulder strap and the glint of a weapon holstered beneath his left armpit.

Ziggy took a step away. "Fine. No money. We can call it quits. I'm through with this. You'll never see me again. Just—"

"It's not as simple as that. Arrogant foreigner, arrogant *gaijin*, you expect me to let you go? Just like that?" He laughed. "No. No, you need to learn about respect. I give you limp in other leg."

Ziggy heard the sound of an engine and saw headlights arrowing down the ramp to pool on the ground just beyond the barrier. He looked up at the gate, but the glare of the headlights blinded him.

"Who's that?"

He looked at Kazuki and felt his stomach turn over as he saw his face. The cocksureness had gone. He looked fearful now.

"Who is it?"

The car rolled down the ramp and turned in their

direction. It was a Range Rover, big and boxy and intimidating. It stopped twenty feet away from them, the high beams still blazing out and making it impossible to see anything beyond them.

"Kazuki? Who is it?"

The man had backed up, his sister falling away with him.

Ziggy stepped even further away from them.

The passenger door and then both rear doors of the Range Rover opened. Three men got out. The engine was still running and the headlights still burned; it was impossible to make out any detail.

The door of the Veyron was still open. Ziggy edged over to it.

The newcomers stepped forward. They were all dressed in the casual uniform of the Yakuza, all sporting extensive tattoos.

One of them was at the front, flanked by the other two. He scanned the space, focused on Kazuki, and spoke to him in harsh, guttural Japanese. Ziggy tried to understand it, but his attention was hopelessly distracted and his vocabulary was insufficient. He picked out a few choice words—"theft," "punish," and a number of imprecations—and watched as the man pointed at the Veyron. He realised what was happening. This man owned the car. He had an air of authority about him, the impression that he was the kind of man used to giving orders.

Ziggy joined the dots.

This new man was Yakuza, too, more senior than Kazuki.

And Ziggy had been sent to steal his car.

He had been sent to steal the car of a Yakuza *wakagashira*.

The newcomer had a pistol in his right hand.

The men behind him were armed, too.

One had a shotgun.

The other had a cleaver.

Ziggy took another step in the direction of the Veyron.

Kazuki dropped the pistol and it clattered to the ground.

The man spat out angry invective.

Kazuki raised his hands.

The speaker advanced, raised his pistol and fired.

The round took Kazuki in the gut.

Shoko screamed.

Her brother took a step back, his hands dropping to his stomach, his fingers lacing across it. He bumped up against the wing of the BMW and stumbled forward.

The man fired again.

A kill shot this time. Kazuki's head jerked all the way back, a mist of blood and bone and brain matter spraying across the BMW's gleaming white paint. He bent backwards at the waist, his arms splaying wide across the hood before his legs buckled and he slid down to the ground, slumped there on his knees.

Ziggy hurried the rest of the way to the Veyron, ducked his head and slid into the bucket seat. He closed the door and locked it and then reached into his bag for his laptop. It was just sleeping; he slapped his hand on the keyboard to wake it up. The screen seemed to take an age to illuminate.

Shoko screamed again from outside. Ziggy looked up for an instant: one of the men had gone to her, penning her back against the wall of the garage. The other two were walking toward him. One of them had the shotgun.

Ziggy opened his app. The car used a rolling code to start the engine. The software was going to have to break it again.

He turned and looked into the barrel of the shotgun. It was aimed right at him, separated by the glass in the window, less than five feet away.

He stabbed at the keyboard over and over, trying to cycle the algorithm faster and faster, but knowing, deep down in his gut, that it was no use, and that he was dead.

"*No!*"

Ziggy cranked his head away from the shotgun to the man who had addressed Kazuki. He was waving his hand as he repeated his warning, and, incredulous, Ziggy understood what he meant.

He didn't want the car to be damaged.

Ziggy reached across and fumbled for the central locking.

The man with the shotgun left it aimed at him while his friend tried the door handle.

The lock thunked into place.

"Open door," the man shouted in poor English.

"Come on!" Ziggy stammered as he frantically hit refresh. "Come on."

The algorithm cycled through and found the correct code.

Ziggy activated it, and the engine awoke with a feral growl.

The man who had shot Kazuki yelled angrily.

Ziggy put the Bugatti into reverse and stamped on the gas. The tyres screeched and then bit. The car lurched back, the man with the shotgun jumping clear just in time. Ziggy had overcompensated, and, before he could apply the brakes, the rear end crashed into the wall. The body of the car was light, made of a light carbon-fibre composite, and it crumpled in on itself. The small rear window was buckled out of shape, cracking down the middle and then shattering into the interior.

He heard a wail of anguish.

Ziggy fumbled the stick, crashing the gearbox into first and stamping down, too firmly again, on the gas. The car shot ahead, the rear end swinging out as he yanked the wheel all the way around, skittishly jerking left and right until he mastered it, pointed the nose at the ramp and let the rubber bite. The car crashed through the barrier, snapping it across the hood, and drew sparks as the underside of the chassis clashed against the abrupt incline of the ramp. Ziggy was dimly aware of the thought that he was wrecking the Veyron and that, therefore, it was more likely that it would cease to offer him protection, when he heard three sharp barking reports and heard the hiss of a round as it passed through the cabin from the rear to the front, punching a neat incision in the centre of the windshield.

The car hit fifty as it reached the top of the ramp, leaping into the air and then slamming down again with a ferocious din as the chassis buckled and the exhausts clanged against the asphalt. Ziggy tried to swing the car around, but it was travelling too fast and he was a poor driver, not nearly good enough to keep it under control. He stamped the brakes and skidded all the way across the road, carving a fortunate path through two lines of slow-moving cars that heralded his short journey with angry blasts of their horns, and came to a stop with a heavy thud into the side of a parked bus.

Ziggy was thrown forward. His head bounced off the wheel and then whiplashed back again.

He sat there, woozy, for several seconds. He was roused by the sound of a car horn and realised, belatedly, that it was from the damaged Veyron. The harsh blare brought him back to himself. He saw his laptop perched incongruously on the dashboard, the screen mangled, and then glanced back at the broken rear window and remembered how it had come to be that way.

Oh, shit.

He tried to open the door, saw that it was crumpled and jammed, and shuffled across the cabin to the other side. The door opened and he fell out, his feet scrabbling on the asphalt as he stumbled away.

* * *

ZIGGY HEADED to Roppongi subway station. The concourse was busy with people arriving for a night out, and he had to force his way through the throng to the gate. He pressed his ticket to the reader; it bleeped, but did not open. He looked at the display and saw that the card was empty.

Shit.

No time to reload it now.

He heard a shout of indignation, turned, and saw the man with the pistol shoving his way through the crowd.

Ziggy gripped the gate, wedged his foot onto a protruding piece, pushed up and hauled himself over it. The effort caused a flare of pain in his bad leg. The guard was in a booth; he saw him and called out for him to stop.

Ziggy did not.

The shaft to the platform was encircled by two floors of shops and restaurants, the escalator running straight down the centre. It was scrupulously clean, the brushed steel polished to a high sheen and even the tables and chairs in the food court at the lowest level seemingly arranged in perfect order. The passengers rode on the right-hand side, leaving a narrow space for Ziggy to negotiate to their left. He looked back behind him as he stepped off and saw the three men following him, pushing a similar path down the left of the escalator.

The corridor was tiled in a dull municipal green and with a black and white floor. It was slick, and Ziggy nearly lost his footing as he barrelled around a corner. A train was waiting on the platform. It had disgorged its last passengers and must surely be about to depart. He ignored the throbbing in his leg and sprinted as hard as he could. The doors bleeped and there came the hiss of their hydraulics as they started to close. He threw himself inside.

The train jerked as it started to move and then, as Ziggy watched with fearful anticipation, he saw the man who had shot Kazuki smash his fists against the window. Ziggy unconsciously scrambled back until he was pressed up against the opposite door, but the train was moving properly now and it wasn't going to stop. His heart pounding, he watched the Yakuza's face recede, twisting with fury, as the train picked up speed.

The carriage was old and in need of a proper clean, the red upholstery of the seating faded in the middle from where hundreds of thousands of passengers had sat. He turned and dropped himself onto one of the empty benches. The carriage was quiet, but the other passengers were looking at him with a mixture of curiosity and alarm. He was sweating heavily and panting from fear and exertion.

The train slowed as it drew into the next station. It was Hiroo. He had ended up on a westbound train. He started to think. He could ride it to Ebisu, then change onto the Yamanote line and head south to Osaki, Shinagawa or Tamachi. He could disembark there, pick up a taxi and then head back to his apartment.

They wouldn't be able to follow him, but he would do a full surveillance check to be absolutely sure.

* * *

HE ALLOWED himself to exhale, closing his eyes and putting his head in his hands.

Stupid, stupid, stupid.

He only had himself to blame for getting himself into this mess and he had been very lucky that he had been able to extricate himself from it. He chided himself again. It was his own stupid greed. He had been doing perfectly well for himself by restricting himself to the opportunities he could find online. He didn't have to leave his apartment to sell a list of credit card details. Car theft? What was he thinking? No, no more of that. He would keep to what he knew best, what he was good at, what was safest. That was what he would do from now on. He knew how to be careful, how to avoid detection.

Goodbye, Tokyo.

Goodbye, Shoko.

The train passed through Shinagawa. A handful of people got off, a handful got on. An old woman, a young couple, a man who was very plainly the worse for drink. None of them looked as if they were the sort to be involved with the Yakuza. Ziggy allowed himself to relax a little.

The train reached Tamachi and Ziggy disembarked. The station was configured with two island platforms that allowed for interchange between the Yamanote and Keihin-Tohoku lines. A train was coming in and, in an abundance of caution, he took it. The carriage, this time, was empty, and, when he disembarked at Hamamatsucho, he was as sure as he could be that he had eluded his pursuers.

The station was directly beneath the World Trade Center and, he remembered, a short walk from the Pokémon Center. He flagged down a taxi and told the driver to take him to Yoyogi Park. It was ten kilometres, and the driver took them along a route that was clogged with traffic. It should have taken thirty minutes, but it was nearly an hour later when they finally arrived. Yoyogi was one of the more exclusive places to live in Tokyo. It was close by the large municipal park and in prime position between Shinjuku and Shibuya. The salarymen in those districts often chose to live here so that they could walk between home and work. Ziggy had always pitied them. The bland man in the apartment next to his got up at six every morning. He heard the shower at six ten, and the sound of the door closing at six twenty. Ziggy was usually bringing his own working day to a close then, and, when the man returned at seven, he would be waking from sleep to start working once again.

He told the driver to skirt his apartment block, staring intently out of the window in an attempt to see anything that might have been out of the ordinary. Shoko had never been to his apartment before, but he was too frightened to cut corners.

He had chosen this area carefully. It was homogenous and dull, and there were enough wealthy international students here that his Western looks did not stand out. There was nothing unusual outside tonight. It was quiet, with few people around—just a few cars and buses going about their business. The driver pulled up outside the entrance. Ziggy paid him and stepped outside into the humidity. His block was twenty storeys high with a communal area on the roof that allowed a splendid vista of the city.

Ziggy went into the lobby, nodded to the concierge, and took the elevator to the nineteenth floor. He hobbled to his door and put his ear to it. He couldn't hear anything, save the quiet hum of the oscillating fans that he always left running. He unlocked the door and went inside. It was just a one-roomed apartment of modest size, with a kitchen-diner, a small square bedroom and a balcony that offered a view out over the park. It was, as usual, stiflingly hot. The banks of laptops and tower PCs that he used for his work were on twenty-four-seven, and they pumped out a lot of heat. He always left the door to the balcony open, but, with the temperature outside just as warm, there was nowhere for the heat to go. The fans were just circulating the hot air.

Ziggy took off his shirt and tossed it over the back of the room's only chair. He went through into the kitchen-diner. It was furnished with high-end appliances and separated from the dining space by a breakfast bar.

His phone blipped.

He took it out of his pocket. He had been getting a lot of spam SMS messages recently, and he expected to find another one waiting for him.

But it wasn't spam.

It was a message from a number that he did not recognise. The message, in English, was simple enough.

WE KNOW WHO YOU ARE.

He stared at the screen in horror, the phone vibrating in his hand as a second message appeared.

GIRL KNOWS WHERE YOU LIVE.

Ziggy bent over the kitchen sink and vomited, a long retching stream of it that kept coming until there was nothing left to come. It filled the basin, stinging his throat with its acid dregs, and, for a moment, he thought he was going to faint. He pushed himself away from the counter, unable to remember if he had locked the door, and hobbled across the apartment to it, turning the key and attaching the security chain. The door looked flimsy, and the chain was cosmetic, no real impediment to an angry gangster who decided he wanted to get inside. He went over to the single armchair and, roughly clearing away the PC towers that blocked the way, he hauled it across the room and shoved it so that it was flush with the door.

Maybe that would buy him some time.

He collected the phone from where he had dropped it and looked at the screen again.

Maybe the messages were gone.

Maybe he had imagined them.

No. They were still there. He hadn't imagined them. They were real.

And then, as he stared with dumb terror at the screen, a third.

WE ARE OUTSIDE.

He went across to the open balcony door. He was about to go outside when he realised that he couldn't do that. What if they *were* outside? Could they have found him? How? He squeezed his eyes shut and racked his brain. What if Shoko or her brother had followed him home? He had always been careful, but what if he had not been careful enough?

It was possible.

He scurried across the room to his laptop and opened it. He had hacked the apartment's CCTV cameras long ago. His first destination was the files that stored all the footage that had been backed up. It was over a terabyte, covering a week's worth of comings and goings, and, undoubtedly, recording him. It would show him in the lobby, in the elevator, which floor he exited on and which apartment he went into. He triggered a subroutine that deleted it and then wrote over the memory so that it was gone for good.

Then, he navigated to the control panel and selected all of the cameras inside the lobby and on the street outside. It took him only three cameras before he found the view he was looking for: there was one on the corner of the building, looking down at an angle that took in the entrance and the street around it. There was a car on the opposite side of the road to the building. It was a Range Rover, big and bulky and with blacked-out windows.

It was the car that had delivered the Yakuza to the underground lot.

He focused on the car and zoomed the camera just as the passenger door opened and a man stepped outside. He was smoking a cigarette and Ziggy watched in fright as he glanced up at the camera, before catching himself, realising that he couldn't know that he was being observed. The man dropped the butt and ground it underfoot. He went around the car and opened the rear door that faced the hotel and the camera. Ziggy got only a glimpse, but it was long enough for him to recognise the slim figure of the woman in the back seat. It was Shoko. There was no doubt about it. She had led them here.

Ziggy stared at the screen, his mind racing through possibilities. Shoko had followed him one time. That was obvious now. But she couldn't know which apartment he was in. Ziggy had tried more than once to bring her back, but now he was grateful that he had failed. There were over a hundred apartments inside the building. He had rented this one under a false Japanese name. The concierge would have no way of knowing which one was his, and the footage that would provide the answer was wiped. How would they be able to find out which one was his? What would they do? Try every door?

He slid down to the floor, slumping back so that he was pressed against the cupboard door.

He didn't know what to do.

Chapter Thirty-Eight

THE VOYAGE proceeded without incident. They had waited inside the metal box for twelve hours, sweltering as the sun beat down on it, before they had been craned onto the deck of the freighter. The ship was the MSC *Maris*, a large freighter with a deadweight of 63,500 tons and capacity for more than four thousand containers. It was owned and operated by a German company, and the crew member who had finally opened the container and let in the late afternoon sun was a big, tattooed Austrian. Milton and Matilda had stepped out and gulped in the air tangy with salt and followed the choppy wake to where the port was a fast-disappearing smudge on the horizon.

They had been given a suite on F Deck. It was generously proportioned, over thirty square metres with a double bedroom, a separate sitting room and a functional bathroom. Milton had insisted that Matilda take the bed, choosing the sofa for himself.

The crossing between Melbourne and Auckland was scheduled to take six days, but the sea was as flat as a millpond and they made good time, shaving off a day en route. It was a comfortable voyage, and Milton took the opportunity to decompress. There was a library in the crew quarters and, to his surprise, he found a battered copy of the Big Book. That wasn't surprising, he concluded when he considered it. There were long periods of inaction to fill during a voyage, and it was no wonder that some crew members might choose to fill their downtime with drink. The previous owner of the book had marked up several passages that Milton also favoured; it was a poor substitute for a meeting, but he felt a connection with the man, whoever he was, the sense of fellowship that was the most powerful benefit of the program.

Milton was the most relaxed he had been for days. There was almost no prospect of threat while they were at sea. And Walter had been as good as his word. The money—plus the threat to his well-being that would have materialised with anything untoward—had served to provide them with safe passage. Milton's anxiety had increased a touch as the skyline of Auckland hove into view, his worry focusing on the practicality of going ashore without arousing suspicion.

As it turned out, his concern had been misplaced. Their Austrian chaperone had led them back to the same container that had been used to smuggle them aboard. They waited inside it once again, listening to the crashing of metal as cranes hauled the surrounding containers off the deck, and then there came the stomach-churning moment as it was their turn. The container swung to and fro as it was hauled into the air. Milton and Matilda anchored themselves to one another and then braced themselves for the thud of impact as they were positioned onto the back of a tractor trailer. The locking mechanism thumped as the bolts secured the container to the trailer bed and then a big engine growled to life. They were jostled together again as the tractor pulled away; their journey lasted an hour before they heard the hiss of the brakes and felt the deceleration.

The doors were opened and the cool night air disturbed the stifling humidity that had left them both covered in sweat. The driver said nothing as they clambered down. They were on the edge of the city, the glow of the neon announcing it to the south. It was a truck stop, their disembarkation hidden among dozens of identical vehicles.

Their own truck drove away, headed south toward Wellington.

Milton and Matilda paused for an hour, refuelling with a quick meal, before beginning the long walk back to the city.

* * *

THE LIGHTS of Tokyo glowed beneath them as the jet descended to Narita airport. Milton knew how big the city was, but it was especially evident from above. It sprawled in all directions, nearly fourteen million people going about their business, a billion busy points of light that glittered and glowed. The perspective was narrowed as the plane closed on the runway and then, as the wheels thudded down, it was reduced to a fast-accelerating parallax as the hangars and buildings and then the terminal rushed by the windows.

The eleven-hour flight from Auckland had been uneventful. Milton had even been able to sleep, which was unusual for him. He awoke to Matilda nudging him with her elbow. They were on their final approach.

The jet taxied to the gate; they disembarked and made their way through the terminal. There was a small queue for the immigration desks, but, with typically understated efficiency, additional staff appeared and the queue dissipated quickly. Milton thought about the fake documents and trusted that they would hold up to inspection. They had stood up to scrutiny as they had passed through security at Changi airport in Singapore. Matilda went up first and her papers were given a brief inspection.

Milton used the pause to consider the message from Ziggy that he had received on board the freighter. The ship's library had two PCs that were connected to the Internet. The message had been left in a forum that they had used to exchange information before. Milton had left the first message and then, with surprising haste, Ziggy had responded. He had explained that he had found himself in a spot of bother, and Milton would need to assist if at all possible. He was brief on the detail, suggesting that he had run into trouble with local toughs and that he was unable to leave his apartment.

Milton had rolled his eyes with mild exasperation. Ziggy was a bona fide genius, but he lacked common sense. That had nearly got him killed in New Orleans on the night before Katrina, and Milton had hoped—vainly, as it soon turned out—that the experience might have taught him to temper his more foolish ideas. Ziggy didn't explain what had happened to him this time, but Milton didn't really need to know. It could wait. And, in the meantime, he would proceed with caution when they got there. Forewarned was forearmed, after all.

The border guard waved Matilda through and tapped on the window.

Milton looked up at him, smiled, and walked forward. The guard said nothing, checked his passport, and handed it back.

"Welcome to Japan."

Chapter Thirty-Nine

THERE WAS a taxi rank outside the terminal building. Milton nodded to the nearest driver, opened the rear door and waited for Matilda to get inside. He followed. Milton told the man to take them to Yoyogi Park. The driver grunted his assent and pulled into the slow-moving snake of traffic that led away from the airport and onto the main road into the city. Milton glanced through the window and took it all in. The vastness of the city, the dazzling Rainbow Bridge in Odaiba, the vaulting skyline and, standing tall in the Roppongi Hills, the stunningly lit ziggurat of the Tokyo Tower.

"This guy," Matilda said as they passed to the north, Tokyo Bay to the right of the cab. "Anything I need to know?"

"He's an acquired taste," Milton said after a moment of deliberation.

"Meaning?"

"He's a bit strange. I can't really describe him."

She looked at him dubiously. "Strange?"

"A mad genius," he concluded.

"And he's worth coming here to see?"

"He is. But you can make up your own mind."

Ziggy's apartment block was near to the park. Milton and Matilda walked down the sidewalk toward it. They were on the opposite side of the street and Milton was paying close attention to his surroundings, just as he always did. There was a gentle flow of traffic in both directions, expensive cars that denoted the money that resided in the neighbourhood. They passed a few pedestrians, salarymen coming back home from work and glossy women walking miniature dogs.

There was a line of cars parked on their side of the

street, but only one of them, a big Range Rover, was occupied. They walked toward it.

"Hold my hand," Milton said, reaching down and taking Matilda's hand in his.

There were two men in the car. Milton quickly glanced in at them as they went by: black hair, medium build, one wearing a pair of sunglasses. The man in the passenger seat, adjacent to them, had his arm hanging loose out of the open window. His skin was coloured by a lurid sleeve of tattoos. He wore a gold Rolex that looked somehow even more obscene against the green and red ink.

Milton led the way across the street and, without looking back, headed into the lobby of the building. It was finished in polished marble, with a leather banquette fitted into one corner. A man was seated there, wearing a tracksuit top with the sleeves rolled up to his elbows. His forearms were tattooed. The man had been dozing, but, as the door sighed closed behind them, he looked up. Milton smiled innocently at him and then looked away, towards the concierge, who sat behind a marble desk. He was reading a newspaper and he looked up quizzically. Milton knew that they couldn't afford to be stopped. If the man realised that they were not residents, he would ask them who they were here to see. He couldn't very well give him Ziggy's name.

Milton put his arm around Matilda's shoulders and drew her closer to him, giving the concierge a confident nod and, without breaking stride, walked on into the elevator lobby.

He summoned the lift.

"The guy back there?" Matilda said as the doors slid closed behind them.

"Not someone we want to stop and chat to."

* * *

MILTON HAD arranged with Ziggy that it would be Matilda who knocked on his door. He waited in the elevator lobby and kept watch as she made her way down the corridor. It was hushed, with just the faintest sound of activity from the nearest apartments. He heard a muffled television, an animated conversation between a man and a woman, the sound of a toilet flushing. He held his breath as he saw one of the elevators ascending from the ground floor, but, as he stood ready for the doors to open, ready to ascertain whether the occupant was a threat or not, the numbers kept ticking up and the lift continued.

He looked back down the corridor. Matilda was outside the door for apartment number 1911. He gave her a nod and, returning the gesture, she rapped her knuckles against it.

The door opened. Milton heard Ziggy's voice and then, cautiously, his head appeared. His face was painted with anxiety.

Milton walked briskly down the corridor, walked on a few paces to check that they were unobserved from both ends, and then returned and stepped inside.

The apartment was almost unbearably hot. As far as Milton could make out, there were two reasons for the warmth. First, and most importantly, was the source: a large number of computers and monitors that must have been pumping out an enormous amount of heat. A quick glance revealed ten different screens of varying sizes, and Milton guessed that there were others around the corner of the room, out of view. The heat needed to be ventilated, but the windows were obscured by thick drapes whose stillness suggested that the windows behind them were closed.

"Ziggy," Milton said, "it's like an oven in here. Open a window." He started for the nearest curtain, but Ziggy intercepted him.

"No," he said. "You have to leave them shut. There's another block opposite us. What if they have someone there, looking into the windows over here? They'll see me. They'll know where I am."

"Jesus, man," Milton said. "How long have you been cooped up in here?"

"I don't know. I've almost lost track. A week."

Milton was about to suggest that Ziggy was paranoid, but he had seen the men downstairs. "You need to relax," he said instead and, gently moving him aside, he pulled the curtain back and opened the French door to the balcony beyond. He glanced across the street to the building opposite; it was possible that they might have a watcher over there, but the room needed ventilation and he was prepared to take the risk. Seeing that Ziggy was about to make an objection, however, he drew the curtains almost all the way together again.

Milton turned back into the room and looked at Ziggy more carefully. He was unshaven and his clothes looked as if he had been wearing them for several days. His eyes were frightened, and, at the sound of a door slamming in the corridor outside, he gave a visible jump.

"Take it easy."

"It's the Yakuza, Milton. The fucking Yakuza."

"The *Yakuza?*" Matilda said.

"Gangsters."

"I know who they are. You didn't say anything about gangsters."

"I didn't know," Milton said.

"So you got me abducted in Australia and now you bring me to the apartment of a man who says he's being chased by gangsters?"

"Abducted—?" Ziggy began.

"It's been an interesting week," Milton interrupted them both.

He went around to the kitchen and rinsed out two dirty glasses. He filled them with water and gave one to Matilda.

"You better tell me what's been going on."

"I got involved in something I shouldn't have been involved in."

"Which was what?"

"I stole a car. Well, a few cars, actually. The last one belonged to a Yakuza. That guy."

He pointed to an open laptop on the table. Milton went over and looked at the webpage on the screen. It was an entry from a database used by the Tokyo Metropolitan Police Department. It looked like a rap sheet. There was a man's photograph and a long list beneath it in Japanese. The man was glaring into the camera, a bored and lazy enmity in his eyes. He was certainly a formidable-looking man.

"His name is Tadamasa Sawanda."

"Never heard of him."

"He's senior. Likes his cars. I stole one belonging to him. And then I wrote it off."

"Not very sensible."

Ziggy shrugged miserably.

"This might be a stupid question," Milton said, "but why did you steal it?"

"I was an idiot. There was a girl. I was trying to impress her and… things got out of hand."

Milton didn't say anything, although his expression was eloquent. He crossed the room and pushed the balcony curtains aside again. He stepped out into the muggy heat and looked down into the street. The Range Rover was still parked on the opposite side of the road.

He went back inside the apartment. "There's a car outside. I saw it when we came in."

"I know. There's been a car outside every day since it happened. A Range Rover or a Lexus. They take it in turns."

"It's a Range Rover today. And there's a man in the lobby downstairs."

Ziggy picked up a tablet from the floor and tossed it to Milton. It was showing the feed from a security camera, with the man that they had passed talking into a cell phone and smoking a cigarette. It was a three-man team, Milton thought. More than enough to keep Ziggy cooped up until he had to make a run for it. Not enough to stop him, though, especially when they didn't know who he was.

"You've been here a week?" Matilda repeated.

"More or less."

"What about food?" Matilda asked.

"Noodles. It is becoming a problem, though. I'll run out tonight."

"Why haven't they asked the concierge?"

"I keep myself to myself," he explained. "I rent under a fake name, and I've always made sure that no one knows which apartment is mine. There are a hundred apartments here. What are they going to do, break down the door to every one?" He shook his head. "They know I'm in the building. They'll just wait for me to come out."

"CCTV?"

"I've wiped it. And I'm piggybacking their feeds now. At least I know where they are."

"Is there another way out?"

"You think I would've been stuck here if there was?"

"No trade entrance?"

"I've checked the plans. It opens out onto the street. They'd see me."

Milton went back to the window and looked down onto the street for a second time.

"Get whatever you need packed up. We're leaving. You need to be ready when we come back."

"When?"

Milton looked at his watch. "One hour."

Chapter Forty

MILTON OBSERVED. He was on the opposite side of the road to the apartment block, on the same side as the Range Rover. Matilda was on the other side, walking in his direction. She crossed and approached the parked car. He watched as she leaned down at the driver's window. Her long legs, bare in the cut-off denim shorts she was wearing, looked golden brown in the glow of the streetlamp overhead. He saw her beam her brightest smile at the driver and, as he turned to her, she leaned forward and rested her forearms on the sill of the window.

Milton set off.

He glanced inside the car as he approached. He couldn't see any weapons. The two men were of modest height and build, average for Japanese. Matilda glanced up for the slightest second, but she did not betray him. She looked back at the driver and gleamed a bright smile that fixed his attention once again. She was flirting with them both, and they had taken the bait.

Milton reached the car. He opened the passenger-side door.

The man in the passenger seat turned.

Matilda reached into the car and seized the driver around the neck. She pulled, dragging him to the side so that his head was hanging out of the window. She held on. She wouldn't be able to secure him there for long, but she didn't have to. Milton just needed him to be temporarily disabled, and her efforts would be plenty enough for that.

Milton grabbed the passenger by the back of the head, drove his face down into the dash and then, as blood splashed down from his crumpled nose, he yanked him out of the seat and tossed him onto the street.

The driver forced his hand between Matilda's arms and

broke her hold. He jerked to the side and, as he reached for the dash to steady himself, Milton was sitting next to him.

His mouth gaped open; his outraged question went unasked.

Milton raised his arm and drilled him in the side of the head with the point of his elbow. His head bounced against the frame of the door and, when it flopped back toward Milton, he elbowed him again. His eyes rolled back as his head was sent back against the door for a second time and, finally, he slumped against it, unconscious.

The passenger was on hands and knees on the road outside the car. He had crawled forward a little so that he was between the door and the chassis. Milton reached over his body for the handle and slammed the door closed against the man's head. It crunched unpleasantly, the man losing consciousness and dropping down so that he was sprawled on the asphalt, his chin propped up against the sill of the door.

Milton reached over and frisked the driver. He found a Sig Sauer 9mm and placed it on the dash. Then he opened the driver's door and pushed the unconscious man out onto the road. Matilda took his place and started the engine.

"Well done," he said to Matilda.

She looked at the two unconscious men and shook her head. It had taken Milton fifteen seconds to put them both out.

Milton stepped out.

"Keep the engine running."

* * *

ZIGGY HAD been watching from the balcony, just as Milton had instructed him to do. He had seen Matilda distract the two men, bending down at the window and saying whatever it was that she had to say. It had obviously worked. Milton had opened the passenger-side door and, a moment later, a limp body had been hauled out and dumped on the sidewalk. Matilda had grabbed onto the driver until Milton had dealt with him, too. And now, with the figures of the two men sprawled out on either side of the car, it was his time to move.

Milton had made it very plain that he wouldn't have the luxury of time.

He collected his rucksack. It was very heavy. He had stuffed as much into it as he could: two laptops, an assortment of other kit, hard drives and cables. He swung it onto his shoulder and took one final look around his apartment. It had been good to him, one way or another. He would have liked to have been able to stay. Tokyo had been good to him, too. If it wasn't for his stupid lust and greed, his egotism and his desire to demonstrate just how clever he was, he would have been able to stay here for as long as he liked. Not now, though. He had poisoned the city for himself, and now he was going to have to leave and never return.

He felt naked as he shut the door behind him. The dimly lit corridor, normally so familiar, now looked like it might hide more of the Yakuza who had been sent to find him. There were blind corners, niches and alcoves that would comfortably accommodate someone lying in wait for him…

Come on, Ziggy, he chided himself. *There's no one here.*

He walked on, into the elevator lobby, and pressed the button to summon a car.

He thought of the man in the lobby. What if Milton was wrong? What if there were more of them, more than just that one man? What would he do then?

He jumped as the elevator chimed and the doors slid open.

There was nothing else for it. He couldn't stay here forever, and if Milton couldn't help him, he didn't know who could.

He stepped into the lift.
Pressed the button for the ground floor.
Closed his eyes.

* * *

THE CONCIERGE was a man named Arata. The corporation that owned the building was not a particularly generous employer, and Arata found it something of a slap in the face that he was paid a relative pittance to guard the apartments of people paid a hundred times more than he was. He smiled at them as they came and went, was pleasant and polite at all times, and cashed his cheque on the first Monday of each new month. He did his job. But, at the same time, he didn't feel any compunction in accepting the ¥200,000 that the gangster had offered him when they came looking for the *gaijin*.

Arata recognised the picture of the man, but he did not know very much about him. He knew that he was a resident, but he couldn't answer when they asked him what apartment he lived in. He said that he would keep an eye out on the CCTV. There were cameras on every floor and, he said, he would be able to at least tell them which floor the man could be found on. Perhaps he would get lucky and a camera would catch him coming out of his apartment. And he said that he had no issue with them stationing a man in the lobby with him.

There was the money, of course, and that was welcome, but he wouldn't have been able to say no to their requests even if they had offered him nothing.

They were Yakuza.

You didn't say no to men like that.

Arata was flicking through a comic book when the door to the lobby opened and a man came inside. Arata recognised him. He had been in and out before, earlier that evening, with a pretty blonde woman. They were both Westerners. The woman, he remembered, was especially pretty. Foreigners were not unusual in the block; it was popular with *gaijin*, the rich ex-pats who could afford the rent to live in a neighbourhood like this. These two didn't live here, he was confident of that, and he assumed that they were just here to visit someone. He would have stopped them to ask them for their identities, but they had walked quickly through the lobby and were in an elevator before he had started out of his chair.

And moments ago, Arata had watched, his mouth falling open, as the man had reappeared through the entrance and walked straight to the leather banquette upon which the gangster was sitting. The gangster had swung around to look at him, but it was too late by then. The Westerner was onto him, standing over him so that it was impossible for him to get up. He had a pistol in his hand. Before Arata could say anything, he drew back his hand and pounded him in the side of the head with the butt of the pistol. The gangster flopped to the side, his legs jacked up and his head lolling against the cushion.

The man turned to Arata.

The elevator chimed.

A car pulled up outside the building. Arata recognised it. A Range Rover. It was the car that the Yakuza had been using.

The *gaijin* the gangsters had been searching for stepped out of the lift. He recognised him from the picture that the Yakuza had shown him. He was carrying a heavy rucksack over one shoulder.

The second man looked at Arata and put his finger to his lips. He turned away, said something in English to the *gaijin* that Arata couldn't hear, and then led the way outside to the waiting car.

Arata stepped out from behind his desk and went to the window. The blonde woman from before was behind the wheel, waiting as the first man got into the passenger seat and the other man got into the back. The car pulled away and disappeared around the corner. Arata looked back at where it had been parked and, as he heard the groans of the man on the sofa, he saw the two bodies sprawled out on the road.

Chapter Forty-One

MATILDA DROVE them out of town. Milton opened the glovebox and found a pistol and a spare magazine. It was good to know that it was there, but he was confident that it wouldn't be needed. There was nothing to suggest that the Yakuza had stationed any more men in the vicinity. They would have expected that a crew of three was more than sufficient to deal with a nobody like Ziggy. There was no way that they could have foreseen that he would have been able to call upon reinforcements, and certainly not reinforcements who were as able as Milton.

That didn't mean that they would just give up, though. They would assume that Ziggy would flee the city. And they would be right. It wouldn't be safe for Ziggy to stay here. Tokyo was closed to him now. He would have to leave.

Ziggy turned as the car passed the turn-off for Narita airport and kept going, headed southwest. "Where are we going?"

"Nagoya."

"Why?"

"They'll be expecting you here. It isn't worth the risk."

"And then?"

"You're going to help me. Like we discussed."

"We didn't really *discuss* it, Milton, did we? You said you needed me. That was it."

"Okay. We're going on a trip."

"Where to?"

"Tel Aviv."

"*Tel Aviv?*"

"That's right. Israel."

"I know where it is, Milton. You want to tell me why we need to go there?"

272

"I'll explain when we're in the air."

"Give me a clue."

Milton turned and regarded him evenly, and Ziggy's mouth stopped flapping. "You're going to hack the Mossad for me."

He fumbled for a response. "The Mossad? Israeli intelligence?"

"You always said you liked a challenge."

* * *

IT WAS a three-hour drive to Nagoya. They spent most of it without speaking, listening to J-Pop on the car's Internet radio station. Matilda was pensive and Ziggy was sour; Milton left them to their introspection and ran through the details of what he was going to propose once they reached Tel Aviv.

In truth, he wasn't absolutely sure what they were going to do. He would make sure that Matilda wasn't involved; she had already been hauled halfway around the world on his account, and that was more than enough. The actual operation—the reason for their journey—would depend on Ziggy.

They passed through Ina, Komagane and Komaki, finally reaching the airport at two in the morning.

Matilda parked the car in the long-term lot. Milton thought about leaving behind the gun that he had confiscated from the driver of the car, but decided that it would be better to be safe. The men he had disabled would have been roused by now, and they would have reported what had happened. They had no way of knowing what Ziggy would do next, of course, but they would likely assume, at the very least, that he would try to leave the city, probably headed for Narita. Milton knew that the organisation had a long reach and, however abundantly cautious it might seem, he wasn't in the business of ignoring even the smallest of risks.

He put the gun into his bag and led the way to the terminal building. He paused and scanned the departures lounge but saw nothing to arouse his suspicion, nothing to suggest that the gangsters had been prescient enough to guess how thorough he would be. He couldn't take the gun any farther than this, so he went into a restroom and dropped it in the trash.

Milton and Matilda were going to pose as tourists when they got to Eilat. A handful of the terminal's stores were still open, so they bought the luggage and clothes that would be expected for vacationers. They stopped in the cafeteria and removed all of the tags from the clothes. They added bottles of sun cream, dark glasses and books.

They bought tickets and checked in together. Ziggy produced his passport from his rucksack, and the smiling clerk made no reference to it or to any of their documents as she quickly examined them. She asked Ziggy whether he wanted to check his rucksack into the hold, as it was too large to be taken on board as carry-on luggage, and he said no, hugging it a little closer to his chest. Milton calmly told him that he could put the most important items into his empty bag, and, after a little extra persuasion, Ziggy took out a laptop and a portable drive and told the clerk to be careful because the contents were fragile. She smiled indulgently, told him that she would, pressed a sticker onto the bag to denote that it was delicate, and then pressed the button to activate the conveyor belt. The bag jerked away and dropped onto the main belt with an audible clatter that made Ziggy close his eyes and mutter a silent prayer.

* * *

THE FIRST leg of their journey was aboard a Thai Air 747, and they had a row of three seats in the middle of the jet. Milton was finally able to relax as the plane hurtled down the runway, launching itself into the air and putting the glowing lights of Nagoya behind and beneath it. The pilot banked them to port and, after a five-minute climb, levelled them out at thirty thousand feet. It would take them six hours to fly to Bangkok, where they would have a nine-hour layover. The connecting El Al flight to Ovda would take another eleven hours. Not for the first time, Milton found himself hoping that the effort to collect Ziggy would be worth it.

And then he reminded himself: he had no other option. Ziggy, for better or worse, was his best chance to eliminate Bachman's main advantage over him.

Matilda wedged her jacket against Milton's shoulder and quickly fell asleep. The flight attendants circulated through the cabin with refreshments. Milton took a bottle of mineral water for himself and another for Matilda. Ziggy grinned at the woman and asked for a gin and tonic. She returned his smile with a perfunctoriness that Ziggy missed, because when she moved on, he turned to Milton and gave him a sly wink.

"What's the matter with you?" Milton asked with exasperation.

"What do you mean?"

"You think she doesn't have to put up with that every day?"

"Come on, Milton. Just a little fun."

"How *old* are you?"

"Not as old as you."

"You're behaving like a teenager. Look at the trouble you got into the last time. Maybe, I don't know, maybe give it a break?"

"Whatever, Milton." Ziggy paused to take a sip from his drink. "What about you?"

"What about me?"

He nodded to the recumbent Matilda and said quietly, "You and her."

"Don't be ridiculous."

"She's gorgeous."

"She's the sister of a friend." He shook his head. "I've got no idea why I'm defending myself to you, of all people."

He grinned. "Sore point?"

"Shut up, Ziggy."

Ziggy had recovered his old spirit quickly. It wasn't that long ago that he had flown to New Orleans to help Milton in his struggle with Bachman, but the intervening months had been long enough for Milton to have forgotten that Ziggy had a particular talent for annoying him. He was always trying to wisecrack, to make a smart comment, to win a point, and it could grow wearying after a while. Milton was no psychologist, but it was obvious, even to him, that Ziggy was driven by the need to find acclaim. He had never spoken of his childhood, but Milton guessed that he had been marked out as different thanks to his geekiness and his intellect. It had not, most likely, been a very happy time for him. He was overcompensating for it all now.

Ziggy stood up, took off his jacket and stuffed it into the overhead compartment. As he sat back down again, an unusual necklace fell free from the collar of his T-shirt.

"What's that?" Milton asked, pointing to it.

Ziggy reached down and slipped his fingers beneath the necklace. He held it up so that Milton could look at it. It was about the size of Milton's thumb, with exposed circuitry and a plug that looked like it would fit into a USB port.

"A thumb drive?"

"Sort of. It's a microcontroller with a USB connector."

"In English, Ziggy. What does it do?"

"What doesn't it do?" He grinned. "If this gets plugged into an open port, it tells the computer that it's a mouse or a keyboard. Fools it into letting down its defences and then it goes to town. It opens the terminal, messes with network settings, installs a backdoor, and then tidies up after itself in about a minute. Works on PCs, OS X, Linux.

Everything, practically."

"What does that mean, Ziggy? What does it actually do?"

"Means I can control the computer. Your computer. Her computer. *Any* computer." He grinned again, even more broadly. "It's called BadUSB. What do you think?"

"I think you have too much time on your hands."

"Been working on it for six months. I've tested it in the field half a dozen times now. Works like a dream."

Matilda stirred, settling herself again against Milton's shoulder.

Ziggy indicated her with a nod. "She just get caught up in your shit?"

"Yes."

"You're bad news. Trouble follows you around."

"You think I don't know that?"

Ziggy cocked an eyebrow, but didn't follow it up. Milton *did* know that, of course. It had been the thing he had found most difficult to get off his mind ever since they had been abducted outside Broken Hill. He had travelled halfway around the world to get away from trouble, but it seemed that he had been wasting his time. There was nothing he could do. He attracted it. It stuck to him the way iron filings stuck to a magnet.

"You want to tell me what you want to achieve when we get to where we're going?"

"I told you."

"Yes, you said you wanted to hack the Mossad. I'm just checking: that wasn't a joke?"

"No. It's not a joke."

Ziggy asked him to elaborate and Milton did. He explained what he wanted to do and, more importantly, why he wanted to do it. Ziggy sat and listened, asking the occasional question, but generally absorbing the information. He was attentive and Milton could see that he was starting to work out a possible plan of attack.

It took ten minutes and, when Milton was done, Ziggy

was quiet for another minute.

"Well?"

"Between you and me," he began cagily, "I might have tried to hack them before. This was a long time ago, when I was working for the government."

"And?"

"They're pretty keen on security, as you might imagine. They get plenty of hostile attention. Everything they have is best in class: firewalls, systems redundancies, network hygiene. They don't cut corners anywhere."

"So you didn't get in?"

"No. And that was with everything GCHQ fired at it. A server room as big as a football pitch. And all I have with me now is my laptop. I don't think there's any way I'll be able to get in from the outside."

"What are you saying, Ziggy? You can't do it?"

"Didn't say that." He tapped his finger against his chest, where the necklace was hidden beneath the cloth of his shirt. "You know me: I like a challenge. I said I didn't think I could get in from the outside. But there are other ways, Milton. Have faith. I have a plan."

Chapter Forty-Two

THEY LANDED AT OVDA. The airport was north of Eilat and the second largest in the country. It would have been easier to take a flight straight to Tel Aviv's Ben Gurion, but Milton wanted to minimise the risk that they might be detected. He didn't think Bachman and his stooges would suspect that he would run to Israel, straight to the bosom of the Mossad, but he couldn't be sure. And, he knew, the passive security at Ben Gurion was state of the art. There was a good chance that he would be identified; his photograph would be captured and sent up the chain. Ovda had always been a little less advanced than its sister facility to the north, more concerned with welcoming tourists to the country than businessmen and diplomats.

That didn't mean that it would be a walk in the park. Milton's working knowledge was out of date and there was a very good chance that the security had been improved since the last time that he had visited.

Nothing to be done about that now, he thought, as he thanked the attendants at the front of the jet and stepped over the sill onto the waiting air bridge. The air was hot, and it washed over him like soup after the artificial chill of the plane.

"You all right?" he said, turning back to Matilda.

"Never better," she said wryly. "Always wanted to visit Israel."

Milton led the way across the air bridge into the terminal building. Their fellow travellers were mostly tourists, with a smattering of businessmen and women. Milton had managed to get a little sleep, but it had not been satisfactory and he knew that he would benefit from a few extra hours. He didn't know whether that would be possible.

They made their way into the terminal building and joined the line for an immigration check that he expected to be particularly rigorous. He knew, from experience, that all Israeli airports had a practice of sending all military-age males with backpacks to secondary screening, regardless of where they were flying from or where they said they were going. They did not fit that profile, but that didn't mean that he wasn't nervous as they shuffled forward. He had reminded Matilda of their cover story and emptied his bag of anything that might have contradicted it. He had been equally rigorous with the litter in their pockets.

He leaned over to Matilda and reminded her quietly, "Be natural."

The border guard looked up at her and beckoned her forward before she could reply.

"She any good at this?" Ziggy said quietly.

"She'll be okay."

"You still want me to head off on my own?"

They had spoken about what Milton wanted Ziggy to do during their conversation on the flight. It would have looked unusual for a couple and a third traveller with no apparent connection to them to check into the same hotel, so Milton had told Ziggy to book into the nearby Hilton. The procedure that they had agreed upon was that the first of them to make it through security would make the arrangements for the trip to Tel Aviv, and then to communicate that information to the other.

"Yes," Milton said. "Just as we discussed."

"Fine."

Milton and Ziggy waited in line as the man checked her papers, scanning the barcode and then looking from her picture to her face and back again. She stood there, her face blank and impenetrable, and Milton silently urged her to smile, to look impatient or irritated, to be *anything*, but she did not.

It was a relief when the man nodded at her to go through and called Ziggy forward.

Milton pretended not to watch too closely. There was nothing for it but to hope that Ziggy wouldn't say anything stupid and that there was nothing in his bag that would have caused him a problem. The guard asked questions, the words muffled by the tinny speakers that broadcast them, and Ziggy answered. He took a little longer than Matilda had, but, finally, the guard gave a nod, slid Ziggy's passport back through the slit in the glass and bid him through.

The man looked up and nodded to Milton.

"Passport."

Milton handed it over.

The man looked at it.

"Mr. Anderson," he said.

"That's right."

"What is your business in Israel, Mr. Anderson?"

"Holiday."

"Where?"

"Eilat."

"Hotel?"

Milton felt the buzz of nerves, but he hid it. "Herods Vitalis Spa."

"You have a reservation?"

"Yes."

The man looked back down at the passport. There would be a button beneath the desk which, when pressed, would summon the agents who performed the secondary screenings. Milton tried not to watch as the guard's hand crept back towards the edge of the desk, paused there for a moment, and then went up to attend to an itch on his nose.

"Good day, Mr. Anderson. Enjoy your vacation."

* * *

MILTON PULLED his suitcase behind him and made his way through customs and into the arrivals hall. Matilda was waiting for him on the other side of the sliding doors. She looked at him with a quizzical expression. He gave a shallow nod and reached down and took her hand as they made their way through the arrivals hall and into the warmth of the evening beyond.

"Ziggy?"

"He got through."

"I didn't see him."

"I told him to go on. We're not staying together. He'll meet us tomorrow."

There was a taxi rank outside. Milton found a vacant car and waited beside it for the driver to disengage himself from a group of drivers who were chatting over cigarettes. He told the man that they wanted to be taken to Eilat. The man grunted his assent and opened the rear door for Matilda. Milton slid in next to her and relaxed a little as the driver pulled out into traffic. There was no need for Matilda to continue with their masquerade now that they were out of sight of the airport's security, but she reached across and took his hand again. Milton squeezed her hand and didn't move to take his away.

The hotel was to the south of the airport. The driver followed Route 12, which cleaved close to the border with Egypt. It was quiet, given the late hour, and they made good time, arriving after an hour. Their destination was a big, lavish hotel occupying an envious position overlooking the Gulf of Aqaba. The driver pulled off the main road and slowed as he approached the entrance to the lobby. A uniformed bellboy emerged as the car drew to a halt, opening their door for them and then going around to the trunk for their luggage. Milton paid the driver with three hundred of the shekels he had converted from his Australian dollars at Bangkok.

Ziggy had already checked into the Hilton and left a message for them at the reception of their own hotel. He suggested that he would pick them up tomorrow morning at nine for the drive to Tel Aviv. Milton was happy with that.

They finished the formalities of registration and a bellboy took them to their room. It was a high-end hotel, and Milton had booked a suite so that they had enough space for them both. There was a large double bed and, in an adjacent sitting room, a comfortable sofa.

"You take the bed," he said as he dropped onto the sofa.

"We can share it," Matilda said.

"No. You have it. I'm fine here. Go on. I sleep better alone."

She shrugged, wished him good night, and went through into the bedroom. She didn't close the door, though, and made no show of modesty as she undressed. Milton felt his self-control erode and, to prevent himself from doing anything that he would later regret, he collected his cigarettes from the coffee table and took them outside onto the balcony for a smoke.

He lit one and inhaled deeply as he looked out across the water. He knew that behind him, 350 kilometres to the north, was Tel Aviv and, at its heart, the headquarters of the most dangerous secret service in the world. It was the reason he had brought Ziggy halfway around the world.

Tomorrow, Milton was going to have to try to infiltrate it.

Chapter Forty-Three

MILTON SLEPT BADLY.

His mind was anxious, full of questions and possibilities, and he woke at four in the morning as dawn broke. He tried to return to sleep, but it was impossible. Eventually, he gave up. He got up and collected his cigarettes from the table. He paused at the door to the bedroom and glanced inside. Matilda was asleep on the bed, lying face down with the sheets pulled down so that her back was bare. The curves of her figure were obvious and eloquent and Milton had to remind himself, once again, why he needed to keep his distance. There were dozens of reasons, but it was still a struggle.

He went out onto the balcony. The spreading glow of dawn revealed the bay in all its glory, the fringe of yellow sand hemming in a sea that was so blue it was almost violet.

* * *

MATILDA WOKE soon after and, after she had showered, they went down to breakfast together. They were both a little subdued. Milton was anxious about what the day might bring, and it was obvious that some of his anxiety had transferred to her.

They were in the hotel lobby at five minutes to nine. Ziggy arrived promptly on the hour. Milton led the way outside; the sun was already burning away the chill of the night and promising another scorching-hot day. Ziggy had hired a large Mercedes people carrier with two rows of seats in the back. He opened the door and slid it back for them. Matilda got in and Milton followed behind her.

"Morning," he said.

"Morning."

He waited until the driver had started off before he spoke again. "All okay?"

"It was fine. You?"

"No problems." Ziggy spoke animatedly, as if he was buzzing. Milton remembered how excited he could get during an operation. It would be something to bear in mind. Excitement could get you into trouble.

"Did you get anything?"

Ziggy reached into his bag and withdrew an iPad. "Quite a lot," he said as he handed it over.

"From where?"

"Best you didn't ask."

Milton took the iPad and started to read.

Of course, he already knew about the Mossad. He knew of its reputation, its methods and the operations that had done so much to protect a country that was surrounded on all sides by states that wished not just its defeat, but that it be erased from existence.

The files were concerned with the director of the agency. Victor Blum had been born on a train between the Soviet Union and Poland during World War Two. His parents were Polish Jews fleeing Warsaw for the Soviet Union as the Germans hurried to implement the Final Solution. It was his impending arrival into the world that had persuaded his parents that they could no longer risk remaining in their home, so they fled. Not all of the family were so fortunate. Many members had been killed by the Nazis, including his grandparents and his two older brothers..

Blum and his parents had survived the war, and in 1950, the family made *aliyah*, a "return" to Israel. Blum had been conscripted into the Israeli Defense Force and had completed his compulsory service in 1966, but was called up as a reservist in 1967, fighting in the Six-Day War as an officer. He stayed in after the end of the war and had commanded an ad hoc undercover commando unit known as *Sayeret Rimon*, whose task was to combat the increasing violence in the Palestinian territories. Later, he had fought in the 1973 Yom Kippur War and the 1982 Lebanon War. He had then held a series of high-level positions in the IDF command, eventually reaching the rank of major general.

The prime minister had appointed Blum to the role of director-general of the Mossad in August 2002. As such, he was responsible for intelligence, counter-intelligence, and counterterrorism activities outside of Israel and the Palestinian Territories and was infamously aggressive in ordering killings of terrorists on foreign soil. Milton had heard of the paradox that, while Israel did not have a domestic death penalty, the Mossad under Blum had carte blanche to target Arab terrorists outside of its borders with complete impunity.

Victor Blum was a killer at the head of an organisation of killers.

And Avi Bachman had been the tip of the spear.

Milton opened another file.

Blum lived in a penthouse in the recently completed Meier-on-Rothschild Tower, a six-hundred-foot-tall apartment block in the heart of Tel Aviv. Prices started at a million dollars per apartment and went far higher than that; it was more, Milton thought, than might have been expected on the budget of a government employee. He suspected that a penthouse apartment, several hundred feet above the ground, had been provided so as to ensure Blum's security. It would be much easier to defend than a ground-level property.

All Milton wanted to do was talk to him.

His residence wouldn't be the place to do it.

He would try something else.

* * *

IT TOOK them four hours to complete the drive to Tel Aviv. The driver took them to the city's main railway station, where they changed to another car. They took that car to the Best Western and checked into two rooms. Ziggy waited ten minutes and then came to the room that Milton and Matilda had taken. He knocked three times, as they had agreed, and Milton let him in.

"Ready?"

Milton nodded.

"What are we going to do?" Matilda asked.

"Not we," Milton corrected. "Just me. You're staying here." He could see that she was going to argue. "Please, Matty. It's safe here. We weren't followed. And what I'm going to do could go either way."

"*What* are you going to do?"

He had been deliberately vague about that until now. "I'm going to talk to them."

"What? Just walk in and ask to speak to someone?"

"Exactly."

"And say what?"

"I'm going to persuade them that they need to stop taking sides."

"And you think they'll take kindly to that?"

"I have no idea. Probably not."

"And then? What happens when they arrest you and tell Bachman?"

"That's where Ziggy comes in."

"Right," she said, not bothering to hide her doubt. "And what's he going to do?"

Ziggy held up a USB stick.

"What's that?"

"We're going to blackmail them," he said.

Chapter Forty-Four

THE MOSSAD'S headquarters were notoriously difficult to locate, but Ziggy had managed easily enough. He led the way to a highway intersection called Glilot Junction, which contained a partially hidden campus of low-slung office buildings sandwiched between the junction, a Cineplex, and a shopping centre.

Milton looked at the bland buildings, all smooth stone walls and tinted glass. The men and women going in and out of the anonymous doorways all wore business dress. It looked as the agency must have wanted it to look: completely unremarkable.

"What do you think?" Ziggy asked him.

"Looks like all the intelligence agencies I've ever seen," Milton answered.

They continued up the street until they were a block away from the building. They reached a kiosk that was selling cheap cell phones and SIM cards. Milton bought a phone, gave it to Ziggy and memorised the number.

"I'll call you when it's done."

Ziggy nodded.

"Do you have it?"

Ziggy reached into his pocket and gave him the USB stick.

"Are you sure it's going to work?"

"Reasonably sure."

"Reasonably?"

"This is cutting edge, Milton."

"You've tested it?"

"Yes." He paused, frowning. "Of course I tested it. But not like this."

"How did you test it?"

"An Internet café in Tokyo."

Milton's stomach dropped.

"But it worked well," Ziggy said quickly. "In theory, it'll work. Get it into the building and make sure it's plugged in."

"And then what? Cross my fingers and hope?"

Ziggy smiled at him. "Have I ever let you down?"

Milton didn't answer.

* * *

MILTON STOOD outside the entrance to the office building. It was a bland, eighties construction, four storeys tall and with mirrored glass windows that prickled in the glare of the midday sun. He had been observing the building for an hour. He had been careful about it, changing his vantage point every ten minutes.

This was one of the most heavily guarded addresses in the world.

The building looked unprepossessing, akin to all the others in this part of downtown Tel Aviv. A pair of revolving doors offered access to the lobby. Milton had walked along the street two times, approaching the building once from each direction, and had fixed the interior in his mind: leather sofas positioned at the perimeter of the room, a marble floor that was polished to a dark sheen, and an impressive marble counter behind which sat three smartly dressed attendants. A steady stream of smartly dressed men and women passed in and out, going about their business. A board fixed to the wall behind the counter announced the businesses that had taken space on the various floors. Milton couldn't read the names from outside, but he knew that they would all be aliases to mask the identity of the building's single tenant. It reminded him of the scruffy office block down by the Thames that housed Group Fifteen. Her Majesty's department of murderers and blackmailers cloaked itself within the fiction of Global Logistics, a front company whose legitimate business interests allowed its agents a pretext to travel the world.

The Mossad would be just the same. A similar fiction. Similar pretexts.

Victor Blum would send his killers around the globe from this faceless building, dealing death and destruction from an anonymous desk somewhere deep inside. Milton knew that the order for his own death warrant, leveraged by Avi Bachman's blackmail, would have been signed somewhere within.

A police car cruised slowly down the street. Milton saw the officer in the passenger seat turn to look at him.

No point in waiting. He had no other cards to play. If he was going to be apprehended, it had to be inside.

He put his hand to the revolving door and pushed.

Inside, it was cool, the air conditioning turned up high to combat the heat outside. A wave of cold air gushed onto him, raising the hairs on the back of his neck. The room was quiet save for the sound of a keyboard being used behind the marble desk, the gentle whoosh of the air conditioning, and the sound of a woman's heels as she crossed the floor to get to the exit. Milton stepped aside to let her pass. He scoped out the parts of the interior that he had been unable to see properly from outside. There was an elevator lobby with four doors, two on one side faced by a second identical pair. There was a guard in the lobby and another near to the counter. He looked up: security cameras all around the room.

Too late to turn back.

He walked to the counter.

"Can I help you, sir?"

Milton assessed him. The man was quite obviously a soldier, with close-cropped hair and a muscular physique beneath the lines of his well-fitted suit. The suit fell smooth and evenly, suggesting that he wasn't carrying a weapon, but Milton had no doubt that he had a handgun within easy reach.

"I want to see Victor Blum."

Milton saw a look of concern flash across the man's face. "I'm sorry, sir?"

"Victor Blum. The director."

The man shook his head. "Who?"

"Do we need to do this? I'm not going to leave until I see him."

"No, really, sir, that's not possible. I don't know—"

Milton spoke over him: "This is what is going to happen." He noticed the man's hand as it slid beneath the counter. "You're going to press your panic alarm, and those two guys over there"—he pointed to the guards—"are going to draw their weapons and detain me. And that's fine. I want them to. And I want you to call up to Mr. Blum and tell him that John Milton is here to see him. Tell him it's about Avi Bachman. He'll know who that is."

Milton saw the two guards step away from the door and start toward him. He kept his eye on the man. "Do you want me to repeat those names? John Milton and Avi Bachman."

The first guard reached him, laying a hand on his elbow. He hadn't drawn his weapon, although it was visible in a shoulder holster beneath his open jacket. Milton could have disabled him easily enough, taken his gun and incapacitated his colleague, too, but that would have gained him nothing. He was hardly about to mount an assault on the Mossad's HQ. It would get him killed. It wouldn't get him to Blum.

"Step away from the counter," the guard said, squeezing his fingers so that they dug into the soft flesh around his elbow.

A little pain flashed, but Milton ignored it.

Milton looked at the man behind the desk. "Call Blum," he repeated.

"Back away, sir."

Milton did as he was asked and stepped back.

"Put your hands up."

Milton did as he was told.

The man frisked him with practiced ease, starting up at his shoulders and working quickly and methodically all the way down to his ankles. The second guard arrived, his hand inside his jacket and resting on the butt of his holstered weapon. They were good. Well trained. Not thuggish, but with the threat of violence obvious and more than sufficient to make it clear that obedience was the wisest course.

"Come with us, sir," the first guard said, impelling him towards the lobby.

Milton didn't resist. They led him to a door that he hadn't noticed, opened it, and directed him down a corridor that led deeper into the building. The passageway lacked the expensive gleam of the reception area. The walls were bare, the floor was treated concrete and the lighting was from harsh overhead UV strips.

The man told him to stop at the second in a series of bland-looking doors, opened it, and nudged him so that he went inside.

Another bland space. A desk with two chairs, one on either side. A dark glass window, opaque from this side, but likely clear from the other. Two cameras fixed on the wall just beneath the ceiling. No decoration. Spare and austere. Milton had been in rooms like this before, sometimes on one side of the desk and on other occasions on the other. It was an interrogation room.

The guard nudged Milton inside and then frisked him again, much more thoroughly this time. He took out his wallet and the USB drive that Milton was carrying in his jacket pocket.

"Wait here," the guard said, closing the door.

Milton heard the lock click.

He didn't know whether his gambit would be successful. He would either see Blum or he would not; if he did not, his long-term prospects would not be very good. With nothing else to do, he pulled out one of the chairs and sat down. It might be a long wait.

Chapter Forty-Five

MILTON HEARD the lock click again and watched as the door opened. The man standing in the doorway was old, but he did not look frail. He was several inches shorter than Milton, but he walked with an erect, proud posture, and there was iron in his eyes.

Milton recognised him at once.

"Mr. Milton," he said, "I'm sorry to keep you. I'm Victor Blum."

Milton stood. Blum extended his hand and Milton took it. Blum's grip was strong.

"Thank you for seeing me, sir."

"Please, sit."

Milton sat down again. Blum pulled out the facing chair and sat down.

"I don't think we've ever met, have we, Mr. Milton?"

"No, sir. I don't believe that we have."

"Of course, I'm aware of your work. The work you used to do, I should say. You don't do it any more, do you?"

"No, sir. Not for some time."

"We heard about what happened, of course. I did meet Control a few times—before his unfortunate end. Was that you?"

"No, sir. It wasn't."

"Still, I should imagine you weren't displeased? I know he wasn't pleased when you decided to stop."

"Not particularly."

"The work we do," he said, waving an arm to encompass the building and what went on within it, "it's not really the sort of profession you can just leave."

"Avi Bachman had the same problem, as I understand it."

The mention of Bachman did not faze him. "That's right, he did. You know I was director of the Mossad then, too?"

"Yes, sir."

"I'm not too proud to say that the whole thing took me by surprise. We thought he was dead. We did for years. He was an extraordinary agent and it was a terrible blow. We investigated what had happened, obviously, as far as we could—this was Cairo, of course—and there was no suggestion that he was still alive. Avi was very inventive about it." He sighed. "A shame, though. A real waste. Men like Avi—men like you, Mr. Milton—are particularly difficult to replace."

Milton held his tongue. The tone of the conversation was amicable, but underpinned by the knowledge on both sides that there was a deeper and more serious topic that was going to have to be addressed. This wasn't a social call.

"I'll be honest with you, Mr. Milton. You are about the last person in the world I would have expected to walk through the doors this morning."

"I would rather not have had to come, sir, but I haven't been left with an alternative."

"Nevertheless, you realise that I can't let you leave?"

"No, sir. You will."

Blum smiled at him as if Milton were a child who had just said something ineffably foolish.

"You killed one of my *sayanim* in Australia."

"They tried to kill me."

"But that's not something I can just overlook."

"Shall we park that for now? It's not going to get us anywhere. I want to talk about Bachman."

"Yes, of course. You killed his wife."

"He told you that?"

Blum nodded.

"It isn't true. He abducted a friend of a friend. I went to retrieve him, and his wife was killed in the crossfire. I didn't fire the shot. Bachman did."

"That's not how he tells it, Mr. Milton."

"Of course it isn't. He isn't going to accept that he's responsible for that, is he? Far better to blame a scapegoat. I was there. It might as well be me."

Blum nodded, indicating that he should go on.

Milton looked at him. "Be honest, sir. What does he have over you?"

"Why would you say that?"

"Because it's obvious. You mounted an operation on foreign soil to break him out of prison. You killed Americans to do it. I can't begin to imagine how far up the chain of command you had to go to get authorisation to do that. And you've backed him to go after me. Four agents in Australia, the *sayanim* you must have activated. The Mossad has no interest in going after me, sir. There's no reason why you would do any of that unless Bachman has threatened you with something very damaging."

Blum steepled his fingers and looked at Milton for a long moment. Milton was aware that he was considering how much he should tell him.

"Very well. Avi took some very sensitive information with him when he disappeared. We only knew that he had it after he had been arrested in Louisiana. He called us and told us that unless we did what he wanted, he would disseminate it."

"What was it?"

"A list of active agents."

"Hardly active. It must have been years out of date."

"Yes, that's true. We've tried to assess the damage that would be caused. Much of the information will be irrelevant, but not all of it. Some agents are still in place. Some have become very senior in their particular roles in the time that has passed. Others have retired, but they could easily be traced. You understand what that would mean for them. Our enemies have long memories. My men and women would be put at serious threat. I care for my agents, Mr. Milton. I respect and honour their service, and I will not abandon them. There are some risks that I cannot take."

"No," Milton said. "Of course not. I understand."

"And we have no relationship. And with respect, Mr. Milton, you mean nothing to me. I don't mean to offend you, but that's the fact of it."

"No offence taken."

"So Avi has leverage. I looked at every option when he came to us. We could have ignored him. He wasn't going anywhere, after all. He was incarcerated. The Americans would have killed him eventually, but that would have taken years. *We* could have killed him. It would have been simple. We could have had an inmate do it. We could have fomented a riot, had him murdered. Such a thing would have been trivial."

"Why didn't you?"

"Avi tells us he has a dead man's switch. An associate. He says if he doesn't report to him regularly, the information will be released."

"And you believe him?"

"I know it to be true. We know who the associate is." Blum laid his hands on the table and drummed his fingers against the wood. "I should be honest with you, Mr. Milton. I don't understand why you have come here. You must have suspected all of this. I'm not sure how you think I can help you. You know I have to hand you over to Avi."

"No. You won't do that."

The drumming fingers stopped and Blum fixed him in a cold stare. "Why is that, Mr. Milton?"

"Your guards took a thumb drive from me. Have you looked at it yet?"

"It's being examined now."

"Let me save you the bother. Avi has his database, but it's old. My stick contains an up-to-date version. It was downloaded yesterday. Operational details. Your Bible, sir.

Who your agents are. Where they are. What they are doing. Everything."

Blum didn't answer.

"Perhaps you should speak to your analyst? It might accelerate things if you know I'm not bluffing. I'm not going anywhere."

Blum narrowed his eyes warily, but took a phone from his pocket and dialled a number. The call connected and Blum tersely explained that he was with Milton, and that he needed to know what was on the memory stick that had been confiscated from him. Milton could hear the buzz of the answer, but it was too quiet for him to distinguish the words. He watched Blum's face instead. He watched as the colour slowly drained from it, as the lips pursed so that they became a hard line, as the frown deepened into a scowl. Blum did not acknowledge the person to whom he was speaking again; he pulled the phone from his ear, ended the call, and put it back into his pocket.

"Sir?"

Blum got up. Milton had no idea whether he had been persuasive enough. He had certainly angered him. Milton had known that a man like Victor Blum would be proud. To last in a career like his for as long as he had lasted would mean that he usually got his way. He would not be used to being defied or, worse, manipulated. But Milton wasn't just manipulating him: he was threatening him. Blum had been reduced to the role of a patsy. He was caught in the middle of a struggle between two others and he had no leverage of his own. He was helpless, and Milton knew that that would be difficult for him to stomach.

He was counting on it.

Blum turned his back and reached for the door.

Had he made up his mind? Was he going to leave him here? What would that mean?

"I'll look at it, Mr. Milton."

Milton knew he had his attention. He decided to risk an escalation. "You've got an hour, sir. Avi isn't the only one with backup. If I'm out of contact for more than an hour, the information is released anyway."

Milton saw the anger flash across the old man's wizened face, but he gave a curt nod and, without another word, he shut the door and left him alone.

Chapter Forty-Six

BLUM SHUT the door to the interrogation room and gestured to the guard stationed next to it.

"If he tries anything, shoot him."

"Yes, sir."

He took the elevator to his office on the fourth floor. It offered a broad view of Tel Aviv, from the elegant and futuristic skyscrapers of the downtown district to the cultural landmarks of Habima Square. He looked east to the Shalom Tower and, beyond it, the Great Synagogue. Blum was old enough that he could remember when the building was always busy. It wasn't the same today. Pious locals had emigrated, and now the services were attended by just a handful of congregants. Blum felt it to be emblematic of a larger problem in Israeli society. Religion was not as important today as it had been when he was growing up. His father had been a rabbi and he had seen to it that his young son was given a thorough and severe religious education. His piety had been the reason he had been able to endure the privations of his military career. His service, however unpleasant, was in honour of God. His standing within the religious community had also been of some benefit to his accelerated promotion and the fact that he had held his position at the head of the Mossad for so many years.

That his fellow citizens no longer put so much faith in God was a matter of great regret, and the subject of many late night rants to whomever he could find to listen to him, but it did not mean that he would countenance—not even for a minute—a lessening of his vigilance. He had stood on the wall for all of his adult life.

He had sent agents to kill and had seen his agents killed.

He was as dedicated to Israel today as he had ever been.

That was why the situation with Avi Bachman had caused him so much dismay.

And now this.

The Mossad was divided into eight separate departments. There was Collections, the group responsible for espionage operations. There was the Political Action and Liaison Department, responsible for relations with foreign espionage agencies. There was Metsada, or the Special Operations Division, tasked with assassination, sabotage, and paramilitary and psychological warfare projects. Blum was responsible for them all, but he didn't need them today. He sat down behind his desk and called the head of the Technology Department.

* * *

"ARE YOU SURE, SIR?"

The man's name was Yossi Levy. He had been born and educated in the United States and then, following some time on a kibbutz, had been recruited to join the Mossad. He had studied computer science at MIT and was a genius programmer. The *sayan* on campus who monitored potential recruits had spoken very highly of him, and had said that he had been raised the right way with the right kind of attitude towards Israel. Blum had told the *sayan* to recruit him, and, with typical discretion, that had been achieved. He had started work at the agency and had quickly risen through the ranks to his elevated position today as the head technician in charge of technology.

"The man who brought that stick is being held downstairs. He is, potentially, significant to our operations. He says that it has information that would be dangerous to our interests."

"He's blackmailing you?" Yossi said.

That irritated Blum, and he frowned. "Yes. He is. How I choose to deal with him depends upon whether he has something on that stick or whether he's bluffing. I need to know."

"You understand my reluctance, Director?"

"You made it plain."

Yossi repeated himself anyway. "We don't know what's on it. We don't know whether there's anything that could compromise our network."

"I'm not a child, Yossi. I need to know what's on it, and I need to know *now*."

"Why not wait until I can test it properly?"

"Because he says we have an hour. If he isn't bluffing and I detain him for longer than that while you work out whether it's safe to look at it, he says his associate will release the information."

"And then he has nothing."

"Maybe it's not everything. Maybe it's something discreet to prove his bona fides? Discreet, but damaging. I can't afford to risk that. And he isn't the sort of man who bluffs. I need to know."

Blum could see that the technician was reluctant to proceed, but they had worked together long enough for Yossi to know that it would have been folly for him to push against Blum once his decision was made. He would simply have to find a way to minimise the risk.

He took a MacBook from his satchel and set it on the coffee table, unfolded the lid and booted it up. The machine played its welcoming note and the screen changed from white to a picture of a woman and two children.

"This is against my better judgment, Director."

"I understand that."

"This machine is air-gapped. That means that it isn't connected to the Internet or the network. It's completely isolated. You could call it a quarantine, if you like. If there's anything on this stick, anything we don't like, it'll manifest itself here, but it will be trapped. It won't be able to propagate."

"Fine," Blum said, waving a hand. He had no interest in the minutiae. He just wanted answers.

Yossi sent the cursor across the screen and opened two applications. "This will check for viruses," he explained, pointing to one window, "and this will analyse the data."

Blum couldn't help noticing that the technician took a breath before he collected the stick and slotted it into one of the laptop's USB ports.

Nothing happened.

Yossi was staring intently at the screen, his fingers flashing across the keyboard as he entered commands.

Blum waited impatiently, drumming his fingers against the surface of his desk.

"There's nothing here," Yossi reported after another minute.

"What do you mean?"

"I mean that I can't find anything. It's empty. There's nothing on it."

Blum scowled. "You're sure?"

"It's empty, Director."

"Check again."

Milton was bluffing? Really? That didn't make any sense. He would come to the Mossad, effectively hand himself over in the sure knowledge that Blum would pass him to Bachman, and threaten him with something that could very easily be proven to be a bluff? No. Something was wrong. Blum knew more than enough about Milton to know that he was smart, and that he wouldn't take that kind of massive gamble without something to back up his threat.

"I need you to be absolutely certain, Yossi. I can't take any risks that—"

He paused, mid-sentence. He heard a high-pitched whining noise.

"What is that?"

He looked at Yossi. The man's face bore an unmistakeable cast of concern.

It took Blum a moment to place it. "It's coming from the computer," he said, pointing to the laptop.

Yossi was ahead of him, his fingers dancing across the keys again. He cursed in Yiddish. "*Fakakta!*" he spat. He held his finger on the key used for powering up and down. It should have taken a second to kill the machine, but nothing happened. It kept playing the sound, that same high whine that was just on the edge of what could be heard, an auditory itch in the back of the head. Yossi looked around the room, saw Blum's computer and the iPhone on the desk, and started to panic, his breath coming in faster and faster gasps. He swore again, picked up the MacBook and, before Blum could say anything to stop him—not, Blum thought, that he would have stopped even if he had asked him—dropped it out of the open window.

All was quiet for a moment, save for Yossi's breathing, and then, just as Blum was about to ask him what in God's name had just happened, the whining noise started again.

Yossi surged across the room, barging Blum out of the way, his face a mask of terror. He bolted for Blum's desktop computer, and, just as he reached it, the screensaver was replaced by a big yellow smiley. It was there for half a second. Yossi yanked the plug out of the wall and the screen flicked to black.

"Switch everything off!" he yelled. "Anything with a chipset—power it all down."

Blum froze, unsure what was happening and paralysed by uncertainty.

The sound played again.

Yossi grabbed the iPhone off the desk and tossed it through the window. He took his own phone and disposed of it in the same way.

Finally, quiet.

"What's going on?" Blum said. "What is it?"

The blood had flooded out of Yossi's face, leaving him as white as a phantom. Wordlessly, he walked to the door, opened it and stood in the doorway, staring out into the open-plan space outside. He closed his eyes, his face set in the fashion of someone expecting a slap, or a piece of the very worst news, then opened them and began to walk. As Blum followed him out of his office, he heard the noise again.

The high-pitched squeal, just detectable, a pulse that nestled in his brain and sent icy fingers to scratch up and down his back.

He heard it again, and again, and again.

Yossi swore again, but quietly, full of dread.

There were forty analysts in the open-plan office. They each had at least one screen, some of them working across two or three. As Blum watched, the documents and programs that they were working on vanished, the screens wiped one at a time and replaced by the same big yellow smiley face that he had seen on his own monitor. The high-pitched tone was like a symphony, all of the terminals playing it from their speakers.

Yossi reached for a desk phone and dialled a number. He turned away from Blum so that he couldn't hear what was said, but, a moment later, all of the power in the room was killed. The monitors all flicked off, save those that were running on batteries. The lights went out. The emergency doors closed.

Yossi called out. "If you have a computer that runs off a battery, take the battery out."

People paused, confused.

"Now!"

They started to move, prising the batteries out of laptops.

Blum crossed to the technician and took his arm roughly. "What's happening?"

The man looked like he was about to cry. "I warned

you—"

"You said it was safe," Blum said, not bothering to hide the accusatory tone. "Air-gapped, you said. Not connected."

"It was. It should have been. This"—he paused—"this is very sophisticated. Beyond anything I've seen before."

"What is? Explain it. *Tell me.*"

"It has been demonstrated, in theoretical experiments, that it is possible to transfer data using high-frequency transmissions passed between computer speakers and microphones."

"So why did you—"

"It's *theoretical*, sir. It's never been done practically. And the experiments only allowed for small data packets. This, though… It's more than that. I'll only know when I look into it, but my guess is that whatever this is, it tries to replicate itself through the network first. If that doesn't work, it transmits sonically. My computer wasn't connected, so it went to plan B. I don't know—maybe it does both right away, doubles its chances. And—"

"What are the consequences?"

"I'll only know when I—"

"Fuck, Yossi!" Blum spat in an overflow of irritation that he could no longer suppress. "Come on. Make an educated guess."

Yossi looked down, chastised. "My guess is that it's opened up our network for someone outside. The first machine was air-gapped. None of these other ones are."

"Can you stop it?"

"We've shut everything down."

"Is that enough?"

"I don't know, sir."

* * *

ZIGGY PENN had his laptop open and an Ethernet cable plugging it into the hotel's broadband connection.

He had no idea whether his little worm would be able to do what he had designed it to do. It was one thing to infiltrate a corporate network. That was easy. He had demonstrated that it could breach the defences of multinationals, but that was easy, too; the firewalls tended to be nominal, justifications for the salaries of the technicians who installed and maintained them, but they were as nothing to a hacker with Ziggy's talents. McDonald's was easy. Apple was easy. But taking aim at the servers of the most secretive and well-defended intelligence agency in the world, though? That should not have been easy.

Matilda was sitting on the bed behind him. "Anything?"

"Not yet."

The worm had taken him a year to perfect. The payload had been rigorously tested in the wild, and he knew that it worked. The script was so pervasive that, as soon as Ziggy had written it, he had almost wanted to fill up his laptop's USB ports with cement. The means of transmission was something else entirely. He had read about the experiments to transmit data sonically and had been intrigued enough to run his own trials. It was high-end stuff, at the outer limits of his skills, and he had called for assistance from others on the hacking fora that he visited. Eventually, he had succeeded in making it work.

In his opinion, even with his vanity taken into account, BadUSB was the most sophisticated piece of malware that had ever been created. It could transmit itself through a dozen different methods and, once it was established, it hid itself among the lowest levels of computer hardware. Targeting BIOS and firmware, it could escape all but the most thorough forms of detection and survive most attempts to eradicate it. The safest defence against it once a server had been infected was to junk every piece of kit that had ever come into contact with it and start over.

"How long before you know?"

"I can't say. It depends on how Milton manages. They might not fall for it."

"And then?"

"And then he's in a world of trouble."

And what would that mean for me? he thought.

Tokyo was finished. He couldn't go back there. South Korea, perhaps. He'd always wanted to go to Seoul. Or maybe China. Somewhere he would be able to disappear. Somewhere—

Wait.

The screen started to flicker as data spooled across it.

"Shit," he said.

"What is it?"

Packets of data were flooding into his computer.

"Shit, shit, shit."

Ziggy was on his feet, gaping at the screen.

He now had complete and unfettered access to the Mossad network.

* * *

ZIGGY HAD been wary of swamping the hotel's connection to the Internet, so he had shut down all other access. No one else—not the hotel staff nor the guests—could get online now. Then he had arranged for the information to be relayed to anonymous servers that would be difficult to trace back to him. He had re-routed the data through a series of relays that further obfuscated his hand in things; by the time the packet of data had been delivered to his laptop it would have been around the world several times. It would buy them a little time until they were detected—and he guessed that would happen quickly. It was already rewriting itself on every machine that it could reach, but, eventually, the system would be shut down and every instance of it would be exterminated. How long did he have? It was impossible to say. Probably a matter of minutes rather than hours. He hunched over the keyboard and worked as quickly as he could.

He had a series of automated scripts on his machine that would do much of the work for him. He set them running, leaving a window open so that he could quickly scan through their results. And then he went into the network himself, trusting his instincts to guide him to the information that he needed. His scripts were sophisticated, but they were unintuitive. They would get to the target eventually, but there was always the chance that he would be able to reach it more quickly than they could.

His fingers flew across the keyboard as he started to arrange the data in the folders that he had prepared. He activated search protocols that would sift and filter it, finding key phrases and identifiers that would alert him that a particular file was worthy of manual inspection. He checked the amount of data that was being pulled in; it had already passed a terabyte. He had four three-terabyte external drives daisy-chained to his machine and, as he saw the volume of data and the speed at which it was amassing, he reached into his bag for a fifth.

The spigot was open. Unless he was careful, it would be like putting a fire hose to his face and trying to take a drink.

"Ziggy?"

"It's working."

"You're getting what you need?"

Ziggy allowed himself a smile at the audacity of what he had just done.

"I'm getting *everything*."

1.3 terabytes.

1.5 terabytes.

1.8 terabytes.

"What about Milton?"

"He's done it."

Chapter Forty-Seven

BLUM WAS gone for a long time. Milton had no idea what his absence signified. It could, for all he knew, have been an opportunity for him to contact Bachman to tell him that Milton had been apprehended. Or, if he was fortunate, it could denote that Ziggy's booby-trapped flash drive had done what it was supposed to do. There was no way of knowing what had happened, no way of knowing whether his gambit had been successful or whether it had failed and he had signed his own death warrant by bringing himself here.

If it had worked? The consequences would cause chaos, and Blum would need to be briefed as to the damage that had been caused. And, if it became obvious that their network security had been breached, perhaps Blum would need to take instructions from the government. Blum had survived as the head of the Mossad for years. That was an impressive feat. Longevity in a role such as that was not common and, to manage that, Milton knew that he would have extensive political contacts. It was not impossible that he would need to take soundings before he could make a decision.

And then the lights went out, the room was plunged into darkness, and Milton knew that the ruse had worked. Ziggy's virus was loose and they were trying to cage it.

Time passed in the darkness. Milton estimated that it was thirty minutes, but it was difficult to be sure. Eventually, the lights came back on again. Some time after that the door was unlocked and opened, and Blum came back inside. His face was a deep purple, the purest fury.

"You are a brave man, Mr. Milton. And one with clever friends." He spoke tersely, his voice dripping with rage. Some of that splenetic anger was reserved for Milton, but, he knew, most of it would have been directed at himself for falling for Milton's artifice. Two hours ago, Milton had presented Blum with the opportunity to rid himself of the problem that Avi Bachman had caused him. Now, because he had been fooled, the problem had been doubled.

"I had no choice. I'm not going to apologise. You put me in that position."

"Quite," Blum said as he sat down opposite him.

"You said it yourself, sir. This isn't my first time doing this. If there's a knife fight, I'm bringing a gun." Blum stared at him evenly, and Milton drove his advantage home. "I don't know how much your technicians have told you, but let me be clear. I'm sure you've been told this already, but the worm on that stick will have replicated itself across your network by now. I noticed you shut off the power, but that won't make any difference. It will have opened a port for my friend, and he will have taken everything that we need. All of your operational data, Director. Everything. We'll go through it all later, but we'll obviously have information in there that you won't want to be publicised. It'll make whatever it is Bachman's been holding over your head look like nothing. But you know that."

"Very good, Mr. Milton."

"As you say, I have clever friends."

"You've put me in a difficult position. Whichever choice I make, there are serious consequences for my agents. For my country."

"Avi is to blame. If you had him under control, none of this would have happened."

"What do you *want*, Mr. Milton?"

"You know what I want."

"I can't give you Avi. And I'm not going to have him killed."

"I don't want you to kill him. He's my problem to fix. I just want a level playing field. I don't want him to have any backup. Pull the agents back."

"I can't. He'll release the information."

"Then you have to think about which set of data is the most damaging. Bachman's data is ten years old. Most of it is historic. I imagine you've already started to take steps to minimise the damage if it ever gets out."

Blum just scowled at him.

"Mine is fresh. You can't take steps to minimise the damage. You can pull your agents out, but it'll destroy everything you've been working on. Every operation, every sleeper you've spent years inserting, every double agent, every mole—I'll burn every one of them. You can insulate yourself with Bachman. It'll be inconvenient, but you'll adapt. But I'll tear everything down."

"So? I call the agents off. Then what?"

"I need a reason for Avi to come to me."

"He doesn't need a reason, Mr. Milton. He's coming whatever you do."

"I want it to be on my terms. I want to control the environment. And I need leverage for that. His associate. Who is it?"

Blum bit his lip, thinking about the request. "Fine," he said, after a moment. "His name is Meir Shavit."

"And?"

"Meir is Bachman's old commanding officer from when he was in the IDF. They were always very close. He was like a father to Avi. He's the only person in the world he trusts."

"Where is he?"

"In Croatia. The Alsatian Coast."

"I'll need everything you have on him."

Blum nodded. "And then?"

"I'm going to go and see him. I'll make sure Avi knows where I am. When he gets to me, pull your agents back. You can leave the rest to me. It's between us now."

"You think it will be as easy as that? 'You can leave the rest to me'? It won't be easy, Mr. Milton. Avi is the most dangerous man I have ever sent into the field. You can't fight him straight up. He'll kill you."

"Maybe. Maybe not."

"He's beaten you twice already. He nearly killed you in New Orleans. And he had you beat in Australia. I know. I read the reports."

"He gave me a bit of a beating. But maybe the third time's a charm."

"I read your file. You were good, but that was a long time ago. Avi never stopped. He stopped working for us, but he's never stopped killing. You know that, don't you, Mr. Milton? Avi Bachman is a machine."

Milton stood up. "You're wrong, sir. I didn't stop killing, either."

Chapter Forty-Eight

ZIGGY HAD set a timer on his laptop for an hour. They were going to leave when that hit zero, regardless of how much information was left to be delivered. He had masked his location as thoroughly as he could, but he knew that once the Mossad brought their systems back online again, they would very quickly be able to find out where all of their secret data was going.

Thirty minutes.

Forty-five minutes.

He adapted as he worked, constantly rearranging the data to be downloaded.

Fifty-five minutes.

He found one particularly juicy piece of information—a list of agents active in the United States, together with Social Security information and images—and decided it was worth waiting the additional time it would take for it to download.

Sixty-five minutes.

The delay was greedy on his part. Almost fatal.

Seventy minutes had passed when he and Matilda hustled out of the hotel and onto the street. Two cars pulled up outside and six men disembarked. There was nothing to mark them out as agents, not that Ziggy would have expected that, but their haste to get inside was evident and, as Ziggy and Matilda tarried a little at the end of the street, they watched as the agents sealed the building and prevented anyone else from leaving.

"Come on," Ziggy said. "We don't want to be here."

* * *

MILTON FOUND a cab on the street. As soon as they had pulled out into traffic, he allowed himself to exhale and relax. The afternoon had been exquisitely stressful. He had known that his life was in the balance and that he had ceded a decision on whether he lived or died first to the scheming of a socially inept hacker and then, second, to a man who was not noted for his compassion. He realised, as the car put the anonymous office block behind him, that he had half expected not to be able to walk out of it again.

He told the driver to stop next to a payphone. While the driver waited, he thumbed in the coins, dialled the number for the prepaid phone that he had given to Ziggy and waited for the call to connect.

"Hello?"

"It's me."

"Are you okay?"

"I'm fine."

"How did it go?"

"He took it. He left me for a couple of hours and when he came back he was very unhappy."

"I bet. You fucked up their network. They'll basically have to blow it up and start again."

"You did it. I was just the deliveryman."

"So they'll stop Bachman? Call him off?"

"No."

"They'll help you, then?"

"Not exactly. But they might not help him."

"They *might* not?"

"I can't say any better than that. That's what I needed most of all. The deck was stacked before. It might be even now. They certainly know I'm serious after what we just did to them."

"So what do we do?"

"We need to give our friend a reason to come and find us."

"How do we do that?"

"I'll explain. But you need to leave the country."

"And go where?"

314

"Dubrovnik."

They had already discussed the safest way to leave, and now Milton told him to put the plan into effect. Ziggy and Matilda would return south to Ovda and leave from there, while he would make his own arrangements. He knew that he would have a Mossad tail now that he wouldn't be able to shake until he had exited the country. But he wanted to ensure that Ziggy and Matilda were able to leave safely. He made Ziggy promise that he would keep a careful eye on her, and he said that he would. Milton didn't think that Matty needed a babysitter—indeed, it would probably have made more sense to tell *her* to look after *him*—but he couldn't help himself. He said that he would call again when he had reached their destination and then ended the call.

Back in the car, he leaned forward so that he could speak to the driver. "Change of plan," he said. "Can you take me to Haifa, please? The airport."

It was a hundred kilometres to the north, and the driver—happy to contemplate the larger fare he would be able to charge—said yes and changed course.

Milton settled back in the seat as they headed out on Route Two, and gazed out the window to the west. The deep blue sea stretched out all the way to an immaculate horizon, a few pleasure craft skirting across the surface. He turned back as a Mercedes with blacked-out windows accelerated by them, matching their speed for a moment before passing and pulling in ahead of them. He wondered whether the car was involved in his surveillance.

Probably.

He would make no attempt to shake them.

It would make no difference. They knew where he was going.

Chapter Forty-Nine

MILTON SHIFTED a little, rearranging himself so that he was a little more comfortable. He was lying on a shallow plateau that jutted out of the steep cliff side that dropped down to the clashing water of the Adriatic below him. He was prone, flat against the stony floor of the plateau, shielded from the scorching sun by the lip of rock that extended above him. He was holding a pair of binoculars that he had purchased at the airport. The sun was overhead, so he wasn't concerned about the prospect of light sparking against the lenses and giving him away. He was hidden.

The villa spread out below him was impressive. The building itself was huge—Milton estimated four thousand square metres—and the grounds led down through a series of terraces to the crystal-clear waters. Trees reached up above bone-white walls that had been bleached by the salt and the sun, and flights of steps offered access to and egress from the terraces to the house and, beyond, the ornamental gardens that had been planted in a cleft in the cliff face. Milton had no idea how much a property like this must cost. Millions, certainly.

Dubrovnik was only a few miles to the north. This was a chic destination now, but it hadn't always been that way. Ziggy had pulled the records of the transaction that had passed the property's title from the previous owner to Meir Shavit. He had been shrewd. The purchase had been made at the height of the war, when the villa was valued at a fraction of the amount it would have made if it were put onto the open market today. Milton had never been one for property, but even he had to admit that the old soldier had been wise in his choice of investment.

He saw movement and jerked the binoculars around,

focusing on the figure that had just emerged from a door at ground level. It was a man, old, but in good shape despite his advanced years. He walked with a confident stride, his back ramrod straight and, if a little slow, he moved with purpose. He was wearing a white robe and slippers.

The man followed a flight of steps down to the middle terrace, and then another that delivered him at the foot of the cliff. Milton twisted the focus. A natural indentation in the rock face had produced a large plunge pool. It was protected from the vicissitudes of the tide by a lip of rock that extended out into the water, a natural breakwater that meant that the water was as smooth as a millpond in comparison with the churn beyond it. A wooden pier had been constructed, stretching out for ten feet into the middle of the pool, and there was a rowing boat tied up at the end.

Milton watched as the man reached the lower level. He took off the robe, revealing a pair of swimming shorts, and then removed his feet from the slippers. He walked to the end of the pier. There was a ladder next to the rowing boat and he climbed down it, dropping the last few feet into the water. He turned over onto his stomach and stroked out into the middle of the pool.

It was Shavit.

Milton watched him as he swam to and from the rocks that formed the breakwater. It looked deep, the light blue of the shallower waters directly below him changing to a much darker hue where Shavit was swimming.

Milton wondered whether now was the time to make his move. He could negotiate the cliff face in fifteen minutes, approach the pool and take Shavit as soon as he emerged from the water. He thought about it, but discounted it. He had no idea how many other people were in the villa. A place as large and opulent as that would certainly have staff, and perhaps Shavit had other guests. Ziggy had promised to hack the security system, and that, together with extended reconnaissance, would give Milton a much better idea of how many people were inside. There was no sense in moving too quickly and making a mistake. It would complicate things horribly to have the local police involved. The property was private and secluded, with high walls and security that would ensure that he and Bachman would be undisturbed when they confronted one another again. Milton did not want to spoil that by acting precipitously.

He took out the cell phone he had purchased in the city and called Ziggy.

"Well?"

"It'll be easy," Ziggy said. "It routes through a local home security firm. I just need to get into their server and I'll be able to see everything they can see."

"How long?"

"Ten minutes."

"Get to it."

"Are you doing it now?"

"Not yet. Tonight."

"What are you doing now?"

"Just keeping an eye on him."

* * *

THEY HAD DINNER together that night. Matilda found a restaurant down by the harbour in the Old Town and the three of them sat on the patio and dined on fish and stuffed calamari. The atmosphere was tense. Milton knew there was a difficult conversation to have, and the anticipation of it was heavy in the air. He had brought the waterproof kit bag that he had purchased earlier that afternoon. It was on the floor next to him, a visible reminder of what he was intending to do.

Milton was the last to finish his main course and he waited for the waiter to clear the table before he began.

"You need to get out of the city," he said to them both

when the man had disappeared into the kitchen. "Tonight."

"What are you going to do?" Matilda asked.

"I'm going to bring this whole mess to an end."

"The old man?"

"Tonight. I'll go and see him."

"See him?"

"He's the way to Bachman. He's the reason Bachman's going to come here. And he's the reason he's going to be off balance."

"And then? When he comes?"

He paused. "And then there won't be a problem any more." He didn't want to speak euphemistically, but he had no desire to describe what they all knew was going to be required if the problem was to be resolved.

"What's in the bag?"

"The things I need."

The waiter returned with the dessert menus. Milton asked for the check.

Matilda was fingering the stem of her wine glass. "How long will it take for Bachman to get here?"

"Depends where he is. If he's still in Australia, it'll take him a day."

"So we'll stay with you until tonight."

"No, Matty. It's too dangerous."

"You'll need help. You can't do it all on your own."

"I can," he said, thinking that he had done much worse.

She started to protest.

"What if it isn't a day?" Milton said "What if they've told him where I am? He could be on his way now. He might be here already." Matilda started to protest again, but Milton stalled her with a raised hand. "No arguments. I don't want you to be involved. Either of you. You should never have been involved in the first place. You need to go."

She started to retort, but bit her lip. Instead, she got

up, folded her napkin on the table and went into the restaurant.

"Ziggy," Milton said, "you have to make sure she leaves."

"I'll do my best."

"You need to do better than that. After I'm gone, you take her to the airport and get onto a plane with her. Promise me."

He looked down and exhaled. "All right. Okay. And then?"

"Get her back to Australia. This will be over one way or another."

"What if Bachman…"

Ziggy didn't finish, but Milton understood what he meant. "It won't come to that."

"I know, John, but what if it does? What if he's still out there and you're not? What happens then?"

"You're planning to disappear, right?"

He shrugged. "That was the plan."

"Make sure you do."

"But what about her? She's not going to want to do that, is she? She's going to go back to Australia and her brother."

Milton took a moment to answer. He had considered the consequences of failure. Would Bachman revenge himself on them, too, even if Milton was dead? He didn't know. The man was a psychopath. He was unpredictable. There was a chance he would consider the ledger still open. There was no profit in thinking about the possibility. There were no other ways to bring an end to what had happened.

That was the thing: he couldn't allow himself to fail.

He stood.

"Are you going?"

"It's easier." He reached down for the kit bag and rested it on his chair. "What we talked about earlier— that's ready to go?"

"You just need to send the email. It's all set up."

Milton collected the bag. "Thanks. You've been great. I wouldn't have been able to do this without your help."

Milton knew that Ziggy looked up to him, and he knew that his praise would mean something to him. He hoped it would cement the last piece of cooperation he needed from him. He needed him to get Matilda out of harm's way.

Ziggy smiled at Milton's gratitude. "You sure you don't need me to stick around?"

"I need you to make sure Matilda gets home. Tell her I'm sorry, about everything that happened. Will you do that, please?"

"Of course."

Milton slung the bag over his shoulder and put out his hand. Ziggy took it.

"Be careful," Milton said.

"And you."

Milton turned and made his way between the tables to the cobbled street that led down to the waterfront. He didn't turn back.

Chapter Fifty

THERE WERE over a thousand islands in the Adriatic within easy reach of Dubrovnik. Businesses gathered around the harbour offered tourists the opportunity to hire speedboats, sailing boats and yachts, some with skippers and others without, so that they could make excursions out to the beautiful and unspoilt beaches that were all within easy reach. Milton wanted a speedboat, although he had no interest in relaxation. He waited until it was just after midnight before scouting the jetties that accommodated the hire craft. He found a Maestral 599, a RIB that was a touch under six metres from aft to stern and powered by a Yamaha outboard motor. He waited until he was confident that the harbour was quiet, tossed the new rucksack down into it and then boarded the boat. He crouched down low and shuffled to the stern and the motor. He popped off the motor cover and dug out the quarter-inch nylon emergency starter rope with a small wooden handle at the end. He turned the valve on the fuel primer to the open position and squeezed the fuel primer three times so that he could hear the fuel squirting. He fixed the knot on the end of the starter rope into a notch on the flywheel and pulled. The engine caught. Milton reduced the revs a touch, cast off the mooring line, and then gave the engine enough revs to edge the boat out into open water.

Milton waited until he was beyond the fifteenth-century fortifications of the Old Town and the Porporela lighthouse and then opened the throttle all the way. The engine growled and then roared, and the Maestral picked up speed, bouncing across the gentle waves. He passed Lokrum, an island that could be reached with a vigorous swim from the city, and headed to the south. He ran dark, with no lights, and maintained a course that kept him around two hundred yards from the shoreline.

In twenty minutes, he was adjacent to the landmarks he remembered from his reconnaissance. The cliffs reached up sharply like crenulated battlements, the villa nestling within their embrace. Milton cut the engine and let the boat drift, bobbing up and down on the swell. The only sounds were the lapping of the water against the hull and, somewhere above, the crying of a gull. He collected the claw anchor from the bow of the boat and tossed it over the edge. The rope unspooled for ten seconds before it went taut.

Milton opened his waterproof rucksack and took out the equipment that he had purchased earlier. He found his binoculars and scanned the coastline. He followed the glow of a car's headlights as it traced the headland before disappearing into a copse of trees. He scanned along the cliffs, across inlets and outcrops of rock, and saw no one. Finally, he examined the villa. There were lights in the windows on all three levels. Milton studied them for five minutes until he was rewarded with a dark shadow that moved across a window on the top level. He was too distant to identify Meir Shavit, but he was prepared to assume that his target was home. Ziggy's investigation suggested that he lived alone. The two pieces of information were all that Milton needed to decide to put his plan into operation.

Milton undressed, folded his clothes and placed them in the bag, then pulled on the wetsuit and zipped it up. He took out one of his two scuba knives and fastened the scabbard around his right ankle. He put his boots in the sack and fastened it all the way around until it was watertight and then he slung it across his back. He put on his flippers, fitted the goggles over his eyes and put the attached snorkel into his mouth. He fastened a weight belt around his waist so that the natural buoyancy of the wetsuit might be neutralised, sat on the edge of the boat and rolled backwards into the water.

* * *

IT TOOK MILTON ten minutes to swim the two hundred feet to shore. The tide was treacherous, with an undertow that seemed determined to sweep him back to the boat and then out to sea. He stayed just below the surface, relying on the snorkel to breathe, and kicked hard until his thighs and buttocks burned.

He finally reached the shore, negotiating the cleft in the rocks so that he could swim past the natural breakwater and into the calmer water beyond. The stone had been fashioned into a smooth slab and the metal ladder that he had seen Shavit use before was fitted into it, descending down into the water. Milton reached up for it and anchored himself, then reached down and removed his flippers. He slid his left arm through the fin straps and the mask, leaving his right hand free to use the scuba knife should he need it, and then slowly pulled himself out of the water. He ascended another two rungs so that he could look over the lip and reconnoitre properly.

He saw two sun loungers, a folded parasol, and the stairs that led up to the first of the three terraces.

He climbed to the top of the ladder and hurried across the space until he was able to press up against the cliff face next to the stairs. He removed the goggles and snorkel, and put them and the fins into his rucksack.

He dug a prepaid cell phone and a balaclava out of the kit bag and left them on the stone. He took a length of paracord, knotted one end through the straps of the waterproof bag and the other around the end of the ladder. He took off the weight belt, put it into the bag with his flippers, fins and mask, and tossed it down into the water. The bag hit the water with a splash and, weighed down by the weight belt, it sank out of sight.

He activated the cell phone, navigated to email and found the draft that Ziggy had prepared earlier. There was no message, just a packet of code that he said would do what Milton had asked him to do.

He sent the email and put the phone back into his pack. He was shrugging it across his shoulders once again when all of the house's interior and exterior lights went out. One moment they were lit, and the next moment they were not. Milton had seen the motion detectors that were connected to big security lights, the CCTV cameras that studded the walls of the house, and knew that there would be a sophisticated alarm system that would summon the local police if it was activated. But the email had wakened a custom exploit that Ziggy had inserted into the programmable logic controllers of the local power company, creating a limited and very targeted blackout. Milton glanced over the water to the clutch of other villas that were perhaps half a mile away around the curve of the bay. They, too, had gone dark. No power meant no lights.

No power also meant no security.

Milton reached down for the scuba knife and released it from its scabbard, holding it in his right hand. He checked again that the way ahead was clear and, satisfied that it was, he turned out of cover and started quickly up the stairs.

* * *

MEIR SHAVIT was tidying up the kitchen when the lights went out. Everything died. The dishwasher stopped mid-cycle and the Internet radio, which had been tuned to Galei Zahal, the Israeli army's own station, went silent. He knew that something was wrong. He put down the cigar that he had been smoking and went to the window. Everything was dark. The lights that illuminated the balcony, the overhead lights above the stairs that led down to the terrace—they were all extinguished. He gazed across the sickle of the bay to the other properties and saw that they were dark, too. A power cut, then. It was odd.

He collected his stick and hobbled across the kitchen

to the door to the larder. He opened it. It was a walk-in space fitted with shelves on all sides. Bottles of wine and spirits were racked in the wall facing him. He kept his shotgun here, on the top shelf, and he stretched up and collected it. It was a Beretta 1301 Tactical, gas-operated and compact, perfect for home defence. He checked that a round was chambered and, the gun in his right hand and his stick in his left, he stepped out of the larder.

When he saw the man, it was already too late. He was dressed all in black, with a woollen balaclava on his head that showed his eyes and nothing else. A hand, fast and accurate, stabbed down for the barrel of the shotgun and grasped it, holding it pointed down to the floor. The motion was quick and forceful and, before Shavit could even try to respond to it, he had been struck on the side of the jaw by the man's opposite elbow. He dropped the gun, which the man deftly collected, and staggered to the side. He turned just as the man drew back his fist. The blow was powerful and accurate, landing flush on his jaw. Shavit dropped, unconscious before he even hit the floor.

Chapter Fifty-One

MILTON PUT the old man in a comfortable chair and waited until he came around. The kitchen was plush. The wooden floor was polished to a high sheen, and the units were white and impeccably clean. There was a big American-style refrigerator, a large range and pendant lights that were suspended from the ceiling on long cords. Everything was freshly painted and in perfect order.

Ziggy's hack had expired and now the lights had come back on again. The villas across the bay were alight again, too, the glimmers shining out across the water. Milton had changed out of his wetsuit and into his normal clothes, and then, once he had satisfied himself that the old man was still breathing, he had started to make his preparations. He had made sure that the alarm was functional, and that the motion detectors in the gardens were activated. He made his way around the room, checking the ways in and out. He tested the windows; they were secured with locks. He had entered through the large French doors. There was the door to the larder and a second door at the other end of the room. Milton opened it and glanced inside. It led to a flight of stairs that descended to the floor beneath this one. He would investigate it properly later. For now, he closed the door and, taking a wooden chair, propped the seat back beneath the handle to secure it.

There would be more to do, but that could wait.

The old man had started to stir.

Milton pulled up a second chair and positioned it directly opposite Shavit. He had the old man's shotgun laid across his lap.

Shavit's eyes flickered open, closed, and then opened again. He looked around calmly. He had experience; it was written in the lines on his face. Milton doubted that this was the first time he had faced down a man with a gun. If it was, the prospect did not appear to daunt him.

He reached up with his fingers and probed his chin. "Did you have to hit me quite so hard?"

"I'm sorry about that. Do you know who I am?"

"Of course I do, Mr. Milton."

"And you know I'm serious?"

"I'm too old and jaded to be frightened by threats. I know why you're here."

"I'm not threatening you. I just want to be sure that we understand each other. I'd rather not be here, but your friend hasn't given me an option."

"You're going to bring him here?"

"Yes."

"You're crazy."

"You're not the first person to say that."

"He'll kill you."

"Maybe. Maybe not."

Shavit paused, but, seeing the iron in Milton's eyes, decided that there was little point in antagonising him.

Milton took out a cell phone and dialled a number.

* * *

AVI BACHMAN and the Rabins landed in Melbourne. Keren Rabin had piloted the Cessna from Adelaide and they had made the short hop in two hours. They left the plane and made their way through the small airport building. Keren called a taxi while Bachman paced impatiently.

He had split the team into two units. Two agents had stayed behind at Broken Hill to keep Harry Douglas under surveillance. Malakhi had tried to persuade him that he should stay, too, and await further information on Milton's whereabouts, but he had dismissed the suggestion out of hand. He needed to be moving. He needed to be doing *something.* He had been furious that the advantage of recapturing Matilda Douglas had been squandered so easily, and he wanted to lead the search himself. Milton would be travelling with the girl. He wouldn't be able to disappear quite as easily as if he was on his own. He would make a mistake, and Bachman wanted to be there to make the most of it.

So they had followed Milton's steps. They had travelled to Adelaide first of all, chartering the Cessna and flying from Broken Hill. They had travelled to the house of the *sayan* who had captured Matilda. Hughes was distraught at the death of his partner. Bachman didn't care about that. He had failed. The thought had crossed his mind that he should just put a bullet into the man's head and put him out of his misery, but he had decided against it. He needed the agency behind him, if only until Milton was located again. There was no profit in killing the man, although he deserved it. It would just have been pandering to his anger. Better that he maintain his composure. He would be able to gratify his emotions later.

Malakhi had received an emailed report as they were driving away. Milton and the girl had been seen in Melbourne. Several law enforcement files had been intercepted and sent to them. The local police department were looking for a man who looked very much like Milton after a branch of a local bank had been robbed at gunpoint. A large amount of money had been stolen. The police had located the car the robbers had used to make their escape. There were several sets of fingerprints inside, but none of them had been identified. The police were making enquiries, but it was obvious from the reports that they had reached a dead end.

Bachman didn't need the prints to be matched to know who was responsible. He had scrolled through the information that Rabin had been sent, pausing on a still that had been taken from the bank's CCTV.

A man facing the counter, a pistol held in his right

hand.

It was Milton.

It wasn't difficult to know why Milton had done what he had done. Standard tactics. He had no money. Neither he nor the girl had cash, credit cards, or means of identification. Milton would not have wanted to stay in Australia, and he would have needed money to leave. This was the easiest way to acquire funds.

The question now was where had he gone? They had *sayanim* stationed at all of the obvious airports that served international destinations. It would not have been possible to leave the country that way without detection, and none of the agents had reported seeing anything. They had agents at the ports, too, and none of them had seen Milton or Matilda, either.

They had just stepped outside to find a car when Malakhi Rabin's cell phone sounded. He answered and handed the phone across to Bachman.

"It's him."

Bachman took the phone. He composed himself, staring out at the wide open green spaces of the airfield, and then put it to his ear.

"Milton," he said.

"We need to bring this to a close." His voice sounded distant.

"Then stop running."

"I have stopped."

"Where are you? I'll come right away."

"Croatia."

Bachman stopped, his mouth open and a sickening churn in his stomach.

"There's someone who wants to speak to you."

Bachman held his breath. There was a pause, with just the noise of static on the line, and then a second voice.

"Avi, I'm sorry."

"Meir?"

"I'm fine. He just got the jump on me."

"Are you okay?"

"Fine. My pride is hurt, that's all."

"It's not your fault."

"Don't worry about me. Don't—"

Shavit was cut off mid-sentence. Bachman gritted his teeth as he heard the old man's muffled protest before Milton spoke again.

"Avi?"

"How did you find him?"

"It doesn't matter."

"No, you're right. It doesn't. You're wasting your time. Do you think I care about him? You know how it is. No attachments. I don't care. You're getting sentimental. Do what you want to him—it won't make any difference."

"I don't believe you."

"I don't care what you think."

"I'm not going anywhere. Neither is your friend."

"He's not my friend."

"Come on, Avi."

"You think I'm crazy?"

"Who else have you got left, Avi? Lila is dead. You want me to kill him, too?"

Bachman tightened his grip on the phone. Malakhi Rabin was watching him anxiously. Bachman hated it. He felt his temper flicker.

"You've got three days to get here. I'll wait for you. If you don't come, I'll kill him and then I'll disappear."

"What about the girl? Is she going to disappear too?"

"Shut up, Avi. I'm sick of your threats. This is the last chance you get."

The call went dead.

Bachman took a moment to compose himself, but he couldn't. He flung the phone at the side of the terminal building, shattering it into pieces. He wheeled on Rabin, his fists clenched, and the agent raised his arms and took a step back. Bachman paused, turned away, closed his eyes, and waited until the threat of an eruption had passed. He turned back. Rabin was still there, a few feet away, cautious of coming too close.

"Are you ready to move?"

"Yes," he said. "Who? All of us?"

"You and your wife. The others stay. Someone needs to stay on the brother in case he's bluffing."

"Bluffing? Where are we going?"

"Croatia."

* * *

MILTON PUT the phone on the counter and opened the door to the larder. There was a narrow aperture at the top of the wall filled with glass bricks that, when it was light, would admit a little brightness.

"Stand up, please."

"You think Avi will stop because of me?"

"I know he won't. I don't want him to." Milton indicated the open door to the larder.

Shavit stood, a wince of pain flickering across his face.

"What is the point of this, then?"

"I want him to come to me."

Milton took the chair he had been sitting on and moved it into the larder for the old man. Then he shut the door. There was a key in the lock and he turned it, sealing Shavit inside. He checked the rest of the kitchen, ensuring that there were no ways in or out that he had missed and, then, finally, he poured himself a glass of water, went out to the balcony and sat down. He looked out at the dark mass of the cliffs, the jagged edges just visible in the dim light that bled up from the grounds of the villa, and then out into the deeper darkness that clung to the surface of the sea. The waves crashed against the rocks, in and out, and Milton allowed himself to close his eyes and relax. He knew that Bachman would be on his way. He didn't know where he was, but he knew where he would soon be.

He had laid a trap, with himself as bait. This would be

the last day he would be able to leave the house until the matter was settled, one way or another. He opened his eyes, took out his cigarettes and his lighter and put a cigarette to his lips. He lit the tip and inhaled, blowing the smoke into the night. Somewhere overhead, he heard the sound of a helicopter and then, with a suddenness that almost startled him, he saw its alternating lights as it clattered out from behind the headland and flew, low and fast, in the direction of Dubrovnik.

He finished the cigarette, flicked the butt over the edge of the balcony, and went inside. He closed and locked the balcony doors and started to go about his work.

Chapter Fifty-Two

THE FASTEST ROUTE back to Australia was to fly from Split. A coach ran from the Dubrovnik bus station, but they had just missed the last of the day. Instead, they bought tickets for the next to leave, departing at just after four the following morning. They had returned to their hotel to get a little sleep. Ziggy had wondered whether Matilda would make their rendezvous in reception at three thirty, but she was there. They returned to the station and boarded the coach. It was quiet, with just a handful of passengers aboard with them, and they had been able to take two seats each.

Matilda had been quiet ever since they had left the restaurant the previous evening, and her pensiveness continued during the journey. She had been angered by Milton's abrupt departure, and her anger had been deflected onto Ziggy when he had explained what had happened. Her initial reaction had been to refuse to leave the city. She said that she would find Milton, that it wasn't right to leave him alone. Ziggy, mindful of his promise, had persuaded her that all they would achieve by staying was to risk the success of whatever it was that Milton was planning. She pressed him for details and he had responded, honestly, that he did not know what Milton intended to do. He told her about the hack that he had prepared for him, but when she asked him for more, he had been unable to elaborate. The lack of information was deliberate. Milton had kept the precise details to himself because he knew that Matilda would insist upon being involved. The less Ziggy knew about what was about to happen, the less he could tell her and the safer she would be. It was sound thinking, but it didn't make for a particularly pleasant evening: she had railed at him for withholding information and, when he had convinced her that he really did know nothing, she had stopped talking to him.

She was asleep now, laid out across the seats with her head rested against her balled-up sweater. Ziggy looked through the window as they headed north, heading through the towns of Neum and Ploce. The dark sea was to their left, with the ghostly shapes of the islands of Otok Sipan and Mljet just visible against the dawn's light on the horizon.

* * *

MILTON SPENT two hours searching the house for anything that might be useful. He had the shotgun and plenty of ammunition, but there were no other weapons to be found. He located the burglar alarm, worked out how to isolate the motion detectors in the garden and activated them. He went from the ground floor to the top, checking that all the doors and windows were locked. Bachman was coming, he knew, and he wanted to make sure that he would not be able to mount an attack without him knowing about it first.

He found a roll of duct tape in a cleaning cupboard. He went back to the kitchen, opened the larder and marched Shavit outside again.

"Sit down, please," he said, pointing to a wooden dining chair.

The old man did as he was told. He saw the tape and realised what Milton was planning. He didn't need to be told what to do; he rested his arms on the armrests and positioned his ankles so that they were pressed up against the chair legs. Milton picked at the end of the tape and wrapped it around Shavit's wrists and ankles, then took the rest and spooled it around his midriff and the back of the chair. When he was done, the old man couldn't move.

"This isn't very comfortable," he said.

"Sorry about that."

"You're wasting your time."

"So you keep telling me. It's getting tedious."

"Just run. Give yourself a chance."

"Be quiet," Milton said.

"Put some distance between you and Avi. You know what's going to happen if you stay here. He'll kill you."

Milton sighed. He tore off a final strip of tape and stuck it over the man's mouth.

* * *

THEY ARRIVED at Split at a little after six in the morning. It would be a long trip back to Australia. The best route appeared to be to fly Qatar Airways to Doha, lay over there for five hours, and then continue on to Melbourne. The trip would take thirty hours, and the first flight out wasn't for another six.

They queued at the Croatia Airlines desk, but then, as they were the next to be called up, Matilda turned and walked away. Ziggy paused, caught between the clerk beckoning him to step forward and the need to follow Matilda. He turned, shrugged an apology, and hurried away to the seating area where Matilda was pacing back and forth.

"What's the matter?" he asked.

"I can't do this."

"What?"

"Leave. I can't."

"We have to leave. You heard what he said."

"I know what he said. But…" She paused. "Look, you know him better than I do, right?"

"Maybe."

"And you're okay with just leaving like this?"

"Milton knows what he's doing. And he can definitely look after himself."

"But you met Bachman."

Ziggy tried not to think about what had happened. "Milton knows what he's doing."

Matilda sat. "What if Bachman doesn't come alone?"

"Look, I don't like it, either." He sat, too. "But you think either of us would be able to help?"

"Maybe we could—"

He spoke quickly, cutting her off. "I thought I could help him, a long time ago. My leg, the reason I walk with this limp—that's what happened when I tried. It took me a long while to realise it. I'm not a hero. I'm not suited to it. And if we go back there, I can tell you what's going to happen. We're not going to help Milton. Not at all. We're going to get in the way. We're going to give him a distraction that he doesn't need, and we're going to make it more likely that we all get killed."

Her eyes, which had been bright and lively, lost their spark as he spoke. Her face drained of animation and, as he finished, her hopeful expression was replaced with disappointment.

"Come on," he protested. "You know this is the best way."

"I can't," she said and, before he could say anything else, she turned and walked back to the exit.

"Matilda!" he called.

She didn't turn back.

Once again, Ziggy was caught. He watched her as she pushed the doors that opened into the bright sunlight outside and knew that he should follow her. But then he remembered where following her would lead—and, more importantly, to *whom* it would lead—and he was frozen to the spot. She paused and, finally, looked back at him. She saw that he was not minded to follow and, without any change in the determined set of her expression, she turned away and walked out into the sunshine.

* * *

AVI BACHMAN and Malakhi and Keren Rabin landed at Split airport. They had flown on diplomatic passports, and Keren Rabin had carried her bags in a white sack that had been printed with diplomatic stamps. The sack was tightened with a drawstring and then secured with a padlock. They had each been scanned, but, thanks to the ersatz letter from the Israeli embassy in Canberra, the diplomatic bag had not been searched. They passed through immigration without incident and made their way into the busy arrivals lounge.

"We need to go south," Bachman said. "Dubrovnik."

The two of them exchanged a nervous glance, and Bachman could see that something had changed between them.

"What?"

"We're done."

"What do you mean?"

"Our instructions were to make sure you arrived here, but that's it."

"Your instructions? Instructions from whom?"

"From the director."

"You spoke to him? When?"

"Before we left Australia. He was very clear. You're on your own now."

"Has he thought about that? Has he thought it through? Has he forgotten what I can do with one fucking phone call?"

"That's not for us to say."

They backed away from him. He felt a blast of heat in his cheeks and he was gritting his teeth so tightly that his jaw started to ache. He closed his eyes and took a deep breath. When he opened them again, he was able to manage a bloodless smile.

"What are you going to do?"

"We've been recalled. We're flying back to Tel Aviv."

He nodded. He didn't need them. He didn't need anyone. He would do it alone.

He took the white diplomatic sack and turned away. He left them behind him without another word.

* * *

ZIGGY PENN was stuck in a slow-moving queue for security. He had already checked in. He had purchased a ticket to Seoul. It was a long flight, with a four-hour stopover at London Heathrow, but he had started to look forward to setting up a new life for himself in Korea. There would be opportunities for him there, chances to build something new without having to worry about the foolishness that he had allowed himself to slip into while he was in Japan.

He took his boarding pass from his pocket and ran his finger against the edge of the paper. He was excited by the possibilities of what he might now be able to do and, yet, there was something that was making him uncomfortable. There was an ache in his stomach. He knew what it was.

Milton.

He thought of what Matilda had said to him before she left to go back to the villa.

He had retorted that Milton could look after himself, and he could—so why did he feel so bad about leaving?

Milton had saved his life in New Orleans all that time ago. He had ignored strict protocol to locate him and then he had ensured that he received the medical attention he needed to save his life. Ziggy had worked with him again in an effort to repay the debt, and maybe he had done that. There had been the situation with the gangsters in Tokyo, and, again, Ziggy had reciprocated with the hack on the Mossad's systems that had led them all to this juncture. They were square. Milton had said so, and Ziggy agreed. He didn't owe him anything.

And yet... why did he feel like such a louse for leaving like this?

"Excuse me," said the traveller behind him. Ziggy

looked at the weary impatience on the man's face and then turned back to see the gap that had opened up between himself and the rest of the queue.

"I'm sorry," he said, and, instead of following the others towards the X-ray machine, he stepped out of line.

The man raised an eyebrow in surprise, but quickly hurried forward. The gap in the queue closed as the travellers jostled for position to present themselves to the ministrations of the machine and the indifferent attendants beyond it.

Ziggy turned his back on them and hurried to the exit.

Chapter Fifty-Three

ZIGGY HAD just missed the bus back to Dubrovnik. He could have waited for the next one, but that wouldn't depart for an hour and he wanted to find Matilda before then. There was a Hertz desk inside the terminal and he went back to hire a car, paying for the rental with one of his fake cards. Matilda had a head start of half an hour. The coach would travel at an average speed of fifty-five or sixty miles an hour and had several stops along the route. If he drove as fast as he dared, he should be able to catch it up before it reached its destination.

He hoped so.

* * *

AVI BACHMAN hired a car from the Hertz desk and set off for Dubrovnik. He drove carefully, below the speed limit. There was no rush. Milton was waiting for him. And haste would get him killed.

He glanced up in the rear-view mirror. A car was approaching recklessly fast. He tightened his grip on the wheel and watched. He was just outside the town of Slano, halfway between Split and Dubrovnik. It was a three-lane highway here: one lane either way, with a third that alternated between northbound and southbound traffic. This stretch of the road offered southbound traffic only on the single carriageway, with two lanes heading north. There was a reasonable number of cars and trucks proceeding in both directions.

The car was an SUV. It closed up to within twenty feet. Bachman looked in the mirror, frowned, and checked for a second time. His face broke into a grin of surprise as he realised that he knew the driver. The SUV swerved out from behind him and passed, just barely merging into the correct lane again before a big eighteen-wheel rig thundered by, its air horn blaring in annoyance.

Ziggy Penn.

What?

Bachman remembered him from New Orleans. He had kidnapped him during Mardi Gras and used him to lure Milton out to the abandoned amusement park where he had meant to kill him. They had spent long enough together for Bachman to extract the information he needed to understand his role in that unfortunate situation, and, now that he saw him again, he was able to make an educated guess as to what had happened to Victor Blum's support. Penn was a hacker.

Bachman had been sure that Milton would send him and the girl away.

What was he doing still here?

Penn and the girl were distractions. They could easily become leverage.

Bachman had dropped the white diplomatic sack onto the passenger seat next to him. He reached over, driving with one hand as he used the other to unfasten the padlock and draw open the mouth of the sack. Inside it was a Glock 9mm and a box of ammunition. He put the pistol on the seat and covered it with the bag.

He looked ahead again. Penn was accelerating away from him. The road was open, the traffic a little more sparse, and Bachman slowly increased the pressure on the gas and picked up speed himself. He would stay a quarter of a mile back. He didn't need to be closer.

He knew where Penn was going.

* * *

ZIGGY PULLED over before the bus turned into the station and waited. It was busier than when they had taken it earlier, and he watched a dozen people disembark before he saw Matilda get off. She paused on the pavement, looking left and right, a little perplexed. She was looking for a taxi. He put the car into gear and drove ahead slowly until he was close enough to wind down the window and call out.

She turned. He realised, as soon as he spoke, that a sudden address like that might frighten her, especially given the circumstances, but the alarm on her face evaporated quickly as she recognised him.

"Shit," she said. "You made me jump."

"Sorry."

"I thought you were leaving?"

"Changed my mind," he said. "You were right. I just missed you at the station, so I drove."

She came closer to the car. "You don't have to be here. You didn't want to."

"I know I don't, and I didn't. And, for the record, I still think it's crazy. I still think Milton can look after himself."

"So?"

"So maybe you're right. I can't just leave like this."

She nodded. "You know the stupid thing? I've been doubting myself the whole way. I don't even know where the villa is. I only realised when I was on the bus. I was just going to ask around."

"Have you called him?"

"I don't have his address or his number," she said. "Have you?"

"I thought about it, but I know what he'll say."

"That we shouldn't come."

Ziggy nodded. "We might as well just go to the villa. We can talk to him there. Get in. I'll drive you."

* * *

MILTON WAS watching the front of the house when the security lights at the end of the drive flicked on. He saw the car turn off the road, heard the crunch of the gravel as it rolled towards the villa. He took his binoculars and focused on the car.

Two people.

He gritted his teeth in frustration.

Matilda and Ziggy.

He had told them to leave. He had been very clear about it. He didn't want them here. He didn't *need* them here. They would make things much more complicated.

He turned back to the room. Shavit was asleep in his chair, the duct tape still secure around his wrists and ankles.

Milton stayed at the window, standing to the side so that he presented the smallest possible target should Bachman be out there with a long gun. He stared out into the darkness beyond the car. There was an outside chance that they were being followed, but the approach was much too dense and gloomy for Milton to be able to see if anyone was sheltering within the margin of the trees. The car stopped next to the Jaguar and Range Rover that had been there before.

Nothing happened. The two of them stayed in the car. It was below Milton now, and the angle made it impossible for him to see in through the windshield, but there was no movement.

And then the doors opened.

Ziggy came out of the driver's door first. Milton was looking down on him and he couldn't see his face. He could see, though, that something was amiss. Ziggy stayed close to the car, looking back inside. His body language was wrong, too. Defensive. Unsettled.

The passenger's door opened and, at the same time, the door behind it.

Milton felt sick.

Matilda got out.

Avi Bachman stepped out behind her.

He had a pistol in his right hand. It was pointed at

Matilda and, as she hesitated, he came close to her and pressed it into the small of her back.

Bachman put a hand on Matilda's shoulder and drew her back so that he could look up at the house.

"Milton!" he called.

Milton gritted his teeth in frustration.

"Milton! I know you're in there."

Bachman moved Ziggy around the car so that the three of them were closer together. He stood behind them both, using them as a shield.

He clenched his fist and drummed it against his thigh.

"You have a problem?" Shavit said. Milton had removed the tape and now he wished he hadn't. There was a mocking tone to the old man's voice.

"Be quiet."

Milton hurried over and collected the shotgun from where he had propped it against his chair.

"Avi is too good for you. I told you."

"And I told you to be quiet. Don't make me tell you again."

"Or what? You'll shoot me? I don't think so, Mr. Milton. You need me."

He went back to the window, flicked the latch and pushed it open.

"I'm here, Bachman," he called down.

"My friend?"

"He's fine."

Milton looked down. The security floodlights lit up the area with the parked cars. Matilda and Ziggy were both looking up at him, their faces pale with fright.

"Let me talk to him."

Milton stepped back and looked at Shavit.

"Kill them and go, Avi!" the old man shouted, his voice an angry rasp. "Don't worry about me."

Milton went over to Shavit, reversed the shotgun and drilled the butt into his unprotected gut. Shavit gasped and wheezed as the air was punched out of his lungs.

* * *

AVI BACHMAN led them around the side of the house. His left hand grasped the girl around the shoulder to keep her close. The pistol in his right hand was pressed tight against her spine.

He had watched as Ziggy Penn had collected Matilda Douglas at the bus station. He had followed them as they drove out of town and forced them off the road when the moment presented itself.

He had them both now.

Penn would have been a good enough prize, but the girl was a bonus. He thought about her. Milton and Matilda had been travelling together when the Rabins had picked him up. What was she? Was she significant to him? Milton denied it, but Bachman didn't believe him. There was something between them. A vulnerability that he would be able to exploit.

"Keep walking," he said in a calm, quiet voice. "Around the back."

Penn was frightened. Bachman could see it in the way that his hands were trembling. It wasn't an unreasonable reaction. Penn knew what Bachman was capable of doing. The girl had more about her. She had held his eye with a steady glare when he had stepped out of his car with the pistol raised, but she was scared, too.

They were right to be scared. He would kill them both before the night was out.

They skirted the edge of the house and reached the grounds at the rear. They were now on the second terrace. There was one above that and one below. He could hear the waves crashing against the rock face and he could taste the salt on his tongue. He removed his hand from the girl's shoulder and angled her to her right, pointing her toward the stone stairs that led to the terrace above them, and, eventually, to the balcony and the French doors that would open into the kitchen.

Bachman told Penn to go first while he and the girl trailed behind, his gun held in a relaxed and comfortable grip.

Chapter Fifty-Four

MILTON HAD OPENED the door so that Bachman, Ziggy and Matilda could come inside. Ziggy entered first, a look of bloodless terror on his face. Matilda followed, her own face written over with anger and a warning in her eyes. Bachman came through the door last of all.

Milton quickly placed everything, fixing the five of them according to their positions in the room. He was at the rear, his back to the front of the house, facing them and the balcony and then the sea beyond. Five feet away from him and to his left, sitting in the armchair with his back to the wall, was Shavit. Milton held the old man's shotgun in a loose, comfortable grip, aiming it squarely at the old man. Milton was so close that he couldn't possibly miss. Between Shavit and the opposite side of the room was Ziggy, and just behind him was Matilda. Bachman was behind them, covering them both with his pistol.

"Hello, John," Bachman said.

"Avi."

Milton smiled. "On your own?"

"What do you mean?"

"No Mossad backup tonight?"

Bachman chuckled. "Ah, yes. That's right. That was a clever trick. Did you see Victor Blum?"

"I did."

"How did you do it?"

"You have information he thinks could be damaging to the agency. I do, too. And mine is more damaging than yours."

Bachman nodded at Ziggy. "Your friend here is very clever."

"He is, but none of that really matters, does it? I thought it would be better just the two of us."

"But it's not just us, is it? You have my friend, I have yours."

"I'll trade him for them."

"Shoot him, Avi," the old man said.

"Be quiet." Milton kept the shotgun levelled, but he didn't take his eyes from Bachman.

"Looks like we have a stand-off, John."

"Maybe."

"What are we going to do about it?"

"I know there's no point in talking to you."

Bachman shook his head. "I think we're past talking, John."

"So do I."

Bachman took a step forward so that he was closer to Ziggy. He shoved him in the back and Ziggy stumbled ahead, limping on his bad leg.

Bachman pointed the gun away from Matilda and aimed it at Ziggy.

"There are too many of us here. I've got her," he said, nodding at Matilda, "and she means more to you. I don't need both of them. Easier if there's just the four of us."

"Avi—"

Milton saw his arm stiffen as he prepared to fire.

* * *

MATILDA FELT the absence of the pressure that had been between her shoulder blades. She could still feel the malign presence of Avi Bachman behind her, but the gun was gone. She watched Milton's face.

She turned her head. Ziggy stumbled ahead of her. Bachman had pushed him. She caught the flash of movement in the corner of her eye.

"Easier if there's just the four of us."

Milton's face changed. Impassiveness to fear.

Bachman stepped up. She could see his arm. She could see the pistol. It was aimed at Ziggy.

Milton took a step ahead. "Avi—"

Matilda launched herself to the side, clattering into Bachman. She caught his wrist with her right hand and tried to force it out of the way.

The gun fired.

* * *

THE PISTOL was suppressed, but the pop of the gun was still horribly loud. Matilda had ruined Bachman's aim and, instead of the head shot he had planned, the bullet went low and caught Ziggy in the back of the knee. It was his bad leg, the left. He yelped in sudden pain as the leg collapsed and he toppled to the floor.

Matilda had her right hand around Bachman's wrist and she reached around with her left to claw for his face. Her nails found the fleshy part of his cheek and gouged down, three red stripes that immediately welled with blood. The blast of pain loosened his grip on the pistol and, as he reflexively reached up to protect his face, he dropped it. Matilda grabbed onto him, reaching for his eyes this time. Bachman had been unseated by the surprise of it the first time, but now he was ready. She had no chance. He instinctively planted his foot to correct his balance, ducked his shoulder into her body, and shrugged her away.

Milton didn't have a clean shot. The shotgun spread would hit Ziggy and Matilda. He would kill them both.

Bachman pushed Matilda away and, taking advantage of the gap that had opened up between them, he lashed out, striking her in the side of the head. She staggered into the kitchen counter, shattering a small glass bowl as she fell to the floor, unconscious.

Still in the line of fire.

Milton couldn't shoot.

The effort of striking her had temporarily unbalanced Bachman.

Milton took advantage.

He charged.

* * *

ZIGGY PENN heard someone screaming, terribly loud, and wondered who it was—until he realised that it was him. It felt as if someone had slid a red-hot poker into his knee, the burning point probing and prodding into the ligaments, scorching soft flesh, rubbing up against bone. He blinked furiously, trying to clear the curtain of white from his vision, and, when he was able to see again, he saw Matilda on the floor. She was lying on her side, close enough for him to reach out and touch, her eyes closed and a vivid purple welt discolouring her temple.

The pain crescendoed and darkness welled up, threatening to wash over him. It was all he could do to lift his head. He saw Milton vault over him, tackling Bachman around the waist and driving him backwards. The pair of them, locked together, stumbled across the room and, as they lost their balance and started to fall, Milton pushed again and propelled both of them through the wide French doors, onto the balcony and into the night beyond.

Ziggy's strength abandoned him and he faded into unconsciousness.

Chapter Fifty-Five

BACHMAN STUMBLED over the step that led down to the balcony beyond. Milton's arms were still wrapped around his waist and he followed him outside, driving him all the way across the space to the glass parapet that guarded the drop to the terrace below. They crashed against the glass and Milton pushed harder, the sudden boost to their momentum sending them both over the chrome rail and into the drop beyond.

It was a fall of six feet to the stone terrace. Bachman struck the ground first. Milton was atop him and he managed to bring up his elbow in the moments before impact, pressing it so that the point buried itself into Bachman's gut. The impact drove the air from his lungs and winded him.

Milton was not dislodged by their landing. He reached up, put his fingers around Bachman's neck and squeezed. He tried to wriggle into a better position, a little higher so that he could press down on Bachman's larynx, but Bachman was too strong. Milton tried to manoeuvre his legs so that he could pin Bachman's legs against his torso, but, before he could, Bachman broke free with his right and crashed his closed fist into Milton's nose and mouth. Milton held on, tried to push down harder, but Bachman punched harder and harder. Blood poured from Milton's nose and from a fresh laceration where his upper lip had been driven into his teeth.

Milton released his grip, rolled off and scrambled to his feet. He hopped back, opening up a little space between the two of them, and spat a mouthful of blood onto the ground. Bachman gasped for breath. Glass from the broken windowpane from the balcony above had scattered across the terrace, and a shard the size of a quarter had lodged itself in his cheek. He reached up and, looking straight at Milton, pulled it out. Blood immediately poured out of the cleft that was left behind, running down his chin and dripping onto his shoulder. Bachman didn't take his eyes off Milton as he tossed the glass aside.

Milton's breath was ragged, and his nose and lip stung, but he took the opportunity to assess his surroundings. The terrace was made of stone and surrounded by a glass parapet that was twenty feet behind Bachman. To the left, a flight of stone steps descended to a second terrace and, as Milton recalled from his journey up the cliff, that terrace was joined by a second stair to a final terrace where Meir Shavit was able to access the natural plunge pool. Milton heard the crash of waves on the cliffs below. The parapet that penned in this terrace guarded a drop of fifty or sixty feet to the surface of the sea. The darkness of the sky on the horizon was demarked by the deep blue of the sea and, in that moment, Milton knew what he was going to have to do.

"Come on, Avi," Milton said. "You can do better than that."

Bachman reached up to his face and dabbed his fingers against the open wound, which was still bleeding freely. He held his hand before him and glanced down at the daubs of red. He looked back up at Milton and smiled. "Look at us."

"It didn't have to be like this."

"You're out of your depth, John, and you know it."

"Stop talking. Do what you need to do."

* * *

MATILDA CAME AROUND on the floor of the kitchen. It took her a moment to remember where she was and how she had come to be there. The whole right-hand side of her face throbbed and it came back to her: Bachman had knocked her out.

She was lying face down, and the tile was cold against her cheek. She placed her palms on either side of her shoulders and pushed, raising her head to look around.

Ziggy was on the floor an arm's length away from her. He wasn't moving. She dragged herself across to him, turning him over so that she could look down into his face. His mouth gaped open and, for a moment, she thought that he was dead. She ducked her head so that her face was just above his and felt his breath on her skin. He coughed, and then coughed again, but he did not awake. She pushed herself onto her knees and, fighting a buffeting wave of dizziness, she looked down at the wound in his leg. Blood had soaked into the beige fabric of his cargo pants and she saw the tiny hole in the material, perfectly smooth around the edges, where the bullet had struck.

She heard voices and looked up. The French doors that opened out onto the balcony had been badly damaged; one of the large panes was missing from the frame and fragments of glass were scattered all around.

The voices were coming from outside.

She looked back into the room. The old man, Shavit, was still taped to the chair. He was struggling with the bonds, unable to free himself.

He looked at her. "Get me out of here. I can help."

She shook her head to clear the wooziness.

"They'll kill each other. I can stop them."

Shavit wasn't going anywhere, and, although Ziggy needed help, she knew that Milton needed it more urgently.

The shotgun Milton had been holding had been dropped on the floor.

She picked it up. She had fired shotguns before and was confident that she would be able to use this one if the moment required it. She held it carefully, aimed down, and hurried out onto the balcony.

* * *

MILTON SETTLED into a defensive posture, his arms raised vertically on either side of his face and his head ducked down between them, presenting as small a target as possible. He knew he was outmatched. He always had been. Bachman was a machine and there was not even the slightest possibility that Milton would be able to defeat him one-on-one like this. But Milton had survived for a long time in a business where longevity was rare. He was resourceful, he was ruthless, and he was not afraid to change the environment and circumstances of an encounter if it improved his odds of walking away.

Bachman, his face a bloody mask, took a step toward him, his fists clenching and unclenching. He pivoted on his left leg and sent out a right-footed kick that Milton deflected by dropping his left arm, absorbing the jarring impact against his triceps. Bachman closed, firing out a left fist and then a right. Milton blocked the first punch with his right forearm, but he was too slow to raise his left arm after defending against Bachman's kick, and the second punch connected with his cheekbone. The blow did not look as if it was thrown with much force, but it was deceptive. Krav Maga was a fearsomely efficient fighting style, and Bachman's mastery of it meant that he was able to deliver powerful blows with minimal backswing. Bachman's knuckles cracked into Milton's face and a blaze of pain spasmed all the way down his neck.

He brought up his guard and opened and closed his mouth as he probed whether his cheekbone had been broken. Perhaps. It was too painful to be sure.

"Come on, John. This is too easy."

Milton fired out a combination that Bachman blocked with ease. He hadn't intended to strike him, just to distract his attention from what he really wanted to achieve. And it worked. Bachman mirrored Milton as he started to circle away from him, the two maintaining the same distance between each other as Milton moved around. He fired in another combination, two left hands around a harder right, and Bachman brushed them away again. Milton moved around again. Bachman followed. By the time Milton was finished, their positions had been reversed. Now he was facing the villa, his back to the parapet. Bachman was facing out to sea.

Milton started to back away.

"This is it, John."

Milton kept going, one step at a time, closing on the parapet, Bachman following.

"You ready?"

Milton lowered his guard and gestured for Bachman to come on.

He rushed him.

* * *

MATILDA LOOKED down from the balcony.

She saw that Milton's back was up against the parapet that guarded the steep drop to the surface of the ocean at the foot of the cliffs below.

Avi Bachman was facing him.

They were both bloodied. Bachman seemed to have been wounded in the side of his face, crimson slipping down the side of his neck and beneath the collar of his shirt. Milton was bleeding from the nose and mouth. He was favouring one side of his body.

Neither had seen her.

The two men closed. Bachman's fists lashed out, a right and then a left. Milton blocked the first with his arms, but not the second; it thudded into his ribs, jackknifing him over the impact, the sound of his breath audible as it was punched out of his lungs.

He stumbled farther back.

Bachman was relentless. He followed Milton, firing out two jabs that both found their mark. Milton tripped, falling backwards, putting out his right arm to support himself.

Bachman kept coming on.

It was hopeless. Milton had no chance against him.

She heard Milton shout something. Bachman responded with a braying laugh.

She had to do something. She raised the shotgun and started for the steps that led down to the terrace, taking them quickly and turning the corner so that she could see them both. The terrace was wide and the combatants were on the opposite side to her. Bachman's position had changed a little; he was still facing away from her, but he had moved a few steps to the left so that he was closer to being side on.

Milton saw her.

"No!" he yelled.

Bachman turned, just enough to catch her in his peripheral vision, but not enough to allow Milton an opening.

Matilda levelled the shotgun. She knew that they were too close together. If she fired, Milton would take just as much of the spread as Bachman. She would kill them both.

She took a step.

"Stay back, Matty," Milton called.

She stopped.

"This is me and him. You need to get away from here."

"It doesn't matter what she does," Bachman said.

"You've got to go now," Milton urged.

"I'll find her if she runs. I want you to know, John—you're first, but she's next."

Matilda's hands were shaking.

She raised the shotgun and slid her finger inside the trigger guard.

Chapter Fifty-Six

JOHN MILTON had done an excellent job of securing Meir Shavit to the chair. He had originally wound the tape around his wrists and ankles, lashing him to the armrests and the legs. There was no play in the bonds and, when Shavit complained that he had lost the sensation in his fingers, Milton had rearranged him. Now, his wrists were bound together, but his arms were otherwise free. He was secured to the chair by the tape that remained around his ankles and the chair legs. Another long span of tape had been unspooled around his chest and the slats of the chair. He could touch the tape around his chest with his fingers, but there was no way he would be able to work it free.

Shavit looked down. The man Avi had shot was still out cold. The girl had checked that he was still breathing and then she had left, following Milton and Avi through the broken doors.

There was a pistol on the floor next to the balcony. Avi's Glock. He must have dropped it when Milton charged him.

He looked at the shattered bowl. It had belonged to his mother. She had inherited it from her mother. It had been left behind when the Nazis took her to the camps, but she had managed to find it again when she had been rescued. It was one of his most precious possessions and, in any other circumstance, its loss would have filled him with sadness.

Now, though, it presented him with something else.

An opportunity.

He had very limited movement, but maybe it would be enough. He started to swing left and right. The chair started to move, slowly at first, and then more noticeably. The legs to the right started to shuffle and scrape across the tiles and then, as he worked harder, they rose up off the floor altogether. Gravity pulled the chair back down onto all four legs the first two times, but Shavit was encouraged and redoubled his efforts.

His momentum raised the legs from the floor a third time. They clattered back down again.

He tried once more, grunting with the effort as he tried to transfer all of his weight to his left, straining against the tape that held him to the chair.

The chair swung to the left, teetered there on the remaining legs, and then toppled over.

He tried to stiffen his neck to absorb the impact that he knew was coming, but he was only partially successful. His left temple bounced against the cold tile and he felt a sudden gust of dizziness that he thought was going to be beyond his capacity to master. The impact slammed his teeth down on his tongue and it was the coppery taste of the blood in his mouth that he focused upon. He anchored on it, squeezing his eyes shut so that he could see starbursts of light against his lids and then, when the moment had passed, he opened them.

He was on his side, still secured to the chair. The shards of the glass bowl were inches away from his face. He reached up with his bound hands, his fingers latching onto one of the larger pieces and twisting until he could wield the sharper, jagged edge. He turned it around again so that the sharper edge was pointed backwards, towards his chest, and used it to start to rip through the tape.

* * *

MILTON GLANCED at Matilda.

Enough.

It had to be now.

He spat out a mouthful of crimson blood. "Avi."

Bachman turned back to him.

"You got any more?"

359

Bachman ducked his head and bull rushed him. Milton started to fall back, but didn't try to evade him. Bachman wrapped his arms around Milton's waist, put his shoulder down and tried to force him to the ground. Milton pressed up until his thighs burned, desperate to stay on his feet, knowing that he was dead if he fell. Bachman pushed down and Milton pulled up, and they stumbled back toward the parapet.

Milton reached down and locked his arms around Bachman's chest.

Bachman guessed what he was doing and redoubled his efforts to force him down onto the ground. He hammered blows onto Milton's torso, pummelling his kidneys, each blow triggering fierce jolts of pain, but Milton did not let go and he did not go down.

Bachman changed tactics, reaching for Milton's legs and trying to trip him.

Milton held on and yanked Bachman up, with a sudden surge of strength that allowed him to lift him off his feet.

Milton staggered another step towards the parapet.

Bachman reached down, pressed his face against Milton's thigh and bit down as hard as he could.

The pain was intense, but it helped. Milton found the strength for one last heave.

The rail of the parapet bumped into his body, against his buttocks and just below his waist, and, with Bachman still held aloft, Milton allowed himself to fold over it.

His feet left the surface of the terrace as he overbalanced, quickly flipping upside down. His shoulders dropped violently and the terrace disappeared as he tumbled to the clashing water below.

* * *

MATILDA WATCHED in horror. Milton had grabbed Bachman around the waist and, with a loud groan of exertion, he pulled up so that Bachman was briefly upside down. Milton stepped back and overbalanced across the guard rail. They both toppled over the parapet and fell out of sight.

She ran the remaining distance to the parapet. She thought she heard a splash, but, as she reached the parapet and looked down, there was no sign of either man. The tide was pummelling the rocks, white froth and spume blasting up, but that was it.

She couldn't see either of them.

* * *

MEIR SHAVIT picked up Avi's Glock and hobbled across the balcony.

He saw the girl with his shotgun.

He saw Avi facing away from him.

He saw John Milton.

Milton had grabbed Avi around the waist and was dragging him back toward the parapet.

Avi didn't know what Milton was doing and hadn't realised the danger he was in. Shavit understood, but there was nothing that he could do to prevent it.

He tried to take aim with the pistol, but Avi was in the way. He didn't have a shot.

Milton gave a big heave. Avi's feet left the ground as he was turned upside down.

Milton overbalanced.

Both men fell over the parapet and disappeared from view. Shavit knew that the drop was fifty feet to the surface of the sea, and the tide there was strong. Too strong for them to swim clear, and that was in the event that they survived the plunge.

He felt hot tears sting his eyes.

He turned, stumbled down the stone steps and, holding the gun out in front of him, approached the girl.

* * *

"DROP THE SHOTGUN!"

The old man was standing at the foot of the steps. He was carrying a pistol and, as Matilda turned to face him, he brought it around and aimed it at her.

"Drop it!" he barked again.

She did as she was told. It would be impossible for him to miss from this close. He held the pistol in a firm two-handed grip and started to walk down the platform to her.

"You killed him."

She could see the tremor of emotion that passed across the old man's wrinkled face: distress and, immediately afterwards, fury. He brought the pistol up a little and walked on, stopping at the parapet. He looked down into the water, just a quick glance. When he turned back again, his face was set into a pitiless mask. She had no doubt that he was going to pull the trigger.

Matilda knew that she was about to die.

She closed her eyes.

There was a loud report, a *crack* that came out of the darkness.

Matilda didn't feel anything.

No pain.

She heard a heavy thud.

She opened her eyes, confused, and saw the body of the old man on the ground. He was face down. Blood was pooling around his head.

She turned. A woman was advancing toward her, holding a pistol steadily with two hands. She saw movement on the balcony and looked up to see another figure looking down at her. A man. She couldn't make out his features in the poor light.

She kept her hands aloft. "Don't shoot."

The woman advanced. Matilda recognised her. It was the woman she had first met on the road outside Broken Hill. Keren Rabin. The man on the balcony descended the stairs and joined her. Malakhi Rabin.

"Bachman?" the woman asked her.

"Dead."

"Milton?"

"The same. They went over the edge."

The man reached the parapet. He kept his weapon on her and glanced down. Matilda looked at him, then at the body of the dead man, and then at the water. Should she jump? Was that her best chance now? Would it afford her an opportunity to get away?

Keren Rabin shared a look with her husband. Something was exchanged, an agreement made.

"I'm sorry about this," she said as she took aim at Matilda's head. "You've been very unlucky."

There was nothing in Rabin's face that suggested empathy. There would be no reprieve. She straightened her arm. Matilda stared into the little inky spot of the muzzle and then closed her eyes.

"Wait!"

She opened her eyes. It was Ziggy.

"Put the gun down."

Malakhi Rabin turned and aimed his pistol back up the steps. Ziggy was at the parapet, his left hand held up before him. His face was bloodless and, as he moved closer, pain distorted his expression.

"Shooting her isn't the right move."

"So maybe we'll shoot you, too."

Ziggy was unarmed. "I wouldn't do that." He started to descend the stairs. "I'm the one who broke into your servers. Took all of your data. And I'm Milton's fallback." Matilda didn't know what that meant, but she registered the flicker of concern that passed across Keren's face. "Milton's no fool. He knew you'd come after us. And I'm no fool, either."

He reached the bottom of the steps and turned so that Matilda could see him fully. He was walking with the stick that the old man had used. His trouser leg looked as if it was sopping with blood. His face was covered with sweat. It looked like he might throw up.

"The information you want isn't even in this country. It's on several servers, in places you'll never find it. I need to check in every six hours or the next thing that'll happen is an email triggers. All the newspapers, TV stations and Internet sites I could think of—they'll get it all. The Mossad's secrets will be broadcast to the world. It'll make WikiLeaks look like a minor diplomatic disagreement."

"You're bluffing."

"Am I? I know Blum has a reputation for gambling. Milton told me. But we both know that he won't gamble on this. So put the guns down, please. We all know you're not going to use them."

The agents exchanged another glance, but did not speak.

Ziggy shuffled, putting a little too much weight on his injured leg, and he winced. He walked away from Malakhi, passed Keren and came to Matilda's side. "Come on," he said quietly, and tugged at her wrist.

She walked. The sensation was weird, as if she was out of her own body. The agents kept their weapons raised, but, as they approached, they stepped apart so that Ziggy and Matilda could pass between them and onto the decked area.

"You're a lucky man," Keren said. "Bachman was an agent, once. And the old man was a soldier, too, a hero, and they're both dead because of you. We won't forget that."

Ziggy swallowed, and Matilda saw his larynx bobbing. He had put on a good show, but she could see how frightened he was. She was frightened, too. She reached out and took his hand.

"You're going to have to help me," he said. "I think I'm going to faint."

She braced him with her arm and he leaned in.

"Where's Milton?" he said groggily.

She bit her lip.

He turned to look at her.

"I think he's dead."

"How?"

"Went over the side with Bachman," she said.

"Did you see him in the water?"

"No, neither of them. And that's a long drop."

They continued through the grounds of the villa, neither of them speaking. Matilda felt an itching sensation between her shoulder blades, as if the agents behind them were aiming their weapons at her, but there was no gunfire and no attempt to stop them. Ziggy grunted with the effort of walking. She braced his weight again and kept them both moving.

Eventually, as they passed around the house and made their way into the gardens at the front, Ziggy broke the silence.

"Come on," he said. "It's Milton."

Matilda shook her head once, wordlessly, and Ziggy looked down at the ground and closed his eyes.

There was no point in pretending otherwise.

Milton was dead.

Chapter Fifty-Seven

MILTON HIT the water and plunged beneath the surface. His momentum was slowly arrested and, as he opened his eyes, he looked, but could not find Bachman. There were lights up on the stone platform, but he was several metres down by now and the illumination they cast beneath the water was minimal. He swivelled left and right, and saw nothing. He had to find him.

He felt a disturbance in the water above him.

He looked up. Another man was an arm's length above him and to the right, closer to the shelf of rock that curved away to demark the edge of the plunge pool. The man was struggling to the surface, his legs kicking without rhythm, desperate and frantic.

Bachman.

Milton kicked his legs and stroked up, quickly closing the distance between them.

They both broke the surface at the same moment.

Bachman gasped for air and reached for the first rung of the ladder.

Milton kicked harder.

Bachman was too far from the ladder and his desperate hand fell short.

Milton's fingers fastened around Bachman's collar. He pulled himself closer, wrapped his right arm across Bachman's right shoulder and his left arm around his waist, cinching his fingers together at a point just above Bachman's sternum.

He pulled.

Bachman struggled.

The waves pushed them up against the rocks. Milton planted his feet and pushed them away, into the middle of the pool.

Bachman tried to prise Milton's fingers apart.

Milton held on. He inhaled as deeply as he could and then yanked back as hard as he could, pulling them both beneath the surface.

They were upside down. Bachman thrashed. Milton kicked, sending them farther down.

It was disorientating: their heads pointed to the bottom and their feet to the surface. Bachman's arms and shoulders filled with a desperate surge of prodigious strength that was almost too much for Milton to withstand. His grip loosened just as Bachman's first surge of strength waned, and he was able to lock his fingers again. They bumped together, Milton's chest pressed up against Bachman's back, and Milton scissored his legs around Bachman's legs and locked them at the ankle.

Bachman found the strength for another attempt to break free. He jabbed the back of his head into Milton's face, but Milton was not about to relinquish his grip. He butted him again, and again, but Milton held on. His shoulders bumped up against the rocky floor of the pool and he squeezed tighter. Bachman turned his head so that Milton could see his face. He saw hatred in his eyes, and panic, the knowledge of impending death.

Milton squeezed tighter, Bachman's mouth fell open and he gulped down a lungful of water.

Milton held on.

Bachman's body bucked once, twice, a third time, and then, finally, it was still.

* * *

MILTON GRABBED the lifeless body by the shoulders and kicked up. He broke the surface flush against the rocks, obscured from the villa above by the modest overhang. The sound of the waves crashing against the outcrop was loud and initially confusing after the eerie silence of their struggle beneath the water. There were a series of natural handholds, and Milton used them, one at a time, to shimmy across to the ladder. He reached for the rope, snagged it, and pulled up the waterproof bag. He untied it and then looped the free end of the rope around Bachman's waist, anchoring him to the ladder until he had prepared himself.

He took out his flippers and put them on, one at a time. He collected his mask, washed it out, and put it over his face with the snorkel close to his mouth. He would have liked to have his wetsuit, but the water was reasonably warm and he didn't have too far to swim. He was less buoyant without it, though, and didn't need his weight belt to keep him below the surface. That was good, because he had another use for that. He removed it from the bag, took a deep breath, and dived down to where Bachman's body was pulling against its tether.

Bachman had drifted away from the rocks, the eddies hungrily sucking him away from land and to the deeper water beyond the pool. Milton looped the belt around Bachman's waist and clipped it together. He untied the rope, manoeuvred himself so that he was facing out through the gap in the rocks to the open sea, and pushed Bachman away.

Milton watched for a moment as Bachman drifted away from him. His arms were wide apart, as if inviting an embrace, and his eyes were open. The body descended, dragged down by the belt. Milton watched as the most dangerous man he had ever known drifted into the deep and slowly faded from view.

Milton stroked back to the surface to untie the other end of the rope, took another deep breath, and then submerged himself again. He kicked, the fins helping him to surge through the water. The eddy caught him and hurried him away from the rocks. He submitted to it and swam for the waiting boat.

Chapter Fifty-Eight

VICTOR BLUM sat at his desk and gazed out the window. A storm cloud had rolled in off the Mediterranean early in the afternoon and now, as dusk descended over the city, the rain started to fall. It quickly gathered in volume until it became a deluge, thundering against the glass and blurring the view that he had always enjoyed. The sky was the colour of a bruise, livid and painful, and veins of lightning crackled across it. In the distance, out over the sea, thunder boomed.

His aide-de-camp put his head through the open door. "They're here, Director."

"Send them in."

He turned away from the window and looked down at the papers on his desk. The report had been filed three days earlier, and it was voluminous. He had requested that its authors attend him this evening so that he could ask a few additional questions. Blum had found through long experience that sometimes the answers were more accurate when the interrogation was face to face.

His ADC returned, paused at the door, and showed the two agents inside. Malakhi and Keren Rabin looked a little nervous, as well they might. Blum's reputation for irascibility went before him, and they must have known that the equivocation in their report would annoy him.

"Sit."

There were two chairs in front of his desk. Keren Rabin took the chair on the left, her husband the one on the right. They sat quietly, waiting for him to speak. The two of them had kept Bachman under surveillance, as he had ordered. Blum knew that he and Milton would meet again to resolve their differences and he wanted to be absolutely sure that his intelligence regarding the aftermath was certain.

"Thank you for your report," he said. "Very thorough, although the lack of a firm conclusion is disturbing. I'll get straight to the point. There was no sign of them? Of either of them?"

"No, sir," Keren said. "None."

"The local police?"

"They were not informed. We didn't think it would be wise."

"No," Blum said.

"I waited for an hour," Keren said, "while Malakhi removed Shavit's body."

"That, at least, is taken care of?"

"Yes, sir," Malakhi said. "We buried him."

He turned back to Keren. "And you saw nothing?"

"Nothing. If they survived the fall, they didn't come out at the property. There was a natural breakwater. They would have had to swim around that and around the bay."

"It was dark, though?"

"Yes, sir, but the property was well lit."

"The sea?"

"Moderate visibility."

"So it's possible they might have been able to swim clear?"

"Possible? Yes, sir. But likely? With respect, sir, I would say not."

"Be clear, agent. You think they're dead?"

Keren held his gaze. "Yes, sir. That would be my conclusion."

He reached for his glasses and perched them on his nose so that he could read the annotations he had made to the summary.

"Matilda Douglas?"

"She has returned to Australia. She flew in to Melbourne, took a train to Broken Hill and was picked up from the station by her brother. They went back to the sheep station."

Blum had wondered whether he could afford to let the girl go. She knew everything, after all. In the end, he had decided that it was a risk he could afford to take. It would have brought unnecessary attention to have abducted her for a second time. And there was little incentive for her to cause trouble.

"And Ziggy Penn?"

"I'm afraid we still don't know."

"You have no idea?"

"No, sir. We couldn't leave the property to pursue them. It would have been a risk until it was cleaned."

"I know that."

"We know that he didn't fly out of the country. We checked airline manifests. No hits."

"Hospitals? He was shot, yes?"

"No sign, sir."

"Make a suggestion, agent."

"It would just be speculation, sir. He knows how to drop off the grid. I'm sure that's what Milton told him to do. He can get money. It might be difficult to find him again."

Blum stood and dismissed them both. He turned to face the window, watching them depart in the reflection in the darkened glass. They were good agents, and they had done almost everything that he had asked of them. The loose ends, though, were displeasing. He didn't like uncertainty.

He gazed out over the rooftops again. Rain streamed down the glass. A peal of thunder detonated overhead, rattling the window in its frame. He put his hands behind his back and clasped them together. Both Milton and Bachman were trained to disappear. Bachman had engineered his own death before and had stayed out of sight for ten years. Milton had the same talents.

The Rabins were sure that both men were dead.

Was that good enough for him?

Chapter Fifty-Nine

ZIGGY PENN had entered the state of Zen calm he always enjoyed when he did his best hacking. His fingers flashed across the keyboard, code spewing forth almost as if his hands and brain were disconnected. The Starbucks shop was as cookie-cutter as all the other branches he had ever been in. It could have been Seattle or Chicago or London, such was the bland sameness of the décor and the coffee and even the other customers arrayed around the nearby tables.

As it happened, Ziggy was in Gangnam, an upmarket suburb of Seoul. The coffee shop was a short walk from the apartment that he had just visited. It was available for lease, was furnished to a high standard and, most important of all, came with a blazingly fast one-gigabyte-per-second Internet connection. It was also correspondingly expensive with a deposit equivalent to six months' rent required before it would be removed from the market. Ziggy needed an injection of funds to make the payment, so he had taken a quick detour.

It was an easy hack. A local restaurant that he had visited the day before was lax with its data security, and he infiltrated their servers and copied the credit card details he needed. He would sell those details online. The purchaser would make five or even six figures if he or she was careful; Ziggy would settle for ten thousand bucks.

He paused for a moment and cracked his knuckles.

Ziggy's leg was still sore, but it was healing well. Matilda had taken him to a hospital in Brgat, where his injury had been treated. There had been no point in trying to disguise what had happened to him. The doctor had identified it as a gunshot wound immediately and had made it clear that the police would have to be called in order that he might be interviewed. Ziggy had not put up any resistance to the suggestion, but, as soon as the man had left him alone to rest for the night, Matilda had smuggled him out of the ward in a wheelchair and then driven him away.

They had travelled north to Zadar and then crossed to Ancona by ferry. From there they had driven north through Italy into Switzerland and on to Bern, where they went their separate ways. Matilda had said that she was going to return to Australia. Ziggy decided upon Korea. He knew what Milton would have advised him to do, and had completed the last leg of his journey in as low-tech a way as possible. He had no cell phone, and he limited his time online to when he could be sure that his activity could not be tracked. He had avoided airports, travelling instead by bus and train to Vladivostok. The trip took nine days and included stops and changes in Basel, Hannover, Berlin, Frankfurt, Brest, Moscow and, eventually, Vladivostok. From there, he took the *Eastern Dream* ferry to Donghae.

Milton had been uppermost in his thoughts during his long journey. Both he and Matilda had debated whether they should stay in Dubrovnik in the event that he hadn't died, but, eventually, they had agreed that it was pointless. Milton was dead. He had to be. Matilda had watched him and Bachman topple over the edge and disappear into the sea below. They knew Milton was resourceful and tough, but there had been no sign of him or Bachman. Even if Milton had survived the fall, the current was hungry and strong and it seemed impossible that he could have beaten it.

Staying in the city would have been dangerous, too. Ziggy had given the Rabins enough doubt that they had allowed them to leave, but there was no way of knowing how their orders might evolve now that both Milton and Bachman were dead. Victor Blum might call Ziggy's bluff. They needed to get away, put as many miles between them and the Rabins as possible.

Ziggy wondered about Matilda. She wasn't going to hide, and he knew there was no point in trying to persuade her that she should. She was going home and damn the consequences. She would be easy to find. Ziggy admired her courage, but thought she was foolish. He would make himself much more difficult to find.

Milton had bought both of them the opportunity to slip into obscurity. Ziggy knew that, and he was going to take advantage of it even if Matilda was not.

So far, Seoul had been everything that he had hoped it would be. It was friendly, the economy was booming, and the weather was pleasant. It was teeming with people, with more than enough ex-pats that another Westerner could be absorbed into the morass without attracting attention. The apartment he had found was luxurious. The women were attractive and his early forays had suggested that the Internet dating scene was vibrant and, even better, it was ripe for a little optimisation. He thought that he would fit in very well here.

He finished inputting his code, pressed return, and stared at the screen. The data would start to flow within the next few minutes and then he would use it to start to build his new life. He would be sensible, stay out of sight, hack only when he had to—and even then, he would take no chances.

He knew he could be happy here.

Chapter Sixty

THE MOTORCADE had driven out from the collection of huts and other ramshackle buildings that comprised the homestead at Boolanga. It was an hour past dawn, and the sun was already starting to bake the sand and rock beneath the wheels of Matilda Douglas's Jeep. She remembered how hot the day had been yesterday. It had persisted deep into the night, pulsing out of the ground as they ate their fry-up of mutton, finished with bottles of beer that had been chilling in an ice bucket.

Matilda had been back on the station for a month. It was coming to the end of the season, and the sheep needed to be mustered so that the rams could be separated from the ewes and the male lambs neutered. They had received a report overnight that five sheep had broken free of the vast 10,000-acre paddock, and that dingoes had been seen in the area. The business was not so flush with cash that they could write off those sheep, so they had determined to go out and find them.

There were four of them that morning: Mervyn and Eric were on motorbikes, and Harry was overhead in the small Cessna that they used to direct operations. He was circling above the paddock, having located the runaways and radioed their location down to the other members of the posse. Mervyn and Eric had gone ahead to round them up. Matilda could still see the long plumes of red dust that were kicked up by the wheels of their bikes. She would find a suitable spot and then take the temporary pens from the trailer and erect them so that the animals could be herded back into captivity. Once they had been penned, they would be driven into the back of the trailer and Matilda would return them to the rest of the flock.

The radio crackled into life. "They're running to the

south," said Harry.

"Roger that," Eric radioed back. "I can see the bastards. We'll loop around and drive them east."

Matilda picked up the radio and spoke into it. "Do it sooner rather than later. It's going to be as hot as Hell today."

Matilda's Jeep was towing a trailer behind it, and the towball rattled noisily in the coupling head as the vehicle bounced across the uneven dirt track. She found a suitable spot and braked to a halt. The landscape stretched on for miles, almost identical whichever way you looked. The sky above was a cold blue, unspoiled by cloud. There were clumps of angry-looking bushes, trees that had been beaten down by the sun, and knots of yellowed, parched grass. There had been a big storm the day before yesterday, and the deluge had painted more green on the landscape than would have been usual for this time of the year. The dusty earth drank the water up, and the ochre had seemed deeper than usual as the first stabs of light had lanced out from the horizon earlier.

Matilda muscled the pens out of the back of the trailer and set them up. They were arranged in a wide V, with the open trailer at the point where the two arms of the V met.

Doves watched from the branches of a nearby tree. A kangaroo regarded her with what she took to be pity as it idled by. It took her twenty minutes to erect the fences and, when she was done, she was damp with sweat. She took a bottle of water from the Jeep and was about to sit down in the shadow of the trailer when she saw a smudge of dust rising to the west. She had forgotten her binoculars in the rush to get going this morning and she cursed herself for it now. It was a vehicle, still too distant to identify, but if she had to guess, she would have said that it was another motorbike.

She leaned into the Jeep and picked up the radio to call her brother, but decided against it. He was out of position, so he wouldn't easily be able to overfly what she was looking at for a second opinion. And he would panic, thinking about what had happened to her, and send Mervyn or Eric, or both of them, back to help. The whole morning's work would be ruined. The sheep would be gone.

No. She'd handle this herself.

Because Bachman was dead.

She had seen him die.

And if the Mossad wanted her, would they really send one agent on a motorbike?

She clipped the radio back onto the dash, reached across for her shotgun and then stood next to the Jeep to wait for whomever was approaching.

Distance was deceptive in the outback, and it was another five minutes before the new arrival was close enough for her to confirm that he or she was, indeed, riding a motorbike. She wished, again, that she had her binoculars, and, instead, occupied herself by breaking the shotgun and thumbing in two shells. She clicked it shut again and then held it across her body, the index finger of her right hand resting over the trigger guard.

Another five minutes passed and now she saw that the rider was a man. He flicked the bike around a depression and then leapt over a termite mound.

Two minutes after that and Matilda recognised him.

She flicked the safety on the shotgun, propped it against the side of the Jeep, and walked out, leaving the blessing of the shade and meeting him halfway.

GET TWO BEST-SELLERS, TWO NOVELLAS AND EXCLUSIVE JOHN MILTON MATERIAL

Building a relationship with my readers is the very best thing about writing. I occasionally send newsletters with details on new releases, special offers and other bits of news relating to the John Milton, Beatrix Rose and Soho Noir series.

And if you sign up to the mailing list I'll send you all this free stuff:

1. A copy of my best-seller, The Cleaner (178 five star reviews and RRP of $5.99).

2. A copy of the John Milton introductory novella, 1000 Yards.

3. A copy of the introductory Soho Noir novella, Gaslight.

4. A free copy of my best-seller, The Black Mile (averages 4.4 out of 5 stars and RRP of $ 5.99).

5. A copy of the highly classified background check on John Milton before he was admitted to Group 15. Exclusive to my mailing list – you can't get this anywhere else.

6. A copy of Tarantula, an exciting John Milton short story.

You can get the novel, the novellas, the background check and the short story, **for free**, by signing up at http://eepurl.com/bvI6gT

IF YOU ENJOYED THIS BOOK...

...I would really, really appreciate it if you would help others to enjoy it, too. Reviews are like gold dust and they help persuade other readers to give the stories a shot. More readers means more incentive for me write and that means there will be more stories, more quickly.

ABOUT THE AUTHOR

Mark Dawson is the author of the breakout John Milton, Beatrix Rose and Soho Noir series. He makes his online home at www.markjdawson.com. You can connect with Mark on Twitter at @pbackwriter, on Facebook at www.facebook.com/markdawsonauthor and you should send him an email at mark@markjdawson.com if the mood strikes you.

ALSO BY MARK DAWSON

Have you read them all?

In the Soho Noir Series

Gaslight

When Harry and his brother Frank are blackmailed into paying off a local hood they decide to take care of the problem themselves. But when all of London's underworld is in thrall to the man's boss, was their plan audacious or the most foolish thing that they could possibly have done?

The Black Mile

London, 1940: the Luftwaffe blitzes London every night for fifty-seven nights. Houses, shops and entire streets are wiped from the map. The underworld is in flux: the Italian criminals who dominated the West End have been interned and now their rivals are fighting to replace them. Meanwhile, hidden in the shadows, the Black-Out Ripper sharpens his knife and sets to his grisly work.

The Imposter

War hero Edward Fabian finds himself drawn into a criminal family's web of vice and soon he is an accomplice to their scheming. But he's not the man they think he is - he's far more dangerous than they could possibly imagine.

In the John Milton Series

One Thousand Yards

In this dip into his case files, John Milton is sent into North Korea. With nothing but a sniper rifle, bad intentions and a very particular target, will Milton be able to take on the secret police of the most dangerous failed state on the planet?

Tarantula

In this further dip into his files, Milton is sent to Italy. A colleague who was investigating a particularly violent Mafiosi has disappeared. Will Milton be able to get to the bottom of the mystery, or will he be the next to fall victim to Tarantula?

The Cleaner

Sharon Warriner is a single mother in the East End of London, fearful that she's lost her young son to a life in the gangs. After John Milton saves her life, he promises to help. But the gang, and the charismatic rapper who leads it, is not about to cooperate with him.

Saint Death

John Milton has been off the grid for six months. He surfaces in Ciudad Juárez, Mexico, and immediately finds himself drawn into a vicious battle with the narco-gangs that control the borderlands.

The Driver

When a girl he drives to a party goes missing, John Milton is worried. Especially when two dead bodies are discovered and the police start treating him as their prime suspect.

Ghosts

John Milton is blackmailed into finding his predecessor as Number One. But she's a ghost, too, and just as dangerous as him. He finds himself in de ep trouble, playing the Russians against the British in a desperate attempt to save the life of his oldest friend.

The Sword of God

On the run from his own demons, John Milton treks through the Michigan wilderness into the town of Truth. He's not looking for trouble, but trouble's looking for him. He finds himself up against a small-town cop who has no idea with whom he is dealing, and no idea how dangerous he is.

Salvation Row

John Milton finds himself in New Orleans with a debt to repay. The family who sheltered him during Hurricane Katrina need his special kind of help. But a man emerges from Milton's past and it might be that he has been given more than he can handle.

In the Beatrix Rose Series

In Cold Blood

Beatrix Rose was the most dangerous assassin in an off-the-books government kill squad until her former boss betrayed her. A decade later, she emerges from the Hong Kong underworld with payback on her mind. They gunned down her husband and kidnapped her daughter, and now the debt needs to be repaid. It's a blood feud she didn't start but she is going to finish.

Blood Moon Rising

There were six names on Beatrix's Death List and now there are four. She's going to account for the others, one by one, even if it kills her. She has returned from Somalia with another target in her sights. Bryan Duffy is in Iraq, surrounded by mercenaries, with no easy way to get to him and no easy way to get out. And Beatrix has other issues that need to be addressed. Will Duffy prove to be one kill too far?

Blood and Roses

Beatrix Rose has worked her way through her Kill List. Four are dead, just two are left. But now her foes know she has them in her sights and the hunter has become the hunted.

Standalone Novels

The Art of Falling Apart

A story of greed, duplicity and death in the flamboyant, super-ego world of rock and roll. Dystopia have rocketed up the charts in Europe, so now it's time to crack America. The opening concert in Las Vegas is a sell-out success, but secret envy and open animosity have begun to tear the group apart.

Subpoena Colada

Daniel Tate looks like he has it all. A lucrative job as a lawyer and a host of famous names who want him to work for them. But his girlfriend has deserted him for an American film star and his main client has just been implicated in a sensational murder. Can he hold it all together?